SUNSET

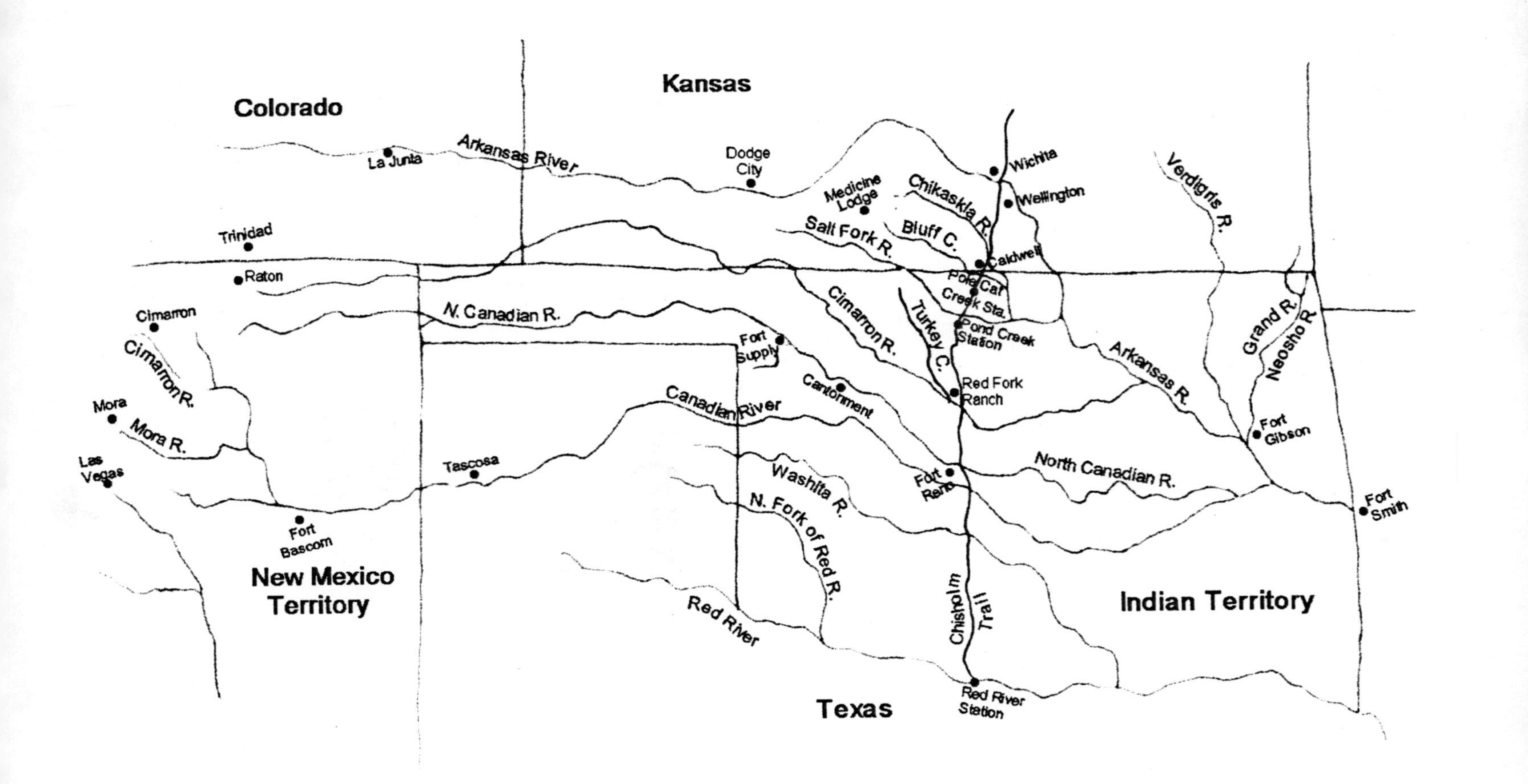
Colorado
Kansas
Arkansas River
La Junta
Dodge City
Medicine Lodge
Wichita
Wellington
Chikaskia R.
Bluff C.
Salt Fork R.
Caldwell
Pole Cat Creek Sta.
Pond Creek Station
Verdigris R.
Trinidad
Raton
Cimarron
Cimarron R.
N. Canadian R.
Fort Supply
Cimarron R.
Turkey C.
Red Fork Ranch
Arkansas R.
Grand R.
Neosho R.
Fort Gibson
Mora
Mora R.
Las Vegas
Tascosa
Canadian River
Cantonment
North Canadian R.
Fort Reno
Fort Smith
Washita R.
N. Fork of Red R.
Fort Bascom
New Mexico Territory
Red River
Chisholm Trail
Indian Territory
Texas
Red River Station

SUNSET

A Novel

GLEN ONLEY

SANTA FE

Cover by Kristina Tripp

This book is a work of fiction. Names, characters, places, and incidents are either the product of the author's imagination or are used fictitiously.

Sunstone books may be purchased for educational, business, or sales promotional use. For information please write: Special Markets Department, Sunstone Press, P.O. Box 2321, Santa Fe, New Mexico 87504-2321.

Library of Congress Cataloging-in-Publication Data:

Onley, Glen, 1943–
Sunset: a novel / by Glen Onley.
p. cm.
ISBN: 0-86534-380-2
1. Young men—Fiction. I. Title.
PS3565.N65 S86 2003
813'.6—dc21

2003008370

Published in

SUNSTONE PRESS
Post Office Box 2321
Santa Fe, NM 87504-2321 / USA
(505) 988-4418 / *orders only* (800) 243-5644
FAX (505) 988-1025
www.sunstonepress.com

This story is dedicated to Don and Gloria White, residents of Caldwell, Kansas and outstanding ambassadors of that Border Queen town and its rich history. They not only opened their home to me but also shared their vast wealth of historical data, including *BORDER QUEEN*, an in-depth account of old-time Caldwell authored by Don.

Preface

This is a work of fiction. Though based on historical events, places, and people, the reader should be aware that the author has of necessity used his imagination in developing characters, creating dialogue, and detailing action. In so doing, the author has investigated many historical writings and records, along with personal interviews, with the intent of capturing the spirit of the time, the essence of the participants, and the significance of the events, trying to portray each as they might have been viewed by the people of the time. Certainly, the author has in no way intentionally depicted any historical character in an unfair or unfavorable light.

Those who moved west, settled, and made their homes on the raw frontier have left us a legacy rich in spirit, determination, and bravery. Mistakes, injustices, and cruelty are a part of that legacy as well, and the brush of history must paint both sides. Civilization has evolved and continues to change, hopefully always to a higher and nobler plane. Looking back, assessing the good and bad, and building on its best is essential to the quality of that process.

This story is an attempt to view the past, but also to sense and feel what it must have been like.

—Glen Onley
Greenville, Texas
November, 2002

Acknowledgements

Those who have contributed to this story are too many to list here; however, the efforts and assistance of some are too important to go unnoted.

Anita Mitchell of the City Library in Greenville, Texas cheerfully contacted other libraries across the Southwest, arranging the loan of some rare and especially insightful books. Particularly beneficial were writings about Las Vegas, New Mexico during the heyday of Vicente Silva.

David Wheaton provided his synopsis of the history of Las Vegas, which yielded an especially insightful look at the town and surrounding area.

Lloyd Corder shared information regarding a colorful character and relative, Black Bill Jones, which included a look at activities around Tascosa and surrounding ranches during the spring of 1883 when many cowboys went on strike. Jones was a cowboy on the LIT until the spring of that year when he became a freighter for W. R. Bolden for three months, then returned to the cowboy life on the Frying Pan Ranch.

Ronald Karron of the Fort Smith Museum of History, Fort Smith, Arkansas, provided a personal tour of the museum while sharing his in-depth knowledge of and enthusiasm for the famous fort and its rich history.

Renee Mitchell, Historic Properties Manager at the Chisholm Trail Museum in Kingfisher, Oklahoma, gave freely of her time and knowledge regarding the famous cattle trail and the prominent stops along its path.

Reverend Carlos Knight provided an invaluable personal tour of the Garrett Historic Home, the residence of several Fort Gibson commanders, as well as insight into the history of the fort and its people.

Lastly, I want to acknowledge family and friends who have rendered unwavering encouragement and advice, along with their labors over various aspects of the manuscript. My wife Phyllis has not only served as a proofreader, but has endured hours of my relating to her each new discovery regarding some character or event related to the story. Also, John and Debbie Boose and Chuck and Nita Dryden deserve special note for reading the manuscript and sharing their *SPANNING THE RIVER*, a history of Dewey County, Oklahoma.

This book, as are most, is born of the efforts of many, and I want to thank each and every contributor.

1

Fort Smith, Arkansas
Fall, 1876

"Samuel D. Brook," the burly judge said, "you have been found guilty of horse theft and murder by a jury of your peers and are now sentenced to death by hanging, punishment to be carried out within the hour. May God, whose laws you have broken and before whose heavenly tribunal you must soon appear, have mercy on your soul."

The stern-faced magistrate then banged his gavel on the shiny oak table and pronounced his court adjourned. A sandy-headed boy seated in the front row stared open-mouthed at the shackled man who slowly turned toward his son. The lad's watery eyes dropped from his father's haggard face to his own hands clenching the court rail. The grimace on the boy's face mirrored the panic sweeping through his body.

Behind him, wooden chairs squeaked as courtroom spectators stirred. Through the fog of their murmuring, the thump, thump of heavy footsteps on the creaky floor brought the boy's head up. Through blurred vision, he watched his father's bristled chin drop to his chest as a deputy led him away, leg irons clanging.

"Judge, sir, what about the boy?" a heavily mustached black deputy marshal asked. "Says he's got no family left."

"Acorns don't fall far from the tree. For now, hold him as your prisoner."

"But, sir, the boy ain't done nothin'," the deputy replied, rolling the brim of his dusty black hat in his powerful hands.

"Then do what you want, Deputy Reeves, but don't set him loose to roam the streets of Fort Smith," the goateed judge replied gruffly and stomped out of the room.

"But I can't . . ." the deputy started to protest, then let out a deep sigh. "Come along, boy."

Leading the way downstairs and to a side door of what was once a Fort Smith soldiers' barracks, the lawman pushed it open and motioned the boy through. "What's your name, anyhow?"

"Everett," the lad replied shakily, tears filling the corners of his blue eyes.

Outside, the deputy untied his blaze-faced bay from the hitching rail and snatched loose the lead rope of a loaded pack mule. In one effortless motion, he swung his muscular, six-foot-two frame into the saddle, then slipped his shiny left boot out of the stirrup. "Climb up, son."

After trotting through a gate in the low stone wall that surrounded the old fort, they turned onto a well-worn path that led down to the street. When they reached the livery stable, Everett slid down with the ease of one born to riding bareback and headed inside.

"Get your pony, and your pa's, too," the trailing deputy called out as he grabbed a pair of scarred saddlebags from across the shoulders of his horse.

The rawboned boy threw a saddle on a buckskin pony, flipped the stirrup over the leather seat, and cinched it down, then did the same with a chestnut mare. Meanwhile, the deputy instructed the hostler to collect his stable fee from Judge Isaac Parker's court.

"Your pa's stuff," the lawman explained as he tied the saddlebags behind the cantle on the chestnut.

Without expression the boy stood staring at his patched boot tops while the deputy purchased a sack of corn for the animals. Leading the buckskin and chestnut, Everett then followed the lawman outside and watched him strap the grain to the pack mule's load.

"Into the saddle, boy," Reeves said as he swung up on the big bay. "We're leavin' town."

As the lad reined the buckskin around, the deputy spurred his gelding from the long shadow of the livery into the sunlit street. For a moment, the lad hesitated, taking a lingering look over at the whitewashed courthouse, then kneed his pony into a trot with the spirited chestnut trailing.

"He really gonna hang my pa?" he asked, having caught up with the deputy.

The lawman tugged on the brim of his hat, cut his eyes over at the boy for an instant, then squinted into the dying sun. "It's the law, son," he muttered.

"Ain't there somebody who can stop it?"

"Your pa killed a man in the Nation and stole his horses, so Judge Parker has the final say."

"What's the Nation?"

"Indian Territory."

Approaching the end of the street, young Everett twisted in his saddle and peered back over his shoulder. Painted on the distant, fire-stained sunset was a black-hooded, lone figure standing on the bleak gallows outside the courtroom. Then a short, stocky man appeared, looped a noose around the prisoner's neck, and slipped the knot down, taking out the slack. The hangman stepped back, then glanced up to an open courthouse window. Barely visible within the shadowed room, the judge nodded slightly. The boy's eyes instantly shifted back to the gallows and glimpsed his father's arrow-straight body plunging downward. The lad gasped as a clanging sound echoed along the street, bouncing off storefronts. With a scream of anguish, he heeled the buckskin into a gallop.

Reeves soon caught up but did not crowd the lad who was hunched over and sobbing quietly. With a sideways glance toward the lawman, the boy dragged his sleeve across his eyes and then stared ahead.

"Need a bandanna, son?" Reeves asked, pulling a blue and white checkered handkerchief from an inside pocket.

Everett shook his head, sniffing and sucking in his quivering bottom lip.

The tough lawman blinked his brown eyes a couple of times as he stuffed the rag back inside his coat.

When they reached the rim of a fifty-foot bluff, the deputy led the way down a narrow path that angled across the cliff wall, ending near the water's edge. After being ferried to the other side on a canvas-covered wagon bed made watertight with pitch and held together with rawhide, they climbed a slope to a dusty road and turned toward the heart of Indian Territory. After a silent hour of riding, Everett pulled his buckskin over alongside the deputy's bay.

"Mister, what're you gonna do with me?"

"The name's Bass Reeves, son, and I'm takin' you to Fort Gibson."

"What for, Mister Reeves?"

"They've got families there. Hope one'll take you in."

"I don't want no family," the boy shot back, turning away.

"How old you be, son?"

"Nearly fourteen," the boy replied, sitting up tall and straight.

"Back East, you might make it, but not out here. Between Indians, murderers, and thieves, a grown man don't have half a chance in this country."

"Why are you here?"

"I got a job to do. And my kind don't get a fair shot most anywhere else."

Everett hesitated. "Hangin' innocent men," he muttered.

"What'd you say, boy?" the deputy asked, reining his horse across the path of the buckskin.

"You and that judge just hung my pa for something he never done," young Everett replied, gazing into the nearby trees.

"That ain't true!" the deputy shouted. "An eyewitness, the forked brand on that gelding's hip, and that jury back there all say otherwise. Now if you know somethin' none of us does, speak up."

"Wouldn't do no good," the boy mumbled. "Pa's dead."

"Dead 'cause he was a killer and a horse thief, but if there's somebody else in on it, just spit out the name. I'll hunt him down just like I done . . ."

Everett's eyes narrowed as he stared at the deputy. "Never you mind. I'll do it myself."

The deputy's dark eyes softened. "Son, I know it's a hard thing, your pa an outlaw and no ma to see after you, to teach you right from wrong. Then seein' your pa meet his end like that. But you can do better. I'll see to it you're put with some good folks."

"Told you, I don't want nobody. Mostly, I've taken care of myself the past two years already."

"Yeah, and within sight of six months, I'd be trackin' you down and standin' you in front of that judge," the deputy barked. "Son, do you know who he is? Isaac Parker, the hangin' judge, that's who."

"Then I guess that makes you his hangin' deputy," Everett said, eyes flashing.

"Come along. Maybe somebody at Fort Gibson can teach you somethin'."

Half an hour later, Everett cut his eyes over at Deputy Reeves.

"You ever a slave?"

"Was once."

"How'd you get yourself freed?"

The deputy stiffened, his dark eyes fixed on the bay's bobbing head.

"Got in a fight with my owner over a card game," he said. "Hurt 'em bad, so I lit out north, crossed the Red, and hid out in the Nation."

"What's it like, bein' a slave?"

"Like a sickness, one that won't go away."

"Sorta like a bellyache?"

"Yeah, one that grips your insides and squeezes them, right down to your toenails," Reeves said, then hesitated. "Son, ain't no use talkin' about it. Bein' free all your life, you can't understand."

"But I ain't free now," Everett said. "I'm your prisoner."

"Ain't the same, son."

"Why not?"

"'Cause when I get you to the fort, you'll be set loose."

Come nightfall, they left the road and made camp in a bend of the wide stream they were following.

"Mister, what river is this?" the boy asked.

"The Arkansas," Bass replied.

"Where does it come from?"

"They say it starts in some mountains in Colorado, snakes eastward to Dodge City, then on to Wichita before it drops down through Indian Territory."

From men who had ridden with his father, the boy had heard talk about wild cow towns, especially Wichita. It might be a place to go, he thought.

"How far to Wichita?"

"Farther than you're goin'" the deputy replied.

"Will Indians kill us if we get on their land?" Everett then asked.

"Gather up some firewood," Reeves said. "We'll be on their land soon, and a few of 'em hate all white men, and maybe they got reason to. But it's the outlaws you gotta worry about. You see, Indian law don't apply to whites, so desperados from Texas, Arkansas, Missouri, and Kansas slip into the Territory to hide out."

"Nobody goes in after 'em?" Everett asked, gathering an armload of broken limbs and driftwood.

"I do," Reeves answered. "And a few others."

The boy hesitated, staring into the first flames. "And you take 'em back to that hangin' judge?"

"Mostly," the deputy replied.

"You ever kill 'em?"

"A few," Reeves said, "those that don't give me no choice."

"How many?"

"Son, I don't carve notches. Killin' a man ain't nothin' to be proud of."

"You ever been shot?"

"No, but shot at aplenty. Once I had a button shot right off my coat, and another time a bullet split my belt. Even got a few holes in my old hat."

"Ma always said gunmen don't live long," the boy said. "You a gunman?"

"Some would say so," the deputy replied. "A farmer's got a plow, a cowboy a horse, and a deputy marshal a gun. And he's gotta know how and when to use it."

"What kind of gun you carry?"

"Two Colts and a Winchester rifle, all .38 to .40 caliber."

"Could I see your revolver?"

"Get your horses unsaddled and cared for," the deputy said. "You got no business handlin' a gun."

After eating they spread out their bedrolls and slipped inside. After a while the boy turned his back to the dwindling flames and lay still, listening to night chatter and the occasional movement of the deputy. An hour or so later the boy noticed the slow, regular breathing of Bass Reeves.

Slowly Everett eased out of his blankets and rolled them up. He tiptoed over to the horses, feeding them corn from his hand to keep them quiet. With an eye on the lawman, he slipped saddles on the buckskin and chestnut, then strapped his bedroll and saddlebags behind. After leading them about fifty yards northwest along the soft riverbank, sticking to sandy patches, he latched the cinches, climbed up, and heeled the buckskin into an easy lope.

Four hours later the boy was nodding in the saddle as he approached a shallow creek feeding into the river from the north. He walked his horses into the shallow stream and splashed along for another half-hour until he spotted a clump of thick bushes off to his left. He turned the ponies out of the streambed and up the creek bank, tying them behind a thicket-formed blind. Soon his bed was rolled out, and the boy climbed in.

Hours later, Everett awakened to the cawing of a crow from a nearby treetop. Startled, he jumped to his feet and headed for his horses, but they were gone.

"Indians," he muttered to himself. "Pa said they always steal your horses."

Instantly, he thought of his father's revolver. In Pa's saddlebags, he guessed. But they were strapped behind the cantle on the chestnut. Beating his hands against his thighs in frustration, he spun around, then heard horses approaching. He dropped to his stomach and crawled under the edge of the thick bushes.

2

Just above the rim of the creek bank, a sweat-ringed black hat bobbed, and then the deputy's face appeared. Everett crawled from beneath the bushes as three bareback horses, led by Reeves, lunged over the crest of the rise.

"Never leave your horse saddled all night," the lawman said. "If you don't take care of 'em, you'll find yourself afoot."

"How'd you find me?" Everett asked, kicking an empty terrapin shell across brown oak leaves.

"Easy. Even a greenhorn could've done it," the deputy replied. "Or an Indian half your age."

"What'd you do with my saddle and stuff?"

"Over there," Reeves said, pointing toward a sprawling red oak.

Turning, the boy spotted his saddles and blankets resting on a long, sturdy limb that swooped to within four feet of the ground. "That judge payin' you to take me to the fort?" Everett asked, glancing back at the deputy.

"Not one cent."

"Then why don't you just leave me be?" the boy asked.

"'Cause I got boys of my own," the lawman replied. "And if I was gone, I'd want somebody to look after 'em."

"Yeah, and if one of them done wrong, you'd want somebody to take 'im to that hangin' judge."

"No," the deputy replied. "I'd take 'im myself."

"Why not just shoot 'im?" Everett quipped. "That'd be better than watchin' that judge hang 'im."

"Let's eat and get back on the trail," the deputy replied. "The sooner we get to Fort Gibson, the sooner you're off my hands."

After a quick breakfast, they saddled up and headed north from the river.

Skirting thick undergrowth, Bass Reeves pushed the bay and trailing pack mule steadily, often calling back to the boy to hurry it up. They soon reached the road and turned northwest.

An hour or so later they met three wagons and a group of mounted soldiers. Reeves stopped and talked to them while Everett remained distant, straddling his horse in the shade of a roadside hickory. When the soldiers rode on, the deputy motioned Everett to come along.

"Who was that?" the boy asked.

"Captain Brown with a detachment from Fort Gibson."

"They out lookin' for Indians?"

"Headed to Fort Smith for supplies. Soldiers from the fort built this road about forty years ago for that purpose."

An hour later, the deputy slowed his bay.

"What's the matter?" the boy asked.

"Crossin' the dead line," Reeves said, pointing to a poster tacked to a tree that read: LAWMEN KEEP OUT.

"What's it mean?"

"We're eighty miles outta Fort Smith, about to enter Indian Territory," Reeves explained. "Outlaws claim everything past this point."

A couple of hours later, Everett nudged his pony up beside Reeves.

"How come we ain't seen no Indians?"

"Just 'cause you ain't seen them, don't mean they ain't out there watchin'," the deputy replied, nodding toward the dense forest alongside the road. "Why an Indian could sneak up and steal the saddle off your spare horse, and you'd never know it."

Stealing a look back at the chestnut, Everett said, "You ain't scarin' me with talk like that."

As darkness settled in, Reeves chose another campsite along the river. Tired and hungry, Everett practically fell from his horse, then slumped to the ground.

"Take care of them horses," the deputy ordered. "Then you can think about restin'."

With the horses fed and tethered, the sullen boy gathered firewood. He ate without a word, then immediately grabbed his pa's saddlebags and opened the flap. His father's holster lay wrapped up in the cartridge belt with a Colt stuck inside. Everett peeled off the leather strap, pulled the thong over the trigger, and slipped out the ivory-handled revolver. He cut his eyes sharply at the deputy. This was not his father's gun. It had been walnut-plated.

Mumbling inaudibly, he broke open the cylinder and found it empty, as were the cartridge slots on the belt. He glared at the deputy, but knew any protest would be pointless. At least it was a gun, he thought, and somehow he would get his hands on cartridges. After snapping the pistol shut and punching it into the holster, he rolled out his bed, turned his back to Marshal Reeves, and within minutes he was asleep.

Hours later, as he turned onto his side, a tug on his arm brought his eyes open. Raising up, he found a cold handcuff around his right wrist with the off-cuff looped through the last link of a heavy chain. When he pulled, the chain tightened, then held firm with its far end looped and padlocked around the base of a hundred-year-old oak. He flushed with anger, but soon simmered down, got comfortable, and dropped off to sleep again.

When Everett awoke to a gray dawn, he quickly checked his wrist and found it free. For a second he wondered if he had had a nightmare, but the cuffs clamped onto the deputy's belt convinced him otherwise.

"Tonight, you'll sleep at Fort Gibson," Reeves said.

Without a word, the boy jumped to his feet, rolled his bed, and headed for the horses. He fed them, and while they guzzled from the clear stream, he cinched on their saddles. Back in camp, bacon sizzled, and steam swirled from the spout of the coffeepot. He poured a cup, stood with his back to the fire, and sipped like an old hand.

After eating they broke camp. While the deputy was packing the mule, the boy strapped on his father's gun belt, using the tightest notch.

"Think you could loan me a few cartridges?" Everett asked, breaking the gun open.

"What for?" Reeves replied, tying a canvas over the supply packs.

"Indians or desperados," the boy replied. "I could help if we meet up with some."

"I've always handled 'em without your help," the deputy replied. "Reckon today ain't no different."

Without another word, the deputy straddled his horse, and the boy slammed the revolver shut and jammed it into the holster. Reeves turned the bay back toward the river, leading the mule.

"This ain't my pa's Colt," Everett said five minutes later.

"It's what he was wearin' when I took him in," Reeves replied.

Everett felt sure the deputy was lying, but he had no way to prove it. That was just one more thing he would have to take care of some day when he would even the score.

As they approached Fort Gibson, long shadows cast by thick, tall pines along the western side of the trail covered the path. Breaking into the waning sunlight, Everett focused on the ten-foot-tall walls of the old stockade lying a hundred yards ahead in an open area. His body tensed while imagining the fierce battles that must have been fought from the weathered, rectangular structure. He could picture long rifle barrels poking out of gun slots cut in the thick walls of the two double-level blockhouses set at diagonal corners. Flame and lead would be spitting from others positioned along the top of the stockade fence formed of pointed, tight-fitting logs. Then his heart leaped when the heavy wooden shutters on the upper level of the southeast blockhouse swung open, and a guard stuck his head out, resting his rifle across the windowsill.

"Goin' soft, ain't you Reeves, bringin' in that peach-fuzz kid?" the uniformed man taunted.

"Better keep your finger on the trigger and your eye down the barrel, blue boy," Reeves called back. "Behind that boy face is a heart dark as midnight, and a draw quicker than Wild Bill himself."

"Maybe I got it all wrong," the soldier said, chuckling. "I thought you was bringin' him in, not the other way around."

"He's my partner," Reeves said. "Between the two of us, we could whip the whole lot of you striped-leg blue-bellies and never break a sweat."

"Guess we'd might as well throw down our weapons and surrender right now," the guard said, withdrawing his rifle and closing the shutters.

Reeves and the boy turned along the stockade wall, following a trail that angled slightly left across flat land, then climbed a mild slope past a long mess hall and a small, disconnected kitchen. The trail continued toward a log house with steps leading to a wide porch, once the home of the commanding officer but now occupied by the quartermaster and his family. The structure was over fifty feet long with an open hallway splitting it in half and a stone chimney on each end.

"Where are we going?" the boy asked as they detoured left past the house.

"To see the commander," the deputy said. "That old stockade is just used for storage now, so he's moved up on the hill."

Continuing, they rode past the quartermaster's warehouse and abandoned earthworks, which the deputy explained had been built during the Civil War. Up ahead, on the side of a long ridge, stood a building with its back to them. In front, the floor of the building was level with the crest of the bluff, while in back it was supported by ten-foot-tall log posts. Beneath the floor, the earth had been dug out and fenced for stables.

"What's that building?" the boy asked.

"Commissary," the deputy replied. "And to the right of it is the powder magazine and then the bakery. On farther down is the hospital."

"Where are the soldiers?"

"In that long, two-story building you see pokin' up from the other side of the ridge."

They angled to the left past a storehouse and a blacksmith shop, and then climbed a steep slope to a road running along the top of an intersecting ridge. To their left stood three two-story buildings, all officers' quarters. Stopping in front of the middle one, the deputy slipped down and motioned the boy to follow.

A man, maybe forty years old and trim in his uniform, answered their knock.

"Hello, Marshal Reeves," the gentleman said without hesitation.

"I need to talk to you, commander," the deputy said, attempting a weak salute.

"Sure, come in," the officer said, "and your young companion."

"His name is Everett," Reeves said, motioning toward the boy. "Son, this here's Commander Coppinger."

Staring past the man into the well furnished home, Everett nodded while his face remained expressionless. Waiting in the hallway while the commander called to his wife, Deputy Reeves removed his hat, then nudged the boy to do the same.

"Rachel, have Nellie entertain young Everett while I visit with the marshal," Coppinger said as his wife descended the stairway directly in front of them.

As the two men slipped into a sitting room to their right, the woman called up to her daughter while guiding Everett to the base of the stairs.

A neatly dressed girl of about ten, with long blond curls, appeared at the top of the stairs, holding a colorful rag doll to her chest. She stopped and stared down at the boy standing blank-faced in his dirty denim pants, torn shirt, and shabby shoes.

"Nellie, this is Everett. I want you to take him up to the widow's walk. After I get refreshments for the men, I'll bring up some lemonade and cookies."

"Yes, Mama," her daughter replied.

Glancing up at the girl, Everett hesitated.

"Go on, son," the woman said, nudging gently with her hand on the boy's back.

At the top of the stairs, Nellie led the way to a door that opened to a narrow, crude stairway that took them to a small landing with another door that opened onto the roof. A white picketed railing bordered a weathered, wooden deck on three sides, while the sloped roof served as the fourth boundary. Three chairs sat around a small table on the otherwise bare floor. The girl walked over to the rail near the edge of the roof and looked out across a treed landscape that dropped rapidly to the edge of a wide river snaking its way from north to south.

After standing quietly for a moment, the girl turned toward Everett who waited some ten feet behind her.

"You know what river that is?" she asked.

"The Arkansas," he replied, joining her at the rail.

"No, the Neosho," she replied proudly. "Some call it the Grand, but Papa says they're wrong."

"It don't matter no way," the boy said. "It's just a river."

"That's not so," the girl replied adamantly. "There are three rivers here, and if you don't learn which is which, you won't know how to go anywhere."

"Learnin' the names of rivers ain't the only thing about knowin' your way," the boy replied. "You gotta know directions, and you can figure that by lookin' at moss on trees and where the sun is. My pa said the stars show you the way at night, if you know how to read 'em."

"You ever go to school?" the girl asked.

"No, but my ma taught me before she . . ."

"If you lived here, you'd have to go to school. Everybody does."

"I don't want to live here."

The door opened and Rachel stepped out with a tray of cookies and a pitcher of lemonade. After sliding the tray onto the table and pouring lemonade for each, she sat down and motioned Everett to a chair, then her daughter.

"Everett, where're you from?" the woman asked.

"Just come from Fort Smith," he replied.

"Your folks back there?"

"Not no more," he replied, turning to look away.

"Do you have brothers or sisters?"

He shook his head.

"Will you be staying around here or traveling on?"

"That deputy says I'm stayin', but I ain't."

"Well, we'd be mighty pleased to have you here with us," the woman said just as she heard her husband call from the porch below. She turned to her daughter as Everett gulped down his drink. "Go ahead and finish your lemonade, dear, while I take your friend down to Marshal Reeves."

The commander and deputy stood waiting just inside the front door. When Everett arrived, they stepped outside and stood on the stone walkway at the foot of the porch, where Reeves turned toward the lad.

"The commander has agreed to board you and feed you so long as you do a day's work in the horse stables," Reeves said. "And he'll try to find a family that'll take you in."

"I can clean stables as good as you or anybody, but I don't want no family." the boy responded.

"Son," the commander said, placing a hand on Everett's shoulder, "I think you'll change your mind when you meet some of the fine womenfolk we have here. You're still young enough to need a woman to fuss over you when you're sick and tend to your clothes."

"Sir, I'll get by just fine on my own."

"Well, we'll see," the commander said, smiling. "And another thing, you'll attend our little school."

"I don't want to."

"I'm taking responsibility for you, son, and that means you will attend school like the other children. There is no need to discuss the matter further."

At the gate Bass Reeves climbed back on his horse and motioned for the boy to follow. They rode down to a large corral full of milling horses. The deputy stopped and pointed to a canvas-covered doorway to a one-room, log shack about thirty feet from the corral.

"You can put your things in there," Reeves said. "Let loose your horses in with the others, so they get regular feed and water."

As Everett rode toward the shack, he watched the deputy trot his horse toward the officers' quarters.

Pushing aside the hanging canvas, the boy stepped through onto a hard dirt floor. It was cramped and drab, but it was better than anything he had slept in for three months. A few pots and pans hung from nails on the well-chinked, log walls. A wood-burning stove with removable cooking discs on top stood in one corner, its front door open revealing a pile of gray ashes inside. Nearby lay a small pile of wood. A straight-back, straw-bottomed chair was pushed up against a three-legged table. A cot with a water-stained mattress filled with cornhusks ran along the far wall, and a lantern hung from a pole rafter in the center of the room.

After throwing the saddlebags on the table and unrolling his blanket on the bed, Everett stepped outside and stripped the horses, chunking saddles and blankets inside the room. At the corral fence he slid back the two top gate-poles, and the horses stepped over the bottom one as he led them into the large pen where he pulled off their bridles and set them free.

Back in the room, he shoveled cold ashes from the stove, then searched the saddlebags and came up with a few matches, which he used to set fire to some small kindling he had placed among the dry wood stuffed into the stove's belly. He pulled the chair up close and slumped down.

Just as he relaxed, a voice at the doorway shook him from his thoughts.

3

"Who's there?" Everett called out, jumping to his feet.

"Deputy Reeves. I've brought you some grub and a couple of army blankets."

The marshal pushed back the canvas, stooped, and stepped inside. He pitched the blankets onto the cot, set four cans of army rations on the table, then added a canister of coffee from his own supplies, along with a wrapped chunk of bacon. He pulled a box of cartridges from his coat pocket and tossed them to Everett.

"You got any money?" the deputy asked.

"What my pa left," the boy replied, having found a few coins in the saddlebags.

Reeves pulled a golden eagle from his pocket and slapped it down on the table. "That'll get you by for a while. I'll be back to check on you now and then."

As abruptly as he had come, the deputy turned and left. The boy stared after him, wanting to thank him but unable to get the words out.

Up early, Everett started frying bacon and heating water for coffee, skills he had learned while waiting in a lonely camp for his father. Sipping from a steaming cup, he peeked out and spotted a sergeant leading two haltered horses toward the pole gate where a couple of officers stood waiting, their saddles riding the top rail of the corral fence.

While the officers saddled their mounts and rode away, the boy finished breakfast, slipped out, and climbed the fence. He headed for the sergeant, now stooped over pouring grain into a long wooden trough.

“Mister,” Everett said tentatively, “can I help?”

The husky man straightened, twisted around, and stared at the boy.

“What’re you doin’ here?” he growled.

“Come to help with the horses,” Everett explained.

“Why, you’re just a towheaded boy. Who sent you?”

“Mr. Coppinger, he called himself.”

The sergeant hesitated, eyeing the boy while twirling one end of his shaggy mustache. “Commander Coppinger?” he asked with one eye narrowed and his bushy head tilted.

“Yes, sir. I think that’s him.”

“Humph. Then fetch this bucket back here full of corn. The crib’s right yonder,” the sergeant ordered, pointing at an old wooden shed with a sagging door.

Everett grabbed the wire handle and struck out. Waddling back across the lot with his right shoulder hitched high and the bucket brimming full of yellow kernels, banging against his leg with every step, he refused the old sergeant’s offered help.

“A bit too much for you, lad?” the fellow asked, laughing.

“No, sir,” Everett shot back, huffing past.

“Then dump it in,” the sergeant said, “and spread it along the trough.”

With a grimace, the boy heaved the bucket up and poured the corn evenly along the wooden feeder, then turned to go for more.

“A couple scoops less this time, boy,” the sergeant said. “You’ll wear yourself out before the job’s half done. There’s three more troughs like this one, and they hold six buckets each. That’ll be . . .”

“Eighteen buckets after this one’s done,” Everett said.

“About that,” the burly man said, glancing down at his fingers, “and four more to fill this one. What’s your name, anyhow?”

“Everett,” the boy called back.

“Well, I’m Sergeant Wilson. When you finish feedin’ the horses, come find me. I might have another chore or two for you.”

Everett continued toward the corncrib, making no response. When he reached the doorway, he glanced back over his shoulder and caught a glimpse of the sergeant ducking inside a room much like his own. I ain’t likely to have much idle time, he thought.

When Everett had finished filling the troughs, he spotted Sergeant Wilson riding the corral fence, running his tongue along the seam of a sliver of paper rolled around a column of tobacco.

"You see that row of horse stalls over there?" the man asked, twisting one end of the paper. "Well, there's a shovel and wheelbarrow leanin' against the outside wall of the first one. When you've mucked out the stalls, spread a layer of clean straw inside. Them officers are picky about such things."

Later, while pushing another load to the heap, Everett noticed the sergeant hop down from the fence and salute an officer who had just walked up. Returning to the stall, the boy watched as the neatly dressed man pointed his way while speaking to Sergeant Wilson.

As Everett lifted another shovel-full to the wheelbarrow, the sergeant appeared in the stall entrance.

"Boy," he growled, "get yourself over to the commander's office. This'll wait 'til you get back."

When the lad reached the gate, the sergeant loomed over him for a moment, then stepped aside. "You smell," he said. "Wash up at that water pump over there."

Cleaned up as best he could, Everett hurried over to the officer who was pacing along the fence with his hands clasped behind his back.

"You Everett Brook?" the man asked.

"Yes, sir."

"Commander Coppinger would like a word with you," the officer said, then turned along a trail that led up the hill.

Standing stiffly on the front porch, the officer clicked his heels and saluted as the commander opened the door and invited them inside.

"Son," Coppinger said, "I hear you've already made yourself useful. That's good, but I think we'd better have a little chat."

He motioned Everett to a stuffed chair in the sitting room while he eased down into another. The officer stood rigid as a rail beside the window, peering out.

"First," the commander began, "I want you to know I'm sorry about your unfortunate circumstance. Second, I welcome you to Fort Gibson.

"Now, we don't ordinarily accept . . . uh, orphans. But Deputy Marshal Reeves assured me you're a good lad who's been dealt a losing hand, and we here at the fort mean to give you a second chance.

"There's plenty work to be done, and a boy needs to be busy. I can't pay you, but I can provide a roof and rations."

The commander hesitated after giving the boy a thorough looking-over. "And I'll see if we can scrounge up a change of clothes for you. Every week, take your dirty ones down to suds row, and the women will wash them.

"Do you have any money?" the commander asked, stuffing his hand into his pocket.

"Some," Everett muttered, recalling the golden eagle Reeves had given him.

"Here's a couple of dollars for you."

The boy took the money and poked it into his front pocket. "I'll pay you back."

"No, son. Consider it hospitality. Now, is there anything else you need?"

"Yes, sir. I have two horses and gear. I'd like to keep the extra horse, but not the spare saddle and bridle. They belonged to my pa. If I could sell 'em . . ."

"Captain Shockley," Coppinger said to the officer, "requisition a saddle with all the trappings. We can always use an extra." Turning back to Everett, he smiled. "Anything else?"

"No, sir."

"Excellent," the commander said, rising to his feet. "You missed school this morning, but tomorrow, and every day thereafter, you'll be at the schoolhouse at half past eight. Is that understood?"

"Yes, sir," the boy mumbled as he stood.

"Now, if you need anything," the commander continued, "just let Captain Shockley know."

Early the next morning, Everett was standing off to the side of the one-room schoolhouse when a tall woman walked up, her gray hair pinned in a bun on the back of her head.

"You must be the new student the commander told me about," she said, smiling.

The boy nodded, glancing down at his shoes.

"I'm Mrs. Weatherly, your teacher," she said. "Come in, Everett."

She opened the door and motioned him inside where he immediately paused, watching her put her things on the small table at the front. She pointed to the end of a bench along the last row of tables and handed him a fat pencil and a few supplies.

Other students filed in, talking and laughing as they took their assigned places. Sitting alone, Everett could feel their eyes on him. He desperately wanted to jump up and dash out of the room.

The teacher introduced him to the class, then began the day. Though she never called on him to answer a question, she often strolled along the back row, glancing at his work, and once patted him on the shoulder while whispering, "Very good."

The next two days were similar with his confidence growing and his affection for Mrs. Weatherly blossoming. The only student that showed much interest in him was Nellie Coppinger who sat on the row in front of him and made a point to walk partway home with him each day.

After school the third day, Everett was feeding the horses when the captain showed up with thirty dollars for the saddle and bridle and a commander-signed note to the commissary officer allocating full soldier rations to Everett Brook. With his stable work done, the lad lost no time in collecting his first allotment of food.

That night in the dim lantern light of his room, the boy spread his money out on the table. Forty-six dollars was more than he could imagine having. With a roof over his head, his wealth spread out before him, rows of rations stacked on a board shelf, and a warm fire crackling, Everett felt more secure than he had with his father who had frequently left him alone for days in some remote camp. Back then, often he had eaten only one meal a day, a bowl of beans with dried crackers or hard bread, and maybe roasted rabbit, if he had made a good shot that day.

Running his small fingers over the coins, he suddenly felt vulnerable in a way he had never known. He remembered his father telling about a man who had killed his partner to get back twenty dollars lost in a poker game, and another who had shot a stranger for half a bottle of whiskey. He must hide his money.

He found a leather pouch in his saddlebags, dropped the coins in, and pulled the drawstring tight and tied it off. Then, with the point of his knife, he cut a few stitches holding the inside liner of his coat and slid the coin bag through the opening. He folded the coat for a pillow and slept soundly.

✪ ✪ ✪

Over the following weeks, Everett settled into a routine of school in the morning, watering and feeding the army's horses in the afternoon, and mucking stalls until dark. He proved to be a good student, especially with numbers. His greatest weakness was lazy pronunciation, so occasionally the teacher had him stay a few minutes after school to practice, most often words ending in "ing." Feasting on her attention, he dedicated himself to pleasing this motherly woman.

In addition to his regular work in the afternoons, he sometimes repaired mule harnesses and saddles and cut and gathered wood for his stove. Mindful of approaching winter, he scavenged enough old boards to construct a door for his room, and with hinges from a dilapidated building, he hung it in place of the old flapping canvas.

One morning Captain Shockley delivered a bundle of clothes with a note from Commander Coppinger pinned to the top.

Henceforth, I expect your attire to be clean and mended when attending school and in the general presence of womenfolk and officers of this post.

Though he was not sure about every word, he got the gist of the note.

The two changes of pants, shirts, socks, and underclothes were hand-me-downs, but clean, pressed, and folded so neatly as to stir remembrances of his mother's smile and delicate touch. Sundays, she had always carefully laid out a fresh change of clothes for him. For a minute, he stood staring at the gray plaid shirt on top, then brushed away a wrinkle. As if from her very hands, he took the clothes and gently placed them on a shelf, then turned away, dabbing his shirtsleeve at the corners of his eyes.

The following Saturday, having completed his corral chores, Everett brought two buckets of water from the well, heated it in a pan on his stove, bathed head to toe, and slipped into the finer set of fresh clothes. Standing just outside his door, he finger-combed and patted down his damp hair, using his shadow as a mirror. To his considerable frustration, the drier his hair got, the more unruly it became, eventually backsliding to its normal dishevelment.

After striding up the hill and turning along the road toward the commissary, his head held high and his back as straight as a lodge-pole sapling, he heard someone call his name. Slowing, he glanced back toward the officer's quarters where he saw the commander's wife, Rachel, striding along with Nellie at her side. Reluctantly, he turned and ambled toward the pair who approached him in their delicate dresses and bonnets.

"Good afternoon, Everett," Mrs. Coppinger called out as they met.

"Afternoon to you, ma'am," he replied, then nodded toward the girl.

"I want to commend you on your attire, Everett," the woman said. "I must say you look quite dapper."

"Thank you, ma'am," he mumbled, looking away.

"But those boots are just awful," she continued. "I'll have to find you something better."

"Mama, he needs a comb, too," the girl chirped. "At school his hair is never in place."

With his right hand, Everett quickly brushed at his hair while his gaze dropped to his clean but often-patched, horse-lot boots.

"Now, now," Mrs. Coppinger said, "We didn't mean to embarrass you. How would you like to come along with us to the store? That is where you're headed, is it not?"

"Yes, ma'am."

"Good, good. Then let's be on our way."

Everett chose the woman's side opposite the girl, but could not avoid Nellie's repeated glances. As uncomfortable as a wild pony strapped to his first saddle, the boy stared straight ahead and tried unsuccessfully to encourage a brisk pace. Inside the store, with great relief, he headed for the footwear display while the woman and girl chose dresses. He had the inventory memorized, having previously inspected them thoroughly at least a half-dozen times, so he grabbed the fore-chosen boots, paid the clerk, then rushed out the door.

Back in his room, feeling his venture into their world a dismal failure, he changed into his work clothes and headed for the stables. He grabbed a bridle and climbed the corral fence. Perched on the top rail, he spotted the buckskin and headed for him. The army horses scattered, clearing a path to the boy's pony, which raised his head as Everett approached and allowed the boy to loop a rope around his neck.

Having led the horse to the nearest stall, Everett bridled him, spread on the blanket, and cinched down his saddle. He then swung up and turned the pony down the slope toward the Neosho. Along the east bank of the river, he followed a narrow, winding trail he had noticed that first day from the roof of the commander's house. Though he had observed other riders arriving and departing the fort by that route, he had never inquired about where the path might lead. At the moment, his only concern was finding an escape route from the fort and away from those critical eyes that made him feel he did not belong, regardless how much he tried or how he dressed. He had felt less alone waiting for days in an obscure camp while his father and partner rode into some town for supplies or for entertainment.

The rested pony was eager to run, and the boy gave him his head. Unsure how long the buckskin had galloped or how far they had traveled, he felt the horse's sides heaving in labored breathing, so pulled back on the reins and guided his mount down to the river's edge. Eager to drink, the horse dropped his head to the flowing stream. Everett slid down and stood patting his horse's neck and shoulders until the pony finally raised his dripping muzzle and perked his ears forward, staring upstream about fifty yards to the opposite shoreline. Following the horse's gaze, the boy spotted three riders fording the stream, their paint horses pushing into the shallow river, heading for the east bank. Each gripped a rifle, wore moccasins, and their dark eyes were fixed on him.

4

Everett snatched the reins and jumped into the saddle. Spinning the buckskin around, he dug his heels into his flanks, sending the pony lunging up the sandy slope to the trail. Stealing a peek up the path, he spotted the Indians flushing out of a narrow stand of trees upstream, and kicked his pony into an all-out gallop.

The buckskin, still weak from his earlier run, maintained a steady pace for only a few minutes, then began to slow. The boy hammered the horse's ribs with his boot heels and whipped his shoulders with the loose ends of the reins, but the pony had nothing more to give.

Glancing back, Everett saw the Indians pursuing, one thrusting his rifle above his head with an indecipherable yell. The boy wished he had strapped on his father's revolver. A few shots would at least slow them down. Terrifying war-whoops reached his ears above the pounding of his horse's hooves, chilling him to the bone. He kicked harder, but when the leg-weary buckskin stumbled trying to respond, he pulled back on the reins.

With the Indians closing in, he turned the buckskin off the trail into the thick trees and underbrush to his left. Bent low over the pony's shoulders, dodging low limbs and vines, he doggedly kept the heaving horse moving ahead toward a sharp rise. Wild-eyed, the pony struggled up the slope, finally falling to his knees. Everett jumped down and led him to the top where he stopped and glanced back. Seeing no sign of his pursuers, he let his horse rest. While watching and listening, he realized the dense forest limited his range of sight to less than fifty feet, so he pushed on.

Easing the pace, they scrambled down the far side of the hill, the boy looking ahead for a hiding place. Spotting an empty six-foot-deep ravine with a gaping gash in its near bank, he climbed into the saddle and reined the buckskin that way. Two quick lurches brought the horse and rider to the bed of the gulch. Thinking the Indians would expect him to head south toward the fort, he turned north.

After several minutes of following the ravine, which gradually doubled in depth, he came to a sharp bend where he spotted a dense growth of bushes shielding a nook sheltered by a twelve-foot-high, rocky overhang. He jumped down and pulled his horse through the scratchy brush into a concealed half-moon space formed by the ravine's curved wall. Out of breath and frightened, he tried to calm his frantic pony. Above their heavy breathing, he listened for approaching riders. Unable to see through the thicket, he looped the reins around a small limb, dropped to his hands and knees, and crawled forward until his head poked out the other side. The first glimpse back up the ravine told him his effort to hide had failed.

There in the soft red dirt of the gulch, his pony's tracks clearly marked their path. Even from the rim above, the hoof prints would be obvious. If the Indians had not lost his trail farther back, it was only a matter of time. Scooting back to his horse, he slumped down, leaning back against the red-clay wall. Defenseless and exposed, he and his tired pony were trapped. From his pocket he pulled a small, single-bladed knife.

As his horse quieted down, darkness began to settle in. Looking up to the sliver of sky above him, he saw heavy gray clouds rolling and heard a rush of wind stir the treetops. A thunderstorm, he thought. It could save him, washing away the tracks.

Suddenly, lightning split the sky, thunder rumbled, and within minutes the clouds burst open. Everett sighed in relief as large drops pelted his upturned face. While relishing his good luck, it occurred to him that the ravine could soon become a roaring stream, trapping him and his pony. Carefully he led the buckskin back through the thick brush and climbed into the wet saddle. Watching puddles as they formed in the creases of the hoof marks and slowly melted them away, he nudged the buckskin on down the ravine, hoping for a place to climb out.

Half an hour later, the gulch now carrying a turbulent muddy flow that swelled above the buckskin's knees, he came to a junction with another ravine, one feeding in a smaller stream of water. Everett turned and followed it until it grew shallow enough for his pony to scale the wall.

For the past year, hunting alone in remote forests while his father was away, he had become somewhat adept at keeping his bearings, but now he found himself unsure. While fleeing from the Indians, he had not kept visible reference points, and had not created a mental map of the path he had followed. Further complicating his whereabouts were the heavy storm clouds concealing any clues from the sun and now a starless night was closing in. He fought off a growing fear that he would become lost in the dense forest and forced himself to focus on past experiences and draw on everything he had observed while traveling with experienced woodsmen.

Follow a stream, he told himself. They always lead to larger ones. He reasoned that going with the current would eventually bring him to the Neosho River, which he then could follow downstream to the fort.

Making his way to the rim of the main ravine, he traced along its bank, eventually reaching a larger stream that flowed to his right. As darkness finally engulfed the woodland, the boy and his horse broke through the tree line onto the trail that ran alongside the big river. Unable to see more than a few yards, he listened for anyone on the path. Hearing no one, he slipped down and checked the soft ground for hoof marks of unshod ponies, but the rain had destroyed any that might have been there, even ten minutes earlier. Back up on the buckskin, he followed the tumbling water southward, hugging the eastern edge of the trail so he could instantly disappear into the dark forest, if necessary.

A little over an hour later, he recognized the natural rock landing at the river crossing just below the fort. He reined his horse into a narrow opening that someone had hacked through a canebrake, then up the slope toward the corral, digging his heels into the animal's ribs to hurry him along. Arriving at the commander's house, he jumped down, ran to the door, and pounded repeatedly.

"What's the matter, son?" asked Commander Coppinger, opening the door while dabbing at the corner of his mouth with a dinner napkin.

"Indians," Everett answered excitedly. "Three of them with rifles. They chased me, but I got away."

"Where?"

"On the trail along the Neosho, to the north. They were headed this way."

"What kind of Indians?"

"I don't know. When they let out war whoops, I slipped into the woods and hid."

Jabbering, gesturing, and pointing, he told how he had made his getaway and had been saved by the rainstorm.

"Did they fire at you?"

"No, sir."

"Most Indians around here are friendly, son. They often come to the fort for supplies and to trade."

"These didn't seem friendly."

"I'll get my horse, and we'll have a look around," the commander replied, showing too little concern to suit the boy.

Soon Coppinger joined Everett, and they rode by the commissary, then down the slope toward the warehouses and corral. Seeing no sign of trouble, they continued to the stockade where some weapons and munitions were stored, along with extra corn, oats, and hay.

As they approached, Everett suddenly grabbed the commander's arm.

"There," he said in a hushed but excited tone, pointing through a gap between the buildings at the northwest corner. "Their horses!"

"Let's check with the guard," Coppinger said, turning his pony toward the block tower at the northwest corner.

"Cherokees from Tahlequah," the sentry explained. "They've come to trade with the sutler for winter blankets. I put 'em up for the night in the old barracks there on the north side."

"But they yelled and chased me!" Everett protested.

"Just funnin'," the guard explained. "They told me they put a good scare into a rabbit-of-a-boy along the trail."

"But sir," Everett started to explain as he followed the commander back up the slope.

"They meant you no harm," Coppinger said, cutting him short.

"Sorry, sir," Everett mumbled as they approached the corral and his little room.

Coppinger reached over and mussed the boy's hair. "Get some sleep, son."

In the coming weeks and months, Everett was surprised to learn that Fort Gibson existed more to protect the Indians from greedy frontiersmen, whiskey peddlers, and ruthless outlaws than to protect white settlers from the Indians.

"The federal government wanted to make room for the growing number of its citizens pushing westward toward the Mississippi River," the commander explained. "But that area was home to many Indians, like the Choctaws, Creeks, Chickasaws, Seminoles, and the Eastern Cherokees, often called the Five Civilized Tribes. The solution was to move them west of the Mississippi."

"So they sent them here?" the boy asked.

"Not at first. You see, the Western Cherokees and the Osages, already in this area, were constantly fighting. The Indians back East sure didn't want to move into that hornet's nest. So the government had to settle that feud before more Indians would agree to relocate this way.

"Well, in 1817, the army sent soldiers up the Arkansas River to Belle Point, where Fort Smith was established. Then in 1822, they sent Colonel Matthew Arbuckle to command the garrison there. He soon realized that his soldiers could do more good if they were farther up the river, in the heart of the troubled area. So in 1824, he moved his men here to the Three Forks and that's how Fort Gibson got started, though it was called Cantonment Gibson back then."

"Three Forks?"

"Yeah, three rivers come together here, the Arkansas, the Verdigris, and the Neosho."

"How did he stop the Cherokees and Osages from fighting?"

"To the surprise of most folks, it wasn't by joining the fight. Colonel Arbuckle was the commander here for nearly twenty years, retiring in the summer of 1841 as a general, and he was mighty proud to say his men never killed one Indian here, and the Indians only killed one soldier.

"Instead of war, he believed in talking, compromising, and negotiating treaties. But he also knew that without the soldiers, enough to fight if he had to, the Indians would not respect him. So he kept his soldiers armed and ready, but they spent their time building roads, surveying, escorting Indians, and standing between feuding parties."

"Why were the Indians fighting each other?"

"Most of the conflicts happened because the Osages and the Cherokees were competing for hunting grounds, for the best land, and for buffalo. Hunting parties would run into each other and someone would get killed. The side losing a brave would then retaliate by raiding the other's village, killing and stealing horses. That's when General Arbuckle and the soldiers would step in and try to put a stop to it."

"Did he get them to quit?" Everett asked.

"Enough to allow more Indians to be moved into the area. Overcrowding of these people who require large hunting grounds was bound to cause more conflict. Then the Eastern Cherokees came, led by John Ross, and set off more feuding with their Western brothers. Add the growing number of white settlers pushing in, the Plains Indians just to the west, and hostilities in Texas to the south, and it was like a powder keg, always about ready to explode."

"But it's not like that anymore, is it?"

"Some still hold grudges, others still quarrel openly, but with time it has settled down a lot. Now the problem is the white settler encroaching on Indian lands, outlaws who kill and steal, and whiskey peddlers who sell firewater to the Indians, in spite of a federal law prohibiting it."

"I thought there was no white-man law here?"

"The criminal court of the Western District of Arkansas has jurisdiction, not only of the western counties of that state, but also of the Indian Territory. For well over a year now, Judge Isaac Parker has presided over that court."

"I know about him," Everett said, dropping his eyes to his shoe tops. "The hangin' judge."

"Son, I know it's difficult for you to understand, but the judge and his marshals have a tough job. Just last year, three of his deputies were killed while trying to uphold the law."

"That don't make it right to hang the wrong man," the boy muttered.

"Everett, maybe there are things you don't understand about your father, about what happened. Maybe when you grow up . . ."

"I'll show them some day," the boy said with clenched teeth. "And they'll pay for what they done."

✪ ✪ ✪

For the next few years Everett remained at the fort, mostly caring for military horses. His fondness for Mrs. Weatherly never wavered, and often in the evening he would join her in strolls about the fort reservation and along the river's edge, always talking about books, about history, and their importance. "The world is much bigger than we know," she would say, "and we need to learn about other places, the ways of other people. Through books we can do that, even through newspapers."

Sometimes she would ask about his past, but he always brushed the question aside with some general statement about the untimely death of his parents. Though never satisfied with his answer, she always moved on to other subjects.

Colonel Coppinger occasionally sought him out, but he was a busy man and spent less and less time with the boy. Reports to him were that young Everett was a hard worker, a dedicated student, and a boy grown up beyond his years.

Deputy Marshal Bass Reeves checked in about every three months, but his stays were brief. He glanced around the little room, asked a few questions, then moved on to the commissary or to tend to his business at the fort.

Everett had chores every afternoon, including Saturdays and sometimes Sundays. He spent very little time with other children, never feeling he had much in common. Nellie sometimes invited him to parties at the Coppinger home, giving her someone her age to talk to while the adults danced and visited. As they grew older, Everett became fond of her, but the social barrier he perceived to be between them prevented him from ever letting her know.

By his eighteenth year he stood over six feet tall with the developing frame of a man and was educated better than most young westerners. The years of hard work left him lean, muscled, and agile, but one thing remained unchanged from the day he had arrived. He was dead set on avenging his father's death.

5

Red Fork Ranch
Spring, 1881

In the late afternoon shadows, a long, lean young man riding a chestnut mare splashed across the Cimarron River at the Chisholm Trail Ford. About half a mile upstream, just below where Turkey Creek joined the river from the north, was the crossing for the Fort Reno Trail, the route used by stagecoaches and the military. Some maps labeled the river as the Red Fork of the Arkansas, and that explained the name of the Red Fork Ranch headquartered about a mile and a half ahead, lying snugly between the two roads.

The lone rider chose the Chisholm crossing because it offered more caution. In early spring the cattle-drive season was yet a month or two away, leaving the trail empty. Also, the cattle trail offered the best vantage point for observing the comings and goings at the ranch prior to riding in.

The mare's hooves churned the shallow water as she surged onto the north bank of the river, entering a natural blind formed by a dense forest of scrubby oaks on both sides that pinched the old cattle trail to a quarter of its normal width. Scanning the shadows under the canopy of treetops, the eighteen-year-old dropped his right hand to his Colt revolver and slipped off the thong looped over its hammer. He had heard too many tales of horse thieves and outlaws who made their dens within the Blackjack Forest, surprising their victims from its darkness.

Half a mile later where the trail gradually widened, the rider veered to the left, using the thick growth of oaks to shield him from view from the ranch. Another mile found him in the edge of the trees carefully scanning a wide clearing where two large buildings sat and a horse corral penned two ponies and a pair of mules. Satisfied, the young man nudged the chestnut forward into the opening and slowly approached the larger building. Pulling up in front of the two-story log structure, he noticed a crude board sign dangling from the porch cover.

RED FORK RANCH
WILLIAMS AND CO.

While the rider carefully looked around the ranch site, a man of maybe twenty-three years stepped through the doorway.

"Howdy," the rancher called out, stopping and leaning against one of six raw oak posts supporting the wood-shingled porch cover.

Swinging down, the young rider smiled and pulled at the brim of his hat, then double wrapped the ends of the leather reins around the iron-rod hitching rail. Draping his saddlebags over his left shoulder, he headed for the three split-log steps fronting the porch.

"Looking for grub and maybe a job," the young rider said, his long stride skipping the middle step.

"Name's Ralph Collins," the rancher replied. "Come along to the cook house and have supper. Then, maybe I can help."

The man led the way to a ten-by-twenty-foot log cabin with walls grayed by years of weather, in stark contrast to the fresh wood of the adjacent two-story building. Inside, the floor was dirt and the eight-foot ceiling consisted of a grid of poles supporting a sloped eighteen-inch-thick sod roof. The log walls stood vertically, stockade style, their ends buried two to three feet into the ground.

The tall rider took a seat on an L-shaped oak bench attached to the wall, the bottom of the L running along a second wall. Pushing his hat back, he dragged his shirtsleeve across his brow while the rancher chunked a few sticks of wood onto a dwindling fire in the belly of an old cook stove. The rancher removed one of two cast-iron discs from the stovetop using a thick rag, and set a pan of beans on to warm. About that time, another young man appeared in the doorway.

"My partner, Fred Williams," the rancher explained, then turned toward his visitor. "I don't believe you mentioned your name."

"Everett," the young man replied, eyeing the fellow in the doorway. "I thought a couple of Caldwell cattlemen ran this place."

"Me and Cousin Fred bought it a while back from John Hood and Johnnie Blair. Hood ran it with Blair putting up most of the money and sending his younger brother Marion down to check on his investment occasionally. Blair's a mighty nice fellow, I hear, but I'm afraid Hood let the place run down some after he sold his herd and pocketed thirty-five thousand dollars. We've added a porch and second floor to the old store, trying to fix the place up a bit."

When Everett did not respond the rancher continued. "We came up from the Darlington Indian Agency, about thirty miles to the south, where our uncle is the United States Commissioner for the Plains Indians in these parts."

"You need any help with the fixin' up?" Everett asked.

"Matter of fact, we do. What kind of work suits you?"

"I reckon I can handle about anything there is to do around a ranch."

"We're expecting a steady stream of steers up the Chisholm Trail this year," Ralph said, "Now if we had a large corral to hold the cattle overnight, one with sections for tallying and branding, the drovers would be more apt to stay over. With the cowboys freed up, more than likely they'd spend any money in their pockets."

"If I was to hire on, what's the pay?"

"Grub and a place to sleep," Ralph replied. "But if you help us build up our little herd, we could pay you cowboy wages."

"How are you growing your herd?" Everett asked, wanting no part of a rustling operation.

"We buy a few tender-footed cows that can't finish the drive, scrounge a few strays from along the river and draws, and we've bought a few bulls to put with the cows."

After hesitating, Everett nodded. He had a few dollars in his pocket from the sale of his buckskin at Fort Gibson, so monthly pay suited him. And he had noticed that the Chisholm Trail ran by the ranch just to the east and the Reno Trail passed about seventy yards to the west. Being particularly interested in travelers, the setup looked ideal.

"Good. You can put your stuff upstairs with ours. Just take those rickety old stairs up. It gets a little crowded sometimes when the stage brings in customers or when cowboys or freighters come in, but mostly, its mighty peaceful out here."

"What about my horse?" Everett asked, rising to his feet.

"Let him loose with ours in the corral back there," the rancher replied.

After gathering his bedroll, slicker, and saddle, Everett climbed the outside stairs and dumped his things inside. Around back, while the chestnut mare ate corn, he pumped water into a barrel halved lengthwise, then led her into a split-rail corral and set her loose with a gray gelding, a brown-and-white pinto, and the team of mules.

"That dilapidated corral across the Reno road, what's it for?" Everett asked as he sat down to coffee, beans, hot biscuits, and two drumsticks of prairie hen.

"It was built by Dan Jones about four years back," Fred said. "It'll hold small herds, but too often the steers bust out during the night, and the cowboys lose half a day rounding them up again."

"Looks like a good wind would blow the whole thing into the river," Everett replied.

"The first herds will show up in about two months," Ralph said. "Maybe you can help us build a new one before then."

"How come this Hood fellow sold out?"

"Just wasn't suited to it. Living by himself out here, he tired of the loneliness," Ralph explained, laughing as he remembered. "Hood said Jones had declared he was ready for a little higher grade of company, and 'now I share his sentiment.' Dan has gone up to Caldwell to be a deputy marshal."

Before leaving the supper table, raw boards lashed together with rawhide and supported by two stacked wooden crates, it was agreed that Everett would begin his morning by scouting for timber to rebuild the old cattle corral. He mentioned that he had noticed stretches of land to the east and west of the ranch house, two to four miles wide and covered with scrawny trees bearing a coat of rough, dark bark and stubby limbs fringed with wide leaves. Blackjacks, he guessed.

"That's right," Ralph said, "and cutting one is like gnawing on a bone, but they're handy and plentiful."

Everett was up early after tossing and turning throughout a night filled with the screech of owls, the howl of wolves, and yapping of coyotes. He slipped out, saddled the mare, and rode to the old cattle corral. The location was good, with trees to the west and northwest to break the bitterly cold winter winds, a nearby stream for easy watering, and a clear path to the big cattle trail. He quickly decided the old pen should be torn down and the rotting poles burned, keeping only what could be cut up for firewood.

Back at the ranch Ralph and Fred agreed, adding that it should be replaced with a much larger corral, one that would hold twenty-five hundred steers.

"Let's make it circular to accommodate the animals' natural tendency to mill, and set a fence dividing it in half to allow for two smaller herds," Ralph suggested. "We'll put gates in the divider so the cattle can be moved from one half to the other during branding, and set some snubbing posts for handling the rowdy ones."

After eating fried bacon with hot biscuits and figuring out the corral dimensions, Everett began gathering tools. With a couple of sharp axes, a wagon, and the team of old army mules, he headed for the Blackjack Forest immediately west of the corral site. He avoided cutting trees along the edge of Turkey Creek, wanting to leave them so their roots would hold the soil against rushing torrents brought on by heavy spring rains. He labored all afternoon, cutting, trimming, and loading the resulting poles onto the wagon, then delivered them to the corral site where he began a stack of new posts. After loading up the wagon with rotten poles, he dumped them in an open area. In the dusk of late evening, he set them aflame.

That night while sitting on the cabin porch watching the fire's waning flickers, the men made more calculations. Twenty-five hundred head of cattle would require a corral of approximately forty thousand square feet, thus a fence of about seven hundred ten feet, plus a cross fence and a fifty-foot entrance wing, a total of close to one thousand feet. Everett had cut and trimmed blackjacks for six hard hours, but had only about twenty poles to show for his effort. They guessed that over fourteen hundred would be required. With the cattle drive season only a couple of months away, even with Ralph and Fred helping when they could, the corral would not be ready.

"I'll ride over to Little Robe's camp," Fred suggested, "and see if he has some young men who would like to help."

"Who's Little Robe?" Everett asked.

"Cheyenne war chief," Fred replied.

"You sure it'll be safe having Cheyenne braves around here?" Everett asked.

"Fred grew up with many of them," Ralph replied, chuckling. "He's never safer than when around his Cheyenne friends. They'd fight for him as quick as they would for family."

"Ralph," Fred said, "you think we could provide axes and rations for the braves?"

"You bet," the rancher replied.

"Will they expect pay?" Everett asked.

"They'd never take our money," Fred explained. "And when they've needed our help, it's always been the same."

Seeing that Everett was baffled by their relationship with these often-feared Plains Indians, Ralph explained that Fred had moved to the Darlington Agency when only ten years old. He had grown up among them, often playing and sleeping in their camps.

"White Shield was his mentor," Ralph said. "Their elders, Lone Wolf, Little Big Jake, The Whirlwind, Stone Calf, and White Eagle, all men of dignity and character, took him into their councils. Like Brinton Darlington, Fred is a Quaker, and the Indians trust him more than some of their own."

The following morning as Everett prepared the team, Fred climbed onto the gray horse and headed for the Cheyenne camp, some thirty-five miles to the west. While keeping an eye on the store, Ralph chopped and hauled old corral posts that were useable for firewood, stacking them against the south side of the cooking house. Meanwhile, Everett hacked away at the blackjack forest, adding to his stack of poles for the new corral.

About ten o'clock in the morning, Everett glanced up from his work and noticed a cloud of dust to the north along the Reno Trail. He rested the axe handle across his shoulder while staring at the growing, reddish-brown mushroom. Soon he could hear the rattle of wheels, the clanging of harness chains, the pounding of hooves, and amidst it all, a man's sharp voice barking commands. Within seconds, a Concord stagecoach broke into view, its wheels a spinning blur and six-member team in full gallop as if being chased. In front of the ranch store, the driver wheeled the coach in a big arc and pulled the team to a stop by pressing his big foot hard against the long brake lever, locking the wheels. The boiling, rust-colored dust cloud, pushed by a south breeze, enveloped the coach and then drifted on northward. The sand-covered coach reappeared only twelve feet from the porch steps.

When Ralph stepped outside, the driver pitched the reins down to him, then grabbed a canvas bag and climbed to the ground, using the wheel rim as a step. Ralph unhitched the team and drove the sweat-lathered horses around to the watering trough.

Meanwhile, anxiously looking up the trail for outlaws or Indians in hot pursuit of the stage, Everett had lodged the axe blade in the top of a stump and headed for the store. As he approached, the driver, a wiry, red-faced fellow wearing a fringed buckskin coat, opened the near-side door, then tipped his hat and bowed to his passengers. Two men stepped out, one handcuffed. The driver, appearing to be in his fifties, strutted about, stretching his legs, twisting the ends of his bushy gray mustache, and brushing dust from his old black hat with its front brim pinned up to the crown to keep it from flopping down over his eyes.

Still intrigued, Everett sidled up to Ralph to help water the team from the half-hogshead trough.

"How come he came barreling in here like that?"

Ralph chuckled. "Dobe always arrives with a flourish. He's brought the usual way-packet and delivered some travelers headed south."

"Dobe who?"

"Don't know his real name. He's called Dobe because he's one of the surviving buffalo hunters of the Comanche attack on Adobe Walls, led by Quanah Parker."

"Wasn't that out in the Texas Panhandle where Bat Masterson fought the Comanches and that Nancy Olds woman decided to stand right alongside her husband rather than save her own skin?"

"Yep, and I hear she's got a restaurant up in Dodge City now."

"What's a way-packet?" Everett asked.

"Mailbag."

"Who are those men Dobe brought in?"

"Deputy marshal from Texas, taking a prisoner back. The stage from Fort Reno will come up tomorrow and take them on down the trail."

Within minutes the team was again hitched to the Concord with Dobe perched on top, stowing a similar canvas bag. The stagecoach completed the circle it had half made upon arrival and turned back onto the road, rattling north.

While the deputy marshal and his captive had supper with Ralph and Everett, the lawman explained that the previous fall his prisoner had killed a sheriff during a chase after a bank-robbery in Denison, Texas. The killer had escaped into Indian Territory and quickly joined a cattle drive headed for Caldwell, Kansas, where he had been arrested after taking a shot at Marshal Horseman.

"Looks like they fed him real good 'til I could get up there," the deputy said. "Not sure why. I'm takin' him back to be hung."

"Won't there be a trial first?" Ralph asked.

"Won't matter none," the lawman replied between bites. "He's gonna swing, legal or not. Folks in Wise County will see to that."

Through the night, Everett repeatedly raised up from his bed and peered out at the lawman sleeping reared back in a straight-back chair on the porch while his prisoner lay in the yard cuffed to a metal ring bolted through the hitching post. He half expected to find the accused killer hanging from one of the cover rafters or shot through the heart.

The next day, the stagecoach arrived from Fort Reno, minus the flurry of dust and fanfare that Dobe had brought with him. Watching closely while setting a corral post, Everett noticed there were no passengers on the coach. The paunchy driver delivered a similar way-packet, picked up the one headed south, then loaded up the marshal and his dusty prisoner.

The next two days Everett cut and hauled poles to the corral site. Then late in the afternoon while pitching the last of a load of fresh poles onto the wagon, he heard riders splashing across Turkey Creek off to his right. His hand flashed to his pistol while his eyes searched the narrow band of trees between him and the stream. Then he recognized Fred in the lead with an old Indian riding alongside, followed by a dozen mounted braves, each with a single feather dangling from his hair and a rifle gripped in his hand. As they broke through the timberline into the clearing, Ralph rushed out to meet them, while Everett held back, watching his friends mingle with the Cheyenne warriors.

Later, as the braves set up camp in a small open area just across Turkey Creek, their chief, Little Robe, visited with Ralph and Fred, who introduced Everett as he joined them.

Soon the ranchers excused themselves and began loading a wagon with food while Everett remained with Little Robe. Uneasy at first, Everett soon chatted casually with the chief, discussing horses, the fate of the buffalo, deer and turkey hunts, and finally the massacre at Sand Creek.

"Many die in our camp, squaws with their papooses. My father, he shot down too," the chief said. "Black Kettle lose much honor among young Cheyenne with his talk of peace. But he again great leader of our people until Long Hair bring soldiers to the Washita to kill him and slaughter women and children in the snow and icy stream."

Everett had no idea how to respond, so he just nodded.

"Old Dog Soldiers not forget," the chief continued, tapping a finger against the side of his head.

Everett listened without comment as Little Robe rambled on about Indian land leased to big cattle companies and the growing unrest among his people.

"They crowd us, leave us too little. They steal our ponies," he said. "The Dog Soldiers talk of warpath, but I tell them the old ways not good. We must parlay with Agent Miles."

"Did you know Agent Darlington, Ralph's uncle?" Everett asked.

"He not like others," the chief said, touching his index and middle fingers to his lips, then thrusting them outward, forking them. "Darlington, he speak truth. He friend to Cheyenne."

"I think Fred must be a lot like his Uncle Brinton," Everett replied, then rose to meet the returning Collins and Williams.

The chief climbed into the wagon and glanced back at the supply of bacon, flour, syrup, sugar, beans, and coffee as they rattled toward the Cheyenne camp.

That night, Little Robe joined his braves as they laughed and danced around their campfire, while Everett and his two friends sat down to eat over at the ranch house.

"I saw four younger boys," Everett said, referring to the gathering of braves. "They look a little young to be wielding an axe."

"They're apprentices. They'll do the cooking," Fred explained. "The rest are fully initiated braves, having been through their torturous Medicine Dance ceremony."

"What's that?"

"They pierce their chest muscles, forming a strip of flesh. Then they run a strong stick behind the strip, its ends poking out on both sides. They attach sinew to the stick ends, which is tied to rawhide ropes used to lift the young men up into the air. They are left suspended from a scaffold until the weight of their bodies eventually rips through the strip of flesh, dropping them to the ground. The tearing of flesh is hastened by the brave jerking his body up and down. If the candidate doesn't do that, he will grow weak and faint, meaning he has failed."

Everett cringed at the image in his mind.

"That's not all," Fred continued. "You'll notice the end of the index finger of the left hand is missing. That's why other Indians call them the Cut Finger people."

The following day Little Robe headed back to his camp while the braves joined Everett in the blackjack forest. He marked trees, the braves cut them down, and then he hauled them to the corral site. Sweating bare backs of the young Cheyenne men sparkled in the sunlight of midday, and their axes played a continuous drumbeat that rang out across the plains and echoed through the oaks. When Everett stopped for his noonday meal, the drumbeat continued.

"When are they going to stop and eat?" Everett asked.

"Tonight," Fred replied. "They drink coffee and eat bread in the morning, then work all day."

Everett did not cut another tree. He stayed busy marking the tough oaks to be used and transporting the fallen and trimmed poles to the corral site. At day's end, he loaded his wagon with more wood discarded from the old corral, and hauled it to the Indian camp, providing firewood for the night.

Twelve days later, with fourteen hundred nine-foot poles ready for the corral, the braves joined Everett in setting them into place, stockade-style, following a circular fence line Fred had scratched into the sand. With Everett's guidance the braves sank the posts three feet into the ground. Ten days later, the corral was finished, including a fifty-foot wing fence to guide the cattle through the main gate.

The Cheyenne would be leaving the following morning, so Ralph called for a celebration. He roasted a side of beef over an open fire, kept several pots of hot coffee ready, and brought out a large tin of licorice candy, a favorite of the braves. They sang, danced, and sat around the campfire telling stories until midnight, long after Everett, Ralph, and Fred had left for the ranch house and their bedrolls.

After breakfast, the Cheyenne braves packed their meager belongings, leaped onto the backs of their ponies, and splashed across Turkey Creek to say farewell. Then Ralph and Fred stood at the creek's edge watching them disappear beyond a distant hillock.

The three men at the ranch spent the next two days building gates for the corral and sinking snubbing posts. With each arrival of the stage, the two ranchers would rush over. Ralph would water the teams while Fred helped with the mail packets and sold any supplies the travelers desired. From a distance Everett would stop, drop his hand to his revolver, and study each passenger emerging from the coaches.

With the corral finished, Everett helped round up the ranch cattle, brand newborns, and pen a few that were sold to the first drover that came along. The corral was used almost daily as the herds began moving up the old trail. Nightly, cowboys sat around campfires close to the store telling stories, sometimes a fiddler sawing out a tune or an old-timer blowing on a Jew's harp. The boys would get up and dance, kicking their dusty heels together, hollering to the wind, and sailing their hats into the starry sky.

Weeks passed with Everett roaming the land, searching for strays and herding them back to the ranch. It kept him away during daylight hours, but every night he returned, always taking a long look at their visitors.

It was mid-July when everything changed.

Late in the afternoon, two riders with a heavily loaded packhorse showed up at the ranch from the north. One, neatly dressed, wore a black vest and matching hat covered with a cloud of trail dust. The other, a sour-looking man in his forties with a coarse face behind a stubble of beard, slouched in his unkempt clothes.

Everett, returning from a natural meadow across Turkey Creek where he had just added five strays to the seventy head of ranch stock, spotted them. The spiffy man stood on the front porch dusting himself, while the other hesitated at the steps, scanning the countryside.

Everett jerked the chestnut mare to a halt in the dark shadows of the blackjacks and slipped the leather thong off the hammer of his revolver.

6

When the men had gone inside, Everett crouched down and headed for the packhorse, keeping the animals between him and the store. Its load was obvious; the smell of rot-gut whiskey reached his nostrils from twenty feet away. He checked the brands on the horses. All three were different and unknown to him.

Silently, he stepped up on the end of the porch, then inched along with his back against the wall until he reached the door. Easing it open, he slipped inside, Colt drawn. Hearing the hammer click back, everyone turned and stared.

"Don't touch that gun," Everett warned, glaring at the rough man whose hand had dropped to his revolver.

The ruffian hesitated, measuring the young man challenging him. When Everett moved two paces closer, the big man lifted his hand away, knowing even a raw kid could put a bullet into this midsection before he could get a shot off.

Everett shifted his eyes to the man's neatly dressed partner.

"Do I know you?" the man in black asked, attempting a smile.

"No," Everett replied, "but your friend does."

"That ain't so. I've never laid eyes on you before," the crude man said, his eyes flashing as he studied the six-foot-two-inch, one-hundred-eighty-pound stranger holding a gun on him.

"In five years, I've changed a bit," Everett said. "I was thirteen back then."

"What's this all about?" Ralph asked, easing along the wall toward Everett.

"My pa hung for a murder this man did," Everett said.

"That's a lie!" the man bellowed.

"His name's Stuart, and he's a killer and a horse thief," Everett said.

"You sure you've got the right man?" Ralph asked.

"Drop your gun belt to the floor," Everett said to the rough man, then glanced toward his dapper partner. "You, too."

"Whatever he's done, I had nothing to do with it," the man's partner said.

"Get their guns," Everett said, nodding toward Fred when two gun belts had hit the floor. "Ralph, tie 'em up."

When the two were bound and seated on crates in a corner of the room, Everett holstered his revolver and turned to Fred.

"That pistol," Everett said, pointing to the one the coarse man had been wearing, "will have a long scratch on the left side of the handle."

Fred slipped the walnut-handled pistol from the holster, glanced at the grip, then darted his eyes up at Everett.

"How'd you know?"

"It was my pa's gun," Everett replied, his eyes fixed on the stunned outlaw.

"You're . . . you're Sam's boy?" the man asked.

"That's right, Stu, and I'm here to collect for him," Everett replied.

"Take the gun," Wiley Stuart said, " and the cartridge belt."

"It's gonna cost you a lot more than that," Everett said.

"What do you mean?"

"You cost Pa his life," Everett explained.

"That wasn't my fault," the man said.

"We're gonna see what that hanging judge in Fort Smith thinks about it."

"What do you mean?" Ralph asked, frowning.

"I'm taking him on a little trip," Everett explained.

"Look," the outlaw's companion said, "I didn't have anything to do with it. You gotta let me go."

"Me and your partner will ride out of here early tomorrow morning," Everett replied. "An hour after we're gone, Ralph will turn you loose."

"Everett," Ralph said, his voice husky with concern, "my Uncle Ben is a deputy United States marshal in these parts. Let him take this guy in."

"No chance," Everett said. "I've waited five long years. Now I'm going to handle this my way."

"Maybe me or Fred should ride along with you," Ralph suggested. "It's a far piece to Fort Smith. Sometime you're gonna need sleep."

"Thanks, but this is a job I've got to do myself," Everett said. "There is something you can do, though. I was once taught to unsaddle and unburden horses for the night, and I don't trust these devils to do it."

Ralph headed for the door.

"Check 'em good for hidden weapons," Everett said.

Supper was simple and brief, the men tense and apprehensive. Afterwards, Everett spent the night astride an upturned cracker crate, guarding his two captives who tossed and turned on the store's hard floor.

When daylight finally speared through the window, Everett pushed the captives outside and tied them to the hitching rail while he saddled Stuart's horse, along with the chestnut. After pushing his prisoner into the saddle, Everett mounted and stared down at the man's partner.

"When Ralph turns you loose, don't try following us. If I spot you, I'll shoot you out of the saddle on sight."

Everett grabbed the reins of his prisoner's brown gelding and heeled his chestnut into a trot toward the Chisholm Trail. Heading south they crossed the Cimarron River, then turned downstream, Everett preferring a path concealed by undergrowth along the river's edge.

Following the stream, they rode all day, seeing no one. In a well concealed camp, Everett untied Stuart's right hand so he could eat, then retied his hands, coiled a rope around him, shoulders to feet, and threw a blanket over him. The next day was the same, and they ended a long ride camped where the Cimarron dumps into the Arkansas.

Supper finished, Everett rested on a log, leaning back against an old oak, and stared at the waning flames of his campfire flickering in a soft, cool breeze. The horses were staked nearby, and his bound prisoner dozed in his bedroll beside the blaze.

Then, amid the harmony of night sounds, he heard a noise that did not fit. He dropped his hand to his gun and eased it out. Remaining statue-still, he listened.

Hearing something stir in the dried leaves to his right, he crouched as he whirled and swung his gun in that direction.

"Drop it," a voice said as Everett felt the cold muzzle of a pistol against the back of his neck.

It's Stuart's partner, Everett guessed, and I fell for the oldest trick in the world, a distracting noise to lure my attention away so he could nab me. Seeing no way out, he dropped the walnut-handled revolver.

"Now, stand up, slow and easy," an unfamiliar voice commanded.

"Who are you?" Everett asked as he turned toward his captor, on whose face danced intermittent firelight and shadow.

"Just do what I tell you, and nobody gets hurt."

"That man over there," Everett said, motioning toward Wiley Stuart, "is a horse thief and . . ."

"I know," the gunman replied as his dark eyes shifted momentarily to the prisoner who was sitting up, "but now he's my prisoner. I'm a federal deputy marshal."

"I never done what he said," Stuart blurted out, straining to see the lawman's face.

"Yes he did!" Everett shouted. "He was my pa's partner in stealing those horses, and he's the one who killed that rancher. If there's any justice in this world, he's gotta be taken to Fort Smith and stood before the hanging judge."

"Young man," the deputy said, "You've got it all wrong."

"No I don't! My pa was hung for a killing this man did, did it with my pa's gun," Everett shouted, pointing to the revolver on the ground.

"Son," the lawman said calmly, "I helped Marshal Reeves arrest your pa."

Everett was stunned into momentary silence.

"But I found my pa's gun on this lying scoundrel!" Everett said, recovering.

"That's right," the lawman explained. "When your pa, along with Stuart here and a third man I'm still looking for, broke open that corral and drove the horses out, the owner rode up. The rancher eased over to the corner of the barn and hid in the shadows. But somehow your pa spotted him and started shooting. The rancher returned his fire, and soon your father had emptied his gun. Seeing your pa's gun belt was empty, Stuart pitched his revolver to him. Your pa chunked his walnut-handled one back and then took cover behind a rain-barrel and kept the rancher pinned down while his partners chased after the stolen horses. The owner had already been hit, so pretty soon your pa finished him off, climbed on that chestnut you're riding, and hightailed it after his partners."

"How do you know this?" Everett asked, unconvinced.

"A neighbor rancher had ridden up with the owner. Unarmed, he hid out until your pa was gone, then rode for help."

"Why should I believe you?" Everett asked.

"I inspected the boot-marks behind that rain-barrel. They showed a chunk missing from the left heel. It matched your . . ."

"He did it chopping wood," Everett said. "The axe glanced off an oak log and caught the inside part of his boot heel. Could have slashed his foot bad, but he took it as a sign of good luck."

"Well, I guess his good luck turned bad," the lawman said.

"Who are you, sir?"

"I'm Ben Williams, uncle to your friend Ralph Collins. He and Fred told me where you were headed."

Everett turned away, staring into the haunting darkness. Suddenly, he was that thirteen-year-old boy again, frightened and lost, watching his condemned father standing alone on the Hanging Judge's whitewashed scaffold with a blazing sunset painting the horizon.

"Come morning, I'll take your prisoner on to Fort Smith and make sure he has his day before Judge Parker," Deputy Marshal Williams said. "You're welcome to ride along."

Everett shook his head, then turned toward the fire as the marshal made his way over to Wiley Stuart and replaced the leather-strap binding with cold, steel handcuffs.

"I never knew who the third man was," Everett said softly. "What does he look like?"

"The rancher said he's medium height, trim, and was wearing a black hat with matching shirt and trousers."

"And there's a scar angled across his chin," Everett said. "He wears black leather gloves, Mexican spurs, rides a big bay, and deals in whiskey."

"Son, you've just described Hurricane Bill Martin," Marshal Williams said. "Have you seen him?"

"Red Fork Ranch, two days ago," Everett replied, shaking his head.

"He and his gang of horse thieves hide out somewhere in that blackjack thicket along the Cimarron River. They take their stolen herds up to Kansas, sell them, and bring back whiskey to peddle to the Indians and soldiers."

"You going back to get him?"

"No, he's long gone by now," the lawman said, handing the walnut-handled revolver back to Everett. "But I'll catch up to him someday."

The next morning, the marshal and his prisoner headed south down the Arkansas River while Everett, uncertain and bewildered, turned upstream.

For five years Everett had lived for the day he would catch the real killer, stand him before Judge Isaac Parker, and clear his father's name. Growing to manhood at Fort Gibson, he had thought of little else. He had chosen Red Fork Ranch, sitting on the north-south thoroughfare of Indian Territory, the land were outlaws reigned, because he guessed eventually Wiley Stuart would show up there. Now, with that hope shattered, eighteen-year-old Everett was lost. He felt as if he were stranded in a vast ocean, surrounded by its endless sameness from horizon to horizon. Suddenly, his life was without a rudder, his sail without wind.

For two days he isolated himself in the wilderness, his thoughts oscillating between his disappointing past and his unplanned future. Finally, he decided to head for Wichita, where he hoped to apply the only skills he possessed.

He rode north along the main artery of the Arkansas River until a tributary, the Salt Fork, joined it from the northwest. After a couple of hours travel up the lesser stream, he came across a bunch of cattle, too many to be strays. He singled out a young brown cow, eased over, and took a look. A 101 brand had been burned onto her left hip, along with an -O- marked on her horns. As he eased through the milling herd, two cowboys approached, their mounts lathered and heaving.

"Howdy," the tall, bushy-faced one called out as they reined their ponies to a halt.

"What's the trouble?" Everett asked after returning the greeting.

"Just settlin' a little bet," the bearded one replied, "on whose pony's the fastest."

"So who pays up?"

"Ain't settled yet," the cowboy replied. "Called it off when we spotted you here amongst the herd."

"Who do they belong to?" Everett asked, glancing at one of the longhorns.

"George Miller. This is the 101 range."

"What's that mark on their horns?"

"Some of the herd was once Bar-O-Bar cattle. Miller bought 'em out about a year ago."

"If you're headin' upriver, best stay away from 101 headquarters," advised the second cowboy, a short squatty one, his jaw bulging with tobacco. "Bad sickness has hit. Three dead a'ready."

"Thanks for the warning," Everett said, tipping his hat as he kneed his horse forward.

He thought it over as he rode on. Those broncs weren't racing; he was sure of that. Those boys were on the run, most likely from somebody at the 101. Maybe he would just stop by and have a look around. After all, the ranch house lay right along his path.

As he rode up, a group of men were gathered just outside a horse barn, their attention focused on a fellow in the center of the circle.

"Now we'll settle this right now," the man shouted, reaching down for a bucket of yellow corn at his feet.

The man then moved along from one cowhand to the next, each taking a single kernel.

"Now you boys hold out your hat," the man said when he had completed the round. "Jim, we'll start with you. Drop your kernel of corn in the hat of the man who stole the payroll last night. Now before you vote, let me remind you. Nobody gets paid 'til that money's back in my hands."

A thin leather-faced man cut across the circle to a barrel-chested fellow and pitched in his yellow grain. One by one, the men voted with most of the corn ending up in the hats of three different men.

"Boys," the boss said, "I ain't gonna hang three men for what was done by one, so you best make up your minds. You've got an hour to decide, then we'll vote again. And I warn you, any man who rides out will be chased down and shot."

"What about Chet and Spud?" the burly cowboy asked. "Maybe their hats would've got the corn."

"Where are they?" asked the boss, scanning the faces around him.

"Lit out, maybe an hour ago."

"Which way?" the boss asked through clenched teeth.

"Don't know."

"What do these boys look like?" Everett asked from the back of his pony twenty feet away.

"Who're you?" the gruff rancher asked.

"Stranger, but I met a couple of boys back down the river," Everett said. "A bearded one, and the other working on a chaw, riding ponies lathered up real good."

"That's them, boss," the burly cowboy said. "And I'll bet my hat them boys got our money."

"Let's ride," the rancher said, heading for a saddled roan.

Everett watched as the men gathered their horses.

"You're comin' along," the rancher said, glancing at Everett, "just in case you're in with them thieves and intendin' on throwin' us off track."

It was dark when the small posse spotted a campfire along the river. After encircling Chet and Spud, the boss edged toward the firelight, a short-barreled shotgun leveled on them.

"Boys, this is Miller. There's a barrel for each of you 'less you throw up your hands pronto," he called from the edge of the darkness. "We've got you trapped, and we mean business."

After the two thieves surrendered, the circle tightened as cowboys crowded into the firelight with their arsenal of six-shooters gleaming. After disarming the two, Miller searched their saddlebags, yanking out a bulging leather pouch that jingled as he shook it. The boys let out a shout, then levered back the hammers on their revolvers.

"Wait a minute, boys," Miller said, pushing the open palm of his left hand toward them. "Back in seventy-two down around San Saba, me and Rainwater had to settle a deal like this. We got our money and let the thief ride. I say we do the same, with the understandin' that if either of you dogs ever shows your mutt face on 101 range again, we'll hang you to the nearest cottonwood and leave you to the buzzards."

Grumbling, his cowboys holstered their guns as Miller walked over to Everett.

"Appreciate the tip, young fella," the rancher said. "I'm just now short two hands. Maybe you'd like to ride for the 101."

"Got my heart set on getting up to Wichita," Everett replied. "But I sure could use a hot meal and good night's rest."

"Come along," Miller replied, watching the two disarmed thieves galloping into the darkness.

Everett got his hot meal and night's rest, then said goodbye to the rancher after a breakfast of bacon, gravy, and hot biscuits.

A hard day's travel took him to a road ranch on the Chisholm Trail. Inside, he learned he was at Pond Creek, a stage station.

"What's on up the trail?" Everett asked J. C. Hopkins, the ranch owner.

"About fourteen miles north, there's Polecat Ranch, run by Henry Stone, and ten miles farther, just across the territorial border, is a store run by Mac McLean. Two miles north of there, you'll find Caldwell."

"What's there?"

"Outside of Dodge, about the only real cow town left. Some call it the Border Queen, but don't let that name fool you."

"What does that mean?"

"Queen of the border towns, I reckon, but this royal lady keeps some bad company. You see, whiskey is illegal down here, and cowboys and freighters work up a powerful thirst crossin' Indian Territory. First thing they see in Caldwell is a saloon. Next to cattle trade, whiskey, gamblin', and dancehall gals make up the most popular businesses in town."

After an early breakfast, Everett saddled his mare and headed north along the cattle trail. Late that afternoon he rode up to the small store at Polecat Ranch, swung down, and stepped inside. The room was crowded with cowboys and freighters, and when Everett asked about a meal, a man wearing thorn-scarred chaps and a dusty hat tapped him on the shoulder.

"For a day's work, I'll see you get a beef-steak tonight and bacon with biscuits and gravy for breakfast tomorrow, along with coffee as hot as the Arizona desert at high noon and as strong as a mule's kick."

"What work you got in mind?" Everett asked, running his tongue over his dry lips.

"Herdin' longhorns up to Caldwell," the man replied, lifting his hat and extending his hand. "Hezekiah Williams."

Everett identified himself and gripped the man's hand. "You lose a boy or two in an Indian ambush?"

Williams laughed. "No, but if I had the pair back, I'd bargain them to the Comanches for a broke-down pony. Two scalawags begged half their pay early, ransacked our supplies in the middle of the night, then up and left camp. I expect they had good reason to avoid the marshal in Caldwell."

"Don't you drive your beeves on up to Wichita?"

"Not since last year. You see, the Atchison, Topeka, and Santa Fe has strung rail on down to Caldwell. Fact is, there's a two-mile spur to the prairie south of town, puttin' to an end all the fuss about Texas longhorns bringin' the fever to Kansas."

"Mr. Williams," Everett said, "I'll be glad to sign on with you."

Everett followed the cattleman outside, and they rode about two miles north where the herd was milling around, pulling at the sparse grass. They dismounted at the chuck wagon.

"I'll introduce you to the boss," Williams said, heading toward a covered wagon some thirty feet beyond the campfire.

As they reached the back of the wagon, a lean woman wearing a man's red flannel shirt and calico riding skirt stepped down.

"This here's Lizzie," the man said, then tilted his head toward Everett. "He's agreed to help with the herd tomorrow."

"What's your name, young man?" the woman asked.

"Everett Brook."

"You know anything about herding cattle?"

"Not much, but I know horses, ma'am."

"Tonight he can nighthawk the remuda and give Charlie a break," the woman said to Williams. "Tomorrow, Charlie can ride drag while this young fellow lends a hand to our wranglers."

"I'll see to it," Hezekiah said as he turned back toward the chuck wagon.

As Everett unbuckled the front saddle cinch, Hezekiah showed up and looped a thirty-foot, coiled lariat over the saddle horn and handed him seven or eight two-foot-long leather strings.

"You'll be needin' these, I expect."

"What are these short strings for?"

"We'll likely pick up a few strays before we get to the railhead. We use those to tie a steer's hind feet together while we slap on our brand. They're called piggin' strings."

Everett met a few of the cowboys while eating and learned that the trail boss was named Lizzie Johnson Williams. She had been a schoolteacher back in

Travis County, Texas. Saving her money, she had invested twenty-five hundred dollars in a cattle company in Chicago. That investment soon turned into twenty thousand, which she had used to buy her own herd, registering the CY as her brand. Later, she had married a floundering rancher, Hezekiah Williams, but retained title to her property, including her herd. In 1879, she had trailed her first drive north to the railhead at Dodge, possibly making history as the first female trail boss.

Later, Everett rode out to the remuda where he met Charlie and told the wrangler he was to spend the night in camp.

"Watch 'em close," the cowboy warned. "There's more horse thieves in these parts than in all the rest of the country put together. Just last year, a Caldwell justice of the peace named Freeman rode into our camp and asked about a horse thief named Brown. The justice said this fellow had stolen his horse and headed south. How'd he know it was Brown who had taken his horse? The fella had been a boarder at Freeman's house, and he'd disappeared right along with the mare."

The wrangler rode off laughing as Everett turned to the remuda of thirty horses, determined that not one would be taken during his watch. About midnight, he heard the footfalls of an approaching pony and dropped his right hand to the butt of his revolver. A young man, maybe twenty-five years old, rode up, explaining that he would take his turn at watch. Everett studied the unfamiliar face with concern, then nudged his mount forward, passing within a few feet of the horse and rider. The brand on the pony's hip was blurred by darkness, but it definitely was not the familiar CY he had seen on the remuda animals. He snatched his pistol from its scabbard and turned it on the fellow.

"I don't recall seeing you in camp," Everett said to the wide-eyed cowboy, "and I ain't turning over these broncs to no hornswoggling stranger."

"It's you who's the stranger," the young man protested. "I've been with this outfit for three years."

"Unbuckle your gun belt and drop it to the ground," Everett demanded.

Fuming, the cowboy hesitated, then dropped his eyes to the gun barrel and complied.

"Now step down," Everett said, then watched the man's every move while he dismounted. "Now climb back up, backwards."

"I ain't gonna do no such fool thing!" the cowboy protested.

"Climb up," Everett said, thumbing back the hammer of his revolver.

Grumbling, the fellow swung aboard, facing the rear of his horse. Everett eased over, slipped out one of the pigging strings strapped to his saddle skirt, tied the young fellow's wrists together, then lashed the binding to his saddle horn. Turning the horse toward the cow camp, he slapped him on the hip, sending the pony dashing away.

Twenty minutes later another rider approached but called out from the darkness, "Hezekiah Williams ridin' in, son."

The cattleman approached Everett, while some twenty feet behind, the young cowboy followed, facing forward on his pony.

"That was good work," the cattleman said, stifling a laugh, "but Vic is one of ours. Come along. He'll stand watch 'til daylight."

Everett returned the fellow's gun belt, then followed Williams back toward camp, explaining along the way that the brand on the cowboy's pony was not the outfit's CY.

"His personal mount," Williams explained, "just like that chestnut you're ridin'."

Back in camp, Everett poured himself a cup of hot coffee, then spread his blankets out and tossed and turned until daylight, catching a few short naps. When the story of his capturing the would-be horse thief made it around, the herders began ribbing him, all except the young wrangler. Wanting to squelch any brewing trouble, Everett walked over to Vic and extended his hand.

"No hard feelings, I hope," he said. "Just a fool shorthorn stunt, I reckon."

When the whole camp roared with laughter, the young wrangler smiled and shook Everett's hand. Moments later, the two rode off together to push the horse herd up the trail with the cattle.

Nearing the railhead south of Caldwell, the point riders guided the cattle off the trail to a grassy depression alongside a dry creek bed. The longhorns dropped their heads and grazed for a couple of hours while the cowboys applied the CY brand to a few strays they had collected. Then they pushed the herd on to Bluff Creek Crossing where the cattle watered. As the sun dipped low in the west, they rounded up the beeves and bedded them down on the prairie about a mile southeast of the creek.

"Why didn't we pen them while we had them there at the corrals?" Everett asked Vic, having noticed the big cattle pens on the high bluff south of the stream.

"Want them to fatten up as much as possible before a buyer sees them," the cowboy explained.

Soon after breakfast the next morning, Hezekiah and a couple of the cowboys rode to the railhead to make sure buyers were on hand. Soon they returned and instructed the herders to rouse up the cattle and push them toward the cattle pens atop the high bluff. Approaching the corrals, the point, wing, and flank riders squeezed the cattle into a long narrow line to ease the task of guiding them along a wing fence that threaded them through the open gates.

With the job done, Everett rode over to the trail boss' wagon, thanked Mrs. Lizzie for her hospitality, pitched the borrowed lariat and pigging strings to Hezekiah, shook the rancher's hand, and then rode toward the creek. Pulling up at the bluff's rim just west of the cattle pens, he stared down at the winding stream below, its far side lined with cottonwoods, willows, and a variety of hardwoods. Looking beyond the treetops, amid a thumb of land in a sharp bend of the creek, he spotted a log structure with a sign out front: FIRST CHANCE SALOON.

Everett laughed while watching the cowboys splash their ponies across the stream and head for the old log building as if it were the finish line of the county race.

7

Caldwell, Kansas
August, 1881

Farther across the wide valley, about a mile beyond the saloon, was another tree-lined creek and just past it was a slow-rising hill. As Everett scanned the landscape and anticipated the delights of his first cow town, Vic rode up.

"What do you think?" the cowboy asked.

"From up here on this bluff it looks like a right pretty place," Everett replied. "I'd heard Kansas was mostly desert."

"We're standing on Manning Peak," Vic said, "named for a cowboy buried here. Got hisself killed by a fellow named Epps, fightin' over a stack of hay down along the creek. This dead cowboy had two brothers, the story goes, and they brought the body up here and stuck it in the ground, sure it wasn't Kansas soil. Then they holed up in a dugout along the stream and threatened to kill Epps, but the old fella went to Wellington and filed a complaint. The sheriff and some boys came down and smoked the Mannings out. On the way back to the county seat, they stopped overnight at Smith's Road Ranch on the Chikaskia River. While the sheriff and posse were playin' cards, the brothers sneaked out a back window and struck out for Indian Territory."

"But I thought we crossed into Kansas a ways back there," Everett said.

"Sure did," Vic replied. "But back then the state line was two and a half miles north of here, in the middle of town. Back in seventy-six, somebody discovered the surveyor had made a mistake, and the boundary was moved down here. The land between the new boundary and the old became known as the Cherokee Strip, and a year later was opened for settlement. When the Manning brothers heard about it, they sneaked back to this bluff, dug up the remains of their brother outta this Kansas dirt, and took him to Texas."

"So, the town's on up there?" Everett asked, glancing across the valley to the hilltop.

"Just past the crest of that slope. Want to ride over and see?"

They turned their mounts and rode along the rim of the bluff to a draw that sloped down to the creek. After splashing across the stream, they continued along a trail with the First Chance off to their right.

"Looks like something burned there by the saloon," Everett said.

"Yep, and it's quite a story," Vic replied, smiling. "A fellow named Curly Marshall owned the saloon back then, and he added a dancehall. While he was gone to Wichita to get some ladies to dance with his customers, a cowboy named McCarty, along with a friend, strolled into Thomas's store off up there on the hill. While the owner was busy takin' a look at the wares of a fellow named Doc Anderson, McCarty bragged to his companion that he could shoot a hole through Anderson's plug hat. Instead, he blew off the top of the man's head.

"McCarty had killed another fellow named Fielder about a week earlier, so the vigilantes took off after him, but he had slipped out and headed south while everybody was seein' after Anderson. Marshall's First Chance Saloon was known as a hangout for outlaws, so the vigilantes headed there first. When the saloonkeeper and some patrons wouldn't let these fellas search the place, the posse gathered up some old quilts, soaked 'em in coal oil, tacked 'em onto the side of the dancehall, then put a match to 'em."

"Did they smoke out McCarty?"

"He wasn't there. But Rohrabacher, the head of the vigilantes, had a couple of fellas slip into the saloon, pretendin' they were ridin' in from Indian Territory. One was named Newt Williams, and he pulled his gun on the bartender and set in to questionin' him. About that time, a fellow named Busey Nicholson rode in and asked for Curly Marshall, sayin' he was sent to collect five hundred dollars owed his boss, less the cost of some supplies. Newt Williams demanded to know who Nicholson was collectin' for, and when the man wouldn't tell, young Newt swung a rope over a log beam overhead and tied off a noose. That loosened the man's tongue. Stammerin' somethin' pitiful, he explained that McCarty had sent him and that the outlaw was hidin' out down at Deer Creek.

"About four in the mornin', the vigilantes found their man nappin' with his horse tied to his saddle horn. The lead rider opened fire, followed by a couple of others, but in their hurry and with only starlight on their target, they missed. Being handy with a revolver, McCarty sprang to this feet, pulled his pistols, and gave a pretty good account of himself, while tryin' to make his way up the rope to his excited pony. Seein' what was up, Newt Williams looped around to the off side of the horse, reached up, and cut the rope, sendin' the bronc tearin' away. McCarty, now shot in the hand, outnumbered, and afoot, threw up his hands. One of the vigilantes asked the outlaw which of his two six-shooters he had used to kill young Fielder. The outlaw smiled and pointed to the one on his right hip. The vigilante snatched it, pressed the muzzle against McCarty's head, and fired."

"I guess they didn't have a hanging judge handy," Everett said.

"Vigilantes don't need one."

"What's this creek called?" Everett asked as they approached the second stream.

"Fall Creek," Vic replied, then nodded his head eastward. "On down yonder it joins up with Bluff Creek."

After crossing a footbridge, they climbed a long slope to the crest of a hill where Everett stared ahead at a wide, dirt street, bordered by several buildings. The first structure on the left was an impressive, three-story, brick building. A sign on the front said LELAND HOTEL, and as they came closer, window signs advertised a barbershop, a billiard room, a dining area, and a bar.

"Runnin' water in every room," Vic said, nodding to the impressive hotel. "It's where the rich cattlemen stay and hold their big-stakes poker games. Some say there's a tunnel under the street connectin' the Leland to the Puck on the other side. When the law makes a raid to stop illegal gamin' in the basement, the boys just sneak over to the Puck."

Across the street from the Leland, next to the Puck, was the Hubbell Mercantile, with A. C. Jones's Blacksmith behind it. On the north side of the street was Gabbert's Drugstore, and Unsell's Lone Star Clothing House. Next to Hubbell's stood a saloon, then a grocery store, and a two-story building with a big sign out front: MERCHANTS AND DROVERS BANK.

A group of people milled about in front of the bank, shouting and pointing while others banged on the locked front door.

"Looks like trouble over there," Everett said.

"Yep. Somethin's wrong, and that's where the cattle buyers transfer money to pay for the herds. Them steers don't sell, us boys don't get paid," Vic replied, then noticed a large CLOSED sign across the bank entrance. "Let's ride over and see what's the matter."

"Why is it locked up?" Vic asked a man at the edge of the street.

"Danford shut it down and skipped town," the man replied. "We've been told the bank has failed, so we're here to get our money."

"There's nothin' we can do about it now," Vic said to Everett. "I'll pass the news on to Mrs. Lizzie when I get back to the herd."

Everett and Vic rode on past a well in the middle of the street in front of the Moreland House, a restaurant and boarding establishment. A saloon stood next door to the east, and then a small newspaper office with a sign in the front window.

CALDWELL POST
TELL WALTON, EDITOR

They continued along the street to the City Hotel, hitched their horses, stepped inside, and took a seat at an empty table in the dining area.

"What's happened to the bank, Mr. Wendels?" Vic asked the proprietor when he stopped by their table to welcome them.

"It's low on cash, so the president, Mr. J. S. Danford, has gone to raise money to reopen," Wendels explained.

"Gone where?"

"Emporia," Wendels said. "Danford has transferred his property deeds to a banker up there for thirty thousand dollars. He'll be back soon, and then folks will get their money."

After ordering their meals, they noticed a heated conversation going on at a nearby table.

"Did that fella say the President has been shot?" Everett asked, leaning toward Vic.

"He said President Garfield was shot in a train station, but he's not dead," Vic replied.

They soon learned that the assassin was named Charles Guiteau, and some speculated the plot was somehow related to an ongoing feud between the President and two New York senators. When President Garfield had appointed James Blaine as Secretary of State, a political enemy of the New Yorkers, the congressmen had resigned in protest, expecting to be reelected in the upcoming November election, thus creating a public denunciation of the President.

"Who'll take over if President Garfield dies?" a man asked.

"Vice President Chester Arthur," another answered, "and he's thick with those New York senators."

Everett immediately recalled the fear and confusion he had experienced as a small child when his father and mother had argued over the assassination of President Lincoln. His father had praised John Wilkes Booth, while his mother had decried the assassin as a coward and he and his cohorts as traitors. His father regretted that Booth had not acted earlier, thus changing the outcome of the war. His mother had countered that Lincoln had only five months earlier been reelected and that democratic elections were the only appropriate way to remove a president from office. Now another one had been shot, no doubt an attempt to take him from office by murder, after having been the voters' choice only four months earlier. Though it all seemed so distant and unrelated to frontier Caldwell, Everett was unsettled by the news, recalling Mrs. Weatherly, his teacher at Fort Gibson, and her repeated praises for the system of government where the people chose their leaders.

"Want to share a room for the night?" Vic asked as they rose from the table.

Everett hesitated, then nodded.

Upstairs, Everett stretched out on the bed as Vic put on his hat and headed for the door.

"Us boys will be paintin' the town tonight," he said. "Want to come along?"

"I paid good money for the use of this bed," Everett replied, smiling, "and I mean to get my money's worth."

Some hours later Everett was awakened by shouts pouring through the open window from the street below. He jumped up and poked his head out. Five or six men were gathered in the street yelling back and forth while others were running east down Fourth Street with guns drawn. Curious about the excitement and concerned that Vic might be endangered, Everett strapped on his revolver and rushed to the street.

"What's going on?" he asked a passerby.

"George Woods has been shot," the man said excitedly.

"Who?"

"The owner of the Red Light Saloon," the man explained and dashed away.

Everett followed the growing cluster of men running down Fourth Street. One block away on the corner, he spotted a milling mass of people just outside the two-story saloon and dancehall. As he approached, the murmuring crowd parted to make way for a badge-wearing man pushing through their midst with a handcuffed cowboy. A young woman stood in the saloon doorway, sobbing and wailing as she stared after the marshal and his prisoner.

"Who's that?" Everett asked a man on the edge of the crowd.

"Lizzie Roberts," the man replied. "That's her lover, Charley Davis, being taken in by Marshal Rowan."

"Why'd he kill the saloon owner?" Everett asked.

"Davis was upset because Lizzie had returned to work at the Red Light. When he tried to get her to go back to the ranch with him tonight, Woods jumped in. From no more than three feet away, Davis yanked out his Colt and fired a gut shot. I expect Woods is done for."

"Think the ruckus will put the place out of business?" Everett asked, scanning the unpainted building with broken windows, a sagging roof, and a row of pathetic-looking hovels out back.

"Humph," the man said. "Not likely. Mag, Woods's wife, is a tough gal. She ain't likely to give up so easy."

As the crowd slowly dispersed, Everett eased inside. A slender woman was kneeling over a man stretched out at the base of a stairway, his midsection soaked in blood. A man and two women stood by, watching while the wife bent over her dying husband to hear his whispered last words.

"What'd he say?" the man asked after the saloon owner's body suddenly went limp.

"He wants me to prosecute his killer," she replied firmly, then dropped her damp eyes back to her dead husband. "And he said for me to do the best I can and be a good girl."

"I'm gonna go tell the marshal that the charge is now murder," the man said bitterly. "Then I'll be back and help you."

"That won't be necessary," Marshal Rowan said as he stepped through the circle of people.

"Marshal, Mag wants Charley Davis charged and punished for what he done," the man said, nodding toward the corpse.

"I expected she would, Spear," the marshal replied, pushing past him.

"Where is Davis?" Spear asked, grabbing the marshal's arm.

"My deputy's holding him," the marshal replied, yanking his arm away. "And I'm warning you. Don't you interfere, or that younger brother of yours, either."

"Marshal, leave my brother out of this. You're still holdin' a grudge 'cause you think David killed Frank Hunt. He didn't, but whoever did was just gettin' even for Hunt's part in killin' Marshal Flatt."

"Frank was a good policeman. Your brother was acquitted, all right, but there's still some who believe he's the killer. Dan Jones said he saw him lurking around outside just before Hunt was shot, sitting in that window right up there," the marshal replied, lifting his eyes toward the north window on the second floor of the Red Light.

After checking to make sure the saloon owner had no pulse, the marshal turned toward the dazed widow. "Ma'am, we'll have an inquiry tomorrow morning, and I expect the justice of the peace will hold over Davis for trial. I'll personally escort him to Wellington and turn him over to the sheriff."

Shortly after Marshal Rowan had gone, Everett found Vic, and they headed back toward the City Hotel. Reaching Main Street, they found Marshal Rowan rushing around calling for a posse. As three men checked the load in their weapons and swung up on their ponies, Everett and Vic learned that Charley Davis had escaped from the deputy, run to Kalbflesch's livery across from the Red Light, grabbed a horse, and ridden south out of town.

"Indian Territory," Everett heard a man say when asked where the small posse was headed. "Bein' here on the border, justice ain't got a chance in this town."

After watching the riders spur their mounts down Main Street, Everett and Vic headed for their room.

"Border Queen town," Everett mumbled, recalling what J. C. Hopkins had said down at Pond Creek.

"Yeah," Vic said. "And she's got a wicked heart."

At breakfast the next morning, they learned from a man at a nearby table that Davis had escaped his pursuers, who had ridden back into town within two hours of leaving.

"I ain't all that sure they wanted to catch Charley," the fellow said. "He was considered a peaceable fella, and there's plenty who feel this town would be better off if the Red Light was shut down."

After eating, Vic asked Everett about his plans.

"I think I'll look around for work," Everett said. "How about you?"

"I'll head back to Texas, but I'll be back this way next year. If you're still around, I'll look you up."

As Vic headed south to join his outfit and report about the bank closing, Everett bought a copy of the *Caldwell Post* and, leaning against the end of a hitching rail, he noticed an article about the prior night's shooting.

The editor, Tell Walton, began his column by condemning lawless murder and questioning the laxness of the deputy for allowing his prisoner to escape. He then proceeded to focus on the Red Light and its crowd.

As James Kelley, Jr., prior editor of this paper, predicted April 8th of last year, this establishment has brought nothing but shame and violence to our town. It attracts notorious men and corrupt women and is a hotbed of vice. It is polluting the very air we breathe. Caldwell is quickly gaining a reputation as a town unsuited for decent folks.

The articled concluded with a fictitious quote illustrating the light in which outsiders must view Caldwell.

There've been only two fights in town this week. Now, the next fellow who says we ain't gettin' civilized down here is liable to get hurt.

Then Everett focused on a column written by Don Carlos, a special contribution from the former columnist of the *Sumner County Press* in Wellington. The rambling, entertaining column related local news, spiced with good-natured tales, and near the end Everett found a paragraph of special interest. The nearby BC Ranch, recently purchased by Johnnie Blair, former postmaster, businessman, and town favorite, had just bought five hundred head of cattle.

Everett wondered if this could be the same Johnnie Blair who had once owned Red Fork Ranch. Ralph Collins had spoken well of the man. In any case, more cattle meant more cowboys, Everett concluded.

Two days later, after getting directions to the ranch, Everett saddled the chestnut mare and headed out of town, riding northwest. As he neared a knoll to the right side of the road, he noticed a burial in progress. He eased off the trail and watched. As the mourners began to disperse, Everett noticed the hotel manager, Wendels, and rode over.

"Whose funeral?" he asked.

"George Woods, owner of the Red Light," Wendels replied.

"But there's two fresh graves," Everett replied, glancing up at the side-by-side mounds of red dirt.

"Fred Kulhman was buried there a week or so back," the hotel manager explained. "He was killed over at Hunnewell at a sister saloon to the Red Light. Fight over a woman there, too. Mag, George's wife, has ordered a two-column, marble monument to set there at the head of the graves. It'll cost her five hundred and fifty dollars, I hear."

Wendels rode on and Everett turned back to the trail, but soon spotted riders approaching from the north, two men with their hands tied to their saddle horns, surrounded by five others.

8

"Who're the prisoners?" Everett asked the lead rider.

"Danford and his cashier from the Drover's and Mercantile Bank," the man replied.

"What're you gonna do with them?" Everett asked, turning alongside.

"They're gonna settle up with the citizens of this town," the man said, raising his voice and glancing at the bankers. "After that, we just might check their neck-size."

Reaching town, Everett rode south where Lizzie Johnson's outfit was camped waiting for a buyer with money, and headed for the trail boss's wagon.

"Ma'am," he said, "they've caught the president of the Drover's Bank. They aim to settle up with him, so if you hurry to town and grab a buyer, you might get your herd sold."

She thanked Everett and ordered her buckboard ready. Her husband, Hezekiah, climbed up and Everett followed them into town. Mrs. Lizzie hurried inside the Leland, then soon emerged with a Chicago buyer in tow, heading for the bank where a hearing was in progress.

"Think Mrs. Lizzie'll get her money?" Everett asked Hezekiah.

"If there's money there, she'll get her share, you can bet your saddle on that."

Half an hour later people poured out the doorway, Mrs. Lizzie near the lead. She smiled as she walked up to Everett.

"Did you get paid?" Everett asked.

"I did," she replied. "But not everybody was so lucky. Some will have to wait for the receipt of accounts payable and sale of other assets. There's a committee, led by Judge Campbell, that's been set up to collect on the outstanding loans, sell-off assets, and disperse payment to those owed."

"What'll they do with the bankers?" Everett asked.

"Some say string them up, but they're the sheriff's prisoners right now. I expect a jury will free the cashier and maybe lock up Danford for a spell."

"Son," the woman called as Everett turned to mount up. "Could I interest you in hiring on and making the trip back to Texas with us?"

"Thanks, ma'am, but I've got my heart set on finding work around here."

"I'd like to have you ride for the CY, but in any case, I want to pay you for coming out and alerting me," she said, handing him twenty dollars.

"Thank you again, ma'am," Everett replied, surprised but pleased.

As Hezekiah and Lizzie wheeled their buckboard around, Everett reined his mare northward, heading out of town.

Something over an hour later, he spotted the entrance to Bluff Creek Ranch. A raw board sign spanned the fifteen-foot distance between the tops of two fresh-cut logs firmly planted into the ground. Burned into the board with a simple, bar-shaped branding iron was BC RANCH in block letters. Extending from the sides of the entrance was a pole fence that formed a large rectangle around a double-sided log house, corral, and bunkhouse. A split-board porch crossed the front of the home with an open hallway down the middle. A burly, tan-colored dog raised himself from the porch as Everett rode through the roughly hewn gate that groaned on its squeaky hinges as the gusty southwest wind gently swayed it back and forth.

Approaching the hitching rail in front, Everett noticed that the log walls, the porch, and the steps showed little sign of weathering. While keeping an eye on the approaching dog, he spotted two cowboys striding over from a long, squatty building off to the right. Both wore revolvers on their hips and dusty hats with the front brims tugged down, shading their eyes. Everett sat waiting, his overlapped hands resting on the saddle horn.

"Hush up, Bruiser," the older cowboy said to the growling dog.

"Looking for work," Everett said as the men stopped some twenty feet away.

"What kind of work?" the old wiry cowboy asked.

"Tending cattle, horses, or whatever needs doing around the ranch," Everett replied. "With the extra beeves, I thought you might need another cowboy."

“Get the boss out here,” the wiry one said to his companion, who hopped onto the porch and disappeared through the hallway door leading into the left side of the house. “What’s your name?”

“Everett Brook.”

“They call me Jed,” the veteran cowboy said as the other one and the owner stepped out onto the porch.

“I hear you’re looking for work,” the rancher said as the dog trotted over, turned, and thumped his tail against the rancher’s leg.

“Yes, sir. I’m willing to try most anything,” Everett replied.

“My name’s Johnnie Blair,” the owner explained, stepping down off the porch and approaching Everett. “Got a startup operation here. I can’t pay much, but I can offer you a place to sleep and regular meals.”

“I’ll start for as little as fifteen dollars a month,” Everett said, sliding down and meeting the rancher with an outstretched hand. “In time, I hope to prove I’m worth more.”

“What brought you out here?”

“I read a piece in the paper, the Don Carlos article,” Everett replied. “Said you’d added some cattle to your herd. Thought I might could lend a hand.”

“Where you worked with cattle before?”

“Down at the Red Fork Ranch,” Everett replied. “Learned horses at Fort Gibson.”

“How come you to leave Red Fork?”

“I finished up my business down there, and wanted to see me a cow town. Along the trail, I joined up with Mrs. Lizzie Williams’s outfit, and . . .”

“Mrs. Lizzie?” Blair asked, interrupting. “My, I wish I’d been in town to meet her. That woman sure could tell a fella how to start up a ranch.”

“I hear this isn’t your first cattle outfit. Didn’t you once run a herd at the Red Fork?”

“With my partner, John Hood, but I had little to do with the ranching operation. There’s gonna be trouble down there, running herds on Indian land. I decided I’d rather own the range I run my cattle on.”

“I reckon you’re right about that, but what about that job?”

“Put your things in the shed over there,” the rancher said, nodding toward the long, squatty building. “This here is Chip, and I think you’ve already met Jed. He’s an old hand, so you’ll get your orders from him.”

"Thank you, sir," Everett said, then glanced up to see a young woman and a little girl on the porch.

"My wife, Katherine," Blair explained, turning. "And that's our daughter, Mabel."

Everett tipped his hat, nodded, and then followed Jed and Chip toward the corral.

"Don't need no blamed woman tellin' me how to run a ranch," Jed grumbled. "Not even Mrs. Lizzie Williams."

✪ ✪ ✪

Everett quickly settled into his new quarters and worked daily alongside Jed, building a barn while Chip rode herd on the new cattle. The old cowboy took a quick liking to his young helper, and just as rapidly, Everett attached himself to the seasoned cowhand, particularly enjoying the cow-trail stories, which the old fellow seemed to have in endless supply.

With construction completed, Everett started cleanup and minor repair work around the buildings and corral. Through these odd jobs he came to know Katherine Blair and little Mabel, often spending the waning daylight hours sitting on the edge of the ranch house porch with Mabel on his knee while her mother rocked nearby sewing or mending some garment. Mother and daughter became especially fond of Everett, but when Katherine asked about his parents, invariably he explained he had some last chore to do.

With work around the ranch house caught up, Everett spent more of his time riding the range with Jed. While traipsing among some red hills one day, Everett's chestnut mare reared up and shied away from a rocky outcropping.

"Rattlesnake," Jed said, when Everett got the mare under control. "There by that rock. Shoot it."

Everett drew his revolver, aimed, and fired. Red dust flew as the rattler tightened its coil and fluttered its noisy tail in the air. Again he fired, and again he missed.

"Not much of a shot, are you?" Jed said as he pulled out his pistol, raised it a little above his waist, and blew off the snake's head.

"How'd you learn to shoot like that?" Everett asked.

"Got my first lesson back in late August of seventy-one," Jed replied. "Wyatt Earp showed up at Stone's Trading Post, outfitting himself for a buffalo hunt on the northern ranges of Indian Territory, south of Medicine Lodge. While buying a wagon, team, and supplies, he talked about Wild Bill Hickok who he had spent time with only weeks earlier at Market Square in Kansas City. 'Hickok is the best,' Earp said. 'I saw him put ten rapid-fire bullets inside the letter O on a sign a hundred yards away. He says to draw quick, but think deliberate. It's clear thinking that makes the difference. In a gunfight, you can't count on gettin' off more than one shot, so your first has got to hit the target. Don't shoot from the hip, and don't fan the hammer. With a natural bend in your elbow, bring the gun waist high or thereabout. Work the hammer with the joint of your thumb.' I've never forgotten what I learned from watchin' Earp that day."

"You said Hickok put ten slugs into that O. Did he miss with a couple?"

"Nope. He drew both guns, emptied the revolver in his right hand, shifted the left-hand gun to his right lightning-quick, then emptied it. Wyatt explained that a gunman worth his salt don't go around with the hammer of his pistol on a live cartridge. He keeps it on an empty chamber so he don't accidentally shoot his own foot."

"Could you show me again how Earp taught you?"

Jed again pulled his revolver, lifted it, and fired, all in one smooth motion. A small red rock shattered into hundreds of pieces.

"You've got to learn the basics, son," Jed replied, "and practice, practice. There ain't no other way."

"Could you teach me now?"

"If you've got a steady hand and the will to learn."

From that time, Everett and Jed found practice time almost every day. "Wear your gun low enough to fit your arm length. Relax your hand. You can be firm without being rigid," the old cowboy advised. "Grab your weapon, bring your gun up while keeping the bend in your elbow, point the muzzle just like it was your index finger, and fire, all in one motion. Don't diddle none, but don't rush neither."

Repeatedly, Everett drew and fired as Jed watched and shook his head. "You've got snakelike quickness, son, as good as I've ever seen. But you've gotta trust your aim and fire without hesitation."

✪ ✪ ✪

Months went by and winter came. Everett and Jed rode out almost daily to check on the cattle. With their work done, they often stopped by the red hill and Everett would practice, shooting at rocks, twigs, and an occasional flower petal. As he learned to relax more and his confidence grew, his aim improved. "You're gettin' to be pretty good, son," Jed would say, "but come summer and warm weather, the rattlers will crawl out from under them rocks, and we'll see if you can shoot somethin' alive, somethin' with enough bite to kill you."

In early December with unseasonably mild weather, Jed invited Everett to go into town with him. As they rode by the cemetery, Everett motioned for the older cowboy to follow over to the graves of George Woods and Fred Kuhlman.

"I want to see this five hundred and fifty dollar monument," Everett explained as they left the trail.

Arriving at the marble marker, Jed whistled through his teeth. "Ain't no man worthy of somethin' like that, 'less he's President."

For a moment, Everett just stared. "What's got me buffaloed is that fresh-looking mound of dirt on Woods's grave."

"Takes a while for grass to grow," Jed replied. "Especially with winter comin' on."

"See that other grave there by it?" Everett said, pointing. "It's got grass, yet it's less than two weeks older."

"Does seem a mite strange," Jed replied, then turned his horse toward the trail. "Reckon it ain't mystery enough to keep us from gettin' along to town."

Riding along Main Street, heading south, they reined their horses over to the watering trough next to the well. Then they veered to the right and hitched their ponies in front of the Moreland House. Inside, they ordered dinner.

"I'm gonna hurry over to the *Post* and get a copy of the paper," Everett said.

When he had returned and taken a seat, he glanced at an article explaining the citizens' reaction to their city council's passing a seven o'clock curfew for boys.

Since some parents will not keep their teenage boys off the streets at night, the police will have to do it. Most folks are in favor of the new ordinance but a few young fellows have already challenged it and spent a night in the calaboose for their trouble.

"Jed," Everett leaned over and whispered while pointing to the article, "I'm just nineteen. Think they'll jail me?"

"I'll swear you're twenty," the old rancher replied, laughing. "Anyways, you're a sight bigger than Marshal Wilson, so I don't think he'll bother you none."

After scanning a few other articles, Everett searched for the column by the entertaining writer, Don Carlos, but found it missing.

"You know a man named Don Carlos?" Everett asked.

"Don't recall nobody with that name."

"He wrote an interesting article in the paper a while back, but I don't see his column in this one."

"Oh yeah, the columnist. His real name is Johnny Sain. Back before Caldwell had a paper, he used to write a weekly article in the *Sumner County Press*, coverin' the local news," Jed replied with a chuckle. "He runs a drugstore here on Main Street. Calls it the Mammoth Cave."

"How come he calls it that?"

"It's a big one and does a mighty fine business. Now days, Sain's so busy runnin' the post office and tendin' to city matters, he has a fella named Mehew run it most of the time. He's a nice enough fella, I reckon, but it's unsettlin' the way he looks at you with that crooked smile when you come in with a throbbing toothache or your gut's tied in knots. And then there's Martha who they say can sell her elixirs to a man three days in the grave, and Sheila who hides behind her white smock and mixes up potions, puttin' in Lord knows what."

"I reckon that's the place to go if you're sickly," Everett said.

"Yeah, or if you want one of them dime novels."

Smiling, Everett turned back to the paper. "What about the Talbot Gang? You ever heard of them?"

"Sounds familiar. A bunch from Texas, I believe."

"It says here that Jim Talbot and six of his gang created a disturbance at the opera house last night. The editor, Tell Walton, says he asked the gang to hold down the obscenities, and the gang leader then threatened him. This bunch of hoodlums, it says, has been in town about six weeks. Talbot, with his wife and two children, has rented the Dan Jones house on the north side of Fifth Street, but he and his boys hang out at the Red Light every night. They've also threatened the life of former mayor and marshal, Mike Meagher."

"They'll find Meagher a tough nut to crack," Jed said. "He was sheriff up in Wichita when it was a wild and wooly town. He got a lesson or two on how to corral gun-totin' cowboys from Wyatt Earp who was a deputy marshal up there at the time and one of the best cow-camp tamers who ever walked the street.

"Meagher was there when Earp arrested Shanghai Pierce and thirty Texas gunmen all by hisself. And I've heard him tell about Earp being challenged to a fistfight by George Peshaur, a big brawlin' Texan. Wyatt ignored the challenge until Peshaur called him a coward. According to the story, Wyatt unbuckled his gun belt and handed it to Dick Cogswell, owner of a nearby cigar store, then invited Peshaur into an empty backroom. Inside, Earp locked the door, and they went at each other. Fifteen minutes later, the door opened and Wyatt stepped out, his knuckles bleedin' and his face puffy. When Peshaur didn't show, his friends went in to check on him. He lay in a heap in a corner, his eyes swelled shut and not a square inch of his face that didn't show a cut or raw flesh. Not even the splash of a cold bucket of water revived him. His friends had to lift him to his feet and drag him to his hotel room.

"So, Meagher has seen some of the worst and knows how to handle them."

"I heard of Dan Jones down at Red Fork Ranch. Ralph Collins said he sold out and came up here to be a deputy marshal," Everett said. "Since Talbot's using his house, do you reckon he's in with this bunch?"

"I doubt it, though the line between lawmen and outlaws gets thin in these parts. And Talbot has a natural dislikin' for all marshals. He was in town back in the spring, March I believe. He got drunk and shot up Main Street before Marshal Johnson threw him in jail for the night. He threatened revenge from the time they slammed the cell door shut."

"Think he'll go after this ex-marshal, Meagher?"

"Talbot's always on the prod. If not Meagher, then somebody else."

While they were eating, a shot rang out on the street. Jed rushed to the door along with several others.

"Just George Spear," the old cowboy said, returning to the table. "Looks like he's celebratin' the end of another all-night drunk."

Before they could finish their meal, another shot exploded from a building just up the street. As customers again rushed to the front windows, a man burst through the doorway.

"There's a fella shootin' up Meagher's Arcade Saloon," the man yelled. "Think it's Tom Love, one of that Talbot bunch."

"Somebody better get the marshal," another man warned. "That gang's been drinkin' all night and threatenin' to kill every lawman in town, startin' with Meagher. There's gonna be trouble."

9

As men poured out the doorway of the Moreland House and other businesses along Main Street, Mike Meagher and Marshal Wilson approached the Arcade entrance, the owner having gone for help when the shooting started. Within minutes, the lawman stepped out with Tom Love in tow and headed for the jail. As they reached the intersection of Main and Fifth, a group of rough-bearded, unkempt men stepped out and blocked their path, their hands resting on their gun handles.

"The Talbot Gang," a man back at Moreland's said. "The tall one is Bob Bigtree, and there's Dick Eddleman and Doug Hill. Bob Munson is the short one, and that's Jim Martin beside him."

"Look," another man said, his voice sounding sharp and strained as he pointed ahead to the opposite side of the street. "There's Comanche Bill Mankin and George Spear. They've been hangin' out with that bunch."

"And here comes Talbot," someone said as the gang leader approached the intersection. "The dance is about to start."

Meanwhile, Everett and Jed had stepped out onto the boardwalk in front of Moreland's as the gang had converged on the marshal and his prisoner. Mike Meagher, watching from the front of the Arcade, saw what was happening and rushed to help. Talbot spotted him, pulled his pistol, and fired. When Marshal Wilson turned to defend Meagher, Love tore away and ran to join his friends.

"Let's give old Mike some cover," Jed said as he headed across the street.

Everett followed, firing twice, but being nervous and on the run, his bullets only kicked up dust short of the gang leader. Reaching the east side of the street, Everett ducked down behind a wood-slat whiskey barrel in front of Hulbert's

Guns and Hardware. The barrel, filled with water to be used in case of a fire, made an ideal shield. Jed crouched behind him, his back pressed hard against the wall.

Firing back at Talbot, Meagher headed toward the opera house on the southeast corner of Main and Fifth. When he turned down Fifth, hugging the north side of the old brick building, Talbot and his boys gave chase.

"Come on," Jed said. "Let's slip through Hulbert's store and catch 'em out back."

As they eased through the back doorway, they saw Meagher scamper around the back corner of the old opera house, and make a run for the foot of the outside stairway. As he bounded upward, two steps at a time, Talbot reached the corner and fired, lead zinging off the metal stairs. He fired again, but too late. The former marshal disappeared inside.

Everett raised his revolver and took aim at the outlaw, but Jed grabbed his arm.

"Don't," he said. "Mike's safe, and here comes the whole gang. You'll draw their fire on us."

With a crowd growing on Main Street, some of the armed men eased down Fifth toward the gang. Seeing a citizen army forming, Talbot called off his men, and they backed their way east down the street to Comanche Bill Mankin's house where they reloaded and grabbed a few rifles.

Everett and Jed slipped back through Hulbert's and onto Main.

"Where's the marshal?" Jed asked Levi Thrailkill.

"Gone to telegraph Mayor Burrus," the local grocer said. "Cass is in Wellington, and Marshal Wilson wants him to gather up a posse and get down here quick. He intends to flush that gang out and round them up."

"I don't think he'll have to flush them out," Jed said. "Them boys have got lots of fight left in 'em. They'll be reloaded and back on the street in no time."

As men bunched up along the storefronts, replaying the events and speculating what would happen next, Marshal Wilson came back out of the telegraph office.

"The mayor will get a posse down here as soon as he can. Until then, I'd like some of you boys handy with a gun to hang around and help me keep that bunch pinned down. The rest of you, get back inside or go home. I don't want a massacre."

Jed nodded toward the marshal, then glanced at Everett. "Let's get our ponies and ride down to the livery. It sits between Talbot's house and the Red Light, and I'd bet my boots those hombres won't go long without more firewater to keep up their courage."

They hurried through the open double doors of Kalbfleish's livery barn and stabled their horses. Everett then followed Jed up a board ladder tacked across two adjacent support posts. Reaching the loft, they crawled across loose hay to a hinged door. Jed unlatched it and peeked out.

The streets lay empty and stayed that way until about an hour after noon when Jed sneaked a look and spotted Jim Martin heading for the Red Light.

"Let's slip down and grab him," Jed said, then crouched over and headed for the ladder.

He and Everett emerged from the side door of the livery and blocked the path of the outlaw crossing the street.

"Hold up," Jed called out with his revolver pulled, "and keep those hands away from your gun."

Everett followed his partner's lead and leveled his pistol on Martin as he and Jed approached the outlaw.

"Watch his back trail," Jed said to Everett as he slipped a revolver from the man's scabbard and retrieved another hidden deep in an inside coat pocket.

"Thanks, boys," Marshal Wilson said as he and Deputy Fossett came running down Sixth Street. "That concealed weapon will get you a few nights in our new calaboose, unless you've got a pocket full of money for Justice Thomas." The marshal then shoved Martin up the street toward Main, his revolver muzzle poked against the outlaw's spine.

Everett and Jed slipped back inside the livery, but within half an hour, Deputy Fossett returned with the prisoner. Everett kept watch from the loft door while Jed slipped downstairs.

"What's that varmint doin' back down here?" Jed asked Fossett.

"Says he's got money to pay his fine here in his saddlebags," the deputy explained.

While the men below were talking, Everett kept watch from the barn loft and spotted Talbot, Eddleman, Munson, and Love slipping out the rear door of Mankin's house, headed for the livery.

"Talbot and his gang are coming this way," he called down from the top of the ladder.

Fossett pulled both his revolvers and quickly whirled his prisoner around, placing Martin between himself and the doorway. Jed flattened out against the inside wall by the front door.

Meanwhile, Everett scrambled back to the loft door, opened it a crack and pushed his pistol muzzle through the slit as Talbot and his bunch stopped just outside the livery. The gang leader, realizing he was caught in the open by four rifles and six-guns behind cover, backed off, his bunch making like a pack of crawfish toward Fifth Street. Turning, the outlaw leader spotted Meagher crouched at the foot of the opera house stairs and fired.

Main Street onlookers heard the shot and rushed onto Fifth Street and began firing into the gang, triggering a blazing gun battle. Unarmed citizens rushed into nearby Hulbert's gun shop and were supplied rifles and ammunition by A. Witzleben. Over at Hardesty Brothers hardware, C. W. Willet armed more citizens who then poured out onto the street to join the melee.

Everett leaped from the loft door to join Jed on the ground, and they crossed to the rear of Hulbert's store, where they fired into the scattering gang. Everett's aim was better this time, and one of the outlaws, Eddleman, grabbed his right side and bent forward. Someone up the street winged Love in the upper arm, forcing him to shoot left handed, and then Jed got off a shot that caught Bigtree in the foot.

Talbot stood in the center of the street with both guns blazing at Meagher. Lead was flying from every direction and ricocheting off brick walls, but the outlaw leader made no attempt to hunker down or shield himself in one of the many nearby buildings. Within minutes the hammers of both his pistols clicked on spent shells. While he fed cartridges from his belt into the cylinders of his revolvers, he stood staunch in the street and hollered for one of his cronies to retrieve his rifle from the rented house.

Hearing the command, Everett raced across the street to cut off the errand runner. Seeing the move to block him, the outlaw fired at Everett who instantly dropped to the ground when the bullet zinged by his head. As the man bounded up on the front porch of the house, Everett fired and the man slumped to the unpainted floor. Just then the door swung open and a cohort fired three cover rounds at Everett, while another dragged the wounded man inside, smearing blood across the raw boards.

Within seconds, another man emerged from the house with two rifles in hand, and ran toward the gang leader while Everett fired three times, missing his target.

With store windows shattering, lead careening off stone and brick, and the smell of gun smoke heavy on the air, Everett replaced spent shells as he ran back to join Jed. Meanwhile, Talbot grabbed his Winchester and, while striding toward Meagher, fired four uninterrupted shots. The ex-marshal headed up the stairs, intermittently shooting back. After about seven or eight shots from Talbot's Winchester, the former Caldwell mayor and marshal came tumbling down the stairs, the front of his shirt soaked in blood.

His primary objective accomplished, Talbot and his gang backed down Fifth Street to the Dan Jones house. Marshal Wilson rushed to Meagher, and finding no pulse, he screamed like a mother catamount hovering over her dead kitten. Leaping to his feet, the lawman gripped both his revolvers and began a steady, determined march toward the outlaw's den, yelling vulgarities, and firing one pistol, then the other until empty. Armed townsfolk, inspired by their marshal, joined him in pouring a hailstorm of lead into the thin-walled shack. With wallboards splintering, windows shattering, and the interior panel of the front door rapidly disintegrating, the furious citizen-army marched on in relentless assault.

As Everett and Jed watched from the rear of Hulbert's, they glanced to the south along Chisholm Street and noticed that Mr. Hubbell had stepped out the back door of his store two blocks down, along with young James Matthews. The two ran down the street and joined Everett and Jed.

"Talbot and his boys have gotta get out of there, and the back door is their only chance," Jed explained. "Let's get down there and cover it."

"They've killed Meagher, so they're ready to get out of town," Hubbell said. "Let's work our way down closer to the livery and pick them off when they head for their horses."

In silent agreement, the four men headed north along Chisholm Street until they saw the outlaws running for the barnyard on the south side of

Kalbfleishch's livery, where several saddled horses stood. Among them, a frantic George Spears was hustling a saddle on a bay mare.

"We're too late. Let's shoot their horses," Hubbell said as he fired into the corral.

"Wait," Everett said as the bay whinnied and stumbled. "Keep Spears busy, and I'll slip around back, open the gate, and flush the horses out."

He ran past the north side of the livery, opened the back gate to the corral, and rushed in among the animals, firing into the air. The ponies raced out the gate and scattered like a covey of quail. Following the horses, Everett glanced back, and there lay Spears beside the dead horse, clutching his chest in agony.

Spotting Everett, Talbot and his men turned their fire on him. He ducked behind the livery and made his way back toward Jed, Hubbell, and young Matthews who gave him cover until he joined them inside the backdoor of the M & S Saloon.

The outlaw gang ran inside the livery and trained their guns on the stable owner, demanding that he saddle horses for them. Talbot climbed aboard the first one and, without hesitation, burst through the doorway with four of his gang trailing him while bent low over their stolen horses' shoulders. In a swirl of dust, the outlaws headed out of town to the east. Eddleman and Love, slowed by their wounds and abandoned by their leader, were late leaving the livery.

Heading for the door, Everett spotted Eddleman emerging with his spurs dug into the flanks of his chestnut mare. Drawing on all the training and target practice, Everett snatched his revolver, swung it up, thumbed the hammer, and squeezed. The outlaw flinched, then tumbled to the street.

Love, following Eddleman, reined up and shot his hands into the air.

"Talbot ain't gettin' away," bellowed young Matthews as he steadied his Winchester on the distant riders and pulled the trigger.

Talbot's horse stumbled, then two strides later, tumbled to the ground, spilling the gang leader. The outlaw scrambled to his feet, swung up behind one of his comrades, and galloped out of town.

Everett rounded up his horse while the marshal and his followers rushed forward and gathered up the two remaining outlaws.

"What about Comanche Mankin and Delaney?" someone asked. "They were in on this, too."

Deputy Fossett and two locals escorted Eddleman and Love toward jail while Marshal Wilson and the others headed for Mankin's house. Soon the man called Comanche emerged with his hands up, followed by Delaney.

While some of the townspeople surveyed the damage to their stores and homes and assisted those with bullet wounds, others began forming a posse. Miraculously, only George Spears and Mike Meagher, along with a couple of horses, had been killed.

"We'll ride south," the marshal shouted to the posse. "They'll turn toward Indian Territory soon enough."

Three miles behind the outlaws, Everett and Jed rode with the posse toward Bluff Creek. Meeting old Mose Swaggart, a well-known trader in the area, riding atop a load of hay with his saddle pony latched to the tailgate, the posse pulled up.

"Mose," the marshal called out, "can we borrow your horse so young John Hall don't have to ride double?"

The old-timer agreed, and the excited young man swung up on the bareback mare.

When the posse reached Shorthorn Campbell's ranch, which was split by Bluff Creek, they borrowed a bridle and saddle for Swaggart's pony. The rancher joined the posse as they continued toward Deer Creek Ranch, run by the Deutcher brothers. About half a mile south of ranch headquarters, the posse spotted the outlaws' abandoned horses at the edge of a deep wash, then noticed Talbot leading his men afoot along the floor of the ravine. They were headed for an old, roofless, stone-wall dugout chiseled into the canyon's north side.

The posse quickly spread themselves along the rim on both sides of the canyon, leaving the gang no escape route.

"I don't see no good way to get at 'em," Jed said to Everett and John Hall from their crouched position on the south wall.

"Maybe we gotta just wait them out," Everett suggested. "They're without food and water, so they've got to come out sooner or later."

"Looks like Campbell's got another idea," Jed said, pointing to the hunched-over rancher approaching a five-foot-high red mound on the ravine floor some thirty feet in front of the dugout.

"Let's go help him," Everett suggested.

Before they could get to their feet, a barrage of gunfire burst from the dugout, and Campbell fell to the ground, clutching his bloody left wrist as red dust shot up all around him.

"He's trapped," Jed said. "Let's cover him."

They began firing and immediately others joined in, pouring a steady stream of lead into the dugout until the rancher had scrambled out of the enemy's range and was climbing out of the canyon.

"Where'd Hall go?" Everett asked, noticing the young man's absence.

"Hightailed it outta here when Campbell went down," Jed replied, pointing to the posse's horses where Hall was swinging into the saddle. "Some find it excitin' 'til they see blood spilt."

With things slowed down, glimpses of the past hour flooded Everett's mind. He swallowed hard, determined to fight off a queasy stomach.

"Go check on Campbell," Jed said, recognizing the symptom. "I'll stay here and keep an eye out for them outlaws."

Everett back-crawled away from the canyon rim, then rose to a hunched-over position and scampered toward the group lifting the injured rancher onto his horse. Two men rode away with Campbell, whose left wrist was shattered, along with several surface wounds, taking him back to town for medical treatment.

"Likely he'll lose the use of that hand, but he's lucky to be alive," the marshal said. "I counted twenty-seven bullet holes in his clothes."

"What'll we do now?" Everett asked.

"We can't get at 'em," the marshal said, "so no need in all of us spending a cold night out here. I need six volunteers to stay while the rest go home, get some rest, and come back at sunup with dynamite. Then we'll blow 'em out."

"Jed Kimble and I will stay," Everett volunteered.

"George, would you guard the horses?" the marshal asked when he had chosen four men, including George Freeman. "We gotta make sure they don't slip up here at night and ride off on our mounts."

With the volunteers stationed on the rim and Freeman guarding the horses, the remainder of the posse left for town, the outlaws' stolen ponies in tow.

As the sun dropped, cold darkness crept across the canyon rim, sinking to its floor below, and the only sound alive on the wide prairie was the moan of a bone-chilling north wind as it dipped and swirled through the eerie depths of the ravine. Staring into the sunset, Everett shivered, remembering his hooded father atop the hanging scaffold, forever painted on the backdrop of a dying sun.

"Wish we had some moonlight," Jed said a couple hours later, easing closer to Everett's position. "I can barely see that dugout openin'."

"You think they'll try to sneak out tonight?"

"Without horses, they'd be easy pickin's, for sure, but I don't know that their chances will get any better with daylight."

"Speaking of horses, I think I hear some coming from the north," Everett said.

Within minutes, Sheriff Thralls and Mayor Burrus arrived from Wellington with a posse of thirty. Two men joined Freeman guarding the horses, while the others spread out along the canyon rim, waiting for daylight.

✪ ✪ ✪

The sun rose in a clear sky and brought welcomed warmth to the shivering men along the canyon rim, inspiring increased alertness. The posse focused on the old dugout, watching for any attempt at escape by the outlaws, but all was graveyard quiet. Growing impatient, two men eased dangerously close along the rim to a point right above the roofless shelter. One sent a rifle shot into the shadows of the stone wall, but the challenge brought no response.

"I'm going down there," Sheriff Thralls said. "If I draw their fire, open up and don't stop until I'm either behind that clay mound or back up here."

The sheriff crept down into the canyon, revolver drawn, and when within forty feet of the red mound, he broke into a sprint, diving behind the earthen shield. The dugout remained silent. After belly-crawling his way to the crest of the knoll, he removed his hat and peeked over. Then he stood, swearing, and banged his hat against his leg.

"The birds have flown the coop!" he yelled to the tense men along the canyon rim, their rifles trained on the empty hideout.

Baffled, some said it was impossible. Guards had been staked all night. No one had seen or heard anything suspicious, and no horses were missing. While the befuddled men discussed what to do, Everett eased over to the rim edge right above the dugout. He noticed boot tracks, but thought little of it until, looking down the steep wall, he spotted a strange smooth place where the wall protruded out toward the canyon interior. He called for Jed.

"Looks like a rope has rubbed against the hard, dry clay down there," Everett said, pointing. "Maybe one of them climbed up, somehow anchored a rope up here, dropped the end down, and the others shimmied up."

"There were guards everywhere," Jed said, shaking his head. "Must have been mighty quiet to not alert anyone."

"But only two guards were over here after the posse left and before the sheriff showed up," Everett pointed out.

"Let's scatter in groups of three," Sheriff Thralls said, "and warn the ranchers around that the Talbot gang is roaming the countryside. They'll be looking for horses, and they won't be particular who they belong to or who they have to kill to get 'em."

After sharing the bad news with a couple of ranchers, Everett and Jed rode on back to town, ate a good meal, and got a room for the night.

The next morning the town was abuzz with speculation and placing blame for the escape of the hated outlaws. Most of the criticism was aimed at Marshal Wilson for letting them get out of town, and then for leaving too few guards at the canyon.

When Everett and Jed stepped through the hotel doorway, the conversation had switched to why Talbot and his gang had descended on their town and why Mike Meagher had been their primary target.

"I heard Talbot was half brother to George Flatt, and the outlaw was gettin' even for Meagher's part in killin' his kin," one man said.

"He didn't bring his whole gang here to gun down Meagher," another said. "He was after the whole Caldwell police force. He intended to take over this town, to punish us."

"Maybe Talbot was just gettin' even for Meagher arrestin' him back in March," Jed said from the fringe of the crowd. "I recollect he swore he would powder-burn Meagher's face for that."

As Everett and Jed turned from the crowd to mount up, a freight wagon rolled down the street. The old driver pulled his exhausted team to a halt beside them.

"Boys, I'm J. K. Harmon, and I need to buy a couple of pullin' teams," the fellow said. "You see, I had to leave two loaded wagons back at Bullwhacker Creek 'cause some outlaws stole five of my horses last night."

A crowd began to gather as the freighter gave a detailed description of the thieves.

"The Talbot gang," Jed said as others pushed closer. "Now they've got mounts and likely are halfway to Texas."

"You might try the livery," Everett suggested to the freighter. "Kalb's got the ones those same fellows left here yesterday. I'd think their rightly yours now."

"I don't reckon I'll be that lucky," the old fellow explained. "They said they'd bring mine back, but I'll never see 'em again."

"That means Talbot and his band walked about ten miles after they escaped last night, and Bigtree with a bullet in his foot," Constable Rhoades said as the freighter pulled away.

"Men," Sheriff Thralls said as he joined the group, "Mayor Burrus has called a town meeting. I think some of you boys might be interested in what he's got to say."

Everett and Jed joined a grumbling crowd of men at the brick schoolhouse a few blocks west of Main Street.

"The city of Caldwell is offering a reward of five hundred dollars for the capture of Talbot and his gang, dead or alive," the mayor announced to a full room, then hesitated before he continued. "And as you know, a while back the state of Kansas made the sale of whiskey illegal, other than for medicinal purposes. Half an hour ago, your city council voted to enforce that law. As of noon today, all saloons in town are closed, indefinitely."

"Mayor, whiskey ain't the problem," a man yelled from the back of the room. "It's the six-shooter."

Over berating shouts and slurs, another man spoke up. "Burrus, if you try to enforce prohibition in this town, you've only got two choices. You can resign or bear the consequences."

The crowd roared, some yelling at the man issuing the threat, but more at the red-faced mayor.

10

"There's gonna be trouble aplenty in Caldwell," Jed said as he and Everett rode north out of town. "Even if the locals would accept prohibition, the cowboys won't."

"But the cowboys can't buy if nobody's selling," Everett said.

"Ever hear of a blind-tiger?" Jed did not wait for an answer. "They operate from behind a locked door with a little slot cut out, just large enough to pass a bottle of rot-gut through. The door makes sure the buyer and seller can't see each other."

"The town belongs to the citizens," Everett replied. "Looks like they ought to run it the way they want to, with or without whiskey."

"But it's split," Jed said. "North and west of Main is mostly homes and businesses for the townspeople who'd like to see the town cleaned up. South and east is mostly for the cattlemen and cowboys who expect to come in after a long drive and kick up their heels."

"What about the farmers?"

"The farmers would like to side with the locals, but they know the railroad wouldn't be here to take their goods to market if not for the cattle and cowboys. There's some mighty good farmin' being done along the Chikaskia River and up Fall Creek. Thirty bushels of wheat to the acre and seventy-five of corn is commonplace. More farmers are comin' and claimin' homesteads, so someday their vote may tilt the scale. Meantime, the town rift is just gonna get worse 'til it finally blows up."

"I guess that new bank that's opening soon, the Stock Exchange, will cater to the cattlemen, adding fuel to the flame," Everett said.

"Its president, Major Drumm, is one of the biggest ranchers in the area, " Jed explained. "He came up on a drive from Texas in the early seventies and started his U Ranch south of town in Indian Territory."

"White man's cattle on Indian land," Everett said, shaking his head.

"He leases it from the Cherokees," Jed explained.

Everett recalled Little Robe's comments about ranchers leasing Indian land. There's another problem on the rise, just waiting to explode, he thought.

Back at the ranch, Everett spent the next two months riding herd on the cattle. The dog, Bruiser, now friendly with him, always followed along. With the cold winter months came hungry wolves, watching nightly from the fringe of the herd for a downed cow or newborn calf. During the day, Everett and the dog napped in a narrow ravine then spent their nights circling the herd, keeping the deadly predators at bay.

Late one Sunday afternoon, with the threat of a winter storm on the northwestern horizon, Everett and his canine friend herded the cattle into a series of wide coulees along the north bank of Bluff Creek, seeking protection from the coming storm. With darkness closing fast, he rode from ridge to ridge, searching for strays. As he scanned the gray landscape from atop a hogback on the southeastern part of the range, he spotted an orange glow in the southern sky farther along the creek. He immediately put the chestnut mare into a gallop, Bruiser scampering to keep up.

Topping a ridge, he stared down at a barn on the opposite side of a wide lowland. In the creeping darkness, long tongues of yellow and orange flame leaped from its doorway and wall crevices, lashing out as if fighting off the cold night.

Lunging down the slope, the horse's sharp hooves sent loose dirt and rock skittering before them while the dog raced ahead. At the bottom he heeled his mare into a gallop across the floor of the wide draw. Suddenly, the barking dog cut sharply to the left, barely giving Everett warning enough to yank his mare to a stop five feet from the edge of a deep ravine that ran north from the creek. Veering left in search of a place to cross, he reached its upper end just as four horses, driven hard by two mounted cowboys, came spilling out. Yelping frantically, Bruiser leaped into the path of the startled ponies, causing them to double back into the ravine. Their pursuers, to avoid being trampled, retreated into the darkness of the deep gully. For a second Everett considered giving chase, but opted to fight the fire. He called the dog away from the heels of the frightened horses, rounded the upper end of the ravine, then thundered across a wide meadow toward the burning barn.

Arriving, he grabbed an empty bucket and joined three others frantically rushing back and forth to the creek, hauling water to dash onto the burning structure. Fortunately, the fire had been spotted early and neighbors had converged to help. The flames were gradually extinguished, damaging only one end of the barn.

"Thanks, young man," the rancher said to Everett as he made his way among the exhausted men. "Don't believe we've met. My name's John Wendell."

"Everett Brook," the young cowboy replied, rising to shake the rancher's hand. "I work for Mr. Blair."

"It's a pleasure," the rancher said. "Johnnie's family. Married my daughter, Katie."

"I'm pleased to meet you, sir," Everett said. "Mrs. Katherine is a fine lady and the best mother little Mabel could ever want."

"Maybe you could give 'em my best, when you get back to the ranch."

"I'll do that, Mr. Wendell, and I'm sure the boss and the boys will be glad to help repair your barn," Everett said, glancing at the smoldering, charred frame.

Before the rancher could respond, a teenage boy ran up. "Pa, the horses are gone!"

"Thievin' varmints!" Wendell bellowed, staring toward a row of stalls about fifty yards to the west. "They set the fire to draw our attention while they stole my horses."

"Coming over I ran into two hombres herding four broncs," Everett said.

"Where?" Wendell asked.

"Yonder at the upper end of that ravine," Everett replied, pointing west. "Bruiser turned the ponies back into the gulch, trapping the riders."

Within minutes Everett, Wendell, and three other men were riding west along the creek bank, approaching the juncture of the ravine and the stream.

"Let's spilt up," Wendell suggested. "Maybe two could head up to the far end of the ravine and shut it off. The rest of us will go in down here and flush them your way."

"What if them thieves commence throwin' lead?" one man asked.

"We've got 'em outnumbered, so don't fire unless you have to," Wendell said. "And be sure who you're shootin' at. I'd rather they get away than us kill each other."

Everett headed toward the north end of the ravine along with another fellow. Heavy cloud cover had turned the night pitch black.

"Them outlaws could be twenty feet from us, and we'd never see 'em," the man said to Everett.

"Bruiser's up ahead," Everett replied. "We'll stick with him, and he'll let us know if they're around."

Following the dog, Everett and his companion reached the head of the ravine, dismounted, and stationed themselves, one on either side. Everett called the dog over and patted him until he dropped to his haunches.

Some ten minutes later Everett heard a rider coming up the floor of the ravine. Kneeling by the growling dog, he slipped his gloved left hand over Bruiser's muzzle, and drew his revolver.

"It's me, Wendell," said the rancher from the darkness. "We've got the horses. No sign of the thieves."

"We'll meet you over at the stables," Everett hollered into the ravine.

With the horses penned, Everett turned to the rancher. "I'll head back to the herd now, but tomorrow I'll ride to headquarters and let Mr. Blair know."

"Before you go, come in and have some supper," the rancher said.

Having not had a home-cooked meal in several weeks, Everett agreed and followed Wendell inside. He hung his hat on a wooden peg to the left of the door, and as he turned around, his eyes settled on a young woman emerging from the kitchen. She had dark hair, brown eyes, and a warm smile on her soft face.

"If you men would like to wash up, we'll have supper on in a few minutes," she said.

"Tabitha," the rancher said, "I'd like you to meet Everett Brook. He rides for Johnnie, and came over to help put out the fire."

The two young people nodded awkwardly to each other, and then Everett excused himself and followed Mr. Wendell to the wash basin.

"A niece of mine," the rancher explained. "Her folks are visitin' back East, so she's spendin' a couple of weeks with us. Her pa, Thomas Nichols, runs the Homestead Ranch."

While eating, Everett's attention often strayed to Tabitha who smiled in return but said little. Only once did she speak directly to him.

"Mr. Brook, are you new to the area?"

"Yes, ma'am," he responded. "Just rode up from Fort Gibson a few months back."

"I hope you're finding our community to your liking," she replied.

"I am. Caldwell's a growing town, and I expect this is a fine place to settle down."

"Caldwell's a cow town, like Wichita and Abilene before it," she said, her eyes steady on him. "Like them, it's got too many saloons, dancehalls, and vile people. Sometimes it's hardly fit for decent folk."

The rancher's wife quickly asked if anyone wanted seconds, and after declining, Everett asked to be excused so he could get back to the herd before the storm worsened.

Riding into a stiff north wind, Everett made his way back to the ravines, old Bruiser whining as he trailed along. After a brief check on the huddled cattle, Everett dropped down to his camp nestled between the steep slopes of a draw. He kindled a fire to life, warmed coffee, and finished off two steaming cups. Then he rode up the slope to its crest where a shower of windblown snow greeted him. Pulling his face down into the warmth of his turned-up collar, he slowly circled the coulees, stopping only twice to add fuel to his fire and to warm up with a cup of coffee. When he rode out the second time, old Bruiser started after him, let out a mournful whimper, then slowly returned to his warm bed of straw.

Later, when a brilliant sun should have been emerging against a blue sky, miserable gray clouds domed their world. Peering through swirling snow, Everett saw a flat landscape dominated by white, broken only by an occasional patch of drooping grass, an up-thrust of rock, or a lone tree. Slowly, the cattle wandered out of the coulees and drifted down to the creek. Filled, they climbed the slopes and pawed at the icy crystals, freeing buffalo grass.

After downing a simple breakfast, Everett lingered by the fire thawing his hands and feet, then climbed back into the saddle and headed for the Blair ranch house. When only half an hour from camp, he spotted an approaching rider leading a packhorse. Soon Everett recognized Jed's pony and nudged the chestnut mare into a trot.

"Thought I'd better come check on you," the old cowpoke called out. "Maybe you'd like a roof over your head for a spell."

Everett welcomed the chance to sleep inside a few nights, so he told Jed where he could find the herd and about Wendell's barn fire, then rode on to headquarters. After telling Blair the story, the tired cowboy headed for the bunkhouse, rolled up in his bedroll and slept until early the following morning. In need of supplies, he saddled a spare horse and rode for Caldwell.

The storm had passed, leaving a five-inch covering of snow, and the sun shone brightly. Though there was only a whisper of wind, the crisp air stung his face as the horse's hooves crunched along over the crusty surface.

Arriving in Caldwell, he headed for Hubbell's general merchandise store, purchased a few supplies, then headed over to Fossett's grocery to stock up on a few food items. From there he rode over to the City Hotel and hitched his horse. As he approached the door, he saw side-by-side pictures of a young man, Asa Overall, and woman, Clara Nyce. Beneath the pictures was a wedding notice for the fifteenth of March.

Before going inside Everett stepped two doors down to the *Caldwell Post* and purchased a paper. Seated at a vacant table, he unfolded it.

The front page carried a story about the rapid growth of the Stock Exchange Bank, opened two months earlier. Secretary-Treasurer Milt Bennett, on behalf of Major Andrew Drumm, thanked their rancher customers, promised to support area cattlemen with loans, meet their banking needs, and provide other "special services." A second story heralded the virtues of the new city marshal, George Brown. A few weeks earlier, Marshal Wilson had abruptly resigned without explanation, but speculation was he had tired of criticism following the Talbot Gang escape. Brown had completed the last month of Wilson's term, and then on the first day of March, Mayor Colson had selected the twenty-eight-year-old bachelor to fill the job for the next year. The editor described the new marshal as educated, gentle, fair, and intolerant of violence. Marshal Brown lived with his sister on the top floor of George Freeman's house at Comanche and Fifth Street, "a convenient arrangement since Freeman is himself a deputy U. S. marshal," the story said.

About the time Everett ordered his noon meal, Tell Walton came in and stepped over. He and Everett had met back during the Talbot gang shootout.

"Mind if I keep you company?" the newsman asked.

"Pleased to have you," Everett replied.

While waiting for their food, they discussed the town's reaction following the escape of the outlaws.

"We closed the saloons, but they were reopened a few weeks later," Walton explained. "The mayor and council were swamped with protests, even threats."

"Tell me about the big wedding," Everett said, motioning toward the pictures.

"Two of our finest citizens," Walton replied. "Asa Overall came here in the early seventies and is known and liked by everyone, and Clara can be counted on to help out with most any civic project. Her father is the assistant cashier at the new Stock Exchange Bank."

"I don't recall seeing Mr. Overall during the Talbot shootout," Everett said.

"He's a farmer, and a good one," Walton said. "He has helped out every time he's been called on. Fact is, when he was in his late teens, he proved himself to be quite capable.

"I believe it was June of seventy-two when George Freeman's sorrel team and wagon were stolen. A posse was quickly rounded up, and young Asa wanted to go along, but had no horse. Henry Stone, one of the founders of the town, saw Asa's eagerness and offered the loan of his pony, provided the young man would promise to stick it out to the very end. Asa didn't hesitate.

"Well, they rode out in pursuit, following the wagon tracks to the northwest, all the way to the Arkansas River just east of Fort Larned. They found the outlaw camp, but a young fella named Dalton was the only one there. Freeman knew he was not the leader, so the posse hid and waited. Sure enough, the man they wanted showed up, swimming his pony across the Arkansas, returning from Boyd's ranch along Pawnee Creek. Cautiously approaching his camp, the thief suddenly became suspicious, turned, and spurred his mount toward some nearby hills. And it looked like he'd make it. Freeman and his men knew that if the outlaw got up in those cliffs, he could hold off the whole posse.

"Suddenly, from out of nowhere, a rider sprang up over a ridge in a dead run, angling his pony to cut off the thief's path. The outlaw fired at the rider several times, but the man didn't slow up or waver. The outlaw leader, seeing he'd never make it to the hills, veered off toward the river and plunged his horse into the flooded stream.

"The rider pursuing the outlaw was soon joined by Freeman. They pushed their ponies into the swollen river and continued the chase on the other side, eventually capturing the thief and bringing him back to camp.

"The rider who rode right into the path of that outlaw and helped capture the noted thief was Asa Overall, not yet twenty years old."

"Who was the horse thief?" Everett asked.

"Tom Smith," the newsman replied. "Young Dalton escaped one night on the trail coming back, but Smith was brought here where a ready mob gathered to hang him. However, using Isaac Cooper's two-seat wagon, Freeman, Dr. Black, Perry Haines, and Dan Carter sneaked the prisoner out of town in the middle of the night, headed for the jail in Wellington.

"When they reached Ryland's Ford on the Chikaskia, they were jumped by a group of armed men who demanded that the prisoner be turned over to them. Freeman had no choice, so he left Smith there with his abductors and went on to the county seat where he notified the sheriff. Come daylight, Freeman and the sheriff returned to the river crossing and found the thief swinging from an elm tree.

"It was then rumored that Tom Smith was actually Thomas Ford, the son of a prominent Illinois politician, and his brother was one-armed Charley Smith, or Sewell Ford. Charley stayed around Caldwell for a while, threatening to get even, but two years later he was captured as a member of the biggest horse-thief ring in Kansas and died in the same manner as his brother."

"One of these days, I hope to meet Asa. Sounds like a mighty brave young man."

Having finished his meal, Everett bid goodbye to Walton and rode north, heading back to the ranch while recalling Tabitha's description of Caldwell. No doubt, he thought, it's a town accustomed to violence and a magnet for those who profit by it. Yet, there are those like the newspaperman, Asa Overall and Clara Nyce, George Freeman, and the new marshal.

✪ ✪ ✪

As the snow melted and the grass sprouted to life, Johnnie Blair and his cowboys prepared for spring roundup, the branding of newborns, cutting out of market-ready steers, and searching for strays.

After two days in the saddle, the cattle were penned in a deep, box-end canyon along Bluff Creek. The cowboys rode among the herd, separating out the new calves, applying the JB iron, and then setting them free to rejoin their bawling mothers. Steers and cows ready for market were isolated and held in the rear of the canyon.

"Don't brand that one," Jed called out as Chip and Everett grabbed a three-month-old calf.

"How come?" Chip asked.

"See that bawlin' cow? That's her calf, and she wears a Homestead brand," the old cowboy explained. "I expect we've got a couple dozen of 'em."

"When we're done here, we'd better cull them and drive 'em home," Blair said to Jed. "Take Everett with you. We'll hold the herd here 'til you get back."

Jed and Everett drove about twenty-five head across the open plain toward the Homestead Ranch, arriving mid-afternoon. The old rancher stepped out, called one of his cowboys to give a hand, then opened the gate to a barn-side corral. The three cowboys soon had the bunch squeezed through the gate and penned.

As Everett was being introduced to the rancher and his cowboy, Bob Jackson, Tabitha stepped out onto the wide porch of the ranch house. When she turned toward the swing, the gentle spring breeze, a crosswind, blew wisps of her long, dark hair across her face.

"Nice meetin' you, cowboy," Jackson said to Everett, then turned his pony toward the house.

Everett tried to pay attention as Jed and Mr. Nichols talked about springtime ranching, but his eyes kept flashing over to the porch where Jackson had leaped down from his pony and was climbing the steps.

"Mr. Blair and Chip are waiting on us back there," Everett reminded Jed, then turned his horse as if to leave.

After farewells, Jed and Everett headed back to the canyon where the JB cattle were penned. Reaching behind the saddle cantle to adjust his slicker-covered bedroll, Everett took one last glance at Tabitha. She and Jackson were swaying back and forth in the porch swing, the cowboy's arm draped along the top rail of the swing.

11

Slapping his coiled lariat against his chaps, Everett pushed the JB herd out through the mouth of the canyon, where Jed turned the bawling cattle southward. Chip and Blair rode point, guiding the lead beeves along the creek. Fortunately for Everett, the ground was still damp, so he was not eating dust as is typical when riding drag.

The next morning, having spent the night along the creek, they forded the stream a few miles south and continued along the opposite side until they reached a gradual slope that led up to the flat plain. It was about noon when they reached the pens at the railhead south of Caldwell.

After selling the stock, they rode into town where people along the street waved at and called out to Johnnie Blair who had originally arrived in Caldwell in 1871, had operated various businesses for ten years, and had served as postmaster for seven. A town favorite, he stopped to visit while Everett and Jed rode on up Main Street and swung down in front of the Arcade.

"I'm thirsty," Jed said.

Everett followed the old cowboy inside and stood beside him at the bar, scanning the room full of men crowded around tables, drinking, talking, and visiting with two flimsily dressed women meandering from table to table, delivering drinks.

"Two whiskeys," Jed ordered.

Everett sipped his while his friend tossed his down, then got a refill. Jed headed toward a doorway draped with a dark green, split curtain, motioning for Everett to follow.

Inside the second room were three tables, two occupied with men playing poker. Jed and Everett took a seat at the vacant one, but soon Jed was invited to join one of the games. Everett watched, amazed at the amount of money on the table and the ease with which it changed hands.

After a while Everett became bored and stepped back outside. There, tying up at the hitching rail, was the freighter J. K. Harmon, the man whose horses the Talbot gang had taken after their escape from the red canyon down at Deer Creek.

"Get your horses back?" Everett asked, remembering that the outlaws had sworn they would return them.

"Beats all I've ever seen," the old freighter said. "Two weeks later a scalawag named Jake Keffer and another fella named Hostetter from Arkansas City ride into town leadin' my five horses. Right off, Keefer claims he'd taken them from those outlaws while they were camped down on Turkey Creek. He asks for a hundred-dollar reward, and if I'd had it on me, I just might've forked it over.

"But I tells him to hold on a minute while I goes over to the bank. While I'm there, Hostetter slips in and whispers to me that those outlaws had handed over my ponies to Keefer to return to me, sayin' they weren't no horse thieves.

"Well, I sails outta there and marches right up to that bamboozler, tellin' him he's low-downer than the worst of that Talbot bunch. I was a'mind to horsewhip 'im right there."

"What'd he do then?"

"He made mighty short his business in Caldwell, an lit out south."

Laughing, Everett walked across to Fossett's Saddle and Boot Shop and admired the fine leather footwear neatly set out in rows on shelves. His were badly scarred with worn-down heels, cracks that leaked, and were patched beyond repair. After fifteen minutes of inspecting various styles, checking prices, and admiring fancy ones he could not afford, he decided on a sturdy brown pair. He sacked up his old ones, and proudly stepped back onto the street, strolling along its western side.

He lingered in front of Unsell's Lone Star Clothing House, eyed the shirts displayed inside the window, and admired an especially attractive gray Stetson hat hanging on a rack.

Shortly, he was distracted by a wagon rattling by. Turning, there was Tabitha Nichols sitting erectly on the wooden box seat beside her father, her dark hair fluttering beyond the edges of her yellow bonnet. She smiled, but Everett was too startled to do better than a blank stare. Watching the wagon pull to a stop next-door in front of Dr. Gabbert's drugstore, Everett turned back to the shop window, suddenly uncomfortable.

Soon curiosity won out, however, and he glanced around at the wagon where Tabitha sat staring straight ahead, her hands folded in her lap, waiting for her father to return. Just then, from the corner of his eye, Everett noticed two rough cowboys leaving Phillips's Saloon across the street. Laughing and pointing, they headed toward the back of the Nichols's wagon. Hearing their revelry, Tabitha glanced back, then toward Everett, a frown twisting her face. He strode over directly, rested his forearms on the top of the front wheel, and smiled at her while clearing his tightening throat.

"Howdy," he said, reaching deep to steady his voice.

"Mr. Brook, I believe," she responded.

"Everett will do," he said, cutting his eyes at the two cowboys now turning and heading down the street. "What brings you to town?"

"Papa's medicine," she replied. "What about you?"

"Drove some cattle to the railhead this morning," he said, nodding to the south. "We'll be riding out soon, I expect."

"I want to thank you for heading off those two," she said, nodding their direction. "Papa's not up to dealing with the likes of them, though he'd have tried."

"Why, you're welcome," Everett said, raising up and standing tall. "I reckon I could ride along with you until you're out of town, if you'd like me to."

"I don't want to impose," she replied. "But if you really don't mind."

"I'll just slip down to the Arcade and let Jed know," he said.

After explaining to his partner, he mounted up and trotted the chestnut mare back to the wagon where Mr. Nichols was climbing aboard. As they rode north, Everett and Tabitha exchanged a few smiles until about two miles out of town where he tipped his hat to them, then broke off onto a trail that led to the BC ranch.

✪ ✪ ✪

The next few months were routine at Blair's ranch. With spring grass plentiful, the weather sunny and cool, mixed with a few showers, the cowboys worked around ranch headquarters, making only occasional jaunts out to check on the grazing herd. Most every Saturday night, the cowboys rode into Caldwell, visited a couple of the saloons, drank a little whiskey, and played a few hands of poker. Jed usually headed for the card tables in the Arcade and fared well enough. Chip preferred the Red Light and usually returned to the ranch in the wee hours of Monday morning, drunk and broke. Everett had joined in the friendly card games in the bunkhouse and gradually tried his hand with the seasoned poker players in town. He lost more than he won but always walked away before his pockets were empty.

Reaching town on Saturday afternoon, June 22, the BC cowboys went their customary ways. The streets were bustling more than usual, the saloons filled to overflowing, and rough-bearded cowboys could be heard yelling, singing, and firing their six-shooters. Inside Horner's drugstore, Everett learned that a large herd of cattle from the T5 Ranch had arrived south of town that morning, and the thirsty cowboys had descended on the cow town with a vengeance. Owners of the saloons, the dance halls, and game rooms were delighted, while other businessmen were on edge.

"Marshal Brown's a good man," a farmer said to Everett, "but he's not the kind to stand up to this rowdy bunch. He ought to have made 'em turn in their guns as soon as they hit town. That's what Bear River Tom Smith did in Abilene."

"Yeah," another fellow said, "but Bear River had fists as big as a longhorn's skull and might near as hard. Without their six-shooters, them cowboys was no match for him. Pretty soon he just rode the streets on his big hoss, Silver Heels, and them bowlegged Texans tipped their *sombreros* and howdy'd him like he was king of the hill."

As darkness settled over the town, a second bunch of cowboys rode in, and the revelry reached new heights. Cowboys spilled out of the saloons onto the street, a bottle of whiskey in one hand and a revolver in the other. Marshal Brown and his deputy, Willis Metcalf, strolled up and down Main, occasionally stopping a fight, encouraging these cowhands to holster their pistols, and keeping an eye on the especially rowdy ones. While the marshal approached the cowboys nervously and spoke apprehensively, his deputy strutted about, bellowed out commands and demanded obedience, seemingly anxious to play the part of a tough, gun-toting lawman.

Recalling the Talbot gang shootout back in December, Everett watched tension grow between the lawmen, the townspeople, and the cowboys. He stepped inside the Arcade and called Jed aside.

"Before the night's over, something is going to explode out there," he said.

"The spark usually comes down at the Red Light," Jed replied. "Stay shed of that place."

"That's likely where Chip is," Everett reminded. "Maybe we'd best go get him and head on back to the ranch."

Jed gathered in his meager winnings, and the two headed for the troublesome saloon, two blocks to the east down Fourth Street. Approaching, they heard a gunshot, followed by raucous laughter. A second shot rang out with more laughter and shouting. A man hurried up the street toward them.

"What's the shootin' about?" Jed asked the man.

"A couple of T5 cowboys, brothers named Bean, are shootin' up the place," the man called back, hardly slowing down. "I'm goin' after the marshal."

"I've heard of them Bean boys," Jed said, tight-lipped. "The Texas Rangers claim they've killed eighteen men, includin' four wearin' a badge."

The saloon was packed with people, some standing in the doorways while others sat in open windows. Drunken men, their arms draped around giggling, scantily clad women, cursed as they struggled along heavily worn footpaths to the hovels out back. From the door and windows, Everett and Jed peeked inside, hoping to attract their partner's attention and entice him outside.

Then, Marshal Brown and his strutting deputy arrived and wedged through the entrance. The crowd peeled back for the lawmen and gradually hushed as word passed from patron to patron.

"Where're the Bean brothers?" the marshal asked.

"Upstairs," someone finally said, motioning toward the inside stairway.

The unfriendly crowd watched eagerly, some laughing, as the marshal and his deputy headed for the staircase.

"Marshal," called out a T5 rider with a stained red bandanna draped around his neck, "why don't you and your puppy just go on back to Main Street and watch after your townsfolk. We don't need you down here."

"We'll be back for you right after we've taken care of your two friends," Deputy Metcalf said, shaking his finger at the sneering man.

As the two lawmen climbed the steps, the crowd whooped and whistled, while some placed bets on whether the deputy would return dead or alive. Customers, hurrying down the stairs, brushed past the marshal and his partner, anticipating trouble.

At the top of the stairs, Marshal Brown eased onto the railed balcony that ran the width of the loft area. Just as the marshal reached the entrance to a long hallway, the jumble of men and women darted into side rooms, leaving Ed Bean standing fifteen feet away, his revolver pulled with his thumb looped over the hammer.

"Hand over that gun," Marshal Brown said, inching toward the cowboy. "And tell your brother to step out and do the same."

"It ain't gonna be that easy," Ed said, wearing a liquor-born grin.

Two paces later, the marshal lunged forward, grabbing the wrist of the man's gun-hand and pinning it against the wall. Jim Bean then stepped out, reaching for his pistol. Deputy Metcalf grabbed him from behind, pinning his arms. As the lawmen struggled with the two gunmen, the red-bandanna man from below rushed up the stairs with his revolver pulled.

"Behind you, Marshal!" someone yelled.

While still struggling with Ed Bean, Marshal Brown turned to look. Seeing the bandanna man, he fumbled for his gun with his right hand. The distraction was just enough for Ed Bean to break the lawman's grip. The muzzle of the outlaw's revolver tilted downward, then spit blue flame amid an explosion. The marshal froze as his eyes stared blankly, then he crumpled to the floor, the side of his head covered with blood.

Deputy Metcalf realized he had no chance, so quickly gave up the struggle and ducked into the crowd on the balcony. The Bean brothers bounded down the stairs, pushed through the crowd to the back door, and ran across to the livery where they hustled up their mounts and rode hard to the south.

Jed and Everett made their way inside as the crowd began dispersing from the death scene. They helped carry the marshal's body to George Freeman's house, where the lawman lived. Freeman's wife, Emmaline, slipped upstairs to get Marshal Brown's sister, Fannie. The young woman rushed down and fell weeping over her brother's body, crying, "No! No!"

"It's a shame," Freeman said, shaking his head as he followed Everett and Jed outside. "That girl thought the world of her brother, and he always saw to it that she was taken care of. They have no family, just each other. Now she's alone. A young single woman in this town doesn't have a chance."

"Who'll replace the marshal?" Jed asked. "This town needs one right now, and that deputy sure don't fit the mold."

"We've had nine in the last two years," Freeman said. "Know anybody who'd want the job?"

Jed and Everett dropped back by the Red Light, looking for Chip Williams. The small crowd that remained was subdued, so the boys had no trouble cornering the bartender and asking about their partner.

"A little while before the shooting, he left with Mag Woods, Poly Bright, and David Sharp," the man explained. "Poly swears a customer told her that George Spears and Sharp, back before Spears was killed, dug up Mag's husband's body and stole the diamond stickpin she had given him. Sharp denies it, but they've gone out to see."

"We'd better get out there," Jed said. "If it's true, there's gonna be another killin' tonight."

Everett and Jed ran to their horses and spurred them into a gallop, heading north on Main Street. When they arrived at the cemetery, candle flame atop the two-column tombstone flickered on the shadowy forms of two women. The cowboys approached cautiously, sneaking up close to a one-horse buggy with a pony hitched to the top rim of a rear wheel. Everett eased up to the horse and recognized it as Chip's.

Watching closely, they saw a man straighten up from inside the grave, dumping another shovel of clay. His hat off, they recognized their fellow cowboy. But they saw no sign of David Sharp.

"Chip," Jed called out from the darkness, "this is Jed. Me and Everett are comin' in."

"Come on. I could use a hand," the sweating cowboy called back.

"Where's Sharp?" Jed asked, as he and Everett approached the pile of freshly shoveled dirt.

"Back there when we turned off the road, he lit out," Chip explained. "I took a shot, but I was just shootin' in the dark."

"No use digging any more," Everett said. "That stickpin is gone."

For a moment, everyone was too startled to speak.

"How do you know that?" Mag Woods asked, her words barbed with anger.

"I'm sorry Mrs. Woods," Everett said, "but a few weeks after your husband was buried, Jed and I rode by here, curious to see that headstone. I noticed the grass was growing right smartly on Kuhlman's grave, but not one sprig on this one. Them being buried within ten days of each other, that didn't seem right. Now I know why."

"If you boys will hand me a couple of ropes," Chip said, "we'll lift this box out and see for ourselves."

With the ropes tied to the end handles, the men lifted it out and eased it onto level ground. They pried the lid off, held the candle over the open box, and stared at the corpse, looking just as it did the day George Woods was buried.

Slowly, Mag Woods reached down and ran her fingertips over the lapel of the black coat. The diamond stickpin was gone.

"George Spears," she said, her voice oozing with hate for the dead man, "after my husband's death, I took you in as a partner, then you robbed his grave. I hope you're burning in hell right now."

With that, she whirled and marched to her buggy, Poly Bright following close on her heels. She climbed in, then hesitated while Chip unhitched his horse.

"Thanks, Chip," she said. "Now I'm going to see Marshal Brown and have David Sharp hunted down like the dog he is."

"Ma'am," Jed said, "the marshal is dead, killed an hour ago in your saloon by the Bean brothers."

"Where was that policeman I pay to stop killings at the Red Light?" she fumed. "Now the city will try to close me down again."

"We'll escort you back to town," Everett said matter-of-factly.

Riding back, Everett sidled over close to Jed. "That woman showed more concern for that stickpin than the marshal's death. Her heart's gotta be as cold as that marble grave monument on New Year's Day."

"Yeah, and as hard, too," Jed said, then spurred his pony forward.

Their horses trotting along Main Street, they spotted a group of men and horses gathered in front of the City Hotel.

"What's goin' on?" Jed asked.

"Tryin' to get a posse to chase down the Bean brothers," Mayor Colson replied.

"It's crazy," a man said. "That T5 outfit has got forty to fifty cowboys, and they stick up for each other like blood-kin. Even if we took an army down there, what could we do? They're in Indian Territory."

"Likely, the Bean brothers are well on their way back to Texas," another said. "The sheriff can wire the Texas Rangers and let them catch those boys."

Finally, after much heated discussion, two volunteered to ride to Wellington and inform Sheriff Thralls. As the crowd broke up, Mag Woods guided her buggy over beside the mayor.

"I want to file a complaint," she said. "My husband's grave has been robbed. One of the robbers was killed back in December, but the other is David Sharp. I want him locked up."

"You'll have to fill out . . ." the mayor tried to explain.

"I've just told you what happened, Mayor," she said, interrupting. "You fill out the paperwork. I'm going home."

As she wheeled the carriage around, the mayor mumbled something about a drink and turned toward the hotel. Everett, Jed, and Chip headed for the ranch.

A few weeks later on a Saturday afternoon, while Chip stayed at the ranch, sick, Jed and Everett rode into Caldwell for supplies and with plans for an evening of poker. At the north end of the street a smartly dressed man in a blue coat with brass buttons, astride a large gray horse, rode over to meet them.

"Name's Bat Carr," the smiling man said, then tapped a metal star on his chest that bore his name and title. "I'm the new marshal."

"Pleased to meet you," Jed said. "I'm Jed Kimble and my friend here is Everett Brook."

"I'm trying to get acquainted with folks," the marshal said. "I know there's been some trouble in the past, but with the help of the good citizens of this town, Caldwell's gonna soon be known as a nice, friendly town."

"We stay on the side of the law, Marshal," Jed assured him. "Most of the trouble comes from Texas cowboys and the Red Light saloon crowd."

"I'm from Colorado City, down Texas way, so I know cowboys," the man replied. "They'll see soon enough that they can't tree my town."

"If we can be of help to you, Marshal," Jed said, "just let us know."

"Welcome to town, boys," the marshal said, as he nodded and pulled at his hat brim.

Riding on, Jed glanced over at Everett.

"He's friendly enough, but unless I miss my guess, he's mighty handy with them six-shooters he's wearin'."

"Did you see the size of his hands and the look in his eyes?" Everett asked. "No doubt, he can take care of himself in a scrape."

"Yea, I'd guess six feet, over two hundred pounds, and a man-sized coat to cover his shoulders."

While Everett gathered supplies, Jed joined a poker game at the Arcade. As Everett was stashing the items in their saddlebags strapped across the chestnut's back, he saw three cowboys riding in from the south. The one on the left was tall and thin, while the one on the right was short and stocky. The middle one was large, burly, and sported a scruffy black beard. Their dusty clothes signaled that they were fresh in from the trail.

Everett piddled around his pony, watching while the men pulled up in front of the M & S Saloon across the street. The three burst through the doors and soon the place erupted with laughter. Everett walked his horse down to Hulbert's, next door to the M & S, to buy some ammunition. As he entered, a shrill scream came from the saloon, then a second. Everett headed for the door, then slowed when he saw Marshal Carr striding across the street.

Everett waited until the marshal stepped inside, then followed, eyeing the lawman as he brushed aside chairs and sent a table reeling on his way to the corner where the three cowboys sat, the big one laughing as he pawed at a struggling young woman.

Suddenly, the room went quiet and men backed away from the trouble they knew was coming. The smaller cowboy was the first to come within reach of the marshal. Without hesitation, Carr backhanded him, sending him sprawling. The tall one jumped forward, snatching out his gun, but quick as a rattler the marshal grabbed him by the shirtfront, yanked him off his feet, and slammed a fist into his face. The cowboy dropped to the floor beside his slow-spinning revolver. The marshal kicked the gun across the floor and faced the big one who sat staring while still gripping the frantic woman's wrist.

With his left hand, the marshal flipped the table aside, sending it crashing against the nearby wall, while his right flashed to his pistol and swung the muzzle end up, stopping it about two feet from the big cowboy's nose.

"Turn her loose!" Carr said, glaring.

The woman stepped away.

"Now, stand up," the lawman said, moving closer.

The bearded man rose slowly, a sneer forming on his face.

"Now," the marshal said, taking a couple of slow steps back and slipping his gun back into its holster, "either unbuckle your gun belt, or draw iron."

After considering his chances, the cowboy reached down to his belt buckle, and his revolver hit the floor with a thud. Turning toward the man's two partners, the marshal ordered them to remove their gun belts, too.

"Outside," the marshal ordered, stepping back.

He followed the three cowboys to their horses.

"Now, get out of town, and if I see you back here, I'll lock you up for six months," Marshal Carr said.

As the cowboys turned their horses, the big one took a swipe at the lawman with the toe of his right boot. The marshal dodged, then grabbed the man's leg and jerked him to the ground. As the burly cowboy struggled to his feet, the marshal landed a vicious blow square in the man's face. A second sent blood spurting from the cowboy's nose. The big man then crawled toward his horse, pulled himself up using the stirrup, and struggled into the saddle. The three spurred their horses southward.

A stunned crowd lined the street, watching. The grim-faced lawman scanned the wall of onlookers.

"It's over," he said, "now get back to your businesses."

Everett turned to go inside Hulbert's just as Jed rushed over.

"You see that?" Everett asked.

"Yeah, and so did half the town," his partner replied. "The rules for cowboys in this town have just been changed."

"You know those fellows he just run out of town?"

"The big one calls himself Stonewall," Jed replied. "Some call him Crazy Carter. He works for a rancher named Harrison, a hard man. Has his spread, the Tin Star, down in Indian Territory."

“Well, I don’t think we’ll see them cowboys back in town,” Everett said.

“They’ll be back. And they’ll bring help. We’re gonna see just how tough our new marshal is.”

12

On their way to Moreland's, Jed and Everett stopped by the *Post* where Everett grabbed a paper. Waiting for their food, he scanned the front page.

"It says here, the Red Light has been closed," Everett announced. "The City Council calls it a public nuisance, and to make sure it stays closed, some residents plan to buy the building, move it, and convert it into a grain storage facility."

"Chip may never come back to town," Jed said, laughing.

"And it looks like Marshal Carr intends to have some help," Everett said, tapping his finger on another article.

Jed scanned the column, then let out a low whistle. "Another outsider. Caldwell's always hired its own, but now Mayor Colson has hired a marshal from Texas and an assistant marshal, this Henry Brown, from New Mexico Territory. It says they're both experienced professional lawmen, though Brown is only twenty-five."

"I'm bettin' he's a gunslinger," Everett said. "He served as marshal of Tascosa, and I've heard that's a tough town. It's got its own boot hill, and a full-time grave digger."

Jed handed the paper back to Everett who flipped to the inside pages.

"How does a flour mill work?" Everett asked.

"Grinds up wheat, makin' it into a powder, I guess," Jed said. "Why do you ask?"

"Says a couple of men, William and Scott Rayholtz, are building one on the Chikaskia, east of town. A farmer named J. T. Sturm is a big supporter of the project. When a committee out of Wellington said the Chikaskia didn't have the flow to support a mill, Strum, having once operated one, challenged the members to come see him and he'd show them six good sites. Looks like he knew what he was talking about."

"After we've eaten, let's just ride out and see it," Jed suggested.

Traveling east from town, they crossed Big Casino Creek and turned slightly southeast. After riding a few miles across flat farmland, they dropped down into a heavily wooded valley and soon came to the river. Turning south, they headed through a stand of tall hardwood trees that lined the high-banked stream until, ahead on the other side, they spotted a part-brick, part-wood structure that rose from the edge of the stream well above the rim of the river bank. A rock-formed levy spanned the riverbed, pushing back a lake. The huge wheel turned steadily, its wide paddles dipping into the massive flow of water diverted to it through a stone trough along the far end of the levy. Massive flat-stone plates turned inside, grinding wheat into powder that dropped into a flume, its spout emptying into huge barrels below.

"Drury Mill, it's called," Everett said, as he surveyed the area. "And this is a right pretty spot."

With the sun dropping, they followed a trail along the river, heading back to Caldwell. Above the lazy murmur of the stream, they suddenly heard a dog barking viciously up ahead, followed by a frantic yell that shattered the late afternoon stillness.

"Sounds like a kid in trouble," Jed said as they spurred their ponies into a dead run.

About three minutes later they spotted a boy beside the river, his dog lying on the ground, bloody and unmoving. A mountain lion, his sharp teeth gleaming, snarled at the frantic youngster crouched with a pitchfork gripped in his hands. Suddenly, the cougar leaped toward the lad who jabbed the sharp tines into its exposed chest. The big cat screamed and retreated a few feet, as if it would give up and leave. Then, as the boy turned toward his fallen pet, without warning, the cougar spun and lunged for the boy who stumbled over the pitchfork handle and fell.

A gunshot shattered the air, and the catamount, claws extended, fell limp across the boy's legs.

Everett and Jed swung down and rushed to the boy whose bloody arms and legs bore long scratches, none life-threatening. The dog's throat was ripped open and hardly a square inch of its body was free of claw marks, fang gouges, and bloodstain.

"Thanks, mister," the boy murmured, his wide eyes fixed on Everett as he pulled the big cat off him.

"What happened?" Jed asked.

"It's all my fault," the lad said, tears coming to his eyes as he rubbed the dead dog's head. "I found the lion in a tree back there. While Butch, that's my dog, kept him treed, I ran home and got this pitchfork. I poked the cat 'til he leaped down and ran. Then we chased it up another tree. Again, I poked it 'til it leaped and scampered away. Then I trapped it here against the river, poked it a good one, and it leaped in. Butch followed. The lion was about to kill him, so I jumped in with my pitchfork and stuck it in the backside. The lion swam to shore while I got my dog out. There it attacked us. I got away, but Butch was just too spent to fight anymore. I tried to stop it by stickin' it real hard in the hip, but then it turned on me. It would have got me if you hadn't shot it, mister."

As they took the boy and his dead dog home, they learned the sixteen-year-old kid's name, Quimby Gillett. He weighed about a hundred pounds, probably twenty-five less than the cougar, which measured four and a half feet long, and a little over two feet from paw to shoulder point.

With the boy safely home, Everett and Jed turned toward Caldwell.

"A fine piece of shootin'," Jed said. "You hit him just behind the front leg, right in the heart. With a lesser shot, that lion would've mauled that boy before we could've finished him off."

Arriving in town after dark, they decided to get a room at the City Hotel. As they stepped through the doorway, they met a man and woman leaving.

"Good evening, Miss Fannie," Everett said, recognizing former Marshal George Brown's sister.

"Mr. Brook and Mr. Kimble," the smiling woman said, nodding her head, "I'd like you to meet my husband, Samuel Swayer."

Everett was stunned to silence, but Jed shook the man's hand and congratulated the newlyweds.

"I'm glad you're happy," Everett finally said to Fannie, recalling the image of her lying prostrate over her dead brother, weeping violently.

Over supper, Everett marveled at how quickly the young woman, who had seemed so helplessly lost after her brother's death, had recovered and married.

"Well, she's now got someone else to see after her, a mighty fine man," Jed said. "Samuel has bought into Hubbell's dry goods business. Already makin' changes. When you walk in, there's a bell on the door that jingles like it was on a lead steer."

"Now I remember," Everett said, his eyes widening. "I heard about Swayer down at Red Fork Ranch. He operated it right after the government had run off Dan Jones. Ralph Collins said Swayer moved into the vacated store and operated it as a trading post and stage stop without a license, along with running some cattle, until the Indian Agent forced him out."

"I've heard worse on men of his position," Jed said behind his hand. "I reckon there's a smudge or two on most our back trails. It's best not talked about."

Everett nodded, though his concern was not what harm might come to Swayer upon such revelation, but what it might forebode for his young wife, Fannie. The image and sounds of her pitiful wailing at the news of her brother's death were still fresh in his mind.

The following morning after breakfast, Everett and Jed headed for the livery and saddled their horses. As they rode into the intersection of Fourth and Main, to their left they noticed a line of riders entering town from the south, spanning the width of the street. A tall, well-dressed man with a full gray beard rode in front with a young man on each side.

"The Tin Star outfit," Jed said, pointing toward Stonewall Carter riding near the middle of the line. "We'd better warn the marshal."

They kicked their horses into a lope over to the marshal's office. Before they could dismount, Carr stepped out.

"What's your hurry, boys?"

"About fifteen cowpokes from the Tin Star are ridin' in, Marshal," Jed said. "They're led by Old Samuel Harrison who's sided by his two sons and Stonewall Carter. Harrison was once a federal marshal, but his outfit is mostly toughs from the other side of the law. You met three of 'em over at the M & S the other day."

"Thanks, boys," the marshal said, then poked his head inside the office door. "Henry, grab a couple of rifles and come along."

"Marshal, do you want us to back you up?" Everett asked, surprised at the lawman's casual tone.

"No, thanks. Me and Henry can handle it," the marshal replied.

A man of average height and build stepped out, a brace of pistols on his hips and a rifle in each hand. When handing one of the Winchesters to the marshal, the deputy's face was stern, his body relaxed, and he ignored Everett and Jed. He lock-stepped with the marshal, walking at an easy pace down the middle of Main Street. Everett and Jed followed along about thirty feet behind, reining their ponies over to the right side of the street.

"Watching those two," Everett said, "you'd think they were going to break up nothing more than a dogfight."

"But it's a pack of mad dogs they're walkin' into. Let's find cover and be prepared," Jed said as they slipped down in front of the hotel and eased over to a couple of slat barrels filled with dirt covered with freshly sprouted yellow flowers.

When the marshal and his assistant reached the watering trough beside the well in front of the Moreland House, they stopped and waited. The Tin Star men continued until only the width of Fifth Street separated them from the two lawmen.

"Marshal," the rancher said. "My name's Samuel Harrison, and I've brought my boys to town so they can celebrate after a long hard roundup."

"Go right ahead, Mr. Harrison," Carr said evenly, "but first you and your boys are going to drop off your guns at my office, and the three I ran out of town earlier are going to jail."

"I won't hand over my gun to you or anybody else," the rancher said. "And neither will my men."

"Then you can turn around and ride out, right now," the marshal replied, glaring at Harrison.

"I was a lawman for fifteen years, a U. S. marshal for six," the rancher shouted, "and this is no way to run a town."

"Being an ex-lawman, you should understand, Harrison. It's my job to keep this town safe. Three of your men came in yesterday, abused one of our women, fired their guns into a crowd, and resisted the law. Now, until you and your men show me that you respect our laws, our citizens, and our property, you will give up your guns while in my town."

"And what if we refuse?" the rancher asked. "I've got fifteen men against you and your deputy, and I don't see any townsfolk backin' you."

"I can count," the marshal said, stepping slightly forward and bracing his feet, "but before you decide what to do, Harrison, remember the counting starts with you."

The rancher's cheeks flushed with anger as the young man on his left pushed ahead.

"I can plug 'im, Pa," he said, smiling.

"Hold it, son," the rancher said. "What's your name, Marshal?"

"Bat Carr."

"Boys," Harrison said, still staring at the lawman, "let's get out of this stinkin' town."

As the cowboys turned their ponies and headed south, a loud cheer rose from the gathered townspeople.

"Everett," Jed said, his eyes fixed on Bat Carr, "now this town's got a real marshal."

"Yeah, and I don't think he needs us," Everett said. "Let's go home."

✪ ✪ ✪

Through the months of August and September, Everett and Jed regularly went to town on Saturday afternoons. While playing poker in the back room of the Arcade, the talk was usually about Marshal Carr and his assistant, Henry Brown.

"What strikes me about our lawmen," Cass Burrus said, "is that neither is a drinker. Prior marshals like Flatt, Horseman, Phillips, and Meagher owned saloons and drank a good share of their own product."

"And they've tamed this town like a pussy cat," said Dr. Schribner, a local dentist. "Cowboys ride in, tip their hats to our lawmen, and keep their six-shooters holstered."

"The only excitement in town these days," said L. G. Bailey, owner of a saddle shop, "is an occasional dogfight, and that ain't much without old Bruiser."

"What's amazing," H. C. Challes said, "is they've done it without killing a single man. A cowboy from Texas told me that Carr is well-known along the cow trails. They say he's a holy terror when riled, that he's whipped brutes half-again his size, and in a gunfight he's unafraid and strychnine-deadly."

"But the man has a gentler side," Schribner said. "He's admired by the women in town, and children flock to him like he's Santa Claus."

"What about his assistant?" Jed asked.

"Brown's different, but no less respected by the cowboys," Challes said. "I'd say he's more apt to go for his gun than face a man down."

✪ ✪ ✪

While in town one October Saturday, the town was abuzz.

"Marshal Carr has gone back to Texas," A. C. Jones, the blacksmith, said. "Gonna sell out down there and invest up here."

"Who's filling in for him?" Everett asked.

"Henry Brown, and he's hired an assistant, Ben Robertson," Jones replied.

"As peaceful as this town is nowadays," Jed said, "I doubt we need another lawman."

"Robertson is temporary," Mayor Colson said. "But through fines, the marshal and Brown have filled the city coffers, not only paying their way but helping the city out to boot."

When Everett arrived back at the ranch, he heard Johnnie Blair call out from the front porch where he sat with Katherine and little Mabel.

"Everett," the rancher said, motioning him to have a seat on the edge of the porch, "Mr. Nichols is ill and shorthanded, and Katherine and me, we'd like you to ride over and help out."

"Sure, if that's what you want," Everett replied. "How long?"

"A week or two," Blair said. "Jed and Chip can handle things here, and I can pitch in, if need be."

"Please don't go, Ev'et," little Mabel said, slipping down from her mother's lap and running to Everett.

"He won't be gone long," Katherine explained, watching her daughter lock her arms around Everett's neck.

After indulging the little girl for a few minutes, Johnnie got up and coaxed her into his arms by offering to take her to the corral where she could pet her favorite colt.

"Everett," Katherine said as he stood to leave, "I was a Wendell before marrying and a relative of the Nichols. Helping them means a lot to me."

"Yes, ma'am," he replied. "I'll do my best."

"I know you will," she said, smiling. "And I hope you'll look in on Tabitha, occasionally."

Everett packed his war-bag and rode over to the Homestead headquarters. He hitched his horse at the yard gate and sauntered up the rock-laden path to the porch. Ruth Nichols answered his knock as her daughter joined them.

"Mr. and Mrs. Blair sent me," Everett explained. "Thought you might could use an extra hand."

"That's so thoughtful of them," the woman said, reaching a hand to her graying hair. "Won't you come in?"

"Thank you, ma'am, but if you'll just point the way, I'll run along and get settled in."

"I'll show him," Tabitha said to her mother, pushing the screen door open.

"How's your pa?" he asked as the door slapped shut behind her.

"Not good," she replied. "I'm afraid he'll never be completely well again."

"Maybe he can get some rest while I'm here helping out," Everett said, fidgeting with his hat. "Now if you'll tell me where to bunk, I'll be getting along."

"Why are you in such a hurry?" she asked.

Startled, Everett looked away, fumbling his hat at his feet. She laughed as he stooped to retrieve it.

"Ma'am, I'm sure there're things that need doing," he said, stepping down from the porch. "And that's what I'm here for."

"You'll find an empty bunk on the west wall," Tabitha said, pointing toward the bunkhouse. "Bob will show you around."

"Ma'am," Everett said, then hesitated. "Thanks."

Walking to his horse, Everett looked back when he heard the door shut, then ambled on to the bunkhouse and stepped inside. Bob Jackson, standing beside a potbellied stove at the far end of the room, held a tin cup in one hand and a smutty blue coffeepot in the other. He turned and frowned.

"I was sent over to lend a hand," Everett said, clutching his bedroll and other belongings.

The cowhand set the coffeepot back on the stovetop, then nodded toward the empty bunk.

"Who sent for you?" Jackson asked, sipping coffee.

"Don't know," Everett replied. "Mr. Blair said Mr. Nichols was shorthanded and asked me to pitch in for a week or so."

"Nichols is down like a sick cow, so he couldn't have ridden over to Blair's place. And Ruth, uh, Mrs. Nichols, ain't been nowhere in a coon's age. Ingle rode out three days ago, so it wasn't him, and sure as shootin' I didn't go beggin."

"I reckon it doesn't matter. Mr. Blair sent me, just the same."

"I'll find out," the cowboy said, his jaw muscles ridging.

Everett rolled out his bedroll and arranged his things while Jackson sipped coffee and watched.

"Don't get too comfortable," the cowboy said as Everett smoothed wrinkles out of his top blanket. "We've lost two newborns to wolves along the creek near Sim Donaldson's place. If you're any good with a rifle, I expect you can thin 'em out in about a week."

Everett slowly straightened his back and cut his eyes over at Jackson. Then he rolled up his bed, gathered his things, and without a word, toed the door open and headed for the corral. Out of the corner of his eye, he noticed Jackson smiling from the doorway as he heeled his pony into a trot.

Everett camped along a small creek, then rode on the following morning. He spotted occasional clusters of cattle bearing the circle H brand, heads down pulling at buffalo grass, already showing signs of curing in the frosty, fall nights. Nearing Bluff Creek north of Donaldson's extensive farm, Everett turned northwest, watching for cattle wearing the Homestead brand. Finding none, he turned back southeast and rode until he found a small bunch of Homestead cows and calves, lazily pulling at grass in a draw that spilled into the creek.

He searched the area for remains of the dead calves Jackson had mentioned, locating none. And he found no distinctive wolf paw-prints with their heart-shaped heel-pads and the four toe-pads, gapped and preceded by claw marks. He had long since learned to distinguish wolf tracks from the smaller coyote's and those of the domestic dog whose back paw was shorter than the wolf's and without claw marks. Making camp at the far end of the draw, he kept vigil through the night, riding the ravine's rim. Only once did he hear a distant wolf howl.

After sleeping through the morning hours, he mounted up and searched for other groups of cattle, but found none along the creek. Back with the main herd, which had now wandered north of the draw where he had found them, he kept watch for two more nights. Finding no evidence of the slaughtered calves or wolf activity, he headed back toward the ranch.

It was late in the afternoon when he reached the crest of a long, bare ridge lying west of the ranch house, rode along its spine for about fifty yards, then dropped down onto a cow trail worn into the side of the slope. The path took him to a tree-lined creek, which snaked along a shallow draw, making its way several miles southeast to Bluff Creek. He let the mare drop her muzzle into the cold, clear water, while contemplating meeting up with Bob Jackson.

"You're back," he heard her say from across the stream.

"Yep," Everett replied, jerking his head up, fixing his gaze on Tabitha and her horse.

"Find any wolves?"

"Nope, and no calf skeletons, either."

"That's good," she replied, nudging her pony forward to the stream's edge. As her horse began guzzling water, she smiled. "I'm glad you're back."

"Your friend Jackson won't be," he replied.

"Don't mind him," she said.

"I'd best get on along." He pulled up the mare's head.

"What's the hurry?" Tabitha asked. "There's a half hour or so of daylight left. Let's ride to the top of the ridge and watch the sunset."

"There's gonna be trouble enough without me cutting in on Jackson's gal," Everett said.

"I'm not his girl!" she replied sternly.

"But I saw you . . ." he said, picturing her beside Jackson in the swing.

"He's just a ranch hand, and not a very good one at that," she blurted out.

"I guess I got it all wrong," he said. "I'm sorry."

Her eyes softened as she turned toward him, allowing a slight smile.

"Want to see that sunset?" she asked.

He reined the chestnut's head around toward the ridge and waited, motioning Tabitha across the creek.

He followed her along the trail as it twisted and turned up the side of the slope. Reaching the top, they slipped down from their saddles and stepped over to a large flat boulder. She sat facing a fading yellow sun that looked like it had burst, splattering the sky orange, pink, and purple and sending spears of brilliant light bouncing off a thin layer of low clouds just off the horizon. Everett stood stiffly beside her, feeling a light breeze fresh on his face.

For Tabitha, it was a splendid moment that required no comment, no amplification. For Everett, it was another sunset of remembrance, one tattooed with the image of his hooded father.

"Was it Jackson that pushed you away?" she asked after a time of quiet.

"I reckon," he replied.

"No need," she said. "He's got no claim on me."

"Ma'am, I'm right pleased to know that," he responded.

"I'd be more comfortable if you'd call me Tabitha," she said, glancing up with a smile.

"It's a pretty name."

After a time of silence, during which he frequently glanced down at her long, dark hair fluttering about her shoulders, he stepped away from the rock, scanning the landscape.

"Someday," he said, "I hope to have a ranch of my own, right here in this wide open country. There's still plenty of unclaimed land, if a man can tame it and hold it."

"That's your dream?" she asked, slipping down from the rock and coming over to him.

"I don't know about dreams," he replied, "But a man's gotta grab onto something in this world, or he'll get tromped on and fill a pauper's grave."

"That sounds harsh," she said. "I dream of something kinder, more peaceful."

"This is not a kind, peaceful world," he replied. "It's full of thieves, murderers, grave robbers, and hanging judges."

"I'm afraid Caldwell has soured you on life, but the world's not all like that. Back on our little farm in Ohio, all our neighbors were good, upstanding citizens. Even out here, people like Johnnie Blair, Ballard Dixon, and Sim Donaldson are fine people."

"I reckon that's so, but I could name two lowdown scoundrels for every one of them."

"Everett," she said, glancing at the fading sunset, "which are you going to be?"

"I expect to do right, the best I know," he replied. "But I sure don't aim to tuck tail and run every time some scalawag hollers 'boo' at me."

"Papa says all this country needs is more good young men with the gumption to come West and the fortitude to stay."

"I mean to stay."

"And so do I."

"It'll be dark soon," Everett said. "I expect we'd better get along."

As they approached the ranch, Tabitha reined her pony toward the corral.

"Ride on over to the house," he said. "I'll take care of your horse."

"Thanks, Everett," she said, "I bet your mother would be proud of you."

"My ma's dead," Everett said quietly. "Pa, too."

"I'm sorry," she said, barely more than a whisper. After slipping down from the saddle, she climbed the steps to the porch, then hesitated at the door.

"Tabitha," he said, grabbing the dangling reins of her pony. "It was real nice, the sunset and all. Thanks."

"There's one every day, Everett," she said, then flashed a smile and went inside.

13

When Everett reached the bunkhouse, Bob Jackson stood leaning against the doorframe, blowing blue smoke-rings and watching them swirl upward, expand, and fade into the soft breeze.

"You kill them wolves?" he asked with the hint of a smile on his face.

"Nope."

"Then climb right back on that nag, and don't show up here again 'til the job's done."

"It's done," Everett said, stopping squarely in front of Jackson. "But there's one more."

Seeing the glare in Everett's eyes and his clenched teeth, Jackson dropped his smoke and twisted it out under his boot sole.

"Never mind the wolves," Jackson said, turning to walk away. "You can ride out tomorrow. You're not needed here."

"I stay until Mr. Nichols says otherwise," Everett said, spinning the cowboy around and shoving him against the bunkhouse wall. "You're the one that's leaving, Jackson."

"What do you mean?" The cowboy's nostrils flared.

"You're going wolf hunting. And you'd best not come back without an ear for proof."

"Don't try that on me!" Jackson bellowed.

"Fists or guns?" Everett asked, dropping his right hand to his revolver.

For a moment, Bob Jackson stared at Everett, sizing him up. He had already considered his physical disadvantage, three or four inches in height and probably thirty pounds of muscle, and now his bluff was being called.

"Look," Jackson said, raising his hands with palms open. "There's no need in us fightin' like this. The truth is, I can handle the work around here, and I got a little upset when you showed up here like I couldn't."

"I didn't come in here to take over your job," Everett replied as he stepped back and relaxed. "And you had no call sending me off on a wild goose chase."

"I did you wrong, sendin' you off out there. I admit that. Now, let's ride to town and cool off with a bottle of whiskey."

"Suit yourself," Everett said. "I'm having supper right here and sleeping inside tonight."

"No hard feelin's?" Jackson asked, offering his hand.

Ignoring the cowboy's hand, Everett brushed past him and into the bunkhouse. Jackson shrugged and headed for the corral.

When Everett awoke the next morning, the cowboy's bunk was unused. After breakfast, he stepped out and went to work on the sagging corral gate, keeping an eye out for Jackson. That done, he started the afternoon resetting leaning posts and reattaching poles. Some were split and some rotting, so he hitched the team to the wagon and headed for the tree-lined creek. After cutting a few posts and trimming several poles, he looped a rope around them and used his horse to drag them over to the corral. Finishing up a posthole, he noticed Tabitha heading his way, so he removed his hat, wiped his sleeve across his brow, and waited.

"Thought you might like a cool drink," she said, handing him a jar of water.

"Thanks," he replied, then gulped down the refreshing liquid.

"Jackson should be helping you."

"He lit out last night," Everett said. "Not sure when he'll be back."

"I was afraid of that," she muttered. "Sometimes he's gone for three days, drinking and gambling. Then it takes him two days to sleep it off."

"I don't think I've seen him around Caldwell," Everett said.

"Mostly he goes to Wellington and hangs out at Gifford's saloon and the Frontier House."

"I'll stay around until he gets back," Everett assured her.

"Papa wants to talk to you. Would you have supper with us tonight?"

✪ ✪ ✪

Everett hauled buckets of water from the well, heated it over the stove, bathed and put on his best clothes. A little before sundown, he stepped outside and spotted Tabitha gently swaying back and forth in the porch swing.

"Come and sit beside me," she said when he reached the porch steps.

She wore a heavy white shawl draped around her shoulders and drawn across her chest, guarding against the sharp bite of a fall breeze. His gray flannel shirt left him slightly chilled, but he had refused to cover his best with his ragged old coat.

"I love sitting out here in the late afternoon," she said. "It's so peaceful. The energy of the sun is dying away, leaving the air lazy, and its brightness fades to something more like a soft, flickering candle. Daytime things are settling in for a restful night, and the wolves and coyotes haven't yet started their nightly prowl."

"Sundown means something else to me. I reckon I see it more as a warning that the bitterness of a cold night is coming on, like the quiet before a storm," he replied, his mind filled with alternating glimpses of his condemned father and a kinder sunset shared with her from atop the ridge.

"I wonder why so different," she said. "Tell me about yourself."

"Not much to tell. I've been on my own most of my life. I sorta grew up down at Fort Gibson, then struck out north, looking for work."

"What happened to your parents?"

"Ma died of a sickness when I was small. Then Pa hit the trail, taking me along. Daytime, I'd hang around camp, mending saddles and such, and do some hunting while Pa and his pal, Wiley Stuart, slept off the night before. Afternoons, they'd ride out again, leaving me to watch after camp. Before dark I'd gather extra wood, and about this time of day I'd build a fire to fight off the cold and dark. I'd wait up, listening to night sounds in the darkness with my old rifle handy, hoping they'd show up before I went to sleep."

He hesitated for a moment, staring into the night while his mind took him to a distant place and time.

"Then, one evening they rode in, their mounts and a couple of extra horses lathered and heaving. Pa stomped out the fire, snatched up everything, and we rode hard all night, hightailing it for Indian Territory. Finally, about sunup we made camp in a thicket of trees and had a cold breakfast. It was then that they spotted two lawmen approaching. Pa and Stuart jumped on their worn-out ponies and took off. Stu, that's what Pa called him, got away, but that marshal caught up to Pa."

"What did you do then?"

"A deputy came back for me and the extra ponies. Then after the trial," Everett said, staring at the fading sunset, "and the gallows . . ." He cleared his throat. "Deputy Reeves took me to Fort Gibson where I tended horses until I was old enough to strike out on my own."

For ten minutes, maybe more, they swayed back and forth, the squeaking swing ticking away time like the pendulum of a clock, and sunset faded to dusk.

"It's getting cold," she said, standing and hugging herself. "Let's go inside."

Everett warmed by the fire and talked cattle and horses with Mr. Nichols while Tabitha helped her mother get supper on the table. The closeness between the two women could be heard in their easy laughter, seen in their gentle touches, and felt when their smiling eyes met.

When everything was prepared, the men joined them in the dining room, Mrs. Nichols seating Everett between Tabitha and her father. They joined hands, and Mr. Nichols gave thanks.

It was the best meal Everett could remember. A warm dining room with a cloth-covered table, the enticing smells of steaming dishes clustered in the middle, and freshly baked bread, thanks said before eating, a family gathered around talking and laughing. He felt like he was somehow a visitor in somebody else's dream of pleasant smells and happiness.

"Everett," Mr. Nichols said, breaking the spell, "Johnnie Blair says you're a good hand with horses and cattle, better than your years. You must like it at the BC."

"Yes, sir. Mr. Blair has been good to me, and so has Jed Kimble. I hope to stay on until I can manage to get my own spread."

"Though I'm feeling much better, Everett, I'll never be able to work this ranch like I once did. And, as you know, I'm down to one cowhand, and he ain't all that reliable. I could sure use a young man like you. Would you object to me asking Johnnie if he'd allow you to help out here on a regular basis?"

"No, sir. I'll leave that to you and Mr. Blair, but I wouldn't change brands without his okay."

"I understand," Mr. Nichols said, nodding.

After visiting a while, Everett thanked the Nichols family for their hospitality, reached for his hat, and headed for the door. Tabitha followed him out onto the porch, pulling the door shut behind them.

"It's mighty fine parents you've got," he said, hesitating at the top of the steps.

"Yes, though I worry about Papa. I hope you'll come and help out."

"I'd like that," he said, twirling his hat. "I'd like it a lot."

"Then you'll be back?" she asked, smiling.

"I ain't quite gone, yet," he said.

"I wish you'd sign on regular," she said, stepping over to the porch rail. "Then Papa could send Jackson packing."

"I've wondered about that," Everett replied. "Why hasn't he already done that?"

"He's afraid what Jackson will do. Papa hasn't said so, but I've seen the fear in his face."

"Well, let him know that while I'm around, he's got no reason to worry about Jackson."

"But you'll be leaving soon," she said, turning back to the door.

"I'll make it clear to Jackson that if he harms your pa or even threatens to, he'll answer to me."

"Good night, Everett," she said and turned toward the door.

"Tabitha," he said, studying the crown of his hat. "Someday I'm gonna have a home like yours."

"And a family?" She hesitated, her hand on the door handle.

He nodded as he slipped on his hat. "Good night, Tabitha."

Bob Jackson returned the next morning about nine and fell into his bunk. Everett noticed, but continued repairs to the corral. Midday, Tabitha brought a jar of cold water and some leftovers from supper. Everett washed up at the well while she spread the food on a small blanket under a large cottonwood. She sat with him while he ate warmed-over potatoes, a chunk of beef, and hot bread.

"This is mighty tasty," he said, "especially the bread."

"It's fresh. I made it this morning."

"Jackson is back," Everett said, finishing off the water.

She hesitated a moment. "When will you be leaving?"

"I'll finish the corral first. Maybe tomorrow."

She nodded, pulled her knees to her chest, and hugged her legs.

"Think there'll be a pretty sunset today?" he asked, glancing up.

"Every day," she replied, looking over.

"Meet you at the creek, half an hour before dark," he said, rising to his feet and extending his hand.

"I'll be there an hour earlier," she replied, letting him pull her up.

Watching her stroll toward the house, he mumbled to himself. "I sure like her gait." Then he chuckled at the compliment only a true horseman could appreciate.

Well before sundown, Everett caught Tabitha's pony and cinched on the saddle. He led the horse to the front porch and tied it to the rail. By the time he had the chestnut saddled, Tabitha was trotting her mount toward the creek. He nudged the mare and came alongside.

They splashed through the shallow stream and followed the cow trail to the spine of the ridge. Sitting side-by-side on the big rock, they faced the fiery western sky. For some time they sat quietly, their moods subdued.

"I'm new to these parts," he finally said, "but I know a pretty girl when I see one." He paused and glanced over at her as she blushed. "And I think you should know my intentions. Someday, I hope you'll be my girl."

"Someday?" she asked.

"Well, maybe we could sorta head that way today, if you're willing."

"I'm sorta willing," she replied.

When he helped her into the saddle, his hand lingered on her arm. She reached over and placed her hand on his, a soft delicate hand.

Back at the house, she invited him to the swing where they talked casually for another half-hour. It seemed there was something more each wanted to say, but the words never came.

"I'll finish up about noon tomorrow," he said. "Think I should drop by the house before I leave?"

"My folks would like that," she replied. "I'll be expecting you."

They hesitated at the top of the steps where they exchanged goodnights.

Lying in his bunk, Everett's thoughts took him back to the rock on the ridge, sitting beside Tabitha. Somehow there was magic in being close to her. Everything turned soft and gentle, and genuine human goodness seemed possible. It was more than he could explain. His eyes closed with a warm sun-painted horizon inside their lids. Then it occurred to him. For the first time, a sunset had not been marred by the gallows.

With Jackson's help, Everett finished the corral before noon. He washed up at the well, packed his things inside his bedroll, and tied it behind the cantle.

Jackson was enjoying a smoke at the bunkhouse entrance when Everett walked over.

"You cause any trouble around here while I'm gone, you'll pay the price when I get back," Everett said.

"You tryin' to start trouble?" Jackson asked.

"Nope. Just letting you know these good folks are depending on you, and if you let them down, I'll consider it personal."

Everett then turned and led his mare over to the porch. He rapped on the door.

Tabitha invited him inside, where he visited with the family for about fifteen minutes. After thanking them again, he stepped out and swung up on the chestnut, Tabitha watching from the top of the porch steps. With a weak tug at his hat brim, he reined the mare around and nudged her into a trot.

Everett spent the following two weeks alone out on the BC range, tallying the herd by marketable steers, mother cows, calves, and expectant heifers. He had volunteered for the job the day he got back, glad to have the time alone to think.

His goal of having a well-stocked cattle ranch with a big log home was a challenge he welcomed. He figured that with hard work, saving his wages, and a little luck, he could do just that in this Kansas country. But Everett's hopes for the future were expanding. He was thinking about Tabitha, and she had asked about a family. Was he ready?

He remembered little of his childhood years, but the brief time around the Nichols family had both warmed him to the idea and frightened him. He could not quite imagine being responsible for a wife and maybe a child, yet he relished the scene, the feelings, the aroma of the meal with the Nichols family, their warm home, the tranquility of that porch swing in late afternoon. And he could not dismiss Tabitha's eyes, her smile, her voice. The memories were like sweet honey on his fingers that could not be resisted, and his appetite grew stronger with each taste.

Back at the ranch, in need of winter supplies, Everett and Jed hitched a team to Blair's wagon and headed for Caldwell. The gossip in the City Hotel centered on Marshal Carr and his deputy, Henry Brown. Sometime after Carr's return from Texas, having sold his holdings in Colorado City, Brown confronted the marshal about retaining Ben Robertson, a tall, lean former companion of the deputy. Carr declined, whether because of cost or personal conflict, no one seemed to know. Without resolving the disagreement, Carr had left for Dallas, Texas in mid-December to be married two days after Christmas.

"While Carr was gone," George Freeman explained, "our City Council up and hired Brown as marshal and Robertson as his deputy."

"Why would they do that?" Jed asked. "Carr has made this town safe, the citizens secure on the streets, and without the usual string of killin's. The outlaws fear 'im, and the locals love 'im."

"Brown must have convinced the city fathers that he's a better man," Freeman said.

"Or that Carr's got a dark past that was gonna catch up to him here in Caldwell," F. G. Hussen said. "When hardened outlaws shy across the street from a man, likely they've rode the same trail somewhere."

"Maybe there's another reason," Wendels, the hotel manager suggested. "Recently, Carr shot three dogs in town, claiming they were mad, but the last one belonged to Isaac Newton Cooper. The *Post* reported that Cooper blew his stack. While the marshal and Mayor Colson were out of town, some say, Cooper cornered a couple of councilmen and demanded Carr be fired. With Brown as a handy replacement, they gave in."

"Whatever the reason," Everett said, "I wouldn't want to be in Brown's boots when Carr gets back."

Before purchasing supplies, Jed went to the Arcade and joined a poker game while Everett grabbed a copy of the *Post* and spread it across the belly of an empty barrel in front of Hulbert's hardware store.

The first article that got his attention was one about the Bean brothers, the killers of former Marshal George Brown. In Decatur, Texas, a group of Texas Rangers had surrounded Ed and Jim inside an old house. Ed was killed, and his brother was riddled with fourteen bullets, somehow surviving. In the back of a wagon, the perilously injured outlaw rode over three hundred miles to Wellington for trial. Two weeks after his arrival, he had succumbed to his wounds. The governor of Kansas had sent a thousand dollars to the Texas lawmen, the posted reward for the capture of the outlaws. Finally, the popular marshal's death had been avenged.

Folding the paper, Everett headed for the door of the hardware store. As he stepped inside, he met two familiar-looking young men. At first he could not recall where he had seen them, but when the younger one spoke, it all came back. He was from the Tin Star Ranch, a son of Samuel Harrison, the one who had threatened to draw on Bat Carr. The second fellow was his older brother who had ridden on the other side of the rancher.

Inside, Everett turned and watched through the front window as the two headed for the Arcade. He decided to follow.

The brothers entered the gambling room and were soon joined by three other men at a table. Everett eased over near Jed's table, but kept an eye on the two cowboys as the saloon owner brought out a fresh deck of cards and broke them open.

After watching the boys for half an hour, the younger, referred to as Brett, was up a few dollars while his brother, Jesse, was a moderate loser, as was a third player. The last player, an older cowboy, held the largest pile of winnings.

Another hour passed, and while the old cowboy's pile dwindled, Brett Harrison's grew. Everett could not swear to it, but he thought he saw the younger Harrison palming cards from a good hand and reusing them to his advantage. The older fellow became frustrated, glaring at Brett from squinted eyes. Finally, the old cowpoke picked up his small winnings and pushed away from the table. Young Harrison goaded him, trying to keep him in the game. Jesse, whose losses had grown quietly, tried unsuccessfully to hush his brother, then stood, caught the fellow by the elbow, and led him toward the bar where he offered to buy him a whiskey.

When Jesse returned to the table, Brett looked at Everett and called him to replace the old cowboy. Staying put, Everett declined.

"You've watched for free long enough," Brett said. "Either join the game or get out."

"Playing with you, a man better watch the cards real close," Everett replied.

"You accusin' me of somethin'?" Brett said, jumping to his feet.

The room went tombstone-still. Then Everett eased away from Jed's table, creating an open path to Brett Harrison. Jesse pushed to his feet, glanced at Everett, then declared the game over.

"Come on," Jesse said, pulling at his brother's shirtsleeve.

Without moving Brett smoldered while his brother left the room.

"Two-bit squaws," young Brett yelled after the quitters.

As Brett Harrison stomped out, Jed stood, eased over to Everett, and motioned toward the door.

"We've got supplies to round up."

Everett slowly followed his partner to the street.

"What do you think you were doin' in there?" Jed asked, irritated. "That kid is a hothead, and if you think he can't use that hog-leg on his hip, you're a fool."

Everett did not respond, striding toward the hardware store.

"And it ain't over," Jed continued. "He'll hem you up, and if he don't kill you, his pals from the Tin Star will."

14

Back at the ranch in the dusky gray of early evening, Everett and Jed were unloading the wagon when Johnnie Blair strolled over.

"Everett," he said, "Nichols from the Homestead dropped by today. Asked the loan of your time. I agreed to every other week, if you don't object."

"Yes, sir," Everett replied. "Starting when?"

"Ride on over tomorrow. I'll expect you back here the following Sunday evening," Blair said. "You'll collect half your pay there, half here."

Soon after breakfast, Everett wrapped his belongings in his slicker, tied them behind the saddle, and swung aboard. Jed ambled out, still irritated with him over the scene with Brett Harrison.

"Best you stay out of town awhile," the old cowboy suggested as Everett turned to leave.

Everett nodded, then spurred the mare into an easy lope. On the northwest horizon, a winter storm was drawing a bluish-purple curtain over the sky. Everett tugged down his hat front and buttoned the top of his coat. Repeatedly he worked his jaws and rubbed his face to fight off the stiffening chill.

Mid-afternoon, he trotted the chestnut through the Homestead gate and up to the rail. He slid down, beat his gloved hands together to restore circulation, and rapped painfully on the doorframe.

Ruth Nichols invited him inside, though he explained he was just letting them know he was on the job and ready for a week's assignment. The house was warm, tempting him to hang around until he had thawed out.

"I'll get on over to the bunkhouse," he explained when a chair was offered, "as soon as Mr. Nichols feels up to pointing me in the right direction."

"I hate to ask you to do it, son," the sickly rancher stepped in and said. "Me and Jackson will see after the horses and orphan calves in the barn, but the range herd needs to be rounded up and pushed behind a natural windbreak. I'm expecting snow, maybe a foot or more, and north winds that can freeze up a cow's breathing. Left exposed to that blue norther, many of the calves and the weaker cows just wouldn't make it."

"Yes, sir," Everett replied, still standing. "I'll get right to it."

"Back in the winter of seventy-one," the rancher continued, "several thousand head of cattle froze to death on the Kansas plains. This ain't like Texas where a rancher can let his beeves see after themselves through the winter."

"I'll do my best to get them sheltered, sir."

As Everett eased toward the door, Tabitha followed, pulling down her coat from a wooden peg. She slipped it on, and they moved out onto the porch.

"It's too cold for you to be out here," he said, buttoning his mackinaw.

"I need to talk to you," she said sternly.

"Shoot."

"I hear you almost got yourself killed over a poker game," she said, turning to face him.

"Who told you that?" Everett asked, cutting his eyes toward the bunkhouse.

"Never mind," she replied. "Do you deny it?"

"Wasn't a shot fired," he said. "I was just standing around watching."

"Standing in the wrong place, watching for trouble that's bound to come," she said sharply. "I thought you were smarter than that."

"I never claimed to be," he replied, his irritation rising to match hers.

"Everett," she said, looking down at her gloved hands, "I don't mean to preach, but poker games, like saloons and brothels, are for cowboys dumber than the four-legged animals they follow around. I took you to be a notch or two higher."

"Will there be anything else?" he asked, turning the heavy coat collar up around his neck. "I've got some riding to do."

After a hesitant, pleading glance at him, she shook her head, and he stepped down from the porch and rode off without looking back.

Stopping by the feed shed, he tied a bag of corn to the saddle horn and set out across the plains. An hour later, he was almost blown from the saddle by a wall of cold, blustery wind. Fifteen minutes more and the rain came down in sheets. He unwrapped his slicker from around the bedroll and slipped it on, draping the long tail over his rolled bedding which had his spare clothes and food tucked inside.

After a miserable night camp, he reached the creek the next day, turned along the northeast side, and headed downstream. He expected that the cattle had sought shelter among the trees on its border or in a coulee or ravine emptying into the stream. His search was rewarded when he located the majority of the herd bunched in a deep draw that ran northwest from the creek bank. Scouting around, he found two more gatherings and guided them to the first, believing their shared body warmth would save a few.

Though the herd was together, the storm current swept down through the ravine that was almost perfectly aligned with it, creating a natural wind tunnel. Everett rode southeast, searching for better protection. Less than a mile away, he found it.

Heavily tree-lined Bluff Creek took a deep bend to the south, gradually curving back to the northeast. The twisting stream formed a fat thumb-shaped haven bounded by tall cottonwood trees and low willows, with sycamores mixed in. The natural stockade wall, though porous, dulled the roaring wind already buffered by the high bluff on the opposite bank. On the right side of the thumb, the land sloped down to the water's edge, providing a natural watering place.

As Everett pushed the mare upstream into the teeth of the windblown rain, he noticed the drops were mixed with sleet. Reaching the herd, he skirted around the huddled cattle and found a brindle steer that earlier had proven to be a leader. He coaxed the gray-streaked longhorn to the mouth of the coulee, headed him downstream, then began pushing the herd out, slapping his coiled lariat against his chaps to hasten the process. Soon the herd was trudging onward toward the protected thumb.

Everett worked his way along the northern edge of the cattle until he reached a point just off the herd's left shoulder. As the lead steer reached the thumb, Everett raced forward, turning it along the peninsula's right edge. Soon the cattle were milling around, pulling at the cured buffalo grass.

As darkness approached, the sleet turned to blowing snow, and Everett set out to find a campsite that would shelter him from the fierce weather. The high bluff on the far side of the creek, across from the right side of the thumb, was his first choice. Fortunately, some prior frontiersman had thought the same, for

Everett found an abandoned dugout that faced southeast across the creek to the herd. He pulled his bedroll down, removed the saddle and bridle, and staked the chestnut along the creek amid a good supply of grass.

Lugging his belongings across the stream, up the sloped bank, and into the shelter took three trips. With dusk turning to darkness, he gathered a good supply of dead limbs, which he chunked into the cave-like dwelling. With a long pole he poked debris from the thin, rusty pipe that angled up through the ceiling of the dugout, exiting horizontally a foot below the rim of the bluff.

Starting a fire, he huddled around it until his clothes dried, then boiled water for his coffee. Reasonably comfortable, he cooked his supper, leaned back against the wall, and ate. Finished, he eased to the doorway of the dugout, all hunched over, and looked out into a snowfall so heavy it looked like a dense fog, forming a wall between him and the cattle.

Curled up in his bedroll close to the fire, he slept fitfully. As long as he kept a lively flame, he stayed warm, so he kept it stoked with broken limbs.

After one last forty-five-minute nap, he turned and peered toward the dilapidated old door. He could see the dim gray light of dawn through its cracks. He pushed the door open a foot, plowing away a snowdrift piled at its base, and stuck his head out. Blanketed in white, the earth lay frozen while a light snow continued. The cattle lay tightly huddled across the frozen creek.

Taking a hatchet from his saddlebags, he squeezed through the opening and made his way to the water's edge. With one foot he tested the ice, and it held. Stepping lightly, he made his way across and up the stream to where the land sloped gently to the water. He hacked at the ice until he had a ten-foot long break that extended four feet out.

He reached for the halter on the mare and led her to drink, then roused the cattle and headed a few to the creek. Others soon followed while he gathered more firewood, dusting off a coat of snow, and lugged it to the dugout.

He spent the day repairing the dilapidated door, watching over the animals, breaking ice along the creek's edge, and warming by the fire. As the day wore on, the snowfall dwindled while the cold grew more intense. Before crawling into the dugout for the night, he used a five-foot length of log to break as much of the ice covering on the stream as possible. With his improved door closed snugly, he cooked his supper, ate, and settled in for the night.

The dugout seemed warmer, though the outside temperature had dropped about fifteen degrees. Maintaining a continuous fire in the small cave-like room had paid off. The walls and floor had absorbed and retained valuable heat, losing dampness in the process.

He slept well, but still kept his fire alive, applying liberally from his ample wood supply. Looking out with first light, Everett was glad to find that the snowfall had ended. After breakfast, he ventured out into the bitterly cold wind.

The cattle were bedded down, steam shooting from their nostrils with each breath. After again breaking the ice along the stream's edge, he saddled the mare. Riding upstream, he found cattle from various other ranches, some from spreads far to the north. In the trees by the stream, he stopped short when he noticed a fresh-born calf shivering beside a downed cow. The mother lay still, her head bent unnaturally against the snow-covered ground. No steam came from her nostrils.

Everett slipped to the ground, eased over to the newborn, looped his arms under its belly and carried it back to his horse. He managed to lift the calf across the mare's shoulders, then climbed up and headed back to his dugout.

He struggled up the slope, pushed the weak animal into the cave, then grabbed a whiskey bottle left by the prior tenant and headed for the herd. He found a cow with a suckling calf and stole some of her life-giving milk. He then cut a finger from one of his gloves, punched a few holes in the tip, slipped it over the bottle top, and bound it snuggly around the glass neck. The newborn soon got the hang of it and emptied the bottle. Everett repeated the process twice more.

That afternoon he ventured out again and found more cattle pushing south to the creek, some crossing on the snow-covered ice and continuing to flee the storm. Everett noticed a family of prairie chickens huddled at the base of a bunch of sage. He rode over and found them frozen solid. Slipping two inside his saddlebags, he turned back to camp where he ate one that night and saved the other by burying it in a snow bank outside his dugout.

The following day began with the first sighting of the sun in three days. Its brilliance on the snow was blinding, but its warmth slowly brought the cattle back to life. The snow turned to steam on their backs as they pawed through more of it on the ground, munching the grass below. Only three cows could not rise from the frozen ground. Everett, using a rope and the strength of his horse, got them to their feet and down to the water. Soon they were foraging also.

He carried the orphan calf to the herd and helped it find an adopted mother, a mature cow with a ready-to-wean yearling. She sniffed the strange calf, but soon licked it clean and stood patiently while it suckled.

By noon of the second sunlit day, the temperature had risen to near thawing, and the herd began to wander out of the thumb-like peninsula onto the plain above the creek. Everett packed his things, saddled up, and started back to the ranch.

Snow-covered patches of solid ice and deep drifts required slow, cautious travel. Along the way he spotted the remains of dead rabbits, coyotes, prairie chickens, and a cow with her young calf snuggled next to her. He made camp among a cluster of trees beside a small stream, and as the sun disappeared he realized how much warmth the dugout had provided. Huddling close, he fed his fire all night.

Passing up breakfast, he saddled the mare and headed out early, reaching the stream west of the ranch house about noon. Stiff and hungry, he swung down and led the mare across the ice. As he strained to climb back into the saddle, he glanced ahead where Tabitha came running toward him, stumbling and falling into a three-foot-deep terrace of snow. Clumsily, he churned through the snowdrift to meet her.

Without words, they wrapped their arms around each other while she cried. His face stayed expressionless, so cold he could do little other than blink his eyes. Through tears, she looked up and brushed ice crystals from his eyebrows and the ends of his hair.

"I worried that you might never come back," she said. "But I kept watch, always scanning the top of the ridge. I almost fainted when there you were outlined against the sky."

"It's good to be back," he finally muttered.

"Come on to the house. We'll get you warmed and fed."

Together, him leading the mare, they plodded through the snow to the corral. He removed the saddle and set the mare free. A wooden trough was half full of corn, and the chestnut began crunching.

Inside, Everett removed his gloves and coat, then his boots. From a rocker he extended his feet toward the hearth. His socks steamed as he sipped a hot cup of coffee.

The family bombarded him with questions. He described the storm, the cattle, the stray herds wandering southward, the death toll. Tabitha showered him with attention while her father praised his courage, his wisdom in saving the herd, and his loyalty. Like the orphan calf, he now had an adopted family.

Warm, fed, and happy, he made his way to the bunkhouse. Jackson had his own questions, which Everett answered as he heated water and took a bath. In clean clothes, he slipped into his bed, instantly falling asleep.

The following morning, Everett packed his things and saddled the chestnut. He led the mare over to the house. Tabitha came to the door, then stopped short when she saw his bedroll tied behind the cantle.

"You're leaving?" she asked.

"I'd best get over and check on things at the BC," he said.

She stepped out onto the porch, pulling the door shut.

"I'm sorry for fussing at you about the trouble in town," she said.

"It's okay," he replied, smiling. "Jed gave me a good tongue-lashing, too."

"I just don't want anything bad to happen."

"I'll side with you on that," he said. "I'll be more careful."

"And you'll be back in a week?"

"Yep, even if there's another storm," he promised.

"Come in and say bye to my parents," she suggested, turning toward the door.

While Everett explained his leaving and plans for returning, Tabitha sacked up some grub and handed it to him.

"Thanks," he said. "I'll be going now."

She stood at the top of the porch steps and watched him ride away, the mare high-stepping through the snow.

The sun was setting when he reached the BC. Jed was out feeding the horses and waved him over. They talked about the storm, the loss of eight cows and two calves from the BC herd, and reports of similar losses from nearby ranches.

"An old fella livin' alone in a thin-walled cabin west of Wichita was found froze in his bed," Jed said. "He'd run out of fuel and had burned most everything in the house. And two army freighters caught out on the plains south of Dodge City froze along with their team of oxen. They'd burned their wagon and tried using their load of corn for fuel."

Three days later, the snow had melted except for protected patches. Jed and Everett headed for Caldwell. The ground was too soft for a wagon, so they rode their horses. Smoke rose from every chimney in town as they rode along Main Street and tied up in front of Moreland's.

Talk in the restaurant was about losses resulting from the storm. Old-timers recalled the two consecutive ones in 1870 and 1871. "Sixty-mile-an-hour wind, and twenty below," they claimed. "Rivers bridged with ice, snowfall so thick it blocked all light. A sight worse than this one."

Then the discussion changed to the return of Marshal Bat Carr to town with his bride, only to find he had been fired and his deputy, Henry Brown, occupying the marshal's office.

"The mayor had Brown break the news," an old fellow said.

"What'd Carr have to say?"

"I heard Brown reached for Carr's badge and ended up on his backside, checkin' his teeth," the fellow said. "Brown got up and threatened to arrest Carr, but when Bat pushed his coattail back behind his revolver, the new marshal had another thought."

"What happened to Carr?"

"They say he's up Wellington way, serving as a special policeman," the old fellow said, smiling. "Close enough to keep Brown in his sights."

"I'd sooner have the devil himself after me," Jed said.

15

Re-supplied and fed, Everett and Jed headed back to the ranch.

"Didn't see no Harrisons in town," Jed said. "But you'd best keep an eye peeled every time you ride in."

After a week of scouring the BC range, finding two more bovine victims of the storm, Everett returned to the bunkhouse wet, cold, and tired. After a good meal, he crawled into his bunk and slept until breakfast.

"Jed," he said as he pushed away from the table, "I'll be heading on over to the Homestead."

"You know, kid, soon you're gonna have to decide which brand you'll ride for," Jed said.

"Why so?"

"Old man Nichols is in his twilight years, and his light's gettin' mighty dim. When it goes out, Jackson's gonna move in on poor Mrs. Nichols and take over. I've seen his kind. He'll sweet-talk her daughter, then steal the two of them blind in sight of a year, unless somebody's there to head 'im off."

Instantly, Everett knew Jed had Jackson pegged right, and it stunned him like a slap in the face.

"Give it some thought, kid," Jed said, then headed for the corral.

Riding to the Homestead, Everett thought of little else. The farther he rode, the angrier he got. By the time he arrived mid-afternoon on a Sunday, he had made up his mind, but found the bunkhouse empty. Jackson is off to Wellington, he guessed. We'll see how long it takes him to get back this time.

Checking in at the house, Tabitha invited him to supper, which turned out to be as enjoyable as the prior one.

"Mrs. Nichols, I can't thank you enough for that fine meal," he complimented.

"Thank you, Everett," she responded, smiling. "But I'm afraid most of the praise rightly belongs to Tabitha."

"Then I thank you both," Everett said, shifting his eyes to her daughter.

"I'd like to accept my thanks from the porch swing," Tabitha said, reaching for her coat.

"Your pa know his lone hand is gone?" Everett asked as they swayed back and forth.

"No, but I saw Jackson ride out Friday afternoon. I don't expect him back for another day or two."

"I'm gonna have a talk with him when he shows up," Everett said. "Think your pa would mind if I run him off?"

"Then what'll we do when you're gone?"

"I expect I can find a replacement in town."

"I think Papa would accept that," she said. "But what he'd really like is for you to be here full-time."

"I reckon I'll have to speak to Mr. Blair about that."

"We're low on supplies, Everett," she said, "and Papa isn't up to going into town. Think you could hitch up a wagon and go tomorrow?"

"Sure. Just need a list of things to get."

"What if I went with you?"

They agreed to leave about nine the next morning, then Everett ambled on over to the bunkhouse and slipped into bed.

After fixing his own breakfast, he harnessed the team to the wagon and pulled it around to the front of the house. Before he could hop down, Tabitha appeared on the porch wearing a blue dress under her coat and matching bonnet. Offering his hand, he steadied her climb into the wagon.

"You're mighty pretty this morning," he said as they clattered along the trail.

"Thank you," she replied, then hesitated as a smile formed on her face. "If asked in town, am I to say I'm your girl?"

"Yes, ma'am," he answered promptly, "and if any of them fellas need convincing, just let me know."

As they rambled down Main Street, a crowd was gathering in front of the store next to Trailkill's place.

"What's that?" Everett asked.

"The sign says an oyster bar with ice cream sodas and lemonade," Tabitha answered.

"Lemonade sounds good to me," he said, remembering the taste from when he had it on the widow's walk with Nellie Coppinger.

Making their way to the door, they overheard that the rather unique business was run by a man named Charles Siringo, an ex-cowboy who had trailed longhorns from Texas to Kansas for the past fifteen years.

"He once rode with Billy the Kid," one man said, a cup of steaming coffee in hand. "Started cowboyin' at the age of eleven down at Dutch Settlement, Texas. While just a boy, he broke broncs on Shanghai Pierce's Rancho Grande at two-fifty a head, sometimes taming five in a day's time. Later, he bossed cowhands for Beals out on the LX near Tascosa."

The customer in front of Everett and Tabitha asked for coffee, black and hot.

"Don't sell nothin' but real cowpuncher coffee," Siringo said from a thin leathery face. "It's so sturdy it'll might near stand by itself."

Everett with lemonade and Tabitha with an ice cream soda, they stepped back out on the street where they saw an Indian and his squaw riding into town with a packhorse loaded with blankets and other trade goods.

"Wonder who that is?" Everett asked.

"A Pawnee called Spotted Horse," Tabitha responded as the Indians turned north toward Market Street. "They come in every so often, usually wanting to be fed."

Back in the wagon, they pulled on over to Morris's Grocery and stepped inside. They had just completed their purchases when Spotted Horse and his wife came in. The man wore a scowl on his face and had his right hand tucked inside a folded blanket held tight against his chest. The woman appeared near tears as she watched her husband pick up foodstuffs with his empty hand. Then Marshal Brown burst through the door, an unarmed older man right behind.

"Spotted Horse," the marshal said firmly, "hand over your gun."

The Indian responded with a sullen stare, tilting his chin defiantly at the marshal.

"Outside," the lawman said, grabbing the Indian's arm and shoving him toward the doorway.

Just as they stepped onto the street, the Pawnee turned and pulled his hand from the blanket, gripping a revolver.

The marshal grabbed his six-shooter and fired four times, staggering the Indian backwards with each bullet until he tumbled to the ground, his weapon slipping free.

Seeing Marshal Brown turn and walk away, Everett and Tabitha rushed out and kneeled at the elderly man's side. His eyes were open and staring blankly, as if in shock.

"How did the marshal know Spotted Horse had a gun in that blanket?" Everett asked.

"He pulled it on Ephriam Beals earlier," another man explained, referring to the old man beside Everett. "Spotted Horse had slipped into Ephriam's home and demanded food from his daughter. When she refused, the Pawnee tried to force her. Ephriam heard the commotion, grabbed a shovel, and ran the Indian outside. Spotted Horse yanked out that gun and would have killed Mr. Beals in his front yard if I hadn't come along."

"Who're you?" Everett asked.

"Grant Harris."

"How'd you stop the Pawnee from shooting Mr. Beals?"

"Shamed him," Harris explained. "What kind of warrior would shoot an unarmed old man?"

By then a crowd had gathered.

"There's a big camp of 'em just south of town," a man said excitedly. "Spotted Horse's wife will go back and tell 'em. Then the whole bunch will ride in, raidin', killin', and likely burn half the town."

Men began mounting their horses, checking their rifles, and then five headed south.

"What'll we do?" Tabitha asked, worry on her face.

"You know anybody in town?" Everett asked.

"The Wendells."

"Let's pitch our supplies into the wagon, and I'll rush you to their house."

"What'll you do then?" she asked.

"If there's to be an Indian attack, every man in town will have to be ready."

After leaving Tabitha with the Wendells, Everett hurried back to Main Street. He ducked into Hulbert's and stocked up on ammunition, then readied himself beside his wagon.

Thirty minutes later the posse of men trudged back into town. Everett walked down to where they dismounted.

"Ain't one blamed Indian out there," one man said. "Every time an Indian starts a little ruckus here, somebody panics the whole town, and in twelve years there's never been a raid."

Relieved, Everett crawled into the wagon and headed over to get Tabitha. After sharing the good news, they headed out of town.

"I've still got my doubts about Marshal Brown," Everett said as they rolled northward. "But I've got to give him credit this time."

"Mrs. Wendells said the marshal is getting married," Tabitha said. "He's to marry Alice Levagood."

"You know this Alice?"

"Know of her. She's a schoolteacher. First at the Wichita Indian Agency, and now she teaches out at Anthony. She was adopted by Mr. Richard Rue, a local brick manufacturer, and his wife."

"She'll be lucky if she's not a widow soon. Marshals don't last long in this town."

"I guess if a woman loves a man, she just accepts who he is and what he does to feed their family," she said, then slid closer and looped her arm through his.

"Even if he's a good-for-nothing cowboy?" he asked, grinning.

"I never said you were good-for-nothing."

"And you never said you loved me, neither."

"How many kids do you think we'll have?"

Everett hollered, "Whoa!" Pulling the team to a stop, he turned and looked into her twinkling eyes, intending to put the brakes on her plan for kids. Instead, he gently touched his hands to the sides of her face and kissed her lightly.

After a brief embrace, he reached for the reins and sent the team forward as she laid her head against his shoulder.

Back at the ranch, he noticed Jackson's horse in the corral. After unloading the supplies at the house, Everett rode over to the bunkhouse and stepped inside. Jackson was asleep in his bunk.

"Get up," Everett hollered, reaching down and shaking the cowboy.

Jackson rolled over, guarding his eyes against the light shooting through the doorway.

"What's this all about?"

"About your leaving, so get your things packed pronto."

"Hold on there, partner," Jackson said, sitting up. "Since when do you do the firin' around here."

"I'm not firing you. You're just leaving, and for good."

"We'll see what the boss has to say about that." Jackson was pulling on his boots.

"You don't understand," Everett said. "This is not up to the boss. I'm telling you to hit the trail."

"And what if I don't?"

"Then you're gonna need a doctor, real bad."

"You're not makin' no sense. Now slow down and tell me what this is all about."

"Think about it. You rode out of here Friday, leaving the Nichols helpless. Then mid-afternoon Monday, you sashay back in and pass out in that bunk, sleeping off a three-day drunk. And this ain't the first time, but sure-as-heck it's the last."

"I'll tote my share of the work, if that's what's eatin' at you."

"How are you gonna do that, spending three days a week drinking whiskey and another sleeping it off?"

"Maybe I need to mend my ways a bit, but . . ."

"Mend your ways?" Everett shouted. "You've gotta shed that filthy skin your wallowing in and become somebody different."

"Tell you what," Jackson said, standing and easing toward the end of his bunk. "I'll straighten up and . . ."

As he turned back toward Everett he gripped a revolver in his hand, but it was too late. Everett hit him square on the chin, sending the cowboy sprawling to the floor. Before Jackson could recover, Everett slammed a boot heel down on the wrist of his gun-hand, sending the pistol spinning across the floor. Everett then drew back his fist.

"No," Jackson yelled. "I'll do whatever you say."

Everett let him up, glaring at his every move.

"From now on, I swear, I'm gonna do my part," he said. "I won't go to town without your say so, and I'll get right back here. You'll see."

"You mess up again, don't even ride back here for your things," Everett said, his eyes fiery. "And if I hear of you saying one word to the boss about this, we're gonna finish this fight."

After that, Jackson was a model cowhand.

"You must have had a talk with Jackson," Tabitha said a week later.

"Yeah," Everett replied, "but right now it's you I want to talk to."

From that time forward, they never missed an opportunity to be together, to talk about their future, their hopes, and their shared dreams. They viewed many splendid sunsets from the boulder atop the ridge, and it was there after a lingering kiss that she surprised him.

"Everett," she said, brushing a wisp of hair from her face. "I love you."

"And I love you," he replied. "Just as soon as I can get enough money to start our ranch, I'm going to ask you to marry me."

"And if you don't wait too long, I'll say yes," she replied, hugging him.

"And what'll we call our ranch?" he asked.

Without a word, she turned and pointed to the fiery glow on the western horizon.

From that day Sundays were both good and difficult for them. He always arrived on Sunday, then left the following one. The weeks they were separated always seemed to have a couple of extra days.

While at the BC ranch a few weeks later and following a steady three days of winter's last hurrah, Everett and Jed prepared to go to town for ranch supplies.

The first place they stopped was Moreland's for dinner. Afterwards, Everett followed Jed to the Arcade. He hesitated before going in, but the cold wind made up his mind.

The crowd in the game room was smaller than usual, so Everett joined in a hand of poker. The room was warm, stakes were low, and laughter rang out with the conclusion of each hand. Half an hour had passed, and Everett was studying his cards when two men came in unnoticed.

At the end of the hand, Jed swept the small winnings he had on the table into his hat, grabbed his empty glass, and left the room for a refill.

“Okay if I join in,” Brett Harrison asked, sliding into the empty chair across from Everett.

Bob Watson, the dealer, welcomed him as Everett glanced over at Jed who stood frowning from the curtained doorway.

16

"One for me," Everett said to Watson, slipping a card from his hand and placing it facedown on the stained, wooden table.

The dealer, wearing a green flannel shirt and an easy smile on his full, round face, had bought the Arcade saloon soon after the death of Mike Meagher. He was now, as he often was, a welcomed player in a game of draw poker.

"I guess you like the cards you've got, Everett," the affable Watson said as he flipped a card his way, then raked in the discard.

An inkling of a smile formed at the corners of Everett's blue-gray eyes. Sitting to the dealer's left in frayed jeans and a faded blue shirt, he slid the card to the edge of the table and turned up one corner, hoping it would turn two pairs, eights and fours, into a full house. Without further expression, he slipped the card into the middle of his hand.

The game was an hour old, and Everett was doing pretty well, a fact that brought a mischievous glint to the burly dealer's eyes as he pulled at his beard. Watson dearly loved the game, studied players' styles religiously, and was trusted by everyone. Bob seldom won in casual games like this, considering it bad for business, but the monthly big-stakes games in the basement of the Leland were a different matter.

The dealer shifted his gaze across the table to the card-wise stranger whose eyes were shadowed by the wide brim of his forward-tilted hat. Watson nodded slightly and waited for the deliberate player.

"Three for me," the solemn, dark-skinned man said, gathering the discards from his hand and carefully placing them facedown on the table.

Watson deftly sailed three cards, one on top of the other, across the table to the black-clad stranger who held the majority of the night's winnings.

"What about you, Brett?" the dealer asked, sweeping in the discards.

Studying his hand, Harrison fumbled with the top button on his red vest, finally undoing it and the two below. Since joining the game, beating Everett seemed to be his only goal. At that, he had not done very well and his voice had taken on an edge. He now considered that his opponent had played to fill out a straight, a flush, or a full house, all of which beat the pair of queens he held.

"Three," he snapped, discarding an equal number from his hand. He picked up the new ones and slipped them behind the two in his left hand, then fanned out the cards.

Everett watched him closely, noticing the three cards did not produce the telltale smile that Harrison had shown earlier with a successful draw. Probably stuck with a pair, he thought.

"I'll take two," the dealer said, replacing the pair he had discarded.

Everett considered the dealer's move. He could be holding three-of-a-kind or possibly drawing to a straight or flush, but he felt sure Watson was playing away from a winning hand, intrigued by the drama building between the two young players.

"Brett," Everett said, "that's the third time I've seen you slip your right hand under the table. Keep your hands in sight or fold and get outta the game."

"Since when do you make the rules here?" Harrison said, jerking his hand back to the table.

"That's my rule, Brett," Watson said. "If you want to play that kind of poker, do it somewhere else."

"Are you accusin' me?" Harrison asked, aiming the question at Everett.

"Just keep your hands above the table," Everett replied, eyes on his cards.

"Come on boys, let's play the game," the dealer said. "It's your bid, Everett."

Everett raised five dollars, his largest of the afternoon. The stranger folded. Brett matched Everett and added ten. Watson folded, then looked at Everett who matched Harrison's raise, then called.

"Three queens," the Tin Star cowboy said, smiling, then spread his cards on the table. "Now, let's see yours, Everett."

"Two pair don't beat three queens," Everett said, "but it beats one pair."

"So what?" Brett asked, reaching for the pot of money.

"Hold on a minute!" Everett shouted. "Bob, I want a count of the cards."

"Simmer down," the dealer replied, glancing at Everett.

"Everybody keep your hands on the table," Everett ordered. "Bob, there's been nine discards and two folded hands. With my hand and Harrison's, that makes twenty-nine. If you dealt from a full deck, there's twenty-three left in the dealer's stack."

"I'll check it," Watson said as he began counting.

"Twenty-two, right Bob?" Everett said when the dealer reached the last card.

"One short," the dealer replied grimly.

There was silence at the table.

Meanwhile, a few drinkers had stepped in from the musty barroom and stood watching, sensing trouble. Others held the green curtains back and peered in from the doorway. One of the bystanders suggested someone go for the marshal.

"Then there'd be a shootin' for sure," another replied.

"For three years now, our marshals have lasted an average of ninety days," said a man at the doorway. "Leave Marshal Brown outta this. He's still got a month to go."

No one laughed, and no one moved.

"Everett," Watson said, "just cool down. Maybe somebody dropped one."

The dealer pushed his chair back and looked down at the floor.

"There it is," he said, bending over his girth and straining for the card.

"Bob, don't touch that card!" Everett said, jumping to his feet.

Watson slowly raised up and stared at Everett while the bystanders crowded closer, the back row tiptoeing to see the card.

"Jed, do you see it?" Everett asked.

"I sure do," his friend replied. "A three of hearts, layin' right there on the floor beside your right boot, Harrison."

"So maybe I dropped it earlier," Brett Harrison said.

"You dropped it just now when you slipped it out of your hand and stuck in one of those queens," Everett said. "One held out of an earlier hand."

"You don't know that!" Harrison challenged.

"I saw you do it a week or so back," Everett said. "Maybe it's become a habit."

"You're a liar!" Brett shouted as he jumped to his feet and moved away from the table.

As the crowd retreated to the walls, Everett stepped back two paces, and slowly lowered his right hand toward his gun.

"Boys, we can settle this," Bob said from near the table, desperate to avoid a gunfight. "Brett, I'm takin' your winnin's and splittin' it amongst the rest of us. You know I don't hold with cheatin'."

"Nobody's takin' my money!" Harrison shouted. "Not while I'm wearin' this gun!"

"Divide it up, Bob," Everett said evenly, his eyes locked on Harrison.

"You touch my money, I'll kill you!" the cowboy said.

"Brett, if you draw iron, you'd better aim this way, 'cause I'm gonna drill you," Everett warned.

"Killin' you is gonna be easy," Harrison responded, a smirk crossing his face. "I've wanted to do that for a long time."

"You won't get a better chance," Everett said, staring coldly.

Suddenly, Brett Harrison grabbed for his ivory-handled revolver. In a blur of motion two pistols exploded with flame and thunderous roar, one seemingly an echo of the other. Blue-gray smoke boiled across the narrow room, and the acrid smell of burned gunpowder drowned that of whiskey.

Brett Harrison's extended right hand slowly relaxed, his pistol rotated backward around his trigger finger and slipped from his limp hand, crashing with a thud onto the saloon floor. His eyes were glazed with fear, his face a frozen contortion of pain. Then his legs gave way, and he crumpled forward against the table. For a moment, he clutched its edge, then his fingers slipped, and he collapsed to the floor.

The crowd stared, first at the fallen cowboy, the youngest son of a wealthy local rancher. Then their eyes shifted to Everett Brook, a tall, rawboned cowboy from the nearby BC Ranch, and of parents unknown.

Everett, his face a picture of shock, stood absorbing the reality of what he had done. His downcast eyes were fixed on the unmoving form at his feet. Slowly he pushed his revolver into its holster, swept the pot, along with his meager winnings, from the table into his coat pocket, and wedged his way through the silent crowd.

"Wait a minute, Brook," someone called out as Everett reached the exit.

He stopped and slowly turned back toward the room, unsure who had called his name. A cowboy, appearing to be in his mid-twenties, stepped from the crowd. Immediately Everett recognized him.

"You can't gun down my brother and just walk away," Jesse Harrison said.

"I got no gripe with you, Jesse," Everett said. "Brett cheated. We all know it, including you."

"Ain't no difference," Jesse replied, lowering his gun hand.

"He drew on me. You saw it," Everett said, his voice strained.

"I saw you kill my brother," the cowboy replied. "Now, I've gotta kill you. Pa wouldn't have it no other way."

"Don't do it, Jesse," Everett pleaded. "You shouldn't ought to die because your brother was a card cheat."

"You never shot anybody before, did you?" Jesse Harrison asked. "I think you just got lucky. Now your luck is run out."

"Jesse, this is crazy. I'm gonna walk outta here," Everett said, starting to turn away.

Jesse Harrison went for his gun. Jed yelled a warning. Everett spun on his heels, dropping into a deep crouch. The Tin Star cowboy's gun blazed. Everett's answered. The explosion shook the room. Then Jesse Harrison's trigger finger squeezed again as he fell forward, the bullet splintering the saloon floor.

Slowly standing upright, Everett stared, his face pale, a wisp of blue smoke rising softly from the muzzle of his revolver.

"Everett," old Jed Kimble called out, grabbing his young friend by the shoulders and shaking him. "You've gotta get goin', boy! Old man Harrison will have a dozen men after you, with orders to kill on sight."

Slowly re-holstering his gun, Everett's glazed-over eyes swept the faces in the room, as if trying to memorize each one. Then, without a word, he turned and walked out, swung up on the mare, and headed north at full gallop.

From the edge of the street, Jed and a few others watched the young cowboy disappear beyond a rise.

"Just a kid, he came here with nothin'," Jed said, as if talking to the wind. "He worked hard, hopin' to make a place for himself. It's a shame, a down right shame. I don't expect to ever see him again."

"Samuel Harrison will make sure of that," Bob Watson replied.

"I taught him how to use that gun," Jed continued, his deep voice monotone with a slight rattle. "Out here a man's gotta protect himself. But I never thought it'd lead to this."

With the chestnut mare at maximum stride, Everett rode through early dusk, the cold air numbing his face. Darkness was settling in when he reached the Homestead. He reined the mare to the water trough, and slipped down. Hurrying along the rocky path to the steps, his heart pounded as if it would explode. He bounded onto the porch and rapped three times on the doorframe.

"Tabitha, I need to talk to you," he said when she opened the door.

"What's wrong, Everett?" she asked, sensing trouble.

He grabbed her elbow and rushed her toward the porch swing, shivering in the cold night air. Seeing her draw her arms about her torso, Everett wrapped his long arms around her shaking body. For a few moments, they hugged in frightened silence.

"Tab, I'm in trouble," he said.

"What kind of trouble?" she asked, glancing up.

"I've killed Brett Harrison and his brother, Jesse," he replied softly.

"Why, Everett, why?" she asked, her voice shrill with alarm.

"There's no time to explain," he said. "I've got to get outta here in a hurry. Old man Harrison will have me hunted down. Tabitha, it was self defense. I swear it was."

"Where will you go?" she asked, her voice quivering.

"I haven't had time to think about it. But I've got to go a long way from here," Everett explained. "Please tell your parents that I feel terrible about letting them down. They've been awfully good to me."

"I'll go with you!"

"No, Tab. They'll hunt me down like I was a calf-killing catamount. You get in the way, they'd kill you, too. I'll be back for you as soon as I can."

"When?" she asked, sobbing. "I want to marry you! Everett, please don't go."

"When it's safe, I'll be back," he said, hugging her tightly. "Tabitha, I love you!"

"Everett, how can this be happening!" she asked frantically.

He held her face between his hands and kissed her forehead. With his finger, he wiped the tears from her cheeks, then turned and leaped from the porch.

Bewildered, cold, and brokenhearted, she watched him climb into the saddle, look back momentarily, and then disappear into the darkness.

Frightened and desperate, Everett turned his chestnut mare west toward the familiar stream where Tabitha had met him in the snow, splashed across, then spurred her up the sharp ridge and disappeared beyond.

Indian Territory, only two miles south of Caldwell, was a haven for outlaws, but the Tin Star Ranch lay that direction. Some of Harrison's cowboys had been in town, and undoubtedly had headed straight for headquarters to inform their boss. Regardless of the explanation, the ex-marshal would hear nothing more after learning his two sons had been gunned down by Everett Brook, a two-bit tinhorn. His only hope, Everett decided, was to ride west into an area he knew well, one in which he could find his way in the darkness, then cut southward toward Indian Territory, escaping Kansas before daylight.

Pushing his horse down the far side of the ridge, Everett thought about Marshal Brown and a posse. He would get one together, but that would take hours, possibly not riding out until dawn. I'll be gone by then, Everett thought.

Harrison, however, was a different matter. He would not wait to send out his bloodthirsty hounds. He would probably lead the hunt himself, and his years of marshaling would have taught him how to anticipate the moves of a desperate man and how to track him down. Come daylight, Everett's trail would be easily found and followed, and Harrison would not stop at the border.

On the flat plain, Everett urged the mare to pick up the pace. He had a few dollars in his coat pocket and a bedroll tucked away in a slicker tied behind his saddle, but he had no food, no water. Afraid of what lay ahead, he was more frightened of what was behind.

With no family to go to, and his friends at the BC and the Homestead ranches sure to be the first ones checked, he thought about Ralph Collins and his cousin Fred Williams at Red Fork Ranch. He could hide out in the nearby blackjack forest, getting re-supplied occasionally from the ranch. But it lay between the Chisholm and the Fort Reno Trails, both heavily traveled by people from Caldwell, and the dense forest, home to cutthroats and renegade Indians, was a dangerous place for a lone man.

Turning along the rim of a ravine, he thought about Johnnie Blair and Jed Kimble back at the ranch. They had been good to him, too, but leaving Tabitha and her family was what tore him up inside. They had been the closest to a family he could remember. And Tabitha's admonition about Caldwell, its saloons, and gambling rooms kept ringing in his head. He had known she was right, yet he had gone back. He was not sure why.

Turning toward Bluff Creek, it dawned on him that he was not only losing Tabitha and her family but also leaving the land where he had hoped to build a ranch. An outlaw now, that dream was gone.

The night air was bitterly cold on his face. When he found a crossing, he let the mare stop halfway across and drink. The bordering trees and steep creek banks protected him from the harsh wind, tempting him to rest there a while. Waiting, he wished he had never coveted his father's revolver, wished Jed Kimble had not drilled him in its use until drawing and blowing the head off a rattler was as natural as swatting a mosquito. Most of all, he wished he had never set foot in the gambling room at the Arcade. He had never won or lost much. It had never really mattered. Why hadn't he just ignored Brett Harrison's cheating? What would it have cost him? Fifteen, twenty dollars? It seemed so simple now.

The chestnut pulled her head up, water dripping from her muzzle, and splashed on across the stream. On the far side, she made three lunges and reached the flat land atop the sloped bank and continued across the open plain. Glancing to the east, dawn hovered on the horizon. He did not know how close his pursuers might be, but, determined to be across the border by sunrise, he heeled his tired horse into a steady lope.

17

Indian Territory
February 1883

An orange glow painted low, thin clouds in the east as Everett pushed his tired pony southward, wondering how he would know when he had crossed into Indian Territory. Neither Indian nor Caucasian considered the boundary a barrier to hunting or pursuing opportunity. Cattlemen had ranches south of the border, and Indians regularly hunted as far north as the Arkansas River. Traders, especially whiskey sellers and horse thieves, traveled back and forth, garnering profits north and south of the border. Once Everett crossed that invisible line, the probability of sighting roaming bands of Kiowa, Comanche, Osage, Cheyenne, and outlaw camps would increase, and they could be every bit as deadly as the posse behind him. About twenty-five miles of open, flat prairie, providing little opportunity for concealment, lay between him and the Salt Fork of the Arkansas. If he could reach that landmark, the river's high banks and narrow canyons would offer reasonable sanctuary.

Knowing he could be spotted from miles away, Everett avoided ridges, bulges, and hills. He sought out depressions of every sort, basins, valleys, and ravines. All day he rode south, varying only slightly when his path became impassable.

With sunlight waning, he spotted a line of trees ahead. Guessing a stream, he hurried his exhausted mare along, anxious to duck out of sight and make camp, find food, and rest. Arriving, he felt sure it was the Salt Fork. After letting his horse drink, he splashed into the water and turned upstream to where the river spilled out of a ravine cut into a wide slope. Concealed within the high walls, he set up camp under a large cottonwood tucked away in a bend carved out by prior, swirling, swift currents.

With the mare staked out in a grassy cove along the water's edge, he set out on foot, searching for food. Though he preferred fresh meat, he refused to risk a shot, passing up a pair of deer. He had heard townspeople in Caldwell talk about forays into Indian Territory for fresh berries, plums, pecans, and walnuts. It was a little early for berries and plums, which many called pawpaws, but he found a cluster of walnut trees. The ground beneath was littered with their fruit, preserved in thick, black shells. Loaded up, he headed back to camp.

For two hours he huddled around his fire, its smoke diffused somewhat by the cottonwood's limbs, cracking hard walnut shells with his gun butt and picking out their rich heart. With his hunger somewhat sated and bitter cold settling into the ravine, he soon crawled into his bedroll and drifted off to sleep.

Sunlight did not reach the deep gully floor until two hours after sunrise. Only then did its rays reach the bedroll, seep through its thickness, and awaken the knotted form inside. Everett pushed his head out, startled at the lateness. He scrambled to his feet, rushed to the rim of the ravine, and peered along his empty back trail. Then he caught his breath when he spotted, maybe three hundred yards to the northeast, a lazy column of smoke rising into the crisp morning sky.

He scampered out of the ravine and headed up the slope of a nearby knoll, squirming along on his belly the last several feet to its crest. Peering over, his eyes locked onto a high, dark tail of smoke and traced it down to a campfire nestled beside a stream where it dumped into the Salt Fork. About a dozen men milled about the camp, some standing, some warming by their campfire, others drinking steaming coffee.

"Stonewall Carter," Everett muttered, spotting a bulky man standing with his back to the blaze.

Evidently, Everett's pursuers had stopped there after losing his tracks where he had entered the river. After breakfast, they would undoubtedly resume their search, half going upstream and half down. Everett's campsite would not be hard to find. As his judge and jury, and his guilt and sentencing already decided, they would need only a strong cottonwood to become his executioner.

Sobered by the thought, Everett quickly slipped back down the slope and into the red-walled ravine. Hurriedly, he threw his saddle on the mare, chunked his bedroll and coat behind, then spurred his horse westward along the stream until he reached a dry gulch joining from the south. Its floor angled upward for three hundred yards where it reached the rolling plains.

Out of the gulch, he reined his pony to the south, heading for a swale where he hoped to drop out of sight. Starved, his plan was to find Turkey Creek, and follow it through the Blackjack Forest to Red Fork Ranch. If he could safely reach his friends, he could sneak in and get provisions for the long journey west.

Everett kept a vigilant eye over his shoulder throughout the morning, even doubling back once, but spotted no one. Early afternoon he reached the dense forest between the two feeder streams of Turkey Creek, and with relief disappeared into its deep shadows. That night he endured a cold camp along the main branch of the creek, knowing he was within a half-day's ride of his friends' ranch. After finishing his supply of walnuts, he snuggled inside his bedroll.

Up at dawn, he proceeded cautiously. Between nearby Reno Trail traffic, hiding outlaws, and roving Indians, he was practically defenseless against sudden ambush, theft, and murder. However, he had one advantage. A lone target, he traveled quickly and quietly, stopping and listening as frequently as needed. And now he was amid a thicket of black-barked trees that would hide his approach to the ranch.

He released a huge sigh of relief when he reached a clear-cut in the forest. He and the young Southern Cheyenne braves had axed the trees to build the stockade-style corral that lay just ahead and east of the stream. Being too early in the year for cattle drives, the big pen was empty and offered a perfect lookout for Everett to assess activity at the ranch store before riding in.

Finding no evidence of visitors, he slipped from behind the corral wall and approached casually. Reaching the building corner, he eased around to the small horse corral on the eastern side where he had just caught a glimpse of Ralph clearing debris from the cleft of the gray horse's left-front hoof.

As Everett swung down, the creaking of his saddle alerted his friend, who spun around, dropping the horse's hoof to the ground.

"Everett!" the rancher called out. "You about scared me out of a year's growth."

"Sorry, Ralph," Everett said. "Guess I was being a mite careful."

"Just passing through or plan to stay a spell?"

"Going west," Everett replied, "and need provisions."

"I thought this was the West," Ralph said, chuckling.

"I'd like to see New Mexico, Santa Fe maybe."

"Lots of rough country between here and there," Ralph said, looking past Everett. "Especially for a man riding alone."

"Where's Fred?"

"Gone to Darlington. He'll be back in a couple of days, and would be mighty pleased to see you."

"I've got to ride out as soon as I'm stocked up," Everett said, glancing at his boot tops.

"What's the rush?"

"I'd like to latch on with some ranch out there in time for the spring roundup."

"Well, we'd better get your supplies before we lose daylight," Ralph said, heading around the side of the store. "Unbridle your horse and let her eat a bait of corn while we fix you up."

Inside, Everett was surprised to see a young boy.

"I'd like you to meet Hubert, my kid brother," Ralph explained. "He's come down from Iowa to see what this country's all about."

"Come by myself," the boy said, proudly, "except later Little Big Jake and Red Lodge got on the train with a bunch of other Cheyenne. I rode the stage from Caldwell where Cousin Sarah lives. Sat up top with the driver most of the way. We turned over crossing the Salt Fork."

What a talkative kid, Everett thought, anxious to get his supplies and move on.

While Hubert Collins told him more about his adventure into Indian Territory, Everett scratched out a list, and then the boy helped the rancher fill it, stacking the items on a table.

"Need a packhorse?" Ralph asked as the mound grew.

"I'll have to do with what I've got," Everett replied, thinking a packhorse would slow him down.

"If you're a bit short right now, I'll loan you that gray mare out there," Ralph said, referring to the plodder Everett remembered Fred riding. "Save me feeding her."

"Thanks just the same," Everett replied.

"Help me out a couple of days, 'til Fred gets back, and I'll practically give her to you," Ralph offered.

"In Indian country, you never know what you might run in to," Everett said. "I'm afraid she couldn't keep up."

"Indians won't hurt you," young Hubert said flatly, while Ralph continued packing.

"Like white men, there's good and bad ones," Everett said, smiling at the boy, then stepped out to the corral to get his horse.

"Who're you running from?" the rancher asked when Everett rounded the side of the store leading the chestnut.

Surprised, Everett hesitated as he tied down his provisions.

"It'd be best that I know," Ralph said, "in case someone comes along trailing you and asking questions."

"Samuel Harrison," Everett said, "and his Tin Star outfit. Be careful of the big bearded one called Stonewall Carter."

"What's Harrison's beef with you?"

"I killed his sons," Everett said softly, then briefly told the story.

"Maybe my uncle can help," Ralph said. "Turn yourself in to him, and he'll see you get a fair hearing."

"It don't work that way in Caldwell," Everett said. "And I'll die fighting rather than let some lawman drag me into that hanging judge's courtroom in Fort Smith."

"You've sure got a dim view of justice," Ralph said, finishing up with the supplies. "If you change you mind . . ."

"I won't," Everett said abruptly, then swung into the saddle.

"You're gonna need more supplies and maybe a safe place to sleep along the way," Ralph said. "If you'll ride up the Cimarron to where a strong stream merges in from the west, then head directly toward the setting sun, you'll soon spot Cantonment on the far side of the north branch of the Canadian. No soldiers to speak of, but there's a school for the Cheyenne and Arapho children. I have a friend there, a Mennonite named Kincade. He'll put you up."

"Much obliged," Everett said, impatiently glancing up the Reno Trail.

"On up the river there's Fort Supply," Ralph continued. "It's a stockade fort, and with good cause. If you'll follow the river and its main western tributary, it'll take you close to the Cimarron Cutoff, the southern route of the old Santa Fe Trail. Be a lot safer if you can latch on with a wagon train headed for Santa Fe."

"Thanks for your help."

"Everett, you're gonna need more help than I can give, so don't turn any down, and always be mindful of your water. The parched bones of too many men litter that country already. Out there you'll find plenty renegade Indians and precious few streams."

"Tell Fred hello for me," Everett said, then reined the mare around and nudged her with his heels.

"Is he an outlaw?" Everett heard the boy ask as he rode away. The words stung deep in his chest.

Staying along the northern bank of the Cimarron River, or Red Fork as many locals called it, Everett rode under cover of the forest. After spending the night in a rocky draw, he headed out early the following morning, making his next stop at the mouth of the stream merging from the west. Soon after daybreak, he crossed the river and followed the creek's main course until it turned south. There he followed along a minor branch, leading west, until it played out. Then setting his course by the sun, he pushed on until late afternoon, when he pulled up alongside the bank of the North Canadian. Across the river was a much-used trail, one he guessed connected Cantonment to Fort Reno. He chose a campsite well hidden from travelers.

After spending the early morning concealed along the river, watching Indian children moving up the military trail, he packed and headed upstream, staying on the northeast bank. Late morning from a hilltop, he spotted the fort across the river. After crossing, he rode into the deserted-looking military post. At the small post store, run by Henry Keeling, he asked about a Mr. Kincade.

The post trader stepped outside and pointed toward a one-room schoolhouse. Everett settled down on the steps of a vacant building and waited until about midday when the children flushed out like a flock of chickens fleeing from a fox. Stepping inside, Everett removed his hat and stood waiting for the tall slender man at the front of the room to look up from a book lying open on his primitive desk.

"May I help you?" the man asked.

"Name's Everett Brook. Ralph Collins from Red Fork Ranch asked me to stop by and meet you, if you're Mr. Kincade."

The man unfolded to his full height, smiled, and stepped toward Everett, extending his hand.

"I'm Morton Kincade," the man said. "A friend of Ralph's is a friend of mine, Mr. Brook. What may I do for you?"

"Just passing through," Everett said.

"We don't get many visitors here," Kincade said, smiling warmly. "Surely you're weary of your travels, Mr. Brook. Won't you have supper with me, and spend the night? Maybe you can update me on my friends on the Red Fork."

"It'd be a pleasure," Everett replied.

After throwing his things inside a vacant room in the officer's quarters, Everett led the mare down to the corral, and turned her loose with about a dozen cavalry ponies. He scooped some corn into a hollow-log trough and headed back, meeting Kincade as he neared his room.

"Left a basin of water and a towel for you, Mr. Brook," the teacher said. "We'll have supper in about an hour."

Everett washed and changed into a clean shirt. He then rolled out his bedroll on a cot, slipped off his boots, and stretched out.

Startled awake half an hour later, he looked up into the face of a young Arapaho brave. As Everett swung his feet to the floor, the Indian lifted his hand, brought four fingertips together with the end of his thumb, then touched them to his lips. Smiling, he repeated the motion. Everett nodded, patting his stomach, yanked on his boots, and followed the boy to the detached house where the teacher lived.

"I suppose you met Clarence," Kincade said, welcoming them inside. "His father, Powder Face, is a highly respected Arapaho chief, and he's asked me to prepare his son for advanced schooling at Carlisle."

Everett nodded toward the young man who extended his hand.

"Nice to meet you," the boy said clearly.

"My pleasure," Everett responded, wondering why the sign language earlier.

"Clarence will be going away to school in the fall. His father wants him to have the best education possible."

"But I will never give up the ways of my people," Clarence said.

While eating wild turkey and corn with hot bread, Everett learned that Powder Face had been a leading Arapaho warrior following the Sand Creek

Massacre in Colorado. Chosen as chief in 1868, he had denounced violent resistance and had defended the Darlington Agency against a Southern Cheyenne uprising during the Red River War.

"He's developed quite a herd of cattle, along with cornfields, vegetable gardens, and meadows," the teacher explained.

When asked about his travels, Everett was vague.

"Spent a little time at Red Fork Ranch, then moved on up to Caldwell," he explained.

"You're welcome to stay here," Kincade said. "There are quite a few cattle ranches in the area and freighting work north to Fort Supply and south to Reno."

"Thanks, but I'll be moving on, come morning," Everett said. "I'm working my way out to the New Mexico Territory."

After spending the night in the cozy room, Everett cooked his breakfast, then stepped out onto the porch, sipping a hot cup of coffee. He was surprised to see a small band of young braves pull up in front of the trader's store. Finishing his coffee, he set the cup on a flat railing and followed the Indians inside.

The braves were laughing and gathering up items, stuffing them inside their loose clothing. A couple slipped outside and headed for their horses. Keeling rushed out from behind the counter and approached their leader.

"You'll have to pay for the goods they've taken," he said, glancing outside.

The brave stared in silence for a moment, then turned to his companions, and spoke in their native tongue. They all laughed and headed for the door, but just then an older Indian stepped through the doorway, a black patch over his left eye.

"Keeling," he said, lingering on the double e.

"Black Wolf," the post trader responded, approaching the old chief. "Last time I saw you was back at Fort Keogh."

"Northern Cheyenne move south," the chief explained, then noticed two braves sneaking toward the door, their clothing bulging with store items. He spoke harshly in the Cheyenne tongue, and the braves stopped, one glaring at the old chief.

Black Wolf took three quick steps toward the brave, grabbed a fistful of his long black hair, and touched the blade of his knife to the warrior's bare throat. He spoke again in low guttural sounds, then slowly released the brave. The group eased toward the counter and slipped the items from their clothing.

One stepped outside and soon returned with those who had left earlier. When all the items were piled on the counter, the band turned and left.

"What was that all about?" Everett asked when the chief had made his purchase and departed.

"Black Wolf is Northern Cheyenne," the young sutler explained. "A few years back at Fort Keogh he was attacked by a white hunter. My brother, Major William Keeling, was the quartermaster, and I was there helping out. With several deep stab wounds, Black Wolf was left to die. I took him to the post hospital where he was treated. He was grateful, though he lost an eye."

"So he just now returned the favor," Everett said. "What'd he say to that brave?"

"Said he'd kill him and every one of his band if they stole a single item," the sutler said. "And they knew he would."

Back at his quarters, Everett was packing when Kincade knocked.

"I was hoping you'd stay around a while," he said, easing through the doorway. "I'd like to take you out to Powder Face's camp and let you see how the Arapahos are adjusting to farming."

Spending another night in the comfort of the officer's quarters appealed to Everett, so he agreed.

While waiting for school to dismiss so they could head for the farm, Everett kept an eye on the military road. He soon spotted a large contingent of Indians approaching from the south, a young, angry-looking one in the lead. They turned into the fort and dispersed, some entering the sutler's store, others gathering in small groups around the parade grounds. Noticing that their positions looked planned, Everett slipped into the store and found Keeling.

"Who's this bunch?"

"White Horse with his band of Southern Cheyenne Dog Soldiers," the sutler replied. "They're all fired up because their food rations have been reduced and the buffalo herds are disappearing. They're waiting for their courier to return from the Darlington Agency with news of their demand to agent Miles for more food."

About that time, the young chief came in and made his way over to the sutler.

"My braves restless," he said. "Our messenger return soon. If our demands not met, we kill every white man on this post."

"Major Randall and his scout, Ben Clark, are on their way from Fort Reno," Keeling said. "They're bringing soldiers with them. Your braves will die if they go on the warpath."

"We starve or we die by the long rifles, no matter," White Horse said. "Our messenger will signal from the hill across the river. If he circles three times and dismounts, the agent agreed. If he makes a fourth circle and rides south, we massacre all. Saddle your horse. You ride fast if trouble starts."

"Is there really help on the way?" Everett asked when the chief had gone.

"Not until tomorrow," the sutler said. "But the post commander, Major O'Beirne, and about a dozen soldiers will be back late this afternoon."

Everett followed Keeling to the doorway and together they looked across the river to the bald hill.

"Get over to the school and warn Kincade," the sutler said. "Get your horse and a couple for the teacher and me. Then keep an eye on that hill."

With warning given and saddled horses in tow, Everett ran to the top of a mound just outside the fort and peered across the river. Half an hour later a paint pony appeared atop the hill, its rider turning him in tight circles.

18

Everett yelled to Keeling and Kincade, and they came running. With hearts pounding they stared across at the brave and his pony atop the hill.

"How many turns?" the sutler asked, grabbing the reins of one of the ponies.

"That's the third one," Everett said, glancing nervously at the gathering band of Cheyenne behind them. "Better mount up."

Across on the hill, the courier pulled his prancing horse to a stop, hesitated, then slipped down.

While the three white men released a huge sigh of relief, the braves shouted angrily and thrust their weapons in the air. Confused, Everett looked questioningly at the sutler.

"They wanted the warpath," he explained. "And if their rations aren't fast in coming, no chief will be able to hold them back."

After returning from Powder Face's farm, an impressive place with a large herd of cattle, massive cornfields, and well-tended vegetable gardens, Everett said goodbye to the sutler and teacher, then turned north on the military road. Two hours later he noticed an approaching dust cloud on the horizon ahead. Turning his horse down a craggy embankment, he splashed across the river and ducked into a thicket of trees, irritated at having to run and hide. Carefully, he slipped upstream through the brush along the eastern bank of the river, holding still while Major O'Beirne and his soldiers clattered past.

Concluding the road was too dangerous to travel, he spent the next few hours tediously twisting and turning through briar-laden bushes and crossing intersecting ravines and small streams until he and his exhausted horse pulled up. For the last half-hour he had led the pony because she had shown a slight limp on her right foreleg. Finding no external problem, he assumed a ligament or internal strain from hurrying his pony down the rocky embankment earlier. To avoid further damage, she needed rest.

While his lame pony drank from a spring-fed stream, he watched the sun drop below the horizon, welcoming darkness as an ally. Slowly, he led the chestnut along a game trail that followed the brook's edge, stopping in a grove of cottonwoods. He staked her among willows along the creek bank, filled her feedbag with corn, then set up camp under the tall trees.

Stretched out beside his fire, he tried to shut out his worries, though Samuel Harrison and his gang were never far from his mind. They were somewhere on his back trail, he was sure, though he had not seen them since that morning on the Salt Fork. He could take a chance and stay put a day or two, giving the mare time to heal, or he could push on at a slow pace, hoping the mare could hobble along until the leg improved. If she did not recover, he would be afoot and an easy target. Though Jed once told him about a man, Martias Dias, back in 1842, who had walked across hostile southern Kansas on foot, both his stolen mule and horse having died, Everett gave himself little chance of survival without a mount. His enemies were too many and too mobile.

Deciding to move on, he led his limping mare upstream.

Two days later while topping a rise in late afternoon, he noticed dark clouds moving his way from the northwest. A couple of miles back he had spotted a dozen head of branded cattle watering along the river, so he guessed a ranch must be nearby. Now he set out in earnest, searching for the nearest shelter.

The wind hit first, pushing a wall of dust that blasted his face, seeping into every crevice of his clothing, and tearing at his skin. Then, huge windblown raindrops splattered his face, streaking downward through a layer of fine red sand. When the sporadic drops turned into a downpour, he considered it a blessing. Wet sand would resist the unrelenting wind.

He pushed on, angling to the east, away from the brunt of the storm. Keeping his hat pulled low, he glanced ahead only occasionally. Gradually the rain became mixed with sleet and small hailstones that battered his hat and pelted his back. Making a dash for a dark clump of trees, he crossed a double-rutted trail, one etched into the earth by the frequent passing of wagons and buggies.

He hunkered down on the southeast side of the largest tree in the grove until the hail played out, then headed back for the wagon path.

Half an hour down the road, drenched and shivering in near darkness, he came to a gate, swung it open, and headed toward a faint glow in the distance, a lighthouse in this sea of land. Getting closer, a window framed the blurred light, one with sashes tied back. Flickers danced on a wet rock porch that ran the length of a peaked-roof house formed of native stone and mud.

With the mare hitched in front, Everett stepped onto the low porch and knocked. A stocky, broad-faced man opened the door and stepped forward, limping on a deformed right leg.

"Need shelter for me and my lame horse," Everett called out over the howling wind and steady drumbeat of the rain.

"Down there," the rancher shouted, pointing to a bunkhouse. "Stable your horse in the barn off to the left."

The door shut, and Everett returned to the storm and led the mare to the barn. He found an empty stable, unsaddled her, scooped corn into a trough, and rubbed her dry with fistfuls of hay. Grabbing his saddlebags, he slung them over his shoulder, tucked his bedroll under his arm, then made a run for the bunkhouse.

Six cowboys sat gathered around a potbellied stove at the south end. They made room for Everett after he dumped his things in a corner behind the door. He had left his slicker wrapped around his bedroll, so he was soaked to the skin and gritting his teeth to keep them from chattering. After breaking the chill, he pulled dry clothes from inside his blankets and hung his wet ones over a wire strung across a corner near the stove.

"You lookin' for work, or just passin' through?" asked a sandy-headed cowboy called Roy.

"Headed west when my horse went lame," Everett said. "I expect she'll be fit in a couple of days."

"Ever work cattle?" asked a mustached man named Caleb.

"Some."

"We're short a hand," Caleb said. "One's gone back East to bury his mother."

"How long?" Everett asked.

"Two more weeks, I expect."

"What does it pay?"

"You'll have to talk to the boss, Hub Guthrie."

Early the following morning, Everett soaped his saddle and rigging that had dried out over night. Then he ran through the cold rain to the ranch house. Inside, he offered to hire on for two weeks.

"Can't stay longer," Everett explained, "and I'll need a mount."

"Five dollars a week," Guthrie said.

"Fifteen for the two," Everett countered.

"I'll have to take out a dollar a week for feedin' your lame horse," the rancher explained.

"Who'll be giving me orders?" Everett asked.

"Caleb Saunders," Guthrie replied, hitching his left shoulder as he got to his feet.

"What happened?" Everett asked, motioning to the man's stiff leg.

"Horse slipped on ice a couple winters back," Guthrie explained. "Penned my leg under him for five hours."

"You seem to manage with it mighty good," Everett said as the man crossed the room at an awkward but steady pace and scribbled on a piece of paper pulled from the top drawer of a chest.

"This slow leg just has to work a little harder to keep up," the man said cheerfully. "Except for old Doc Chandler, I'd be flat of my back, or likely dead."

Everett made his way back to the bunkhouse and asked Saunders which horse he should throw his saddle on.

"In the barn you'll find a chocolate-colored pony with a blazed faced, about fifteen hands high," Caleb explained. "Ride over to the Skeeter ranch. They're holdin' a few head of ours. Bring 'em back and corral 'em here."

With directions and a note to Horace Skeeter, Everett slipped into his slicker and saddled up. He rode north into a soft rain, arriving late afternoon at the ranch headquarters, which lay in the edge of low mountains along the south bank of the Cimarron River. He handed over the note and was pointed toward the corral in which about thirty-five head of soaked cattle were penned. After spending the night, he eased into the corral, cut out seven wearing the HG brand, and turned them south, the cold wind to his back. Arriving at the Guthrie ranch after dark, chilled to the bone, he swung the corral gate open and pushed the bunch inside.

The following several days he rode out with Roy, searching for strays hiding in ravines and clumps of trees, bringing in a dozen to fifteen head each day. The weather was miserable, but Everett was glad to be out on the range, working cattle.

His chestnut mare healed in a few days, but Everett decided to let her rest. The middle of the second week, he turned the chocolate pony loose in the corral and saddled his mare. He trotted her around, seeing no sign of a problem, then walked her back to the corral.

"Everett," Caleb Saunders called out from the doorway of the bunkhouse.

Everett veered to the right and met the ranch foreman.

"While you were out, two fellas dropped by lookin' for you," Saunders said.

"Who?" Everett asked.

"Didn't give names," Saunders said, "but one was a large burly fella and their horses wore a four-point star brand."

"Stonewall Carter," Everett mumbled. "What'd you tell them?"

"Told 'em I didn't know no Everett Brook," the foreman said, smiling. "Said their posse had tracked you to Cantonment, then lost your trail in the rain. So they had split up, checkin' all the ranches around."

"I'd like to collect my pay," Everett said.

"I doubt they'll be back."

"I'd best be moving on."

While Everett packed, Saunders picked up his pay from the owner and delivered it to him, along with a three-day supply of food.

"I don't know what you're runnin' from," the foreman said to Everett, "but you've been a good hand in some mighty poor weather. I hope you'll stop this way again."

After extending his hand in thanks, Everett swung up and reined the mare north toward the distant, low mountains bordering the Cimarron River. His thought was to hide out in the hills north of where Harrison and his boys were searching.

Tired and cold, he made camp that night under a cluster of trees along a small stream, its icy waters flowing east just beyond the southern edge of the mountains. Seeing no evidence of pursuers, he gathered dead limbs and soon had a warm fire crackling and sizzling as the wood gave up moisture from the recent rain.

With daylight he planned to move up into the hills to a better hideout, one with a good view of any approaching riders. Everett lay in his bedroll, using his saddle for a pillow, when the imposing figure of the old marshal flashed hauntingly into his mind. Where were his men? Were they on their way to the Skeeter ranch? Realizing they could be close by, he quickly kicked sand on the flames, and buried himself inside his blankets.

Morning's first light glistened on the frost coating his bed tarp, and his stomach growled with hunger. His concern for Harrison's men convinced him to skip breakfast, so he packed and saddled the mare. As he slipped his foot into the stirrup, he glanced to the west where a column of smoke was curling into the cold, blue sky. Pursuers or Indians? Indians would likely camp along the North Canadian, much farther to the west or along the Cimarron to the east. He reined the chestnut toward the mountains, kicking her into a full gallop.

Concerned about his recently lame horse, he slowed her after a mile or so, keeping an eye on the dwindling column of smoke. Reaching a stream, he and the mare took a long drink, then splashed up the creek toward the hills. Half a mile later, he reined the mare out of the stream to the north side and proceeded cautiously, watching for tracks of unshod ponies or a still-warm campsite.

Reaching the base of the hills, he followed along the stream, twisting along a gently rising crease formed by the junction of two of the low mountains. Half an hour later and five hundred feet higher, he slipped down and climbed to the rocky crest of the highest peak, belly-crawling the last few feet. Peering down on the Skeeter ranch, which lay nestled beside a clear stream splitting a fertile meadow on the Cimarron side of the mountains, he spotted three men out front, standing at the head of two saddled horses, talking and arm-gesturing.

A wide-brimmed gray hat identified one as Horace Skeeter. Everett was unsure of the other two until they turned and headed for the barn. The man with the bushy beard was Stonewall Carter.

After searching the stables and then wandering through the corralled horses nearby, Carter and his partner mounted their ponies and headed south. Everett guessed that Skeeter had identified him as the cowboy who had picked up the HG strays a week earlier, and his pursuers were now headed back to Guthrie's ranch.

Everett turned his pony to the north, then pulled up. Carter would be angry, knowing Hub Guthrie had misled him earlier. If he regrouped the Tin Star posse and descended on the HG Ranch, the rancher, Caleb Saunders, or some of their men who had helped him would likely get shot. Everett turned back and set out on a path to cut off Carter and his partner.

Riding hard, he thundered off the mountain, split two hills, and splashed through the little stream. Pushing the chestnut up a rise, he kept her in full gallop for two miles, reaching the main trail between the two ranches. Hoping he was ahead of Carter and his partner, he climbed up a hillock, ground hitched his horse and eased to the crest of the peak. Looking back, he soon spotted the Tin Star cowboys. Everett pulled out his rifle and hunkered down, waiting.

As the two riders passed below, Everett raised up and shouldered his Winchester. A shot rang out, and sand jumped right in front of Carter's roan. The two men grabbed their six-shooters and turned. After two shots, they realized Everett was out of pistol range.

"Drop those shootin' irons, boys," Everett hollered, taking a bead on Carter's left shoulder. "And shed your rifles, too."

The bearded man's partner dropped his revolver, but Carter raised his and fired his response. Everett squeezed the trigger and the big man tumbled from his horse, clutching his shoulder.

"Shuck them rifles," Everett called louder, "or I'm gonna adjust my aim."

Carter made it to his feet while his partner pitched his rifle aside, then did the same.

"Help him into the saddle," Everett shouted to the man on the horse, "then you boys hightail it out of here."

Carter's partner slid down and helped the bearded fellow onto his horse, then jumped back onto his own.

"Brook, I'll get you if it's the last thing I do," Carter bellowed, stuffing his bandanna inside his shirt covering the wound.

Everett raised his Winchester to his shoulder and took aim. Watching the two Harrison men spur their ponies into a dead run, he slipped his finger off the trigger.

After gathering up their weapons, Everett headed north, knowing Carter would round up the posse and pick up his trail, abandoning plans to take revenge on Guthrie and his boys. He hoped for a two-hour head start.

He planned to ride day and night in an attempt to reach Fort Supply the next day. There he would get a fresh horse and stock up for a lengthy trip across No Man's Land, that narrow strip of desolate plains stretched across the northern border of the panhandle of Texas.

The sun was setting when Everett reached the big westward bend in the North Canadian. As darkness settled in, he crossed the river and followed the military road upstream, hoping for no nighttime travelers. As he neared the fort, well before sunrise, he eased over beside the river and made camp, giving him and his spent pony much-needed rest.

After only three hours of sleep, Everett woke to a chilly dawn. Anxious, he fed his horse, ate breakfast, and saddled up. From a knoll south of the post, he watched early morning stirrings. The ten-foot stockade walls formed of sharp-tipped posts and two corner blockhouses emphasized the necessity for fortification in this hostile land, yet several unprotected outbuildings and military tents bordered the wooden citadel. Just to the west of the outpost, Indian tepees encircled an early morning cooking fire, and to the north covered wagons sat scattered about.

As he crossed Wolf Creek and approached the main gate, a blue-clad soldier was hoisting Old Glory to the top of the flagpole that was the centerpiece of the fort's interior. From the sergeant at the gate, he got directions to the tent of a horse trader who regularly sold horses to the cavalry. Everett focused on a young black mare the chunky man offered even-up for the chestnut, or for fifty dollars cash. Cracks at the edges of her hooves suggested she had been shoed for the first time in the past few days and missing were typical saddle marks found on most cowponies. Everett guessed she had recently belonged to an Indian. Stepping up to check her teeth, he noticed she had a cloudy left eye, matter bunched at the corners.

"She's half blind," Everett said. "My chestnut is worth double your mare."

"She's young, spirited, and the fastest horse at this post, including yours," the trader countered.

"She'd break a leg in a prairie dog hole, or stumble over a rock, or likely run into a tree or over a cliff. She ain't worth twenty dollars."

"I'll swap and throw in fifteen dollars to boot," the trader said.

"She's an army reject," Everett replied, guessing. "So you're stuck with her. I'm offering twenty cash."

"I'd shoot her before I'd sell her for that," the trader replied. "Thirty-five."

"Twenty-five, and I'll take her off your hands," Everett offered, knowing she would do as a packhorse, and if he could cure the eye problem, he might have two good mounts.

"I'll throw in a saddle and bridle for another forty," the man said.

"Don't need it, but I could use a pack saddle, if you've got a good one for ten."

"I've got a sawbuck and practically new packs for fifteen, including a halter and lead rope."

"Let's see it," Everett said, pulling out his money.

The pack outfit was not anything to brag about, but it was functional. After paying, Everett doubted he had enough money left to cover the supplies he needed.

He showed the two spare rifles and revolvers to the sutler. The man offered thirty dollars.

"I need about twenty dollars worth of provisions," Everett said. "The guns should cover them, plus another twenty."

He gathered his provisions and twenty dollars, then switched the packsaddles to the chestnut and cinched his saddle on the black mare. Cautiously, he slipped his left foot into the wooden stirrup and pulled himself up. The black pony bowed her neck and reared up, her front hooves pawing air only a couple of feet off the ground. Everett patted her neck, gave her plenty of rein, and maintained a steady stream of soothing talk. After prancing around a bit, she settled down, and he turned her toward the post corral, leading the chestnut.

Locating the sergeant in charge, he asked if the post had anyone who might look at the black's cloudy eye.

"Already checked it, and there ain't nothin' he can do," the sergeant replied. "She ain't gonna see out that eye ever again."

A bit discouraged, Everett turned his ponies toward the west bank of the river, which the sergeant had called Beaver Creek, and headed upstream, keeping a lookout along his back trail. The spirited black set a lively gait, which she maintained throughout the day.

After a good night's sleep, Everett again saddled the black, and hit the trail. By day's end, the new pony had shown good strength and enviable endurance.

The next day Everett switched back to the chestnut and continued across the flat, arid terrain. A few bare mesas and hills broke the monotonous landscape, but Everett continually felt exposed to anyone within two miles. Though it slowed progress, he avoided the few ridges, sticking to the swales, ravines, and dry creek beds where possible.

Mid-afternoon he found himself in a basin, so he turned his horses across the western side, staying just below the crest of the ridge, and headed for a low outlet at the southwest edge. Suddenly, a band of seven Indians popped up over the west rim, trotting their ponies down the slope toward him. First instinct told him to turn and run, but he knew he would never get away.

Checking his weapons, he sat and waited.

19

No Man's Land, (Oklahoma Panhandle)
May, 1883

The Indian braves pulled up abreast about thirty yards ahead of Everett, each with a ready rifle. At the command of the taller one in the middle, the line closed in while bending around him and forming a loose circle. He wanted to yank out his revolver but knew he would be dead before getting off a shot. With his left hand gripping the reins and his right lying relaxed against his thigh, he sat tall with his shoulders back and chest out and set his eyes firmly on their leader, determined to hide the fear rampaging inside his veins.

While the braves squeezed the circle tighter, the tall one broke rank and pushed in front, stopping some ten feet in front of the chestnut. He spoke in his native language, and then one of the braves rode over and reached for the lead rope of the packhorse. Everett jerked the line away and pulled the black pony up beside him. The brave raised his rifle and leveled it on Everett, glancing at his leader.

Everett ignored the brave and his carbine.

The tall brave kneed his pony forward, his dark eyes glaring at Everett.

"We take pony," he said, raising his own rifle.

Matching the leader's gaze, Everett eased his right hand to the handle of his revolver.

"I'll kill you if you try," he said, rising anger fighting back fear.

The leader sneered and swung his hand around his circle of friends, clearly indicating the numbers were in his favor.

"We take pony. You ride away," he said, his tone guttural.

"No deal," Everett said through clenched teeth.

As the tall one's face hardened, one of his braves eased closer, staring curiously at Everett, then spoke to his leader, who nodded in response.

"You know Red Fork?" the brave asked.

"I've got friends there," Everett said. "Ralph Collins and his cousin Fred Williams."

"You make corral?" the brave asked, drawing a large circle with the index finger of his left hand, the end missing from the last knuckle.

"Yes," Everett replied, recognizing the brave as a member of the Cut Finger band.

"Me help," the brave said, pushing his chest out and pounding it with his clenched left hand. Then he turned to his leader and explained.

The Indians were a band of Cheyenne, three of whom had been among those who had helped Everett construct the huge stockade corral at Red Fork Ranch.

"Come with us," the brave said, kneeing his pony alongside Everett and following the band of braves as they turned and headed west.

A couple of miles later, they dropped down into a fertile draw and followed its descending floor to its mouth where about twenty tepees were clustered, the river only thirty yards beyond. A herd of horses grazed along the stream as several boys kept watch. The river split the floor of a canyon, its vertical red walls some forty feet high, forming a natural protective barrier.

When Everett dismounted, he slid his rifle from its scabbard. The braves seemed unconcerned as they each headed for their respective shelters. The leader soon reappeared with a graying, wrinkle-faced Cheyenne.

"Chief Bluecoat," the tall leader explained with obvious pride. "He rode with Dull Knife. We Dog Soldiers."

Everett knew a little about Dull Knife's refusal to stay on the southern reservation, and his leading of a hostile band of Northern Cheyenne on a determined trek north to their former grounds. Half starved by scarcity of food and weakened by the bitter winter, many had been rounded up and killed by the army, but eventually their valiant struggle had led to securing their own northern reservation. As a survivor of that ordeal, Chief Bluecoat undoubtedly held a deserved position of honor among these eager warriors.

Speaking through the young brave, the chief asked where Everett was going, where he had come from, what was in his packs, and did he know Little Robe.

"We spoke at Red Fork once," Everett said after explaining his plans. "His braves helped me build a corral."

The chief's intent eyes studied Everett as the brave interpreted, then he smiled.

"We eat," he said, turning toward the cooking fire.

Though free and unwatched in his separate camp in the draw, Everett hardly slept and rose early, rolling his bed and saddling his ponies. As he led them to the river for a drink, the leader of the braves came over to him.

"You ride away and not come back," he said, motioning toward the western horizon. "You not bring others to Cheyenne camp."

Everett nodded his agreement, then pulled on the reins to turn the black mare. Suddenly the warrior grabbed the bridle side-straps, halting the startled horse.

"Bad eye," he said, peering into the pony's cloudy left pupil.

Everett relaxed the reins as the brave led the pony over to a tepee just beyond the fringe of the others. He motioned Everett to wait as he stepped over to the lone dwelling and called out. An old Indian pushed back the flap and stepped through the opening. After a brief conversation, the medicine man stepped over to the black and examined the eye. Returning to his tepee, he soon came back with a watery mixture. With the brave's help, he twisted the horse's head to the side and dripped the liquid into the cloudy eye.

The black flinched and tried to pull away, but the young Indian held firm. The medicine man trickled more of his remedy into the wild eye. When the pony had settled down, the brave released his grip, and the old man handed a small pouch of powdery substance to Everett.

"Add water," the brave explained, stirring his fingertip in his cupped palm. Then closing his fist around the imaginary potion, he turned it up, pointing to the small opening formed at the base of his clenched little finger. "Each sunrise, put in eye."

Everett thanked the Indians and headed up the draw.

Reaching the rim of the canyon, he followed the river west until he came to a series of rapids, the first beginning about forty feet above the canyon floor. Tired and hungry, Everett turned the mare down the gradual slope to the water's edge and swung down. Stepping upstream from his guzzling horses, he hand-dipped a drink for himself, then splashed cold water over his face.

While the two mares cropped at the skimpy blue stem grass along the stream, Everett ate some dried beef and a cold biscuit, then filled his canteen. Running low on food and money, he hoped to find work soon but had not seen a ranch building or range cattle in days.

Up ahead he spotted a stream flowing into the river from the southwest. Though he had ridden a hundred miles west since last seeing Harrison's men, he decided to leave the river and splash along in the shallow stream for a mile or so, hiding his trail.

As daylight played out, so did the stream, its headwaters being a strong spring. Everett watered his horses, filled his canteen and then headed away from the stream. Reaching a dry gulch, he eased down to its floor by way of a cut in its red wall and searched for a good campsite. After some time, he discovered a shallow cave burrowed into the west-side bank. Revolver in hand, he gathered a fistful of sagebrush, set it afire for light, and ducked inside. It was empty except for a rattlesnake, which he quickly eliminated.

After stuffing his things into the shelter and staking his horses, he headed over to some cottonwoods that flourished around the spring. He gathered an armload of firewood, then returned to camp. Just then, he remembered something Keeling had told him while at Cantonment.

Years back, while transporting seven thousand dollars of quartermaster money from the post to Fort Leavenworth, Kansas, Keeling's traveling companion, Bad Face, had noticed they were being followed. The Indian had suggested they continue and act as if they were unaware. Then as dark had settled in, they had made camp. After building a good fire, they had slipped away and continued another five miles before setting up a cold camp, losing their four pursuers in the process.

Everett chose a spot near the spring and built a fire. He piled on two armloads of wood, and then brushed out his tracks with a tree branch while returning to his dugout. He started a cooking fire, ate, and then kicked sand over the flames. To keep his coffee hot, he nestled the pot down among the hot coals beneath the dirt.

When morning came, Everett stepped out and prepared to drip the last of the mixture in the black mare's eye, but froze when he heard voices. He jerked his rifle out and sneaked over to where he could look down on the diversionary campsite. A group of men milled around, one kicking at charred stick-ends surrounding a smoldering pile of campfire ashes.

"Done rode out," one said.

"We waited around out there all night in the cold for nothin'!" another said bitterly. "We should've rushed 'im, first thing."

"Only a fool barrels into a man's camp when you can't see 'im," Stonewall Carter said, reaching a hand to his aching shoulder. "He was hidin' out, waitin' for the flames to light up our faces so he could cut us down."

"Or maybe he tricked us," another said. "Could've built a fire and hightailed it."

"Won't work next time," Carter said, turning his pony to the west. "Let's ride. I gotta get this shoulder seen to."

When they were out of sight, Everett scampered back to his camp, dripped the mixture into the pony's eye, then threw his things together and swung up. With Carter and his bunch headed west, he turned south, believing the main branch of the Canadian River lay close by.

About noon he found the stream which was bordered to the south by a well-traveled road, the trail from Fort Smith to Santa Fe. Through the afternoon, he rode with the sun, and when only a couple of hours of daylight remained, he noticed a small town amid a grove of tall cottonwoods across the river, about a quarter of a mile distant. Needing supplies and money, he splashed across the shallow stream.

As he turned onto a dusty road, a raw-board sign tacked to a four-foot post read, TASCOSA. Up ahead strode a man wearing black, carrying a bible, and followed by a wagon loaded with a board coffin. Five or six people, including a veiled woman, trailed the wagon. Everett reined the mare off the road and removed his hat while the procession passed.

As he headed toward a collection of buildings lining the street on both sides, he glanced back. The funeral group had climbed the flank of a rocky hill and was headed for a fenced patch where a pile of red dirt and surrounding wooden grave markers stood silhouetted against the western sky, undoubtedly Tascosa's Boot Hill.

"Who died?" Everett asked the clerk in the Cone and Duran Mercantile.

"Nobody just dies in this town," the man replied, "leastwise not naturally."

"Gunfight?" Everett asked, nodding toward the funeral in progress.

"Ambush," the man said, stepping around and extending his hand. "J. W. Cone's the name. Don't reckon I caught yours."

"Everett Brook."

"Pleased to make your acquaintance, Mr. Brook," Cone said. "Our marshal got himself killed yesterday. You ever wear a badge?"

"Not me," Everett said. "I'm looking for cowhand work."

"You sure picked a bad time," Cone replied, laughing. "Cowboys for all the big outfits around here are on strike, demanding fifty dollars a month for cowhands and seventy-five for their bosses."

"With their regulars on strike, maybe the ranchers are hiring," Everett said.

"The LIT headquarters is just four miles east of here," Cone said, "but you're gonna make a passel of enemies if you replace one of them strikers."

"I've got trouble enough," Everett said. "And I'm headed the other way."

"A new ranch, the XIT, is startin' up and headquartered over at Buffalo Springs, if you want to give it a try," Cone said.

"Thanks," Everett said, figuring Harrison's men would check out all the big ranches.

"If you're lookin' for honest work," a fellow said, "The T Anchor is hirin', and the boys there ain't a part of this fight."

"How come they haven't joined in?" Everett asked.

"Their boss allows his boys to brand mavericks as their own and run them on his range," the man said. "The big ranchers have put a stop to that, triggering this feud."

"Sounds like the boys have good reason to strike," Everett said. "How do I find this T Anchor outfit?"

"Follow the river west about ten miles. You'll see a signpost pointin' south. Follow the trail to headquarters in Spring Draw, down on the Tierra Blanca."

"Is it a big outfit?"

"The range runs from Palo Duro Canyon into New Mexico, an area called Little Texas."

"Little Texas?"

"Yeah, it's land in New Mexico Territory that's mostly range to Texas ranchers."

"Who do I ask for?"

"Jud Campbell," the cowboy said. "Tell 'im Black Bill Jones sent you."

"You one of the striking cowboys?"

"Not now. I quit the LIT and latched on to a job with W. R. Bolden, runnin' freight between here and Dodge," Jones said, chuckling. "Our loads are mostly to and from the LIT, so I reckon that outfit's still payin' my wages."

Everett tipped his hat to the man, and stepped outside. Noticing the left-side pack hanging lopsided, he stepped over to the black mare and adjusted it. As he rubbed the pony's neck affectionately, she twisted her head and looked back at him.

"Why Blackie," he said, surprised. "That eye is as clear as rainwater."

Taking a long look at his horses, Everett decided they could use some rest and a bait of corn. Looking around, he spotted a livery four doors down the street and led his horses that way.

"Your sign above the door says McCormick's Livery," Everett said, looking around at a makeshift bar, several tables, and a gambling room off in a corner. A small woman with black hair in a bun on the back of her head stood beside a monte table, fingering a deck of cards.

"It's around back," the rather short man replied, brushing at his dark, curly hair. "Name's Mickey McCormick, and this is my wife, Frenchy."

"I'd like to leave my horses for the night," Everett explained, nodding to the woman. "They've been on the trail a spell and could use a good feed, a place to roll, and a thorough brushing."

"Just take them around the corner there, and through the gate. The hostler will see to them," McCormick said.

With his horses cared for, Everett grabbed his saddlebags and headed up the street to the Exchange Hotel. After washing up in his room and slipping into a fresh shirt, he stopped by the front desk.

"The food good down at McCormick's?" Everett asked the man named Russell behind the desk.

"Yeah, but if you're figurin' to sit a spell at Frenchy's gamblin' table," Russell replied, chuckling, "you'd best pay for your room right now."

"She run a crooked game?" Everett asked.

"Not that anybody's ever proved," Russell replied. "But I've seen her pocket eighteen hundred on a good night."

"Where'd she learn to handle cards like that?" Everett asked.

"Nobody rightly knows," the man replied, leaning across the counter. "Mickey found her at Mobeetie a couple years back. Says she brought him good luck at the gamblin' tables. He calls her Frenchy, but Scotty Wilson, justice of the peace hereabouts, says her marriage license reads Elizabeth McGraw. Scotty says that ain't her real name neither, but we ain't likely to ever know the name her mother gave her."

Everett was intrigued, though he had no intention of gambling. After a good supper in McCormick's dining area, he eased over to the open doorway of the gambling room. Frenchy was standing beside Mickey who was seated at a poker table. Judging from the stack of money in front of him, he was enjoying a run of luck.

About ten minutes later, Frenchy stepped out of the room. About that time a woman dressed in a dancehall outfit brushed past Everett, and noticing Mickey's winnings, she eased over, looped her arm across his shoulders, and offered to help him spend the money. Mickey laughed and kept playing.

Three losing hands later, Mickey called for Frenchy, who returned to his side. When her beloved husband lost again, she glared at the woman at his other shoulder. Suddenly, Frenchy reached over Mickey's head and shoved the dancer away. After another losing hand, Frenchy ordered the woman to leave the room. When the dancer protested, Frenchy flashed a knife and took off after her, flushing her through the doorway, almost running over Everett. With order restored and Frenchy at Mickey's shoulder, he won the next hand.

Shaking his head in disbelief, Everett headed for the exit.

The next morning, with his horses refreshed, Everett packed and headed for the river, following upstream until he found the arrow-shaped sign that read, T ANCHOR. He turned onto the dusty wagon trail and, an hour later, rode down a barren slope and through an open pole gate on the edge of a grassy valley surrounded by scruffy, brown hills.

A cottonwood log home, a rundown sod bunkhouse, and a rectangular pole-corral beside a barn rested in the bend of a lazy, shallow stream. About a dozen horses stood swishing their tails in the corral, and scattered bunches of cattle pulled at patches of grass along the fertile draw.

Everett crossed the sandy creek bed, and approached the house. A short, brawny man answered his knock, and Everett explained he was looking for work and mentioned the names Black Bill Jones and Campbell.

Jud Campbell stepped outside and offered his hand.

"Where'd you meet up with Black Bill?"

"Tascosa. Says he's freighting up to Dodge for Bolden these days."

"Good hand," the rancher said. "Helped me build the drift fence along the north boundary of the ranch."

"What's a drift fence?"

"A barrier to stop northern cattle from driftin' down on our range, usually runnin' from winter storms. It's north of the river and starts at our border with New Mexico and goes east to Indian Territory, built out of whatever's handy."

Everett proposed to work for room and board for himself and his horse, plus twenty a month. Campbell asked a few questions, took a look at Everett's horses and rig, then offered a job helping with a summer roundup. The rancher said the job would take about a month, but being short-handed, he might have steady work for a good cowhand. Everett agreed, but explained he would be heading farther west after the herd was gathered and sorted.

Everett threw his supplies and bedroll into the dirt-floor bunkhouse, hung his saddle and bridle on the corral fence and set his horses free in the pen. As he turned for the bunkhouse, a tall, lean cowboy headed his way.

"Boss put you on the payroll?" he asked, his voice deep and scratchy. "Name's Jim, but the boys call me Frog."

"Just for the roundup." Stifling a laugh, Everett then introduced himself.

Later two more cowboys showed up, a young one named Willie and a veteran called Hensley. The night meal was warmed-up stew and cornbread, but Everett enjoyed it as if it were a king's feast. After making three trips to the big cast-iron pot simmering on the wood-burning stove, he felt full for the first time in weeks.

Sitting out on the porch later, Hensley explained that they were short two hands since one had been killed by a band of roaming Comanches returning to

Palo Duro Canyon, and a second, who had barely escaped, had lit out the next day. Between the LIT's, the LS's, and LX's appetite for cowboys and roving Indians, the T Anchor often found itself shorthanded. The strike had just made things worse since cowboys from the big outfits resented the Anchor boys not joining them.

"More Indians than cowboys out here," Frog said. "Gotta keep your eyes peeled and your rifle handy."

After sharing stories for a couple of hours, Everett stretched out his bedroll on a rickety cot and crawled in. He felt like he was on the outer edge of the world, beyond the reach of Harrison's boys. For the first time since leaving Caldwell, he slept without concern.

Early the next morning, he joined his companions in scouring the nearby range. At sundown he found himself pushing a gathering of cattle along the stream in the valley. Noticing the other cowboys' constant search of the horizon, Everett was reminded of Harrison's posse. When they did not find him at one of the big ranches, the XIT, LIT, LX or LS, they would likely head for Tascosa and ask questions. Would Cone or Black Bill point them toward the T Anchor?

For a week their sweep reached progressively farther out on the range. As the gather dwindled each day, Everett's anxiety grew.

"Better pack for a week's ride," Hensley said that night, indicating the roundup would extend to the extremes of the range for its final sweep.

For Everett, the change was welcomed, though he was enjoying sleeping inside and eating regular meals. In some remote camp, he would be less likely to be trapped by Stonewall Carter and his cohorts, and on the range he always rode prepared to make a run for his life at a moment's notice.

He found that the lingering, torturous sun of summer days on the wide-open high plains burned to a crisp everything below. The hours dragged on monotonously. Drifting in and out of ravines, pushing through mesquite brush, and scanning the empty horizon for cattle afforded Everett time to think about the mess he had made of his life, about his dream of owning a ranch back in Kansas, and about Tabitha.

A sick feeling filled his stomach when he thought of all he had lost. Could he ever go back? Would it ever be safe? Or was he following in the footsteps of his father, doomed to die swinging from the end of a rope?

And Samuel Harrison and his men began to weigh more on his mind. Maybe they had checked the other ranches and turned back to Caldwell, but Everett could not convince himself of that. The old marshal would have threatened his boys that they were not to return until they had avenged his sons. Though it might take months, the posse would eventually ride into Tascosa, get a tip, and would show up at the T Anchor. They would ask questions, and Everett could not expect Campbell to protect him. He had to move on before that happened.

One night, sitting around the campfire, the boys got to talking about cattle rustling and horse stealing. Hensley had seen his share, as had Frog.

"Things have settled down around here since that bunch led by Billy the Kid got busted up," Hensley said. "Back in seventy-eight the Kid and his boys brought in a hundred and twenty-five horses rustled over in New Mexico and hung around town sellin' them to local ranchers, along with a bill of sale."

"Out of horses to sell, they'd steal ponies right out of our corrals," Frog remembered, "drive 'em back into New Mexico Territory, trade 'em for Mexican ponies, then bring them here and sell 'em to the same folks they'd robbed in the first place."

"What stopped them?" Everett asked, when the laughter died down.

"When the Kid headed back to New Mexico Territory, three of his boys, Fred Waite, John Middleton, and Henry Brown, stayed in Tascosa. Eventually, Brown became deputy marshal and sent a posse out and rounded up what was left of the gang," Hensley said. "He collected the reward money put up by local ranchers, payment intended for the posse, and skipped the country with it. Then folks figured out how he knew where to trap the thieves. It seems he hadn't completely reformed."

"The deputy had ridden with them when they stole the horses," Frog said, shaking his head. "Then with most of the herd sold, he figured it was more profitable to arrest them and pocket the reward."

"Anybody go after him?" Everett asked, realizing the man they were talking about was Marshal Brown of Caldwell.

"A posse chased 'im all the way to the Kansas border, but never caught 'im."

The eighth day out, Everett was flushing five cows and three unbranded calves out of a copse of mesquite brush when he spotted an unfamiliar rider approaching. He eased his hand down to his revolver and slipped the thong off the hammer. The stranger pulled up, his brown horse lathered and breathing heavily.

"You Brook?"

Everett nodded.

"I hired on two days back," he explained. "The boss sent me out to lend a hand."

"You need to see Hensley," Everett said, somewhat relieved. "He gives the orders out here."

"I done seen him," the man said. "You're to ride in. I'll finish up here."

His thoughts a jumble, Everett headed back to camp which was set up near the mouth of a deep draw where they were penning the cattle.

"The boss sent a message," Hensley said, waving a piece of paper. "Some men stopped by the house, askin' about you."

"Did he say who?"

"Armed posse. Their leader, a big fella with a bandaged shoulder, went on a rampage, swearin' you was on this ranch and demandin' Campbell turn you over."

"What did the boss do?"

"Campbell told the brute this is a big ranch, but he's welcome to comb every acre if he's up to fightin' Geronimo's Apaches to the west and Comanche renegades to the east."

20

Everett knew that the threat of Comanches and Apaches would not stop Crazy Carter. He and his bunch would come searching for him.

"Thanks, Hensley, but I'll be moving along, now. If you would, thank Campbell for me."

"Sure. Maybe you'll come back after these boys have had their look around," Hensley said. "You got any money, Everett."

"A little."

"I'd say you've got ten dollars wages comin'," he said. "I can't pay you, but you're welcome to sack up some grub to get you along your way."

Everett cut his black mare out of the remuda, tied the packs on, then stuffed in a two-day supply of food. He swung up on the chestnut and turned her to the west.

Staying half a mile south of the river road, he maintained a good steady pace until dark when he set up camp in a dry ravine. Though the warm day turned to a cold night beginning with sundown, he avoided a fire, eating beef jerky with cold bread.

The next two days Everett pushed his mount farther west, tracking parallel to the river and risking its edge only to fill his canteen and water his horses. At dusk the second day he approached old Fort Bascom, lying on the south side of the Canadian in a wide, desolate valley.

He approached the abandoned buildings with caution, found them empty, but then noticed fresh hoof marks of unshod ponies in the dry sand. Keeping an eye out, he watered his horses and headed up an incline to the south.

Rock-infested mountains bounded the valley on both sides. Their slopes lay cluttered with huge chunks of stone long since broken off and tumbled down from craggy outcroppings higher up. Soon he settled in behind a cluster of boulders, each larger than his horse. Shielded from anyone in the valley below by his stone fortress, he started a small cooking fire.

With daylight he continued upstream until the river split, one branch heading northwest and the other tracking the path of the afternoon sun. After crossing over to its north bank, he stuck with the westerly course, putting the river between him and the road.

The second day he topped a rise and, off to the northwest, he noticed a dark column of smoke. After riding to the top of a high mesa, he saw a cabin burning with five mounted Indians circling. With little thought, he thundered down off the mesa and headed for the flaming building. As he approached from a knoll about a hundred yards from the cabin, he lifted his rifle and, with little effort at accuracy, fired three rapid shots. As the Indians scampered away, stampeding two loose cowponies, they returned his fire, none taking effect.

The cabin was a smoldering heap of charred logs, the ground littered with the homesteader's ransacked belongings. A man's body lay out back, three blood-circled bullet holes in his shirt. A patch of hair was gone from the top of his head, and his empty rifle lay beside him.

While checking for other victims, he found a three-drawer chest toppled backwards. He pushed it upright, and pulled out each drawer. In the last one, a yellow bonnet lay folded across other feminine clothing.

He began digging through the rubble, looking for the charred remains of a woman, but found none. Desperate to know what happened to her, he expanded his search. He found a footpath that led a couple hundred yards down a slope to a small spring where an empty pail sat beside the pool of water.

He called out, hoping the woman was hiding in one of the many surrounding clumps of bushes. Twice more he tried to coax the woman to join him, but got no response. Knowing she had not been with the Indians when they rode away, he guessed she had spotted them early and had managed to escape, possibly to a shelter planned for just such an occasion.

Upon failing to locate such a hideout, he climbed back up the hill, swung up on his pony, and started for the river, planning to comb the area along the way.

"Please don't leave me," a voice called out.

Turning, he spotted her easing out from behind a thick bush, her fearful face tear-streaked, her long dress ragged and dirty, and her hands bloodstained.

"Are you okay?"

"They didn't find me," she said, nodding.

"What happened?" Everett asked, slipping down.

"Kiowa attack," she said. "I gave them food a week ago, but this time I was at the spring and Jim refused. There were too many of them."

"Can you ride?"

"Yes. My husband worked for Mike Slattery, foreman of the Bell Ranch. I've been around horses all my life."

"You got folks in these parts?"

"A sister in Las Vegas," she replied.

While she packed a few things from the chest, Everett grabbed the rifle, inserted a few shells, then helped her into the saddle on the chestnut.

"Here, keep this handy," he said, handing over the rifle.

After rearranging the packs on the black mare, he swung up and glanced around. On two sides high rock cliffs towered over the basin floor, and on a third side, boulder-laden mountains rose thousands of feet into the sky. They were in a hole practically encircled by a harsh wall of rock.

"Is there a way out without following after those Indians?" he asked.

The woman turned to the west and pointed. "We can go by way of Corazon Hill."

"Where's that?"

"Up there," the woman said, indicating the tallest point on the rock cliffs.

"You sure?" he asked, seeing no way to scale the harsh, craggy wall.

"There's a trail," the woman said.

"You lead," he said. "And don't hesitate if we meet up with any Kiowa."

Reaching the base of the towering cliffs, she reined the chestnut behind a wall of boulders and onto a narrow path spiraling upward, clinging to the edge of the mountain. For an hour they twisted up the trail, squeezing between boulders and hugging the rock wall as their horses trod along on a flat shoulder only five feet wide. Glancing to his left, Everett swallowed hard. Less than a yard stood between him and an unbroken drop of nine hundred feet.

About three-fourths the way up, they reached a flat area protruding outward from the mountainside and supported by a rock pedestal. Stopping to rest, Everett looked back, his eyes following along the beautiful valley engulfed in a soft blue haze and stretching for miles to the south.

With energy restored, they climbed on to the summit where the land flattened to enormous, treeless hills that formed a rolling grassland larger than Everett had ever seen. He marveled at its striking contrast to the rugged world below the cliffs, some two thousand feet down.

With daylight waning, Everett and the woman arrived in Las Vegas. After seeing her to her sister's house, he headed for the plaza.

With twenty dollars in his pocket, he bought a meal and a few supplies, then at Danzinger's store, he asked about work. A large bearded man and his thin companion invited Everett to ride along to their camp west of town.

"The SP ranch ain't far, and some of the boys know the boss," the bearded one assured Everett.

The men camped along a narrow stream that followed a deep, twisting canyon cut through harsh mountains.

"What makes the water so warm?" Everett asked the thin fellow who had accompanied him to the stream to fill their canteens.

"Hot springs up on the side of Montezuma Hill," the man replied. "Best bath a man ever had."

Later, Everett made his way upstream until he found the flow of warm water tumbling down a steep slope. He climbed up and found the springs, the larger being an eight-foot-wide pool. He stripped and slowly slipped into the hot water, which nature had spiked with soothing minerals.

At first the elevated temperature stung his chilled skin, but gradually it relaxed him to the point of sleepiness. Not since a warm bath at Caldwell had he enjoyed anything so refreshing and tranquilizing.

The next morning, the bearded man guided Everett to the SP ranch, as he had promised. The owner, Seth Palacious, offered him fifteen dollars a month plus room and board. Everett remembered the fifty-dollar demand of the striking cowboys at Tascosa, but with the lure of a bed and hot meals, he accepted without haggling over the terms.

"We'll be driving some cows up to the high country," Palacious explained. "You and Butch will have 'em to yourselves 'til we bring 'em back here in the fall."

For two weeks they gathered the herd, rounding up cattle in the valley, cutting out those to be pushed north to market and those to be held at headquarters for beef. With the sorting complete, Everett and five others herded the cattle to be kept up a narrow, climbing canyon. Two days later they reached a mesa seven thousand feet up, and settled into camp along a fifteen-foot-wide stream. The following day, four of the cowboys headed back to headquarters while Everett and the cowboy named Butch stayed with the herd.

Through summer the two rode the boundary of the mesa, keeping a tally of the herd, helping birthing cows, and protecting the calves against cougars, black bears, and coyotes. The weather was cool and dry, the most comfortable summer Everett had ever experienced.

With early fall, the nights became bitterly cold, and four cowboys showed up to move the herd back to the valley. Everett and a cowboy named Curly Washburn headed for a draw at the far northern section of the mesa to search for strays. A light rain, turning to sleet and snow, was falling from a gray sky, while a sharp northwest wind cut at their faces. They rounded up about thirty cows and half that many calves, pushing them back toward the main body of cattle.

As they approached the stream, now stretched to a width of twenty-five feet by a recent downpour farther up the mountain, Everett became concerned. Glancing at Washburn, he realized the cowboy intended to drive the cattle into the raging creek. Everett kicked his horse into a full gallop, intending to head off a likely disaster.

"Curly," he called out, "it's too deep and strong for the calves."

"They've crossed here lots of times," Curly called back.

"On downstream it widens and shallows out. Let's cross down there."

"The weather's gettin' nasty, and we're runnin' out of daylight. We're pushin' them across right here, then we'll bed 'em down in a sheltered canyon on the other side," Curly replied, irritated at being questioned by a newcomer.

In any case it was too late to head them off. The cattle pushed on toward the stream until the lead cow, nudged from behind, plunged into the swift water. As others reached the stream's edge, those following pushed them in, like driftwood being swept over the precipice of a waterfall. The cows swam frantically, struggling to keep their heads above water as the current carried them downstream. The lead cows finally began crawling out on the far side.

Everett focused on a newborn thrashing beside its mother, gradually falling behind. When it reached the heart of the current, the calf was suddenly swept away, its head dipping below the rolling water's surface, then bobbing up again. In less than half a minute, it disappeared beneath the turbulence one final time. Several of the young calves suffered a similar fate.

Curly joined Everett in trying to head off the remainder of the herd from the deathtrap, but the cattle stubbornly plunged ahead, as if linked tail-to-nose. On the other side of the stream, the cows that had lost calves turned back into the emerging mass, bellowing for their offspring. The herd panicked, some trapped mid-stream by the mass of cattle ahead. Finally, the two cowboys swam their ponies across, broke loose the logjam of cows, then rounded up and bedded down the milling herd in a shallow canyon.

"I'm going on downstream," Everett said, "and search for any calves that might've made it ashore."

He combed every nook and cranny along the stream until darkness put an end to the search. After finding seven dead calves, he saved one, hoisting the drenched calf across his horse's shoulders. Back at the ravine, the shivering newborn bawled until its mother found it and licked it clean. The cowboys spent the night with blankets wrapped about their shoulders while drying their clothes by the fire and watching over the restless herd.

The next day, amid a steady snowfall, they drove the cattle to the big mesa where the other cowboys held the balance of the herd. Smithey, the senior cowhand, asked about the delay.

"Had some trouble crossin' the stream," Curly explained.

Smithey noticed several bawling cows without calves, their utters bulging. Suspicious, he counted the little herd before letting them merge into the others, then rode over to Everett and Curly.

"What happened to the calves?"

"What calves?" Curly asked, eyeing Everett.

"The ones that belong to these cows. I'd guess a dozen of them had a suckling calf no more than two days ago," Smithey responded.

"Maybe the mountain cats and bears got 'em. They're bad up there," Curly replied.

“What about it, cowboy?” Smithey asked, turning his eyes on Everett.

“We lost a few crossing the stream,” Everett said. “It was deep, and the current was stronger than we expected. The small calves just couldn’t make it.”

“Yeah,” Smithey said. “Well, you boys owe the boss for those calves. Even my grandma knows better than to drive newborns off into a stream when it’s up. I figure you lost a dozen. At three dollars a head, that’s thirty-six dollars, with half owed by each of you. Curly, I’ll be takin’ it outta your pay. Everett, I’ll hold your black mare ‘til you’ve earned enough to pay your part.”

Riding for the ranch, Curly threw angry glances at Everett who had made up his mind that no one was taking his black mare. If necessary, some night he would pack up, take his horses, and slip away.

After dinner that night, Everett lay on his bunk, mulling over how he could settle the debt without losing the black. Suddenly, Curly stepped over and glared down at him.

“Get outta that bunk, greenhorn. You cost me a month’s wages, and I’m takin’ it outta your hide.”

“Curly, I told you not to drive ’em into that stream,” Everett replied, swinging his feet to the floor. “So don’t try to lay the blame on me.”

Curly reached for Everett’s shirtfront with his right hand. With a swift upward swing of his forearm, Everett knocked the cowboy’s hand away.

“Keep your paws off me,” Everett said, clenching his teeth.

“Stand up, you yeller skunk!” Curly yelled, stepping back.

Everett jumped up, and the two moved cagily toward the center of the room, their fiery eyes locked in a hard stare. Then Curly charged Everett, and the two cowboys crashed into the wall and spilled back onto the floor. Jumping to their feet again, fists began to fly. Most punches missed, but finally Everett landed a solid right to Curly’s jaw, buckling his knees and dropping him to the floor. Everett shook his hand in pain as he stepped outside.

Minutes later the bunkhouse door swung open, and Curly stepped out, his gun strapped on.

“Here’s yours,” the cowboy said, pitching Everett his gun belt. “You got lucky in there, but now I’m gonna kill you!”

“Curly, there’s no call for this,” Everett said, slowly strapping on his revolver. “I warned you those calves couldn’t make it. You know I did.”

"That don't matter! You didn't have to go and tell Smithey! You've got a big mouth, and I'm gonna shut it for good."

A few of the other cowboys stepped out, anticipating trouble.

"Boys, don't do this," an old hand said. "It ain't worth dyin' over. Sleep on it, and tomorrow it won't seem so blamed important."

"I'm gonna kill this yeller-bellied squealer right now!" Curly blurted out.

"Curly, don't touch that gun," Everett said. "I've already killed two men, and you ain't as fast as either of them."

"So you're a killer, are you? Well, that'll just add to the pleasure of drillin' you!" Curly bellowed.

"Curly," the old-timer said, "Everett here looks like he can handle a gun. You'd best cool down and walk away." He then glanced at Everett. "Young fellar, we don't need no gun-slick around here. It's time for you pack up and hit the trail."

"I'll be gone as soon as I get my things. But I'm takin' my horses."

"Okay," the old cowboy said. "I'll get 'em for you. Just get packed up. Come on, Curly. Let's take a walk."

Shooting a snarled look over his shoulder, Curly followed the old cowhand toward the corral.

Everett had stepped inside and was packing when a couple of the boys eased through the doorway. Never mind Curly, they insisted. He's just a hothead. And they reminded Everett that they needed every ranch hand available. Everett thanked them while stuffing his things inside his bedroll. Finished, he stepped outside with a group of the boys following.

"Hey, we know you done got a raw deal," one of them said, approaching Everett. "And we know you're broke. Here's a few dollars, and Butch is sackin' up some grub for you." He pushed a handful of coins toward Everett as Butch came out with a bulging white sack.

"Thanks a lot, fellas," Everett said, surprised.

As he accepted the bag of foodstuff, the old cowboy returned leading the saddled black and chestnut loaded with the packs. Curly stood back, leaning against the bunkhouse, while Everett stuffed his things into the boxes and tied his bedroll behind the saddle cantle.

Pulling himself up, he glanced around at their faces, tugged at his hat brim, and nudged the mare forward.

"Everett, keep a sharp eye out for Indians," Butch called after him. "Ridin' alone, you'll be a mighty easy target."

Everett headed west along the valley, reaching the foot of the Sangre de Cristo Mountains the second day. A light snowfall was spreading a white blanket over the ground, and the nights had grown bitterly cold. The mountains blocked his path, unless he chose to climb higher, but the peaks had long since disappeared behind a veil of white that also hid any possible mountain passes.

Stalled, he holed up in a small canyon protected from the harsh winds. After building a lean-to using cedar branches, he gathered a good supply of firewood, huddled around a warm blaze, and resigned himself to wait out the storm. If Harrison's men are out there, they won't find me here, Everett concluded. The snow would slow them, and it had already covered his trail.

For two days the storm held on, and Everett was running short on food. Soon, he would have to return to Las Vegas or find a way around the mountains.

The third day the storm ended, leaving ten inches of snow and drifts that could swallow a horse and rider. Having exhausted his at-hand supply of firewood and with deadfalls buried beneath the snow, Everett wandered into the trees along the edge of the valley, breaking low, dead limbs off old pines. Just as he reached to snap off a brittle branch, he heard a horse whinny. The direction told him it was not one of his own, so he dumped the wood, slipped behind a snow-draped cedar, and pulled out his revolver.

Three riders with buffalo robes draped over their shoulders appeared through a narrow window between the evergreens. They reined up, having spotted Everett's camp. He stepped out, his revolver leveled on the lead rider.

21

"Easy there, friend," a red-bearded man said, staring down at the muzzle of Everett's revolver. "We mean you no harm."

"What can I do for you?" Everett asked, holding his gun steady.

"Some hot coffee, maybe," the man said, "and a warm fire."

With the barrel of his pistol, Everett waved the men down and over to his smoldering fire. "Help yourselves."

Everett slipped the revolver back into its holster but kept his coattail pushed back. He gathered up the wood he had spilled earlier and met the visitors in camp. With one of the sticks, he pointed to his only cup, then fed limbs to the low blaze as their leader poured coffee.

"Where you boys headed?" Everett asked.

"The boss has some horses up in a mountain meadow," the redheaded man said. "We're on our way to see about 'em."

"What outfit are you with?"

"The Monte Largo," the cowboy said. "I'm called Red. This here's Tomas Lucero and he's Wolf Medran."

"I'm Johnny," Everett said, deciding on an alias.

"You're a little off the main trail, ain't you friend?" Red asked.

"I'm new out here. Got caught in the storm," Everett explained.

"This snow has caught us all a little off guard," Red said. "Maybe you'd like to join our bunch."

"I'd take a job," Everett replied, "if one was offered."

"You ride in to headquarters," the man suggested, "and ask for El Romo. Tell him Red sent you."

The cowboy gave directions to the ranch while his partners drained the coffeepot, then the visitors climbed up on their ponies and rode out.

The following day, Everett broke camp and headed for the Monte Largo. Two hours later he approached a clutter of buildings and a corral squeezed between two foothills. The buildings looked like miniatures against the towering mountains beyond the hillocks. He rode through a pole-framed entrance that had an iron VS hanging from the horizontal overhead beam. Pulling up at a hitching rail in front of the main building, he tied his ponies next to two others standing three-footed with their tails pushed between their hocks by the brisk breeze. Spotting a fellow just outside a small blacksmith shop, Everett headed over and watched him pry debris from the cleft of a brown and white filly's left front hoof.

"Hello, I'm Johnny Caruthers," Everett said, sticking with the false name. "Fella named Red told me to ask for El Romo."

Ignoring Everett, the cowboy picked up a horseshoe. After positioning it on the upturned hoof, a tack appeared between his lips. He took it and pounded it into place, then reached for another. When the shoe was firmly attached, the man let the hoof drop to the ground, moaned as he straightened his back, spit two more tacks into his hand, and turned to face Everett.

"I'm Zim. Romo's over to the house there," the man said, eyeing Everett.

"Much obliged to you," Everett said as he headed toward the white adobe structure.

A short, lean man answered his knock and stared at Everett a moment before speaking.

"Yeah, what do you want?" The man's tone was sharp, his voice gruff.

"You El Romo?" Everett asked.

"And who are you?"

"Johnny Caruthers. Red said you might need another hand."

"Where'd you see Red?"

"Back a ways, in the edge of the mountains. Red, Tomas, and Wolf were headed up to see about some horses."

"You a bronc buster?"

"Can't say that I am, but I'll give it a turn, if need be. I've done about everything else there is to do on a ranch."

"I don't need no tenderfoot, boy. I could use a cowboy that'll work hard and mind his own business. I don't allow no carousin', and you'd better be handy with a gun. This here's tough country."

"I don't go looking for trouble, but if it comes my way, I won't shy off," Everett said, dropping his hand to his revolver. "I can handle the job, if the pay's right."

"Ain't one in ten worth the grub they eat," Romo said, then pushed the screen door open and stepped out.

"I've ridden for three brands," Everett said, "and ain't nobody said I don't carry my weight."

"I'm offerin' a line job. You'll be stayin' in a cabin up there," the rancher said, pointing toward the mountainside. "You'll keep the cattle from wanderin' off into higher meadows and gettin' trapped in a storm. You gotta watch out for bears, coyotes, and the mountain cats. Kill 'em, run 'em off, or whatever, but keep 'em away from the stock. Keep a tally on the cattle and play nursemaid to the sick ones. They'll make it on buffalo grass and blue stem, even if it's covered by snow. I'll see to it you have plenty grub and ammunition, but otherwise you'll be on your own. Think you can handle it?"

"I reckon I can. As I said, if the pay's right."

"Ten a month with food, shelter, and an extra horse with ridin' gear. You'll cut your own firewood, do your own cookin', and you'll stay up there 'til winter's blowed itself out. Take it or leave it."

"I'm worth twenty, and I don't see nobody else waiting to sign up," Everett responded.

"I don't need help that bad. I'll make it twelve if you're on the job right now."

"Fifteen a month, and I use my own saddle and riggings."

El Romo stared at Everett long and hard, then nodded.

"And I want my horses fed before I go," Everett said. "I'll be ready to head out just as soon as you get my grub together, but I want the first month's pay up front."

"Tell Zim you're hired. He'll see to your supplies. And I'll pay you six now, and the rest when you get back, assumin' you stay through winter," the rancher replied, digging into his pocket for the money.

"I'll see you in the spring," Everett said, extending his right hand. The rancher smiled as he slapped six coins into Everett's palm.

"I'll keep your black pony here, just to make sure," the rancher said.

Everett put the black in the corral, dumped a pail of oats in a trough for her, then set a second bucket on the ground in front of the chestnut. He headed over to where Zim Walls now sat on the stoop of the bunkhouse, sipping coffee.

"Step inside," the foreman said when Everett explained he had been hired, then followed him through the doorway. "In that corner closet are spare gloves and some old boots. Help yourself while I sack up your grub and oil for the lantern. And you'll need a map to the place."

With his gear rounded up, Everett followed the foreman to the corral. Zim suggested a bay gelding for his packhorse. The chestnut finished the bucket of oats while they packed and strapped down the supplies on the gelding. Everett climbed into the saddle, clutching the lead rope for the packhorse.

"Come spring, I'll be back," Everett said, reaching down for the hand-drawn map.

"I'll send more grub up in about a month," Zim said. "Be careful. There's trouble aplenty for a man off up there by himself."

Everett followed the sketchy map and arrived at the line shack the next day. It sat on a stony mountainside bench, a couple of hundred feet up from the valley floor. A noisy stream tumbled down the slope just east of the sturdy log cabin, which faced the valley and was covered with a wood-shingled, V-shaped roof. Inside was a cast-iron stove with firewood stacked just to the right of the door. Soot-covered pots and pans hung from wall nails, and an old cot stretched across the back wall. Heavy wooden shutters covered two small windows, one centered on each side wall. Protection against Indians, Everett guessed. An old lantern hung from a thick beam above a small, three-legged, oak table, centered in the room and accompanied by two old cowhide-bottom chairs pushed against it. The rough, split-log floor felt solid.

Everett removed the packs and saddles, then turned the horses loose in a pole corral attached to a lean-to that, with some repairs, would offer the ponies decent protection from the weather.

Each day after taking an initial tally of the herd, he rode among the cattle down in the long valley, getting familiar with the layout, watching for newborns, and checking for predators. Late afternoons he chopped wood, determined that he would at all times have enough to get through a three-day storm. Nights, he sat at his table, enjoying the cozy cabin and reading dime novels some previous cowboy had left.

One morning while riding near the north end of the valley, Everett spotted two riders approaching a small gathering of cows and calves grazing alongside the stream up ahead. Not sure who the visitors were and hoping they had not spotted him, Everett slipped into a grove of pines and watched.

One rode into the herd, pointing, while the other slipped his rifle out. Unsheathing his Winchester, Everett spurred his pony out into the clearing and headed for the men. The one with the rifle glanced up, then balanced the gun across his saddle front while his partner dismounted and knelt down, apparently studying tracks in the damp soil beside the stream.

"What's going on here?" Everett asked, his eyes on the one with the rifle.

"We ride for a brand up the valley a ways," the man explained. "A big cat has killed three newborn in the last month."

"Think he's headed this way?" Everett asked.

"Yeah. He made a kill early this mornin'," the cowboy said. "We followed his bloody tracks this direction. We figured he might've stopped here for a drink."

"I haven't seen any sign," Everett said, "but I'll keep an eye out."

When Everett turned and rode south, pushing the little herd along, the tracker remounted, and they headed north. Everett glanced back, and when the two were out of sight, he rode back to where they had met along the stream. He swung down and checked for lion tracks. Boot marks scuffed the sand, and a few cow tracks, but no paw prints.

That afternoon, he again headed up the valley to the north, looking for evidence of the cat or its killings. Seeing fresh horse tracks along a narrow trail, he followed them up the mountainside and into a thick grove of spruce trees. Continuing on the path for some time, he spotted a gutted deer hanging from a tree. Nearby, bear hides stretched taut across pole racks. Looking closer, a cabin lay hidden behind a thick row of spruce. With his rifle pulled, Everett approached the half cabin, half dugout. Finding no one around, he soon turned back down the trail toward his herd.

Two days later with a light snow melting, a bawling cow at the north end of the valley got his attention. Arriving, Everett recognized the agitated longhorn and guessed that she was searching for her near-weaned calf. Soon he spotted a splotch of blood on the brown grass. Checking closely for paw prints and claw marks, those characteristic of a bear or cougar, he became puzzled at finding none. But he did spot broken blades of dried grass, then beneath them, marks of boot heels sunken into the soft ground.

Suspicious, he headed for the hidden cabin, but before he got there, he ran into four men on the trail. He recognized the pair of trackers riding ahead, but not the two fellows behind, each wearing a badge.

"What have they done?" Everett asked the sheriff.

"Theft, and maybe more" the lawman said. "They rob folks along the trails, then disappear into their hideout up there. And they kill deer, elk, bear, even pine martens, and sell their hides in Las Vegas."

"What's a pine marten?" Everett asked.

"Little black bird, a furry thing. Good market for their hides."

The lawmen then explained how they caught their prisoners.

Earlier, the prisoners had stopped a couple on the Santa Fe Trail and looted their wagon. The following day, the man who had been robbed recognized the thieves selling hides to a dealer in town and alerted the lawmen. Finding the robbers gone when they arrived, the sheriff and his partner hatched a plan. First, they had removed their badges and stepped inside the tanner's store.

"There ain't no black pine martens around here," the sheriff had said, approaching the hide dealer.

"You're dead wrong," his deputy had countered. "I've seen 'em."

"I'll bet you ten dollars," the sheriff had challenged.

"Ten for every hide I find?" the deputy had asked.

When the sheriff had nodded agreement, the tradesman had turned toward them.

"You lose," he had said to the sheriff, smiling.

"What do you mean?" the sheriff had asked.

The man had then pulled out two small, black, furry hides.

"That's twenty dollars you owe me," the deputy had crowed.

Shaking his head, the sheriff had handed over the money, then turned to walk away.

"You sure those hides are from these parts?" he had asked the dealer.

"Yep. Couple of hunters from up in the wilderness brought 'em in," the man had said, lowering his voice. "And I know hides. These are fresh ones."

With a little prodding, the tanner had revealed the hunters' names and had given directions to their hideout. The two lawmen had stepped outside, where the deputy had returned the sheriff's twenty dollars, mounted up, and they had headed for the hideout.

"Did you see any evidence of a butchered calf around their cabin?" Everett asked.

"Matter of fact, we did," the sheriff replied.

"I think you can add cattle rustling to the charge," Everett said.

The lawmen followed Everett to the bloody spot while he explained about his prior meeting with the hunters and his suspicions. The prisoners denied having killed the calf, but the lawmen seemed convinced.

The following morning Everett decided to ride up to the hunter's hideout and look around. After checking on the herd, he headed up the mountain where six inches of fresh snow had collected. He searched the cabin, finding hides of various animals, mostly elk and bear, and those of three calves scarred with the VS brand.

He remounted and headed back toward the trail. As he crossed a narrow valley, he spotted a man on a lame mule leading a burro and wearing a priest's frock. Concerned, Everett rode along in the edge of a grove of spruce, avoiding the deeper snow and hoping to intercept the slow-moving priest. When he found the trail, he waited in the trees until the clergyman and his limping mule rounded a shoulder of the mountain. Spotting Everett, the man stopped abruptly about thirty feet away.

"Hello," Everett called out as he approached the priest.

The man waited in silence.

"What's the problem with your mule?" Everett asked.

"Stepped into a drift back there a ways," the clergyman explained. "But he's getting along okay."

"Where you headed?"

"Mora."

"How far?"

"About fifteen miles."

"If I'm any judge, you'll never make it."

"Once we head down the mountain, the snow won't be so bad. I'll get down and lead him."

"There's a vacant cabin across the valley," Everett said. "You could hole up there 'til that leg gets better."

"I'm awfully short on supplies," the priest said.

"I've got some in my saddlebags," Everett said. "Enough to hold you over a couple of days."

The priest nodded his head, and Everett turned and led the way. When they reached the hideout, Everett slipped down and untied one of the pack boxes on the burro.

"I'll get that," the priest said, rushing his way.

"I don't mind," Everett said, straining to lift the box, which carried most of its weight in its bottom.

"What's in this thing?" Everett asked, struggling toward the door.

"Please, just set it down," the priest said, blocking Everett's path. "If you'll be so kind as to care for my mule, I'll get the boxes."

Lowering it to the ground, Everett headed over to the lame mule while the priest struggled to maneuver the box inside.

When Everett had unsaddled the mule and checked his swollen leg, he went back around and got the burro. By that time the clergyman was dragging the second box toward the cabin.

With the animals cared for, Everett grabbed his saddlebags and stepped inside. He pulled out some coffee, bacon, and cold biscuits he always carried in case Harrison's men should suddenly show up, and set them on the table while the priest reached inside his frock.

"I don't have any coins," the man said, handing over a small leather pouch.

"No charge," Everett said. "You can return the favor on down the road."

"My conscience insists," the priest responded, pushing the pouch into Everett's coat pocket.

With the clergyman settled and daylight waning, Everett said goodbye and headed back to his line shack. It was dark and bitterly cold when he stepped inside, lit his fire, and pulled off his coat. Hanging it on a nail, he remembered the pouch. Stepping over to the lantern, he loosened the drawstrings, and poured its contents into his palm. He let out a shrill whistle.

Gold dust.

22

Everett bolted upright on his rickety cot. The night air was a chilly twenty degrees, yet his face was soaked in perspiration. In the nightmare from which he had just awakened, a half-dozen of Harrision's men, led by Stonewall Carter, had trapped him in a box-end canyon.

Returning to reality, Everett lay back and closed his eyes, but could not sleep. Was it a forewarning? Should he pack up and ride out at sunup? He rolled out of bed, dressed, rebuilt his fire, boiled water for coffee, and then sat sipping from a tin cup when he remembered the pouch of gold dust.

After emptying the bag's contents onto the table, he stood admiring the glittering mound. He guessed it amounted to two or three ounces, worth thirty to forty dollars. Where did the priest get it? Was there more in those pack boxes? The lure of gold strengthened while the fear spawned by the nightmare weakened. After winter, he just might go back up there where he met the priest and look around.

Breakfast over, he slipped on his coat, gloves, and chaps, then stepped outside. The air carried a deep chill, even while the half-hour-old sun glared off heavy frost, almost blinding him. Saddled up, he headed down to the pastureland, then turned north to take a fresh tally of the herd.

He found a group of cows and calves huddled for warmth, thirty-two mothers and about half that number of offspring, all less than a year old. Soon he spotted four other clusters of cattle, a total of maybe three hundred cows and a hundred twenty calves.

Farther on, he rounded up twenty more cows, most with newborns, and pushed them back to the main herd. After making a similar gather to the south, the herd totaled five hundred twenty-two cows and two hundred sixty-five calves. He knew of only the one loss, and the tally was now eighteen above his original one, newborns accounting for the addition.

Throughout the winter, the cow-count in his weekly tallies never varied more than three, counting errors he guessed, while the number of calves grew steadily. Finding scraps from deer carcasses in a remote meadow, he followed cougar tracks, made easy by the almost-constant snow cover, but gave up each time when the trail climbed into the deep snow high on the mountainside. The weather was biting cold, with frequent snowstorms, but each produced only a few inches of groundcover. The cattle managed amazingly well, pawing through to the cured buffalo grass below.

After the nightmare, he kept an eye out for Stonewall Carter and his band of riders, but as weeks passed Everett grew lax and unconcerned. Throughout winter only one passable path led to the line shack, and the north window gave him full view of it for at least seventy yards.

The one thing that haunted him was his concern for Tabitha. During long winter days and nights with the wind howling outside and snow thrashing against the north window, he often sat by his old stove, warming and thinking. How he wished he could see her, talk to her, reassure her. But Samuel Harrison had money and power, and no doubt he and his men had poisoned the minds of everyone who had listened to their slanted story. Probably Tabitha had heard their side of what happened. What did she think now?

From that cold evening when he had ridden away from her, hope of returning had driven him to survive, to keep ahead of Harrison's pack of bloodhounds. Doubt that he would return to her waiting arms had never entered his mind. But now, isolated in a bitterly cold mountain wilderness hundreds of miles away, months having gone by, he wondered. If he ever got back there, would it be too late? Was it already too late?

Once while returning from the herd with a sickly newborn calf across his horse's shoulders and its bawling mother following, he remembered that winter day when he had ridden in from the snow-covered range and Tabitha had met him, running and falling in the deep snow. She had hugged him, and it seemed everything changed between them after that. He wished she would be standing outside the cabin now, waiting.

About the end of January, a cowboy from the ranch brought more supplies. Before giving him a rundown on the herd, Everett asked of any news from headquarters. He was relieved at no mention of a posse asking about him. The following day, after a hearty breakfast and soaking up warmth from the old stove, the visitor returned to the ranch.

Everett had no calendar and made no attempt to count the days, but with the first extended warm-up, the ground thawed, and new grass sprang up almost overnight.

After one last inspection and tally of the cattle, Everett packed up, saddled his pony, and arrived at ranch headquarters mid-afternoon of the next day. He headed over to the horse corral where the foreman was hanging on the fence, watching some cowboys reacquaint a couple of horses with a saddle and a curb bit. Everett slid out of the leather seat and climbed up beside his boss.

"Well, Johnny, it looks like you made it through the winter. Any problems with the cattle?" Zim asked, catching Everett off guard with the alias.

"Nope," he said. "We started the winter with about five hundred and twenty cows and two hundred and thirty calves. Last count I made showed we'd lost a couple of cows, but the calf count was up to about two hundred and sixty-five, with only one loss that I know of."

"That's better'n most years. I'd say you did a right good job, cowboy."

"What's next, boss?"

"Roundup, countin', and brandin', but we'll let the land dry a little more before we head out. You can help with repairs and breakin' these new horses until we head for the range. Find an empty cot in the bunkhouse and chunk your things on it. I'll see to your horses."

"Boss, if I can collect my pay, I'd like to ride into town and get a few things," Everett said.

"You're due a day off," Zim said. "I'll see El Romo about your wages."

When Everett had put his things away, he eased back to the corral where the chestnut and bay were crunching oats. Searching for the black mare, he pushed through the throng of horses, but she was not there.

As he scaled the fence and made a beeline for the ranch house, Zim stepped out the front door and headed his way.

"Where's my black mare?" Everett asked, angrily.

"El Romo said she needed exercise, so he told Martin to ride her a few days," Zim replied, handing over the balance of his pay.

"Who's Martin?"

"He does the horse buyin' and tradin' for Romo."

"When I get back from Las Vegas, I expect her to be in the corral," Everett said sternly.

The following morning Everett headed for town. He stopped by the Montezuma hot springs and took a long, soothing bath. In town he headed for the bank, where he set the pouch of gold dust on the counter.

"Where'd you come by this?" the attendant asked.

"A priest," Everett replied.

The attendant laughed at the seemingly preposterous answer, then slipped through a doorway and disappeared into a back room. Two minutes later, the man returned with a bank officer.

"Harry says you got this from a priest," the owner said, raising his left eyebrow. "Where?"

"Met him on a trail up in the wilderness," Everett replied. "He had a lame mule and needed supplies."

The man nodded, and a smile broke across his face. "Father Tafoya. Says he goes up to give spiritual service to the sheepherders up there. Some folks in Mora say he's got a hidden gold mine, a good one. I never believed it."

He handed the pouch to the attendant and instructed him to weigh it. The teller soon returned and handed over thirty-eight dollars. Everett stuffed the money into his pocket, remembering that when he had met the priest, the herders had long since taken their sheep down from the mountain.

Everett bought his supplies and got a room in the Plaza Hotel. After a good meal, he slipped into bed, relishing comfort he had not known in quite some time.

After an early breakfast, he saddled his horse and headed back for the ranch. Reaching the entrance, he put the chestnut mare into an easy lope right up to the corral gate. A quick search told him the black mare was still missing. He spurred the chestnut over to the ranch house, hit the ground on the run, and banged on the door.

"Johnny," Romo called out through the screen door. "What's the . . ."

"Where's my black mare?"

"I thought Martin would be back by now," he said, stepping out. "Zim!"

The foreman came striding across the dirt yard.

"Have you seen Martin?" Romo asked.

"He's in the bunkhouse."

Everett leaped down from the porch, heading that way.

"Johnny," Zim said, catching his arm, "the black mare's gone."

"What do you mean?" Everett asked, jerking his arm free.

"Stolen," the foreman said. "She, along with four other horses, was taken by Apaches who raided the corral out at the western line shack."

"You owe me twenty-five dollars," Everett said, turning to Romo.

"Sometimes horses get stolen," the rancher said. "Could happen to anybody."

"I want my horse or my money, and I want it now!"

"Who's gonna pay me for the four I lost?" the rancher asked.

"That's your problem," Everett replied.

"Look, Johnny," El Romo said, stepping down from the porch. "We bring lots of horses in here. You hang around, and I'll see that you get a good one."

"I won't be here that long," Everett said, grabbing the reins of the chestnut and heading for the bunkhouse.

He chunked his things onto his blanket, rolled and tied it, threw it on the chestnut, and galloped her through the ranch entrance. He did not slow down until he reached Las Vegas. In the Imperial Saloon on Moreno Street, angry and tongue-loosened by whiskey, he told his story to a couple of tough-looking cowboys.

"Indians never stole your horse," one said. "That rancher done it, him and his buyer, El Moro."

"Martin," Everett corrected.

"Martin Gonzales, but he's called El Moro, The Moor," the man explained. "He knows this country like its creator, every hidin' place within three hundred miles. And that's likely where your black mare is now, in one of his hideouts."

"Maybe not," the second one said, then lowered his voice. "There's a ring of horse thieves around here. I've heard that the Monte Largo is somehow in cahoots with them."

"Who's their leader?" Everett asked.

"Fella named Vicente Silva," the man whispered. "He owns this saloon, but stays hid out. I've seen him around a few times late at night. And some of his boys come in here, now and then. You say I told you so, I'll swear I've never seen you."

"Any of that bunch here now?" Everett asked, glancing around.

"Don't see one," the man said, "but come Saturday evenin', I expect they'll show up."

Everett, somewhat sobered by the information, thanked the boys and lumbered to his room. He hung around the next couple of days, spending time in the saloon and, after swearing to secrecy, received a fair description of Silva and a couple of his bandit cowboys.

About sundown on Saturday, Everett headed for The Imperial, got a drink, and squeezed in behind a corner table. An hour later, a couple of rough-faced, unkempt cowboys came in. They had the markings, so Everett watched them closely. When he had about decided they were no different from half of those around, the bartender, Gabriel Sandoval, grabbed a bottle and stepped over to his table. While the man refilled his glass, Everett kept eyeing the pair of newcomers.

"Those two," Sandoval whispered, then nodded his head toward the backs of the two rugged cowboys, "they work for Silva."

Everett paid for the refill and the information, then grabbed his glass and headed to the bar where the two stood gulping down their whiskey.

"Okay if I join you boys?" Everett asked.

"You buyin'?" one asked.

"Bartender," Everett called out, "refills for my friends."

"You two look like cowhands," Everett said. "And I'm fresh outta work."

"We've chased a cow or two," the older one said.

"Any ideas where I might land a job?"

"The Monte Largo, maybe," the man suggested.

"I've worn out my welcome there," Everett said. "Your outfit short-handed?"

"The boss is mighty particular," the older one said with a warning glance toward his partner.

"I'm hard up, boys," Everett said, shaking his head. "Would you put in a good word for me?"

"Sure," the man replied. "You stayin' around here?"

"The Plaza," Everett replied, "but I'll be broke in a couple of days."

"Got a name?"

"Just ask for Johnny, here or at the hotel."

The older one sniggered. "Just Johnny? The marshal know you're in town?"

"I ain't on the best of terms with the law," Everett said, leaning close to the older one. "I find horses a lot friendlier."

Everett then motioned for the bartender to refill the cowboys' glasses.

"Keep 'em full until this is used up," he said, pitched two coins onto the counter, and walked out.

Two days later a neatly dressed man called on Everett at the hotel.

"You Johnny?" he asked.

"I am."

"I'm Vicente Silva," the man said, brushing past Everett into the room, then turned. "I hear you need work."

"That's right," Everett said. "And I ain't particular."

"Can you handle that six-shooter or does it just balance the gold in your left pocket?"

"Too good to suit the law," Everett replied to the first part, and was instantly mighty curious about the second.

"Let me see your pistol," Silva said, reaching out.

"I don't hand my gun over to anybody," Everett replied. "My gold neither."

"How do I know you can use it?" Silva asked, cutting his eyes down to the revolver.

"Stand any man you've got in front of me," Everett said, "and I'll put him down."

"That include me?" Silva asked, smirking.

Everett glared at Silva for a second, then backed up a couple of paces and squared himself in front of the large man.

"Some other time, kid," Silva said, his face turning solemn. "You ready to ride?"

Everett grabbed his saddlebags, hat, and bedroll. He followed the man downstairs, paid the desk clerk, then stepped out where the chestnut was hitched. Everything latched down, he climbed up, and trailed Silva out of town, heading north.

A mile later, the man doubled back toward the mountains, explaining he never rode straight from town to camp. Watching their back trail, they rode hard for the canyon west of town. By dark, they had broken off into a tree-choked side canyon. Twenty minutes later, they came to Silva's camp.

All evening the man kept a cautious eye on Everett who did his best to fit in with the rough gang. After coffee and bacon the next morning, they saddled up.

"Johnny," Silva said, "I have a few horses in a high mountain meadow. Some of the boys watch after them, break them that needs it, and shuffle some down to the ranch. It's blasted cold and lonesome up there. Most don't like it none. But, I expect you might be different."

"What's the pay?"

"Twenty-five a month, if you mind your work and don't ask questions. Supplies are brought up regularly, and there's a couple of cabins."

"Sounds like my kind of place, but I'm worth more than twenty-five."

"You prove yourself, there're be a fat bonus for you."

"I'll remember that," Everett said, his eyes narrowing. "And see to it that you do, too."

"Librado," Silva said, glaring at Everett, "sketch him a map and write a note tellin' the boys in the high meadow to let this fella in. Whether he ever rides out is up to them."

From his shirt pocket, Librado Polanco pulled out a piece of wrinkled paper, and with the stub of a pencil, he scratched out a map and a short note, handing the folded paper to Everett.

"I'll be ridin' over to headquarters," Silva said, turning to the other boys.

"Where is that?" Everett asked.

"You don't hand over your gun," Silva said, sneering, "and I don't leave my door open to strangers."

Everett nodded with a smile, then watched the man climb up on his horse.

"Now, it'll take you two, maybe three days," he said to Everett. "There's a pass up about eight thousand feet. This time of year, you'll find snow, lots of it in places, so stay on the main trail."

Everett stared at the map for a moment. From his wanderings into the wilderness while at the line shack, he recognized some of the trail. He stared up at the mountains, trying to memorize the layout.

"Who do I ask for?" Everett wanted to know.

"Go to the cabin circled on the map, and ask for George. He's the boss up there. Just show him the note."

Everett stuck the paper into his shirt pocket.

"One more thing," Silva said. "Don't go snoopin' around. Just do your job, and mind your own business. The boys up there ain't very sociable."

The winding path up the mountainside quickly became steep and slippery. Near the pass, the snow was five feet deep in places, so staying on the trail was impossible. But, each time Everett strayed, he managed to get back. Making camp required pushing back two to three feet of snow, and the bone-chilling nights seemed endless. Firewood had to be gathered from horseback, breaking off low limbs from pines. Often a howling wind swept across the slopes, whipping up surface snow like a dust storm and forcing him to pull up behind a large, snow-capped boulder for protection.

Four days later in the dusk of late evening, he found himself on the high rim of a narrow valley, peering down on a herd of shaggy horses milling around in the meadow, pawing at snow to reach grass a foot below. A narrow stream split the banana-shaped hollow, flowing from snowy peaks to the west. Tired and saddle-weary, Everett checked the map, then turned along the rim and soon spotted the circled cabin. Cautious but eager for warmth and food, he made his way over. About fifteen feet from the door, he swung down, looped the reins around the hitch rail, and headed for the dark entrance. The levering action of a Winchester cracked the winter air, causing Everett to whirl around.

"Hold it right there, cowboy," a scratchy voice said.

Everett could barely make out the image of a bearded man half hidden behind a large pine, aiming a rifle at him.

"What's your business here?" the man asked.

"Vicente Silva sent me," Everett replied. "I'm to ask for George."

"Slip your gun belt off and drop it to the ground."

"I just told you Silva sent me. There's no need . . ."

"Drop your gun belt, or I'll fill you with lead, cowboy."

With his eyes glaring and his teeth clenched, Everett unbuckled it and let it fall.

"Turn around and face the door," the man instructed. "Now move, but take it slow."

Everett eased toward the door, crunching along in the snow while the man behind snatched up his gun belt.

"I'll open it," the bearded man said, nudging Everett to the side with his gun barrel. "Bein' a stranger, you might catch a belly full of lead."

Keeping his rifle trained on Everett, the man rapped on the door.

"This is Red. I'm comin' in," the man announced as he lifted the latch and pushed open the door. "Got a lost cowboy with me."

Lamplight poured through the doorway as Everett stepped in, momentarily blinded. When his eyes adjusted, he faced three men standing behind a table across the room. Each wore guns low on their hips, the bottom end of their scabbards strapped to their legs. Everett recognized two of them, the one called Wolf and his partner Tomas. The one behind him with the rifle, the bearded man, would be Red. They had stopped by his camp during the snowstorm and told him about the Monte Largo ranch. The middle one in front of him, the largest of the men, with a coarse round face, a full black beard, and small dark eyes, he did not know.

"Bandanna," Red said, "he says Silva sent him. He asked for George."

"What're you here for?" the black-bearded man asked.

"To help out with the horses," Everett replied.

"You don't look like no bronc buster to me. You ever broke a wild horse, a stallion?" Bandanna asked.

"I can do anything you boys can," Everett replied, forcing a smile.

"Bet you can't do this," Bandanna said, snatching the revolver on his hip in a flash and training its muzzle dead center of Everett's midsection.

Everett flinched, then anger flared inside him as the men belly-laughed.

"You're only half right," Everett said, a hard ridge running the length of his jaw, "which makes you dead wrong."

Laughter stopped. Bandanna George moved slowly around the table, pushing Tomas aside, and stood facing Everett from across the room. With his eyes fixed hard on the young cowboy, he holstered his revolver.

"And just what part am I wrong about, you wet-eared pup?" Bandanna asked.

"Give me my gun, and I'll show you," Everett replied, matching the dark-eyed man's stare. Everett then extended his left hand back toward the man holding his gun belt.

"Give it to him!" Bandanna blurted out.

Red eased it across Everett's open palm, then sidestepped three feet to the left.

With anger somehow settling his nerves, Everett strapped it on, never taking his eyes off Bandanna.

The big man's nostrils flared, and his jaw muscles bulged as he flexed his right hand.

23

Horse Thief Meadow
April, 1884

"I didn't come here looking for trouble," Everett said, his eyes steady on the big man, "but if that's what you want, I won't turn tail."

Slowly, he eased his left hand into his shirt pocket and pulled out the note.

"Maybe you ought to take a look," he said, pitching the note across the dirty floor.

The chestnut whinnied outside; the wind moaned. Inside, no one moved until Bandanna motioned for Wolf, a stocky man wearing a bearskin coat, to pick up the note.

"It's sure enough from Silva," the man said. "It's signed by Polanco and says this Johnny fella has been hired. Bandanna, you're to send El Indio back to the ranch."

"Boss," Red said, "we've got a good thing here. Why go and mess it up?"

Still the big man smoldered, glaring at Everett. Then his eyes shifted to Wolf as he reached for the note.

"Kid, you're lucky today," Bandanna said, looking up from the paper, "but if you ever cross me, I'll kill you like you was a snake."

"I've killed a few rattlers myself," Everett said, then managed a faint smile.

"Get 'im outta my sight!" the big man bellowed, grabbing a chair and slamming it against the wall.

Red motioned Everett outside. "I'll take 'im over to the cabin on the north ridge," he said, then pulled the door closed behind him.

"I've never seen him so mad," Red said to Everett who was untying his horse. "He wanted to kill you, real bad."

"I knew he wasn't going to draw," Everett said as Red headed for his mount.

"What?" the man asked, spinning around on his heel.

"When a man hesitates that long, he starts to doubt, maybe even think about dying."

"Not Bandanna," Red said. "He's ain't afraid of nothin'."

"Then, why didn't he draw?"

"I just don't know," Red said after giving it some thought. "Let's get you outta here before he changes his mind."

Everett swung up on his horse while Red climbed aboard a roan, and they headed out along a narrow, winding trail that traced the rugged mountain rim overlooking the dark meadow.

Riding along in the dark, Red twisted in his saddle and glanced back at Everett.

"Look," he said. "Bandanna's bad, a man-killer. And Wolf's a back-shooter. You've done crossed 'em, so I expect you better ride outta here, come mornin'."

"How come you're still here?" Everett asked, realizing the man was trying to help him.

"I've worked for Silva a lot longer than Bandanna, and no man lives after crossin' Vicente Silva."

"Since Silva hired me," Everett said, laughing, "I reckon I'd better stay, too."

Red stopped his pony and looked back at Everett.

"Would you have drawed down on Bandanna?"

"He never doubted it," Everett replied.

Red smiled, then shook his head. "You must be fast, kid, real fast."

The cabin at the north end of the valley rested on a high, rock-formed promontory at an altitude just over nine thousand feet. The site offered an excellent view of the meadow, which was bounded by mountains on three sides, and directly overlooked the north pass. The deep, narrow stream meandered through the lush pasture then fell through the pass, its noisy rapids settling into a narrow canyon rivulet some two hundred feet down the mountainside. The only entrances to the meadow were from the rugged trail Everett used earlier and the north pass.

"Wait here," Red said, sliding down and making his way to the cabin door.

Within minutes, a Comanche wearing Mexican-style clothes stepped out, glanced at Everett, then disappeared around the corner of the cabin, soon returning with a saddled horse. After latching a bedroll across his mount's hips, he swung up.

"Indio," Red said as the man turned his pony toward the trail, "hold up. I'll be ridin' back with you."

Alone, Everett stepped inside the cabin. The sturdy structure was outfitted with a wood-burning stove, a small table with two chairs, a cot, and a lantern that sat on the table along with a couple of pans for cooking, and a blackened kettle. Its two windows were small and smoke-stained.

Outside, a pole corral without a shelter for his horses abutted the back of the cabin. The boulder-covered ground wore a blanket of snow, though north winds often raked the exposed ridge, blowing most of the flakes into rock crevices and onto the harsh slopes.

Though the prior confrontation with Bandanna and impending showdown wore on Everett's mind, a roaring fire in the old stove warmed the room and soothed his mind, and he soon drifted off to sleep.

Up early, he had breakfast, then stepped outside onto a granite ledge protruding over the edge of the pass. Though his job had not been defined, the purpose of the site was obvious. He must guard the entrance, keeping the horses in while shutting out intruders. Harsh travel conditions and remoteness were likely to preclude casual visitors, but Silva had said ranch horses were taken to and from the high meadow. Likely they came through the north pass. He wondered about the source of new horses. Surely some were wild mustangs, but he was just as certain that others wore brands of area ranches.

He saddled the chestnut mare and followed a steep trail down to the meadow. Before he reached the horse herd, something ripped through the snow-laden grass just ahead and thudded into the soft ground, followed instantly by the boom of a rifle that echoed through the valley. Everett jerked his eyes to the high rim where the east cabin sat, settling on the huge form of Bandanna. When the man raised the rifle to his shoulder again, Everett spun his pony around and rode back to the promontory.

He spent the rest of the day, as well as the next several, roaming the area around the pass and becoming familiar with the layout, but he avoided the valley floor. Using limbs from nearby spruce trees, he fashioned a shelter for his horses, then swept and dusted the unkempt cabin and built up his reserve of firewood. All the while, the others hung out around the east cabin.

Then a couple of weeks later, Red showed up at the north cabin.

"Thought I'd best check on you," he explained to Everett, "and let you know that tomorrow we'll be splittin' the herd and takin' about half down to the ranch."

"Want me to lend a hand?" Everett asked.

"Orders are for you to keep away from the operation," Red replied.

The following morning Everett watched from the granite ledge as four cowboys separated out a little herd and drove it through the pass beneath him.

A week passed with no other visible activity, leading Everett to wonder if he was the only cowboy left in the high, mountain meadow. Curious, he rode over to the cabin on the east rim. It was vacant.

Turning his pony, he headed down the steep slope to the meadow below. He roamed through the horses, an eye out for his black mare. She was not there, but he noted something especially interesting. The horses all wore a recently applied brand, the VS.

Right after lunch one afternoon, Everett heard the pounding of hooves, along with the shrill whistles and shouts of men. They were coming from the dense forest below the north pass. From atop a large boulder, he scanned the approach, readying his rifle and six-gun. Soon a herd of maybe thirty horses broke through the timberline, following a narrow trail alongside the stream. Red, Bandanna, Wolf, and Tomas trailed the ponies, swinging coiled lariats overhead. The horses thundered through the rocky pass into the lush meadow, the snow mostly gone now. Everett scanned the ponies for any blacks while Red turned his mount up the steep trail toward him, leaving his partners to follow the band of ponies.

Approaching Everett, the haggard-looking cowboy rode slumped in the saddle.

"We've brought in a new bunch, kid," Red said. "Watch the pass real close. There might be trouble from some boys who tried to rustle them from us back there a ways. If you see riders, fire two rapid shots, wait for a count of three, then fire two more. Hold 'em off the best you can. We'll come a'runnin'."

Everett nodded, and Red turned to leave, then stopped and glanced back.

"The next couple of days, we'll be brandin' the mustangs. Just do your job and don't go meddlin'."

Nighttime came, and the thin mountain air turned crisp. Everett sat on the large boulder overlooking the pass, gazing at the huge western sky, the stars brilliant against its flawless purplish-blue background. A half-moon glowed so bright that he could easily make out individual horses in the meadow, the silvery light gleaming on their shiny backs.

Near midnight, Everett sat bundled on the boulder, every breath turning to steam. While scanning the timberline bordering the peaceful meadow, a blur of movement about a hundred feet up the west mountainside caught his eye. Watching closely, he spotted a cougar cautiously padding his way down toward the lazing horses. Everett snatched his rifle, jumped on the chestnut, and scrambled down the steep incline toward the meadow floor.

As he charged up the valley, the languid horses stirred from their rest, watched curiously, then trotted away to the far end. The alert mountain lion broke off his planned attack and bounded back up the steep slope, disappearing into the black shadows of the trees.

Everett turned to trail the big cat but soon thought better of following it into the dark forest. Back in the meadow, he eased among the now quieted horses. In the moonlight, he hoped to get a closer look at the three black ponies he had spotted earlier. He soon realized that he could not distinguish between deep brown, blood-red bay, and black ponies.

Locating the brand on a pony's hip, his finger traced a T resting on top of a W, the middle point of the W supporting the pedestal of the T. The brand meant nothing to him, other than it was not Silva's VS. Also, these were not unbranded mustangs.

Back at the cabin, he kept a vigilant lookout for the big cat, but it must have gone in search of other prey. As daylight eased over the eastern rim into the meadow, Everett stood on the granite ledge, his blurred eyes searching the band of horses. Based on age, size, and coloring, he felt sure he had spotted his young black mare. Anger boiled in his chest, tempting him to dash down and grab her, but an inner voice convinced him that Bandanna and his thieves would give chase. If there was to be a showdown with the bandit leader, let it happen here, the only chance he had of riding away without keeping a lookout over his shoulder.

All day Everett kept an eye on the north pass from his guard post, while sneaking peeks at the horse herd and yearning for a closer look at his black mare. Further, he guessed that if the so-called rustlers showed up, their mounts would wear the TW brand.

The second day the four cowboys from the east cabin rode down into the meadow and cut out ponies for the re-branding process. Everett watched anxiously, ready for a fight if they included the black mare. Maybe because she wore no brand, they passed over her in favor of ridding the herd of the TW brand.

Two days later, half an hour after midday, Everett again stood on the granite ledge, watching the pass. Suddenly, he heard the squeak of saddle leather from the rim trail behind him, and whirled around while drawing his revolver, a split-second blur of motion.

"Don't shoot!" Red called out, lifting his hands shoulder-high. Then as Everett put his gun away, the cowboy swung down. "You're quick, kid. Maybe you are quicker than Bandanna."

"I'm sorry, Red," Everett said, walking to meet him. "I'm a little jumpy, I guess."

"You've a right to be," Red replied. "I'm on my way to Mora, a small town about twenty miles away. I thought you might like to ride along."

"I guess I'd better keep a lookout," Everett said.

"Horsefeathers! Them rustlers ain't comin'. They'd have been here already, if they was. Come along with me. I could use some company."

Reluctantly, Everett saddled his mare and followed Red down the slope to the north pass. After changing trails three or four times, crossing two streams, and riding down a deep canyon, they broke through the tree line onto a heavily used trail that took them to Mora.

Red made a beeline for the hitching rail in front of the adobe saloon, then stepped inside while Everett hung back on the boardwalk, scanning the street. Spotting a general store, he headed that way, slipped inside, and tested a couple of new hats. He left the store, then slouched back against the side of the building, lifting his old gray hat and blowing dust from its crown and brim.

He glanced up as a cowboy slid down off his buckskin pony, hitched the reins, and headed inside. The man's pant legs were tucked inside his decorated boot tops, which clearly bore the letters T over W. Everett eased over to the buckskin and ran his hand across the now-familiar brand.

While keeping an eye out for Red, Everett waited around until the TW man came out the front door of the store, a package in his hands. Seeing Everett standing beside his buckskin, the cowman hesitated.

"I'm new to the area," Everett said. "What does the TW stand for?"

"Tom Worlon, owner of the ranch. Why the interest, stranger?" the man asked.

"The TW sell horses?"

"We sell beef," the cowboy replied, stuffing the package into his saddlebags and swinging up on the buckskin. "But we've had a few horses disappear lately."

"Sorry," Everett said. "I was just wondering where a man might buy a string of good ponies to start a little ranch."

"The only ranch in these parts that sells many is the Monte Largo. Leastwise, that's what I hear," the man replied, reining his pony around.

"Thanks," Everett said as the man spurred the buckskin.

Everett headed over to the saloon and drifted inside where he spotted Red seated at a table being mighty friendly with a young woman. Everett stepped up to the bar and ordered a whiskey, then seated himself at an empty corner table.

Red noticed his partner alone, sipping his drink. He and the young woman came over, Red clutching a near-empty bottle.

"Maple, I'd like you to meet my friend," Red said, his speech sluggish.

"Mabel," the woman corrected.

"Uh, what's your name, kid?" Red asked.

"Johnny," Everett lied.

"Yeah, Johnny," Red said, clasping his hand on Everett's shoulder. "Johnny, this here woman is Marble. No, that's not it."

"It's a pleasure, Mabel," Everett said. "I once knew a sweet little girl with that name."

"Not sure I was ever that, but it's good to meet you, Johnny," she replied, smiling. "You must be new in town. I don't think I've seen you around."

"Yes, ma'am. My first visit to Mora, a nice, friendly place."

"Some of us are," the young woman said with a wink.

"Well, Johnny. Your glass is about empty. I'll fill her up for you," Red said, strangling the neck of the whiskey bottle as he swayed it over the glass, some finding its target but more splashing onto the old table.

Then Red turned the bottle end up, emptying it into his own glass until whiskey spilled over the rim. Closing one eye, he peered into the dark bottle, then tossed it over his shoulder, banging it against the wall.

"Let's drink to pretty women," he said, sloshing whiskey out as he lifted his glass in Mabel's direction. "To you, my lovely lady."

"We'd better be going, Red," Everett said, draining his glass as he stood up. "Nice to meet you, Mabel."

"Okay, okay," Red said, wobbling to his feet. "Where's my horse, kid?"

"Tied up outside, I expect," Everett replied, shaking his head, "'less he's up and run off, dragging the hitching rail and a string of other ponies with him."

"Took the others with him, you say?" Red asked, steadying himself against Everett's shoulder.

"If so, they'll likely hang you for horse theft, since it was your horse that done it."

"Come on. Let's get outta town, kid," Red mumbled.

"Climb up on this one right here," Everett said when they reached the roan. He then guided the man's left boot into the stirrup and pushed him into the saddle.

Red slumped forward as Everett climbed onto his mare, grabbed the reins of the roan, and headed out of town.

It was late when they arrived at the north-pass cabin. Everett helped Red down from his horse, guided him through the doorway, then dumped him onto the cot. Everett yanked the drunken cowboy's boots off and grabbed a blanket. Red was asleep by the time the cover settled over him.

Everett then built a fire, pulled a chair close, and relaxed. Soon he dozed off.

As morning light broke across the mountains, Everett stepped out into the brisk, fresh air. From the big, flat boulder he looked down at the horses in the meadow. The TW doesn't sell horses, he thought, yet those wear their brand, or did a few days ago.

Then he heard pounding hooves approaching along the rim trail. He quickly ran to the cabin, strapped on his gun, grabbed his rifle, and called to Red, but to no avail. Outside he faced the path, waiting.

Bandanna and Wolf, riding hard, broke through the trees, and headed toward him. They yanked their horses to a stop some twenty feet away.

"Have you seen Red?" Bandanna barked.

"He's asleep inside," Everett replied, nodding his head toward the cabin.

"What's he doing here?" Bandanna questioned.

"Sleeping off a couple bottles of whiskey."

"Drunk! How'd that happen?" the big man demanded to know.

"Mora. We went there last night."

"And you got him soused."

"He proved quite capable of that on his own."

"What'd he tell you?"

"We didn't discuss business, if that's what's eatin' at you," Everett replied.

"Wolf, get Red outta there and on his horse," Bandanna ordered.

Wolf slid down and started for the cabin door, while Everett stood staring at Bandanna, ignoring his partner.

"By the way, I met a man in town who says he's missing a few horses," Everett said, then cut his eyes toward the herd in the meadow.

"Them horses are none of your business, greenhorn. And you'd better remember that," Bandanna replied.

"But maybe they are," Everett said. "After all, I'm part of this operation. Now if those are stolen broncs, then somebody might decide I'm a horse thief, the same as you."

"You callin' me a horse thief?" Bandanna yelled, leaping from his saddle.

"Yep, I reckon I am," Everett said calmly. "Some of those ponies down there wore the TW brand, same as the buckskin that Worlen cowboy was riding in town last night."

"I bought them horses from the foreman at the TW. Bought 'em myself. Now, you still callin' me a horse thief?"

"And there's a black mare down there that looks mighty familiar," Everett replied, nodding toward the meadow. "Yes, I'm saying you're a horse thief."

Wolf and Red struggled through the cabin door, Red trying to shake off the effects of the night before. Wolf started toward his horse, but Red stopped alongside Everett, sizing up the situation.

"I'll kill you for that!" Bandanna shouted.

"I thought you might feel that way about it," Everett replied.

Wolf spun around and faced Everett, standing about five paces to Bandanna's right.

"Wolf, you interfere, and I'm gonna plug you," Red said, surprisingly sober.

"Red, I should've killed you years ago," Bandanna growled. "And right after I've finished off this greenhorn, I'm gonna do just that."

Red smiled. "Bandanna, I don't think you'll be alive long enough. I've seen the kid draw, and I've seen you a time or two. He makes you look like cold molasses creepin' out of a small-mouthed jar."

"Drawin' on a man wearin' a gun is different," the big man said. "I've seen his kind. He ain't got the nerve for it."

"Suit yourself, Bandanna. But you'll never clear leather," Red said, smiling.

"Back me up, Wolf. Don't let Red wing me while I'm finishing off this greenhorn," Bandanna said.

"I ain't no gunfighter," Wolf replied nervously.

"You've killed aplenty before!" Bandanna said, fuming.

"Not in no stand-up gunfight. Not against the likes of him," Wolf said. "Bandanna, you'd better back off this time."

The big man's eyes glazed over, hesitating. "I swear, I'll kill you one day!"

"Bandanna, if not now, you never will," Everett said.

The bearded man turned to walk away, then suddenly whirled as his right hand dropped to his gun. Everett had watched the big man's every move, and in a blur of motion his gun came up and a blue blaze leaped out its muzzle. The boom echoed through the trees. Horses in the meadow lifted their heads and warily pushed their ears forward. Bandanna's right hand lay limp on the handle of his pistol, its barrel dangling in the mouth of its holster. Then he crumpled to the ground.

"Bandanna went for his gun first, kid. Tried to sucker you," Red said, grinning widely. "It was a fair fight. Don't you agree, Wolf?"

"Yeah, a fair fight," Wolf replied, staring down at his boss' limp body.

"Boys, I'm no horse thief," Everett said. "And I don't intend to be hung for something I got no part in. Now that black mare down there is mine. I'm taking her and heading outta here."

"Red, we can't let him leave like this," Wolf said. "He'll ride into town and send a posse up here after us. We got to kill 'im, Red."

"You seen him draw!" Red shot back. "Wolf, we better get outta here our own-selves."

"I got nowhere to go," Wolf pleaded. "This is a perfect setup. And what about Tomas? He's over there waitin' for us. This kid's fast, but he can't take both of us. We gotta stop 'im."

"No matter, I'm gettin' out," Red said. "The TW's gonna figure this out soon, and I got no hankerin' to be strung up to a cottonwood."

"Suit yourselves, boys," Everett said, glancing across at Wolf.

He then hurried inside and packed his things, taking liberally of the supplies. When he came out, Wolf and Red were gone. He loaded up the chestnut, then headed for the meadow. He slipped a halter on the black mare, then looped his lariat around the neck of an unbranded white stallion, figuring it to be the only pay he would get. Up on the chestnut, he rode through the north pass, leaving Horse Thief Meadow.

He set out on the same trail he and Red had taken to Mora. Along the way, he thought about his new situation. He had killed another man and had stolen a horse, but more threatening were those involved in the horse-theft ring. Unlike Harrison and his men, Wolf was the kind to hide out and ambush his enemy. Red and Tomas were of little concern, but what about Vicente Silva? It was his operation, and he was a dangerous man.

24

Anxious to put some miles between himself and Vicente Silva, Everett kicked his horses into a gallop, heading for Mora. Knowing the outlaw leader and his bandits frequented that town, his plan was to make a brief stop, gather valuable trail information, and then keep moving, either west or north. He was gambling that he had a few hours before word of the gunfight would ripple across the territory. As if it were a horrific monster in a nightmare, he had to somehow outrun the news.

Mabel was his best bet. Surely she knew the kind of man Red was, and while in a drunken stupor, he likely had told her about Bandanna and the horse theft operation. Everett had a feeling she would be sympathetic to his plight. In any case, he had no other choice.

The street was practically empty when he tied his three ponies to the saloon's hitching rail. He pulled his hat brim down, slipped inside, and eased down to the far end of the bar where he could view the room from its darkest corner. Making every effort to appear casual, he leaned against the bar and scanned the room. Spotting Mabel clearing a table, he nodded when she looked his way, then ordered a whiskey.

The barman filled his glass as he slapped down a coin. Just as he lifted the drink to his lips, he felt a light touch on his left arm.

"I believe the name's Johnny, right?" Mabel said.

"Yep, and I'm back a bit sooner than I expected."

"I'm glad." Her voice seemed velvet-soft. "What brings you back to town?"

"I didn't get along very well with the boss up there."

"So, will you be looking for work around Mora?"

"I'd like to move on north, but I don't know this country. What do you suggest?"

"If you'll stay around," she said, snuggling his arm against her body. "I'll be your girl."

"I can't stay, Mabel."

"Sounds like trouble," she whispered in his ear. "Buy me a drink, and we'll slip over to a table. You can tell me all about it."

The bartender filled a second glass, and they found an empty corner.

"Now, what's the matter, Johnny?" she asked, inching her chair next to his.

"Them fellas up there think I might blow the whistle on them. The one they call Wolf, another named Tomas, maybe even Red, they can't let that happen."

"Red likes you. He told me so."

"Yeah, but he's got other friends."

"What do you mean?"

"Ever heard of a man named Vicente Silva?"

"Sure. A saloon owner and big horse trader, some say. Others say a lot worse."

"I just busted up his operation," Everett said.

"Johnny," she said, frowning. "If you've crossed Silva, any one of his forty bandits might be after you. There's the Indian, Icicles, Owl, Pussy-foot, and Hawk, some of the most cold-blooded killers in the territory."

"I figure I've got an hour or so before the gossip riders hit town, but I need some advice. Where can I go and hide out for a spell."

"You could follow the river through town to La Junta, then head north on the Santa Fe Trail. It'll take you to Colorado. A less traveled road would be the cutoff at La Junta that leads to Kansas. Or you could go northwest into Moreno Valley. There's lots of abandoned miner's shacks in the mountains and hideouts in the river canyon that leads to Cimarron."

"Thanks, Mabel," he said, finishing his drink. "I'll be going now."

She followed him to the door where she caught his arm.

"Be careful and come back to see me sometime," she said. "And don't worry about me. I'll swear I haven't seen you."

He hesitated, glancing back at her. Sunlight fell flush on her face. A faint smile curled the edges of her mouth and wrinkled the corners of her sad, blue eyes. Suddenly, he realized she was younger than he had thought, and prettier.

"Mabel, I hope you find yourself a right nice young man, one who'll see after you, and take you away from here."

"The nice ones never stay," she said, glancing away.

He climbed into the saddle, pulled at the brim of his hat, then headed for the river road.

"Goodbye, Johnny," he heard her say.

In La Junta, he found a buyer for the white stallion and pocketed forty dollars. A beautiful, high-spirited animal, he knew it was worth more, but clearly it was wild, and he was in a hurry. He headed up the Santa Fe Trail, counting it as money Silva owed him, but he knew the law would see it otherwise.

Two days later he rode into Cimarron and hitched up in front of the St. James Hotel. In Lambert's restaurant, he ordered a hot meal, savored every bite, then headed across the river to the general store where he bought some trail food. When he stepped back out, he noticed a woman and a boy at the back of a wagon, struggling to load the first of several sacks of oats. After stuffing the supplies into his saddlebags, he walked over.

"Ma'am, my back's better made for lifting. Could I load that for you?" he asked, then bent down, grabbed a sack, and pitched it into the wagon.

"Thank you," the woman said as he stacked the last bag.

"You're quite welcome," he replied, turning to face her.

For a moment, he stared, hardly able to catch his breath. She reminded him so much of his mother. Her soft tanned skin, the dark hair shimmering with early strands of gray, the kind brown eyes, all so familiar.

Speechless, he tipped his hat and headed for his ponies.

"Young man," she called after him. "I believe you're new to Cimarron. I'm Amelia Bannister."

"Johnny," he said, hesitating. "Just rode in."

"Will you be staying?"

"That depends," he replied. "I'm looking for work."

"We own a ranch south of town, and the spring roundup starts soon. Have you ever been in that line of work?"

"Ma'am, that's about all I've ever done," he replied.

"If you're interested, follow along."

"I'll do that, ma'am," he replied, helping her into the wagon.

As she and the boy pulled out, he untied his packhorse, jumped on the black mare and trailed alongside across rolling plains. About an hour later, they turned onto a wagon lane that took them toward the nearby mountains. After crossing a narrow stream, they headed into a wide-mouthed canyon cradled between the sloped shoulders of two peaks.

When they arrived at the sprawling adobe ranch house, the woman and boy hustled inside while Everett waited beside his horses. Soon she reappeared on the veranda with her husband, a tall, stern-looking man.

"Son, I'm Elliot Bannister. My wife says you're a ranch hand looking for work."

"Yes, sir," Everett replied.

"Roundup will start in a few weeks, and it'll last a month, maybe more. You ever been on a big gather?"

"A couple, back down the trail."

"It pays twenty a month with meals and a bunk. You provide your own horse, saddle, and rope. On the trail, you'll sleep under the sky, and the nights are cold, so you need a good bedroll and weather gear. If it's to your likin', throw your things in the bunkhouse over there. The workday starts at sunup around here. The name is Johnny, right?"

"Johnny Caruthers," Everett replied, and then glanced over at the woman as her husband turned back toward the house. "Where should I unload the wagon?"

"I'll get one of the boys to help, then he can show you around," she said, turning toward the corral.

A young cowboy named Woody headed over with his shock of blond hair tossing in the wind and a smile on his broad face. His legs, molded by spending most of his nineteen years wrapped around a horse's belly, churned awkwardly. After they had unloaded the oats into a storage crib, he led Everett over to the bunkhouse.

"The Bannisters are mighty good people," Woody said as Everett unrolled his blankets along a bunk and stowed his things underneath.

"What's the boy's name?" Everett asked.

"Chet," the cowboy replied. "And his sister is Rosemary."

Two more young cowboys bunked there, Woody explained, one named Tom Beasley and the other they called Chap. They were out on the range with the ranch foreman, a fellow they called Vaquero.

For two weeks, Everett worked around the corral and barns, helping replace rotten posts and split boards. He put up hay, repaired a wagon wheel, greased axles, and soaped saddles. Often, young Chet hung around, asking questions, handing him tools, and explaining what he would grow up to be, "pretty soon."

One morning, with the fix-up work done, Everett ambled over to the ranch house and knocked.

"Ma'am, is your husband in?"

"Elliot," Amelia called out, "Johnny is at the door."

The rancher showed up with the boy alongside.

"I've about got things patched up," Everett said. "You got anything else needs doin'?"

"That spring up there on the ridge needs cleanin' out," the rancher said. "It's our only source . . ."

"Oh, Elliot," his wife interrupted. "Let the boy have some time to look around. He's done nothing but work since the minute he set foot on the place."

"Ma'am, I don't mind," Everett said.

"Can I go along?" Chet asked.

The rancher and his wife looked at Everett.

"Sure. I doubt I'd ever find it without you."

After saddling the chestnut and a short-legged pony for the boy, Everett grabbed a shovel and they headed up the canyon, following the stream. Half an hour later, Chet pointed to a manmade pool, which was fed by the spring up another hundred feet on the mountainside, tucked away behind a thicket of willows.

They slipped down and led their mounts up the steep slope, squeezing through the bushes to the water's origin. Everett began digging, creating a four-foot-wide, circular hole around the water source while the boy told him how he had once sneaked up to the spring and found bear tracks in the surrounding damp sand.

"Pa saw him later, a huge cinnamon," the boy said, then stretched his hands nearly two feet apart. "His paws were this long."

Everett chuckled and continued digging until he reached a depth of five feet. By then the stream of water had increased to five times its prior volume. Worn out, Everett dropped the shovel and leaned back against a boulder, ready for the next tale.

"A few summers back, the water just about played out," the boy started, pushing his hat back and settling in beside Everett.

"Shhh," Everett said, opening his eyes.

The clang of horseshoes striking rock, mixed with voices, rose from the trail below. Everett eased over to the willows, removed his hat, and parted the flimsy limbs. With the boy's cowlick tickling his chin, he focused on two riders.

"It's Woody and Sis," the boy said.

"Yeah," Everett whispered, watching the young cowboy riding up the path, followed by a girl on a bay horse. She looked to be about fifteen, had her brown hair done in pigtails, and wore jeans, a plaid shirt, and boots.

"Reckon it's okay, don't you think?" Everett whispered, lifting his chin slightly to give the boy's renegade hair more freedom.

"Uh huh," the boy mumbled.

"Your ma and pa know?"

"Sis said she'd kill me if I told."

"Then we'd best keep this our secret, right?"

"Uh huh."

When the pair had disappeared around a bend, Everett gathered his things, and he and his junior partner started back down the slope, their ponies in tow. Glancing to the right, Everett smiled when he spotted Woody and Rosemary standing at the edge of a promontory, hugging. Reaching the trail, he and Chet raced back to the ranch, the boy winning by a neck. While the boy ran in to brag to his mother, Everett began brushing the mare.

"Hello, young fella," an old cowboy said, strolling over.

Zeb, who had been away visiting family in Raton when Everett had arrived, explained that he was the cook, or "coosie." He had once been a full-fledged cowboy, but no longer rode the range, though he still made the roundups and cattle drives aboard his chuck wagon. The rest of the time, the old fellow did the bunkhouse cooking and cleaning, along with repair work around the ranch.

"Looks like you kept up my chores while I was gone," he said to Everett, "but I doubt you're much of a cook."

"The boys swore they'd go on a hunger strike if you were gone another day," Everett replied.

"Them boys will swear to most anything," the old fellow said, laughing as he headed back to his old Dutch oven.

The next morning Everett woke to the aroma of coffee, the sounds of sizzling bacon, accompanied by a crackling fire in the old cast-iron stove. He swung down from his bunk, dressed, and offered to help, but Zeb preferred to handle things his own way.

By the time Everett had cleaned his boots and washed up, Zeb was calling the boys to breakfast. They rolled out and gathered around the table, Everett straddling a corner leg.

With breakfast finished, the cowboys stepped outside to a beautiful sunrise, a clear sky, and crisp, fresh air. As they saddled their ponies, Vaquero, pushing forty and as tough as leather, according to Zeb, invited Everett to ride to the south end of the ranch with him. The Anglos found the wiry cowboy's Mexican name to be more than a mouthful, thus he had become Vaquero, "cowboy" in his native language.

"You'll get a look at the lay of the land," the veteran cowhand said, "and I could use some help huntin' down a catamount that's been driftin' down out of the mountains, killin' newborns."

After tying on a sack of supplies Zeb had prepared, they headed out, Everett on the black mare.

"We'll skirt the foothills," Vaquero said, "and check the canyons and ravines in the edge of the mountains. Cougars don't stray far from cover."

The open land of rolling hills and sweeping valleys was treeless except along streams and where some moisture collected in ravines and sandy washes that occasionally cut across its face like age-wrinkles. To the right, running north and south, rose a string of mountains dotted with scruffy pinions, cedars, and scrub oaks, and just beyond them, a row of towering peaks covered with a forest of pines, spruces, and firs.

"How far south does the ranch go?" Everett asked.

"To the Rayado, maybe fifteen miles," Vaquero replied, "and we share range east to the Cimarron."

"How far to Las Vegas?" Everett asked, thinking about Vicente Silva.

"Two-day ride along the Santa Fe Trail. Three through the backcountry."

With afternoon light fading, they spotted the first sign of a kill. A bloody trail streaked the scant grass leading toward the mountains, the path along which a big cat had dragged a carcass. For an hour they followed, finding soiled places with bits of hide and flesh where the lion had stopped and fed. Well up on the mountainside among the pines, the trail signs ended. The wiry cowboy pulled up and pointed to a limb fork twenty feet up a big tree where the remains of a three-month-old calf lay draped.

"Tonight, the cat will come back to feed," Vaquero explained, "and we'll be waitin'."

After setting up camp a couple hundred yards down the slope, they relaxed until dusky dark. With their rifles, they returned to the lion's cache, climbed a couple of nearby trees, and leaned back.

As darkness settled in, Everett buttoned his coat, turned up the collar, and tucked his hands inside its pockets. Comfortable and relaxed, he almost fell out of the tree when Vaquero's rifle rang out. Then Everett saw the big cat tearing up the mountainside. Some thirty feet later, it stumbled, struggled to its feet, then collapsed and lay still.

"A mighty pretty animal," Everett said, as they inspected the cougar.

"And about the best killer in these parts," Vaquero said. "They can take down a grown cow, even a horse."

The next morning they returned to the base of the mountains and continued south to Rayado Creek, lined with tall cottonwoods and bordered with bushy willows. They watered their ponies, refreshed their canteens, then turned upstream.

"The creek is a favorite place for lions to attack," he said. "They wait for a thirsty animal, then leap from a low limb onto the back of their prey."

They soon found evidence of an old kill, but the trail was too cold to follow, so they turned back through a crease in the mountains to the flat land, arriving at the ranch a couple of hours after sunset.

For the next two weeks, Everett regularly rode out with Vaquero, checking for predators. They helped birthing cows, matched orphans to adopted mothers, pasted salve on cuts and gashes, but found no more kill sites.

Back at headquarters, Everett was bracing up a sagging corral gate when Elliot Bannister walked up.

"We'll be heading out on the roundup soon, and we need a passel of supplies." He handed over a list. "Rig up a wagon and get to town before dark. Take one of the boys with you."

With the wagon and team ready, Everett checked with the cowboys, and Woody jumped to his feet, volunteering. They arrived in Cimarron, bought the supplies on Bannister's account, then started back.

"Let's stop by the Saint James," Woody suggested. "A glass of whiskey would taste mighty good right now."

"I'll wait in the wagon," Everett responded. "Too much invested here to let some scalawag help himself to it."

Thirty minutes later, darkness was settling in, and Everett was growing impatient. Ten more minutes passed, then he jumped down and marched into the saloon.

"Anybody seen Woody?" he asked the bartender. "He's about twenty, blond hair, a friendly sort."

"Upstairs," the bartender replied. "He's with Frankie, his regular girl."

Everett stormed up the stairs and started checking rooms, embarrassing himself and a few customers.

"Woody!" he bellowed. "Get yourself dressed and downstairs in five minutes, or I'm leaving without you."

Still steaming, Everett climbed back onto the wagon seat and twirled the reins off the brake handle. Minutes later, just as he rippled the reins along the backs of the team, Woody came running and tumbled into the rolling wagon.

Half an hour later Woody broke the silence.

"Sorry partner. I don't get to town much, and I sorta lost track of time."

"That's not good enough!"

"What do you mean? There's no harm done."

"It's bad enough you can't tell time, but what you done is worse."

"You mean that gal back there? She ain't nothin'."

"She's a sight better than you, and what about Rosemary?"

"What's she got to do with it?"

"I know about you and her," Everett said. "Now you make up your mind right now. Which is it going to be, Rosemary or that Frankie back there?"

"You ain't gonna tell, are you?"

"No, but you are."

Not another word was spoken.

After breakfast the next morning, Everett noticed Zeb loading the chuck wagon with food supplies and cooking vessels. He stepped over to a collection of coiled ropes, branding irons, rain slickers, a spare saddle, and a small reserve of firewood.

"Johnny," Zeb called out, "maybe you'd like to help. You don't seem to have nothin' else to do."

"If you'll get in the wagon," Everett said, "I'll hand up these things to you, and you can stack it however it suits you."

Zeb nodded, then hesitated at the tailgate.

"Need some help?" Everett asked.

"Son, I'm grayed some, and my eyes have dimmed a tad, but the day I can't climb up into my chuck, they'll be shovelin' dirt in my face."

Everett and Zeb spent the next half-hour loading up. Finished, Everett was amazed at how much they had stuffed into the old wagon.

Early the next morning, the cowboys left for the range, Zeb and his chuck wagon given a half-hour head start. Near mid-afternoon, they reached the mouth of a box-end canyon, split by a narrow stream that dropped sharply down from the mountainside. They set up camp near one of two sturdy pole-corrals built against the south wall of the canyon, a regular roundup site.

Spare horses were herded into one of the pens, then the boys teamed into groups of three, each with a designated leader and an assigned area of the range to scour for cattle. Everett was teamed with Vaquero and Tom Beasley. Woody, still leery of Everett, made sure he was on the other team.

Vaquero led his partners east along the Rayado toward its junction with the Cimarron River. They crossed the Santa Fe Trail and continued across the undulating plains, passing bunches of grazing cattle.

"We'll catch 'em on the way back," Vaquero explained.

They made camp that night where the little creek emptied into the river. Though they had not eaten since sunrise, they ate lightly.

"A man will starve ridin' with Vaquero," Beasley grumbled.

But Everett liked the old cowboy, who said little and asked nothing but a hard day's work. Riding with the veteran for the past couple of weeks, he had learned to dry strips of meat over a low, night fire and chew on it throughout the day.

"Whose ranch is that across the river?" Everett asked Vaquero, having noticed a wire fence that crisscrossed the winding stream.

"Mr. Chase and his partners, Dawson and Maulding," the old cowboy replied. "Fifty thousand acres, all enclosed by either wire or mountains. They run between twenty-five hundred and three thousand head."

"That's some herd," Everett said with a soft whistle.

"But there's more. Chase and his partners own another ranch, half a million acres, with twelve thousand head of cattle, in addition to a big sheep ranch to the south, over a hundred thousand acres of grazin' land, with fifteen thousand sheep on it."

"How does a man ever see to that many animals?" Everett asked.

"With a herd of cowboys," Vaquero replied, smiling. "Now, let's get some shuteye."

At daybreak they were in their saddles, splitting up to cover more terrain. Everett took the path nearest the stream, Vaquero the middle one, and Beasley, riding ahead some thirty yards, the outermost strip. Sweeping a wide path back toward the mountains, they gathered cattle, pushing them along using the stream like a wing fence on a corral.

Everett had to contend with the trees, deadfalls, and bushes along Rayado Creek. The willows formed thickets and the cows would burrow beneath their umbrella of limbs, hiding themselves in the dark shadows. His mare could not penetrate their fortress, so he had to climb down, hunch over, and drive the cattle out. They would then double back on him, until he caught the mare and re-gathered them. He wished for old Bruiser to send in after the cattle, but instead compensated by calling out commands to the rider-less mare to herd the cattle as they emerged from the brush. Occasionally, a cow would plunge into the stream and cross over, Everett getting doused with splashing water as he pursued.

Meanwhile, Vaquero swept back and forth across eight hundred to a thousand yards of hills, ravines, and plains, pushing the cattle ahead. To his right, Tom Beasley covered a similar swath of mostly open land, always herding the cattle inward toward Vaquero and Everett.

Finding a good open pasture covered with new spring grass beside the stream, they rested their ponies, drank from their canteens, and let the cattle graze. Soon they continued, the herd having grown to several hundred, until they approached their canyon camp. Others rode out and helped them wedge the herd into the mountainside corral.

They spent that night in camp. Relaxed around the fire, Everett listened to old Pecos Bill tales in which he performed feats of Paul Bunyan magnitude, about stampedes, Indian raids, burned out ranch homes, and scalped cowboys and frontiersmen, men who lived about as savagely as the Indians. And they commemorated the vastness of the West, the enormity of the mountains, the swiftness of the rivers, and the fickle weather that blessed or punished at will. Most of the exaggerated stories were familiar ones, yet each storyteller's unique style was reason enough for laughter, and somehow encouragement for the hard work ahead. They always spoke with pride in being a character upon that stage. After the telling, sleeping on a cold, stony bed under a vast, starry sky seemed within a lariat's throw of paradise.

After breakfast the next morning, Everett, Tom, and Vaquero rode north, along the base of the mountains, driving a second herd of cattle to the canyon. This continued day after day, always riding farther from camp. The more distant cattle proved to be the wildest and most difficult to handle, and trail camps were often out in the open, so one cowboy had to ride night-herd while the other two slept.

One day Vaquero spotted about ten cows huddled in a clump of trees. His attempts to drive them out set them to bawling and darting in and out of bushy thickets. One cow, protecting her two-week-old calf, which was bedded down nearby, swung her long horns at Vaquero's horse, coming too close for comfort.

Finally, the veteran cowboy called his partners for help. Together they pushed the cows out, all except the defiant one and her newborn. Vaquero then threw a loop around her horns, wrapped the near-end of the rope around his saddle horn, and began backing his horse, trying to pull her out of the trees. The cow set her cloven feet into the soft dirt and resisted with all her strength.

Suddenly the cow changed her tactics, charging toward Vaquero and his horse. With her head dipped slightly, her sharp horns were aimed at the belly of Vaquero's gelding. With the sudden loss of tension in the rope, the horse tripped over a dead log and fell, trapping Vaquero's right foot beneath its body. While the cowboy struggled to get free, the enraged cow charged, her sharp horns lowered.

25

With Vaquero's leg trapped under the fallen horse, he snatched up a four-foot limb snapped off the dead log when his pony fell. With the cow charging full tilt, the old cowboy pulled the stick back like a bat, then with a blood-curdling yell, he swung with all his strength. The brittle limb cracked across the bridge of her nose just as a rope sailed through the air, fell softly over the long horns, and jerked taut with a zing. The cow's head snapped around against her shoulder, then her body whipped past, coming to a jolting halt against the horse's raised head. Vaquero's eyes closed as he collapsed onto his back.

The instant the loop had settled over the cow's horns, Everett had yanked slack out of the rope and whipped the near-end around his saddle horn. Then, before the cow could fully recover and brace herself, he anchored her by reining his horse around a six-inch oak, twisting the rope around its trunk. When the startled cow began fighting the lariat, Everett took up slack, inch by inch, drawing her closer and closer to the tree.

With the mother's fury focused on the rope, Vaquero managed to free his foot and get his horse up. Back in the saddle, the wiry cowboy worked around behind the cow and brought his rope taut again, stalemating her movement.

The cow under control, Tom crawled into the brush and eased the calf out. When the two cowboys relaxed their ropes, the mother headed for her offspring. While she inspected it, the cowboys flipped their ropes off her horns.

Reeling his rope in, Vaquero rode over to Everett. "Thanks, Johnny. She would've gored my horse and likely killed me to boot."

"Glad to help. Maybe I'll need you to get me out of a jam sometime," Everett replied.

The situation created a bond between the three cowboys, especially between Everett and Vaquero. Though unspoken, each realized how dependent he was on his partners.

While two groups continued to gather cattle, the third stayed in the canyon, sorting out those destined for market and branding newborns along with mavericks that, lost from past drives, had joined with the herd during the winter. Everett was thankful to be riding the range rather than wrestling steers in the dusty canyon.

The roundup lasted five weeks. At its end, marketable steers, along with a few older cows, were driven north toward Pueblo where they would be sold, loaded on a train, and transported to Kansas City, Chicago, Saint Louis, or farther east. Hired only for the roundup, Everett and two other cowboys, along with Vaquero and Woody, rode back to headquarters.

The next day Elliot Bannister stepped out into his front yard, money in hand, to pay off the temporary help. Vaquero stood at his side while the cowboys gathered and, one by one, received their wages. The old cowboy whispered advice to the rancher as each made his way forward.

From the back of the line, Everett noticed that the rancher's daughter, Rosemary, had come out onto the veranda. Dressed to ride, she stood watching.

As Everett approached Bannister, Vaquero leaned over to the owner and shared a thought, as he had with the others. Bannister listened, then handed Everett sixty-five dollars.

"Cowboy," the rancher said as Everett turned to leave, "would you like to work a while longer? Most of the boys will be off on the cattle drive for the next few weeks, and Vaquero could use some help around the ranch."

"Yes sir, Mr. Bannister. I'd like that."

After thanking the rancher and nodding to Vaquero, Everett led the chestnut and black mare over to the bunkhouse where he unpacked. As he walked the horses toward the corral, he noticed Rosemary heading his way.

"Johnny, it looks like you'll be staying around a while," she said, smiling.

"Vaquero put in a good word for me," Everett replied.

"I'm glad it worked out," she said, then hesitated. "I'd like to talk to you."

"Shoot," Everett said.

"Could we take a ride, just you and me?"

"I don't know," Everett said, glancing across at her father.

"I'll speak to Pa," she said, and proceeded to do so.

"He said to be back before supper," she reported, then motioned toward the corral.

"I guess you want the bay mare," Everett said, swinging the gate open.

With the bay saddled, Everett swung up on his black mare, and they turned up the canyon trail.

"The mountains are my favorite part of the ranch," she said, then put her pony into an easy lope.

They followed the dusty, hoof-worn path next to the stream as it climbed up a seam formed by two mountains welded together. Slowing the pace, they wound along its path past the spring, continuing until they reached the rocky promontory overlooking the valley below, the spot where Everett and Chet had seen her with Woody. She swung down, and he followed suit.

"Everything down there looks so small from up here," she said.

"I can't imagine owning something like this," Everett said, recalling his ranch dream.

"I love it here," the girl said. Then she turned to face Everett. "My brother sure likes you. Pa and Ma, too."

"They're good folks, and have a right handsome family. Maybe this is a place I can settle down in," he said, remembering the long months he had been on the run.

"Ma says I need to spend more time in the house," Rosemary said. "Says I'll be marryin' age before long."

"You'll make some lucky cowboy a mighty fine wife, I'm sure."

"What about you? You got a girl?"

"I had one, once."

"What happened?"

"Maybe some other time," he replied.

"I had a talk with Woody last night."

Everett hesitated to comment, so she continued.

"He said you know about him and me, and you don't approve."

"It's not for me to say," Everett responded.

"He said you threatened him."

"Did he say why?"

"I was hoping you'd tell me."

"It's better if he does that."

"He did something bad, didn't he?"

"We'd better head back," Everett said. "Be suppertime before long."

"I'll find out. You'll see."

Back at the ranch, he saw Rosemary to the house, then took care of the horses.

Over at the bunkhouse, Vaquero was seated on the top step drinking coffee when Everett walked up.

"Johnny, I believe Mr. Elliot is inclined to offer you a permanent job. Would you like that?"

"I'd be glad to settle right here," Everett replied. "Vaquero, you've been good to me, and I'm gonna do my best to prove deserving."

As the days passed, Everett and Vaquero kept watch over the remaining herd, repaired feeding troughs, storage buildings, saddles, bridles, and wagons.

While replacing old boards on a corncrib one afternoon, Everett noticed Rosemary and Woody heading up the canyon. When Vaquero dropped by and suggested they call it a day, Everett lingered, saying he would be along when he had finished the repair job. Taking his time with the last board, he kept an eye out for the return of the young couple.

The task done, Everett turned and looked into the disappearing sunset. Where was Tabitha? Was she now resting on that boulder atop their ridge, gazing upon the same horizon, her eyes somehow meeting his upon its soft glow? How he missed the magic of sitting beside her, the tender, warm feeling, the gentleness that she had brought to his world.

As darkness approached, he dropped by the bunkhouse and told Vaquero he was going to take a ride up to the spring. With concern growing, he saddled the chestnut and headed up the canyon trail. At the promontory he found only fresh tracks, so continued up the trail until it played out in a narrow walled-in canyon. Just as he turned to go back, thinking he had missed an alternate path, he heard a scream.

Kicking his horse into a gallop, he headed farther into the canyon, though he knew its darkness could turn deadfalls into trip-lines and gopher holes into lame ponies. When he heard a second scream, he slapped the loose ends of his reins against the pony's shoulder. She laid back her ears and lengthened her stride. Minutes later, Everett caught a glimpse of Rosemary's red shirt at the mouth of a deep crevice in the canyon's back wall.

Reaching a steep slope that rose to the base of the wall, he leaped from the saddle and scampered up toward the opening.

"Stop right where you are!" he heard Woody yell.

"Rosemary, you okay?" Everett asked, panting.

"He won't let me go," she cried.

"Turn her loose, Woody."

"You stay outta this," the cowboy yelled. "It's all you fault, anyhow."

"Let her go, then you and me can talk about it," Everett replied, easing toward the dark crevice.

"You stay back!" Woody shouted. "Or I'll hurt her bad."

"Think about it, Woody. You harm her, and you won't live ten minutes. Send her out. That's your only chance."

While the cowboy was thinking it over, Everett heard horses approaching. Looking back to the canyon entrance, he made out the images of four riders. In seconds, Everett picked out Elliot Bannister, Vaquero, Zeb, and Beasley, approaching at full gallop.

"Woody, this is your last chance," Everett said. "Here comes Bannister with help."

For a minute, there was no response.

"Don't shoot, Johnny. I'm coming out," Rosemary shouted, stepping from the crevice and leading the bay.

The girl ran to meet her father while Everett grabbed the reins of her pony, then joined them.

"What's going on?" Bannister asked, hugging his daughter.

"She can explain on your way back to the house," Everett replied. "Woody's still in there. I'll get him out."

After some argument, the rancher, his daughter, and the boys rode away.

"They're gone," Everett called to Woody. "Now come on out and let's talk."

The cowboy eased out and worked his way down the slope.

"I told her I'm sorry," Woody explained. "But now she hates me."

"Woody, when you make a mistake, there's a price to pay," Everett said. "Saying 'I'm sorry' is just the down payment."

"I can't go back down there," he said, tears coming to his eyes.

"Come along," Everett said. "I expect you'd best stay in town a few days."

"I ain't ever comin' back here."

Together they rode down to the ranch, Woody ducking in behind the bunkhouse while Everett gathered his things and brought them out to him.

"Woody," Everett said, thinking of his own past. "A man can only run from his mistakes so long, then he's gotta clean up his back trail. Good luck."

The next day Everett was hanging on the corral gate, studying the horses, when Rosemary walked up.

"I want to thank you," she said, smiling sheepishly.

"Everything is going to be okay. He's gone."

"I was foolish," she said, looking down at her boot tops.

"I know the feeling."

"Johnny, I hope you stay. So does Ma, Pa, and little Chet, but you're thinking of leaving, aren't you?" she said, gazing off at the mountains.

"They're good people, and the boys have all been more than fair to me," he replied. "But I expect I'll be moving along soon."

"Why?"

"Need to straighten out a few foolish things I've done."

"That girl in your past?"

He nodded. "She's part of it."

"I hope you'll come back someday, Johnny."

He considered telling her his real name, then thought better of it.

Two days later, he packed up, drew his pay, and rode away, unsure of how to go about what he needed to do. He wanted to go back to Tabitha, but all he could offer her was a life on the run. Somehow he had to settle with Harrison, and there was still Vicente Silva. Undecided, he turned his horses toward Cimarron.

As he rode into town, he passed the Saint James Hotel. Turning his pony, he pulled up at the saloon attached to the side. Standing at the bar drinking a whiskey, he noticed a woman and a young cowboy talking at the foot of the stairs. The image of Mabel's face flashed into his head, and he turned back to the bar, considering a ride to Mora.

Then he heard a pop, like an open hand slap, followed by a woman's shriek. He whirled around and saw the girl clutching her face, blood spurting from her nose. The man struck her again, this time sending her tumbling against the steps.

Men turned and watched. Another woman stared from a nearby table. But nobody moved.

When the young man standing over the girl drew back his hand, Everett burst across the room, sending chairs skittering across the floor. He grabbed the cowboy by the coat collar and the back of his belt, lifted him and slung him across a nearby table. The fellow tumbled headfirst onto the floor and lay addled.

"You okay?" Everett asked, turning to the young woman.

Sobbing, she nodded and headed up the stairs, steadied by the second woman.

As Everett turned to leave, the hushed crowd pushed back, except for a young man who blocked the doorway.

"Hey, tough boy. That gent you just throwed aside is my friend," the youngster said, a slight smile on his face and his hand resting on the butt of a holstered Colt. "Let's see if you can use that six-shooter or if it's just decoration."

Concerned about getting caught in a crossfire, Everett took a quick glance back at the boy on the floor. He still lay limp.

"Maybe you ought to go see about him," Everett said to the bright-eyed youngster, maybe seventeen.

"He'll wait," the boy said in his shrill voice, "until you apologize."

"He's got no apology coming," Everett said. "Now, I'm walking out of here, through that doorway. You can either move or get trampled."

Keeping his eyes fixed on the boy's, he started forward, ready to draw if he had to. The boy tensed, but as Everett came within a stride, he darted aside. Passing through the doorway, Everett heard laughter behind him. Without looking back, he swung up on his horse and headed for the river.

Back in the saloon, a tall man seated at a corner table stood and eased over toward the youngster where he stood peering out the doorway.

"Count yourself lucky, son," the man said. "He'd have shot you dead before you could've got your gun out."

"You know him?" the boy asked.

"He used to call himself Johnny. I seen him draw twice. Once on a man called Bandanna, a badman mighty good with a gun. He's dead now. Never cleared leather."

"You said you seen him draw twice," the boy mumbled, reminding the tall one.

"Yeah. The other time he drew on me," the cowboy replied with a twisted smile on his face.

"If he's so fast, why ain't you dead?" the boy questioned.

"He let me live, just like he did you," the tall one answered, turning and plopping his empty glass down on the bar. "Fill it up. One for the kid, too."

"What's your name?" the boy asked.

"My friends call me Red," he said, lifting his hat momentarily, revealing a shock of unruly, sandy red hair.

Meanwhile, Everett had crossed the stream and pulled up at the mercantile across from the stone courthouse that had the name, COLFAX COUNTY, etched into a limestone slab above the entrance.

Two men, one short and old with a full beard and a younger fellow, were tying up at the railing in front of the mercantile. The squatty fellow was riding a mule and leading a burro, while the younger was swinging down from a roan, his burro in tow. Their loads were half the size of their pack animals with picks, shovels, and mesh wire contraptions hanging all over.

"Where you fellas been prospecting?" Everett asked.

"In them mountains over yonder," the older one said, pointing west. "But now we're headed for a new field."

"Whereabouts?"

"We hear there's still some gold in the mountains out west of Trinidad."

"I wouldn't know," Everett said. "I prefer cowboying to swinging a pick."

"You sound like my partner," the old fellow said. "He's lookin' to sell out, land a job on a ranch, and let his hoss do the work."

"There's a good ranch a ways down that trail," Everett said, nodding toward the road to the Bannisters's place, "and they're a cowboy short, right now."

"The name's George," the younger man said. "I'd sure be obliged if you'd point me in the right direction."

Everett described the route. "Just ask for Elliot Bannister or Vaquero when you get there."

"You wouldn't be interested in buyin' me out, would you?" George asked, motioning toward his burro.

"I don't know prospecting," Everett replied.

"Josh can teach you everything there is to know about it," George countered, referring to his old partner.

"Just not my line of work," Everett explained, glancing at the burro. "Besides, I'm a little short on cash."

"I tell you what," George said. "I'll trade you my burro, all my tools, and twenty-five cash for that black mare you've got."

Everett hesitated, thinking that disappearing into the mountains for a few months might be a good idea. It might give him time to come up with a plan, and if Harrison's boys were still trailing him, they would never come looking a couple thousand feet up on a mountainside.

"Join up with me," Josh said, "and I'll see that you don't go hungry, and you just might line your pockets with a few ounces of gold dust."

Fifteen minutes later, Everett was riding west alongside Josh Clawson, the burro trailing behind, while George Pratt was heading toward Bannister's ranch, leading the black mare.

26

"We got to get some things straight," Josh said to Everett. "The claim is my property, but otherwise, we share equally. We share in any gold we find, and we share in the cost of supplies. That okay by you?"

"Seems fair to me."

"George gave up on our claim," Josh explained. "But I've worked those hills in Colorado, and I'm right pleased to be down here."

Along the palisades in Cimarron Canyon, they stopped and let the animals quench their thirst while Everett admired the sculptured walls and watched in awe as heart-shaped cottonwood leaves twirled in the breeze. Leaning back on a boulder, Josh rambled on about the fabulous gold finds in the area, such as the Aztec and Black Horse Mine.

"Still fortunes buried up there. Just the easy ones are gone," Josh said with a glint in his eye.

Near the western end of the canyon, they started up the mountain to the north, winding their way through tall pines, firs, spruce, and occasional aspen groves. Daylight was waning when they reached a sharp bend in the trail and then dropped down a steep slope to a noisy stream.

"The claim ain't more'n a cannon shot on up this creek," Josh said, leading the way alongside the brook.

A quarter of a mile later, they reached an elbow in the stream where the water cascaded down noisy rapids. Less than fifty yards ahead the gulch widened. The stream held snug to the right wall, while to the left the floor rose to a flat-topped knoll on which sat a cozy log cabin. Two flat boards nailed across the door horizontally sealed the entrance.

Grabbing a crowbar, Josh pried off the lumber and swung the door open.

"Pitch your stuff in and make yourself at home, partner," old Josh said.

Everett hesitated, staring at the dank room with a dirt floor, a broken-legged table, two old rusty cots, an ash-filled stove, and smoke-stained windows. Fighting the urge to turn and ride away, Everett ducked inside, slid the windows open, propping them with sticks conveniently left on the sill, then stacked his things on one of the cots.

He hauled the table outside, grabbed a saw from Josh's pack, and took off in search of a replacement leg. A few minutes later he was nailing a four-inch cottonwood limb in place.

"Got any chairs?" Everett asked.

"Broke down, so we used them for firewood last winter."

An axe in hand, Everett climbed to the rim of the ravine and soon returned with two logs, each a foot thick. With a crosscut saw, they sliced off the ends, making twenty-inch-tall stools, and set them beside the table.

While Everett had been gone, Josh had rounded up firewood and started a good blaze. Now he began cooking while Everett filled the lantern with coal oil, rolled out his bed, arranged his supplies on a dusty board shelf, and staked the animals near the stream.

After breakfast the next morning, Josh showed Everett the basics of panning. On the second attempt, he pointed his stubby finger into the pan.

"See that?" he asked.

"See what?"

"Gold."

Straining, Everett spotted a tiny fleck glittering in the sunlight, and nodded while wondering how long it would take to collect even one ounce.

"The mine is upstream a ways," Josh said, heading that way.

They spent the day digging at the back of a twenty-foot deep shaft tunneled into the west bank of the creek, sifting out the larger stones, and washing the fine sand. They bagged maybe half an ounce.

"What does it sell for?" Everett asked.

"Twenty dollars in Trinidad, maybe eighteen locally."

For two weeks, they continued digging, sifting, and washing, but the return on their efforts was meager.

"We're running a little short on supplies," Everett said.

"We'll ride to E'town and cash in for what we need," Josh explained.

By late morning, they reached the little town on the hillside of a narrow valley to the north, sold their gold, ate, and bought their supplies. After each paying for a shave and bath, they headed back with less than twenty dollars.

"This old mine about played out?" Everett asked as they approached the shaft the following morning.

"It's got another couple months in it, I expect."

"How long you been working it?"

"I reckon I've seen about six full moons here, maybe seven."

"We won't ever get ahead this way," Everett said. "And come winter, I expect we'll be shut down."

"It don't take much to get by, hibernatin'," Josh said.

After supper that night, Josh retired to his cot and was snoring within five minutes. Everett walked down by the stream, moonlight shimmering on the rippling water. An owl hooted upstream, and he spotted a coyote lapping water at the brink of the rapids down below. The air was crisp, a light breeze stirred the aspen leaves, and birds roosted in the pines up on the rim. The stream gurgled, the sky crowned the world in brilliance, and the night insects sang their songs. Creation wooed him, but he was restless.

Though well hidden from Harrison's men and Silva's bandits, Everett fretted that his trail had taken him farther and farther from Tabitha. He had been running for a year and a half, his life seemingly in a downward spiral. Nothing mattered unless he could return to Caldwell and reclaim her love.

"One more payday," he whispered to himself. "Then I'm heading out."

For three more weeks he slaved in the dirty shaft, sunlight to sundown, swinging a pick and shoveling his diggings into a rickety wheelbarrow. He would push it down to the stream and slowly spill its load into a board flume through which water was channeled. A long tom, Josh called it. He would watch the dirt and rock wash down to a mesh-wire trap where Josh would discard the debris while the fine sand filtered through into a bucket. Gold was then laboriously panned from the black sand and stored in a pouch that filled at a miserably slow rate.

"I'll get some firewood," Everett said at the end of a hard day.

"Okay, and I'll get a blaze started and heat some water," Josh offered, gathering a few small pieces of wood and stacking them with charred stick-ends from the morning fire.

When Everett returned with a bundle of broken limbs, Josh had suspended a blackened kettle from the bottom of an S-shaped hook that hung from a metal rod that spanned the fire. The rod rested in the forks of two limbs stuck into the ground.

"Tomorrow," Everett said, "I'll take my half and ride out."

Josh just nodded and went on with his cooking.

Soon a hissing kettle announced that hot water was ready. With a blacksmith's heavy glove, Josh retrieved the old kettle, and shortly they were drinking steaming coffee.

After eating, they sat quietly, sipping from their cups and listening to insect chatter as a cold night settled around them. Josh lifted his gaze from the flickering flames and tipped his hat back.

"It was a stormy day, spring of last year, and I was workin' a shallow, high-banked stream on the other side of the mountain," he said. "I was by myself, but pocketin' a fair share from a little shaft over there.

"I was quite a ways down the mountainside, breakin' my back, swishin' a pan, and lookin' for anything yeller. I heard somethin', a low noise, but a man can't go chasin' every sound he hears, so I keeps right on workin'. It gets louder, but I supposes it was just a big wind comin' across the mountain, and the trees was a givin' me fair warnin', so I pays it no mind. But that noise was gettin' bigger and comin' closer. Well, I straightens up and takes a look upstream, feelin' a mite shaky. Suddenly, around a little elbow up the canyon, I seen a wall of water comin' at me. I tried to get outta the way, but there just wasn't no time. It hit me, knocked me down, and sent me tumblin' head over heels. I finally lodged against a big rock and pulled myself out, cold, wet, and beat-up.

"Almost as sudden, the water dropped back to near its normal level, but it took me two days to find my pan and eight more to rebuild my washin' trough.

"Now what caused that stream to swell was a heavy rain shower farther up the mountain, though not a drop where I was. All that water up there had collected itself into that little canyon I was in, and come a'roarin' down on me.

"A man might fend off a black bear or a cougar, but they is things a lone man just can't fight."

Without another word, the old prospector got up and went to his cot.

After another hour of sitting by the fire, thinking about his plight and that of old Josh, Everett went to bed, sleeping fitfully.

Up early, he packed his things and was ready to ride when Josh came out. The old fellow poured himself a cup of coffee from the pot Everett had brewed.

"This ain't a life for most folks," Josh said. "But there's gold up here, son. It's here but it's hid. You just never know when the next swing of yore pick, the next shovel full of diggin', or the next pan of washin, will be the one that glitters with a nugget.

"The failin' of most who go lookin' fer gold is they expect to walk up and find it waitin' fer 'em. But a man's gotta dig, gotta wash, near breakin' his old back. Then, if he's lucky, he gets rewarded."

"If I find somebody down there wanting to give it a try, I'll sell out and send him up," Everett said.

"Don't send no cowboy," Josh said, resigned that his partner was leaving.

On his way down the mountain, Everett met a couple of fellows riding up, one tall and thin, the other a burly sort.

"You have any luck?" the tall one asked, noticing the burdened burro.

"Not much," Everett replied.

"Givin' up your claim?"

"Never had one."

"We hear there's some good ones up this way."

"I'd sell out at a fair price," Everett said, motioning toward his burro.

"I've got no use for a dumb donkey," the tall man said, snickering.

They rode on up the trail while Everett continued down. Then it occurred to him that though the men had showed no interest in mining tools, they certainly might be after the fruits of a miner's labor. For half an hour, he tried to put these concerns out of his mind, but could not, so he turned and headed back up the mountain.

When he reached the point where the trail dipped down into the little canyon, he veered left and hurried along its rim. Up past the cabin, he spotted the two men following Josh upstream toward the mine, the tall one gripping a revolver. Hurrying, Everett tied the burro to a sapling and rushed the chestnut mare to a clump of pines just above the mineshaft. The pony tied, he pulled out his Winchester and eased over to a boulder, giving him an easy view of the approaching men.

Hidden by the huge rock, he waited until the men had passed him, then stood, looking down on them some thirty feet below, and lifted the rifle to his shoulder.

"Hold it right there, boys," he hollered.

The two whirled around, lifting their gun barrels toward the canyon rim. Everett squeezed the trigger, and the tall one staggered backwards. The burly man fired and lead zinged off the granite rock. Everett's Winchester rang out again, and the burly man spun halfway around, then fell to his knees, clutching his left shoulder. Everett scampered down the sharp incline holding his rifle overhead, then stopped dead in his tracks when another shot boomed, echoing through the canyon.

Josh stood over the burly man, holding the tall one's revolver.

"You okay?" Everett asked his partner as he approached.

"Yep, no thanks to these low down skunks."

Everett turned to check on the two fallen men. The tall one lay unmoving in the edge of the stream, his face half under water. Blood stained his shirtfront. He was dead. The second was stretched out on his back, a bullet hole in his left shoulder and a second one right through the heart.

Everett turned toward Josh, a questioning look on his face.

"They aimed to take my gold and bury me," he said. "They got what they had comin'."

Everett stepped over to the mineshaft and grabbed a shovel. He climbed up a little knoll and began digging. Soon, Josh joined him, starting a second grave.

"They'd have left me for the buzzards," he grumbled.

Everett pitched the shovel down and went for the body of the tall one. He dumped him into the shallow grave.

"Cover him up," he said, turning to get the second corpse.

With the dead buried, Everett headed for the canyon wall.

"Thanks, partner," Josh called out.

Everett glanced back, then continued up the slope. He collected the chestnut and the burro, then headed for the trail that led to the streambed. Reaching the campsite, he swung down and untied the packs.

"I'm mighty grateful to you," Josh said. "But it ain't necessary . . ."

"Josh, I'm staying, but I ain't going back into that worthless mineshaft," Everett said, interrupting the old prospector. "We gotta find a real mine."

For two weeks they sampled up and down the stream, finding little sign.

"I've got a few ounces of gold put away," Josh said, "and we're runnin' low on grub. I'm goin' to town and stock up. Want to come along?"

Everett shook his head. He was frustrated and welcomed the time alone.

Josh saddled his mule, loaded up his burro, and disappeared down the trail.

While Josh was gone, Everett decided to search for another stream. Rather than walk downstream to the trail or upstream to the mineshaft where the canyon walls were less steep, he headed for the near-vertical wall right behind the cabin. Using rocks jutting from its face as handholds and footholds, he slowly moved upward. About ten feet from the top, he stretched his right foot to a protruding, sharp-edged rock and lifted himself up another three feet. Then the stone tore free, leaving Everett holding on with his hands and left foot as he watched the rock tumble downward. Shoving his right foot into the hole left by the dislodged stone, he pulled himself to the rim.

After catching his breath, he headed for the top of a ridge to the west. The other side sloped down to a dry ravine, and farther west was heavy forest. He headed northwest and searched for a couple of hours, then returned disappointed.

He stood on the canyon rim briefly, then climbed down, using his prior footholds. Reaching the base of the wall, he stopped to rest on the rock that had dislodged earlier. Straining to turn the big rock to a flat side, he suddenly caught his breath. Right before his eyes, something yellow glittered in the sunlight.

27

With gold stuck to the embedded side of the dislodged rock, Everett concluded that more must be in the hole it left in the wall. With that in mind, he clawed his way back up and stared into the crevice. Seeing nothing but dark shadows, he stuck his hand in, scraped up some loose pieces, and pulled out a fistful. Among the litter of dirt and rock he spotted two pea-sized chips of gold. He stuffed them into his right shirt pocket, then filled his left one with a handful of loose diggings, and climbed down.

He emptied his left pocket into the pan, dipped its edge into the stream, and rotated it round and round, dipping the pan rim to spill out dirt and pebbles. He twisted slightly so the sun came over his shoulder and struck the pan contents, glittering off four little nuggets. He let out a low whistle, then with shaking hands he reached in for one, almost dropping the pan and spilling it all into the stream. After easing back from the water's edge and setting the pan down, he yanked off his shirt and spread it on the ground. Carefully, he dumped the pan contents onto it. After admiring his find, he gathered the shirt around it and headed for the cabin where he found a pouch and carefully tucked away the gold.

With the little bag deep in his pants pocket, he ran to the mineshaft, grabbed up a pick, and hurried back. He slipped its handle inside his belt, snatched a couple more leather pouches from a nail inside the door, stuffed them into his pocket, and frantically pulled himself back up the canyon wall. After hacking a ledge to stand on, he picked away at the hole, soon returning to the stream to wash his diggings. Over and over he climbed, chipped, and washed until two pouches were bulging with twenty ounces of gold.

Back on the ground, he considered what to do. It figured to two hundred dollars per hour, so he knew he had found a rich deposit, something much better than the old mineshaft. This one could hold thousands of dollars of gold, maybe tens of thousands. Rested, he took a couple of old cans back up and filled them, producing another eighteen ounces. He emptied the leather pouches into an old jar, sealed it, then scratched out a hole under the wall of the cabin where he buried his gold. After smoothing the disturbed dirt with a cedar branch, he hung the empty pouches back on the nail.

As he considered disguising the vein of gold by filling the hole with loose dirt and rock, he heard Josh's mule bray. He stirred the coals in the campfire, chunked a couple of limbs on, and watched them flame. When Josh rounded the bend, thirty yards away, Everett called out nervously. From the back of his mule, the old miner waved.

"Let me get those supply boxes," Everett said, meeting Josh and helping him down.

Carrying a pack of supplies to the shack, Everett glanced up at the hole. Late afternoon shadows blended it into the wall. With the foodstuff unloaded, Josh stood by the fire, warming his hands while Everett gathered firewood.

After flapjacks and salt pork, Josh sat by the fire sipping coffee while Everett added limbs to the blaze.

"What's botherin' you, Johnny?" Josh asked.

"Nothing, nothing at all."

"Quit stirrin' about. Sit and enjoy the fire."

"Truth is, I'm thinking about making a trip to town tomorrow."

"I just packed in a month of supplies, and all our tools are in workin' order. What's the need?"

"I'm getting a little cramped up here," Everett replied.

"Okay. I reckon I can work the old mine while you're gone."

"I'll get on back. We've gotta find a likely spot and sink a new shaft, Josh."

The conversation drifted and soon enough, they were in their bedrolls, though Everett tossed for an hour.

Up before daybreak, Everett eased outside, saddled the chestnut, crept over by the south cabin wall, and dug up his gold. As dawn broke, he headed down the trail with Josh watching through the smoky window.

Twice along the trail, he considered turning back and telling Josh about the find. When he reached the valley floor, Everett rode north to E'town, crossed the little river, and headed up Main Street, becoming apprehensive. Would the clerk require the name of his mine? If identification was demanded, should he reveal his real name? After the banker assayed the gold, weighed it, and placed it inside a black vault, he handed over seven hundred sixty dollars, without a single question.

Crossing back over the river, Everett considered heading for Caldwell. That's what Pa would do, he thought. He had enough money to keep himself fed and clothed for two years, maybe enough for a good start on a ranch, but the more he thought about it, the worse he felt. When he reached the base of the mountain, he turned the chestnut up the trail.

Back in camp, Josh was eating supper when Everett rode up, glancing up at the hole on the wall. It looked undisturbed. Everett sat down by the fire, then glanced over at his partner.

"Josh, I've got a confession," he said. "While you were away yesterday, I struck gold."

Josh took a sip of his coffee and poked at the fire with a long willow limb.

"I took a small sample in today," Everett went on. "The assayer says it's might near pure."

"I know," Josh said.

"You do?"

"Saw you dig it up this mornin'," the old fellow said. "Wondered if you'd come back."

"It's up there on that wall," Everett said, pointing. "The mother lode, I think."

"Nope, but a right smart pot of it, from the looks of that dislodged rock. Could be a vein close by."

"Here's your share," Everett said, starting to count.

"Let's just call it your finder's fee," Josh said, pushing the money back. "There's plenty left up there for the two of us."

"But this is rightly yours," Everett said, stuffing a hundred dollars into Josh's coat pocket.

Everett was up early, cutting a couple of straight saplings. He leaned them against the wall to make sure they would reach the hole, then notched them every two feet. While Josh cooked breakfast, Everett hacked down a third, then cut it into two-and-a-half-foot rungs. After eating, he fit them into the notches, securing them with nails.

Setting the ladder in place, he climbed up, a bucket in one hand and a pick dangling from his belt. For an hour, he pecked away, three times filling the bucket, which he lugged down where Josh was set up with the long tom trough and riddle to filter and wash the ore.

The old miner let out a shrill whistle when he saw the first finished pan agleam with nuggets and hundreds of smaller flecks. Slowly and with great care, he extracted the precious gold and stuffed it deep into a leather pouch.

At day's end Josh estimated they had sixty-five ounces, over a thousand dollars. That night the old prospector sat around the fire, cutting and sewing five more bags.

The next day's labor produced close to eighty ounces, and for the next two weeks they worked sunlight to sundown, averaging forty ounces per day.

"We'd best cash in," Josh suggested after a particularly productive day.

After filling the hole with brush to camouflage it, they headed for town. Josh and Everett grabbed a bite to eat while the assayer and banker evaluated the gold and counted out their money. Back at the window, the clerk handed over a heavy bag and an attached note.

649 Ounces
$18 per ounce
Total: $11,682

Everett hurriedly calculated half that number and added the six hundred sixty he already had, arriving at one dollar over six thousand five hundred for his share.

"Josh," he said, back in camp discussing their good fortune, "I know there's more gold up there, but I've got to take a trip, and I don't know if I'll be back."

"Just remember," Josh replied, "there's a place here for you if you ever want it."

The following morning Everett said a warm goodbye to his partner and left.

Stopping at the Saint James Hotel in Cimarron, he bought himself a bath, a shave, a change of clothes, and a room for the night. The following morning while having breakfast, he heard soldiers talking about Geronimo's recent escape from White Mountain Reservation.

"They say he's headed this way," one soldier said. "No doubt, he'll round up some of his old renegades and be attackin' ranches, settlements, and travelers."

"Yeah, and he'll inspire Apaches everywhere to go on the warpath," another said. "The Jicarilla reservation is just west of here."

Feeling a little uneasy about traveling alone, Everett rushed through breakfast, climbed on the chestnut, and headed for the Bannister Ranch, leading the burro. He had been around Indians, the Cherokee, Chickasaw, even the Cheyenne, Osage, Arapaho, and Comanche. But Apaches were different, so he had heard, especially those led by Victorio, Cochise, and now Geronimo.

Arriving at the ranch, Rosemary answered his knock.

"I'm not looking for work this time," he said, after exchanging hellos. "I've come to buy back my black mare, the one I swapped to George Pratt, a cowboy that rode out this way."

"He's out on the south range," she replied. "Won't be back for a couple of days."

"I'll ride out that way," Everett said, turning to leave.

"No need," she said. "Pa bought the mare from him the day he showed up. I begged him to get her for me."

"I've got this donkey to trade," he said, nodding at the burro, "but I'd expect to pay some to boot."

"She's not for sale," Rosemary said, a slight smile on her face.

"I'd really like to have her back," he said, then went on to explain how he got her, the bad eye, and the Indian's cure.

"I'm afraid I've become attached to her," Rosemary replied. "She means a lot more to me than a packhorse."

"And to me," he said, "or I wouldn't have ridden all this way to get her back."

"You'd just sell her again, the first time you ran out of cash," the girl said. "I've seen drifters like you before."

"I can see how you might think that," Everett said, "but you don't know the straight of it."

"Suppose'n you tell me, then," she said, tilting her head slightly.

"First, you need to know my name is Everett Brook," he said, watching her chin drop. "Johnny is a name I've used now and then because there are some bad men following me, intending to hang me."

He went on to explain the gunfight in Caldwell, his flight across Indian Territory, even his shooting of Bandanna in Horse Thief Meadow. He neglected to mention the gold or the two graves up on the mountain.

"Now, I mean to go back to Caldwell," he said.

"Why? Won't they just hang you on sight?"

"Maybe," he agreed. "But there's that girl, and I've got to know if she's still waiting for me."

Rosemary's face brightened as she walked to the end of the porch, staring toward the mountains beyond the corral. He had declined to tell her about the girl when she had asked up on the mountain, but now she meant to find out.

"So you're really going back," she said when he ambled over. "You know she might not be waiting."

"I expect she is," he said.

"How long has it been?"

"Going on two years."

"What's her name?"

"Tabitha."

"What does she look like?" Rosemary asked, enjoying herself.

"Brown hair, pretty eyes, soft skin," he said, then turned to leave. "I'll be going now."

"The black mare is out there in the corral," the girl said. "Take her and the packs."

Surprised, he turned and looked back.

"Give her to Tabitha," Rosemary said, smiling. "Tell her she's a gift from the Cimarron Rose."

"I'll leave the burro," he said, then laughed. "It's slow, but a fine pack animal."

Soon Everett was on the road back to Cimarron. From there he followed the Santa Fe Trail toward Raton, and rather than risk a camp attack by rumored Apaches, he spent the night at the Clifton House. Up early he continued north, climbing up over the seventy-eight-hundred-foot pass and down into Trinidad.

Asking about a room and meal, he was directed to Red Bransford's boarding house.

Over supper with Dr. Michael Beshoar, who made the boarding house his bachelor home, Everett learned that Red was an Ogalala Sioux Indian, sister to Chief Red Cloud. Before marrying Uncle Billy Bransford, the doctor explained, she had been the common-law wife of Marcellin St. Vrain, the noted frontier trader.

By the time Everett hit the trail the next morning, he was convinced that the Indian woman, with jet-black hair and in her late forties, was about the best cook he had ever known. Pulling out of Trinidad, he turned northeast, beginning a two-day ride to La Junta, a town along the Arkansas River.

Though he had no map, he had seen an old one tacked on the bunkhouse wall at Bluff Creek Ranch. Printed by the Atchison, Topeka, and Santa Fe Railroad Company, it had included portions of Colorado, Kansas, New Mexico Territory, Texas, and the Indian Territory. It highlighted the railheads, the cattle trails from Texas and New Mexico Territory, and the Santa Fe Trail.

From La Junta, Everett planned to follow the river, then leave it just east of Fort Dodge, where it bends sharply to the northeast. At that point, he would head southeast across the rugged countryside to the Homestead Ranch, northwest of Caldwell.

From Trinidad, he guessed he was nearly four hundred miles from Tabitha, ten days of riding, maybe less by switching horses daily.

Feeling safer now that he was out of New Mexico Territory, he made camp along the trail, rose early, and rode steadily. Years of wind and erosion had left the arid land broken by buttes, mesas, valleys, and arroyos, all with crumbly, fragile walls, forcing him to waste hours skirting impassable terrain. With very few streams handy, Everett always returned to the river. The harsh land offered little encouragement for settlers, yet it had a stark beauty, a comforting quietness.

Long days in the saddle offered him time to think and reconsider. He had enough money for a good start toward a ranch in Colorado or up in Wyoming, even Montana. Back in Caldwell, Harrison and his bunch would likely hear about his return, and they would come after him. Yet he rode on, reaching Dodge City mid-afternoon of the fifth day.

The rough town immediately lived up to its reputation. Three cowboys were racing their ponies up and down the street on the south side of the railroad tracks, firing their pistols into the sky, yelling, and chasing pedestrians off the street. One of the riders even reined his horse onto the boardwalk and along the storefronts, sending folks ducking through doorways.

Everett pulled up at the west end of the street and watched the revelry, amazed that no one seemed interested in putting a stop to it. Then it occurred to him that the railroad divided the town, the cowpunchers on the south side and the townspeople on the north. Shortly, he spotted the Dodge House across the tracks on the north side of Front Street and headed that way. One of the cowboys noticed and spurred his mount toward Everett, yelling and firing his gun into the air. Everett reined up as the cowboy whizzed past, coming within a foot of a collision, then continued after a quick glance back.

The reveler turned his horse and charged again from the rear. Anticipating this, Everett had untied his lariat and now casually shook out a nice loop with his right hand while gathering the remaining coils in his left.

As the cowboy came thundering by, he reached out and knocked Everett's hat off. Just then, Everett swung the big loop above his head once, then flipped it forward while releasing a few smaller coils with his left. The noose dropped over the cowboy's raised right arm and fell around his chest while Everett whipped the near rope end around his saddle horn. The lariat jerked taut, snatching the cowboy over his saddle cantle and sending him crashing to the ground in a stunned heap, losing his gun and hat in the dust.

The chestnut mare automatically backed up, dragging the cowboy through the sandy street as if he were a roped steer. Everett halted his pony, then nudged him forward a couple of steps, creating slack in the rope.

The cowboy yelled obscenities while getting untangled, then stood facing Everett who sat on his horse reeling in his rope, loop by loop, recoiling it while keeping an eye on the angry man below.

People eased out of the stores onto the boardwalk, some spilling into the street, all watching curiously.

"I oughta kill you for that!" yelled the reveler as he brushed dust from his pants and shirt.

"You ought to be glad I didn't shoot you, cowboy," Everett responded.

"Let me find my gun, then we'll see who stops lead," the man shouted, spotting his revolver half-buried in the powdery dirt.

"I wouldn't do that," Everett said as the cowboy reached down for his pistol.

The reveler glanced up, staring into the barrel-end of Everett's Colt.

"Pick it up slowly, with two fingers," Everett said, "then put it away."

The cowboy complied, then found his hat, brushed it off and started for his horse.

"Now, get my hat," Everett said, "and bring it to me."

The cowboy's two companions had taken notice and made their way over.

"What happened?" one asked.

"This here varmint roped me from behind," the reveler explained, having made no move toward Everett's hat, which rested upside down in the street.

"My hat," Everett reminded.

"Get it yourself," the cowboy replied, now sided by his partners.

Everett fired, and the reveler jumped to the side as the bullet exploded a puff of dust within inches of his right foot.

"Why, you coyote," the cowboy bellowed.

"My hat," Everett said, nodding toward it.

"Better get it," one of his buddies advised. "That hombre's holding all the aces right now."

The cowboy hesitated before retrieving the dusty hat, then grudgingly handed it up. Taking it with his left hand, Everett slapped it against his leg a couple of times, then put it on. Pushing his gun back into its holster, he nudged his horse, and rode past the three cowboys, headed across the tracks to the hotel.

"I'll get you for that!" the cowboy yelled after him, as the crowd broke up.

Everett continued toward the Dodge House without looking back. Sliding down, he hitched his ponies, slung his saddlebags over his shoulder, and stepped up on the boardwalk, glancing over his left shoulder. The three revelers watched him disappear inside.

Registered, he deposited his money in the hotel safe, then took his key and headed up the creaky staircase to his room. Inside, he stepped over to the window, carefully pushed the thin curtains back, and looked down on the street. The three cowboys were making their way to the hotel, intending to check the register, Everett guessed.

After a brief rest, he grabbed his saddlebags, stuffed in fresh clothes, then headed downstairs. Keeping an eye out for the three cowboys, he led his ponies over to the livery and had them cared for.

After a haircut, shave, and bath at the barbershop, he headed back toward the hotel when he spotted his three adversaries idling near the doorway. When he stepped up on the boardwalk, one of them slipped over, blocking the entrance.

"We want to talk," the man said, as his partners closed in.

"Just do it fast," Everett said.

"Everett Brook is how you signed the register," the cowboy said. "We ain't never heard of you."

"I'm new to Dodge, and won't be here long."

"You a gunfighter?" a second one asked.

"If I have to be."

"I think you're a yeller coward," said the one he had roped earlier.

"I'm done talking. Get out of my way," Everett said.

The man blocking the doorway faked a punch, causing Everett to lift his hands in defense. The diversion allowed time for the one on Everett's right to snatch his gun. In the blink of an eye Everett was disarmed while the cowboys trained three revolvers on him.

"What's the problem here?" a tall man asked, stepping up on the boardwalk.

"We've got you a gunfighter here, Marshal Tilghman," one of the cowboys said. "I'd bet my supper you've got a wanted poster on him."

"What's your name, son?" Tilghman asked.

"Everett Brook," he replied, hoping Harrison had not posted a reward.

"What's your business in town?"

"Just riding through."

"Where from?"

"New Mexico Territory."

"You'd better come down to the office with me," Tilghman said, then looked at the cowboys. "Hand over his gun."

Everett brushed past the three cowboys and followed the lawman south across the tracks to the jail. In the marshal's office he took a seat while Tilghman searched through a stack of papers, finally settling on one.

"Marshal Henry Brown of Caldwell, it says here, wants you arrested for murder," the lawman said, twisting the end of his mustache. "There's a five hundred dollar reward, dead or alive."

"Self defense, I tell you," Everett explained. "It was shoot or be gunned down."

"I'll telegraph Caldwell, but if this warrant is still good, you'll spend the night in jail," the lawman replied.

"But Marshal Brown is a horse thief," Everett protested. "He's wanted down at Tascosa where he rode with Billy the Kid."

"I don't have no warrant for him," the lawman replied. "Besides, there's plenty lawmen who've rode a spell on the other side."

After a cold supper, Everett laid back on his cot. He doubted the notice for his arrest had been withdrawn. If taken back to Caldwell where Harrison held sway, would he stand a chance? The fact he had run would make him look guilty to most, but a few who saw the fight might take his side. It might not matter, because Harrison's boys likely would carry out their own form of justice with a strong limb and a hangman's noose.

An hour later, Tilghman verified the notice for Everett's arrest.

"Come mornin', we'll be takin' you to Caldwell," the lawman said, holding a telegraph message in his hand.

I can't let them take me back, Everett decided. I'd rather be shot trying to escape.

28

Everett suppressed the desperation pounding in his chest, cleared his mind and concocted a plan. Gripping the cell bars, he called out to the night jailer. After the second call, the man appeared in the office doorway and headed down a narrow hallway that fronted three consecutive cells.

"Look," Everett said, "back in Caldwell the Harrison boys drew on me first. Those who saw it, men like Jed Kimble and Bob Watson, will back me up on that."

"How come the Caldwell marshal sees it different?" the jailer asked with evident contempt for yet another prisoner's plea of innocence.

"They were sons of a wealthy rancher and ex-marshal. Old Harrison's word weighs heavy back there."

"Even if that's so, there's nothin' I can do about it," the man said. "That notice says you're a wanted man. Save your story for the judge in Caldwell."

"But your job is to protect folks here in Dodge," Everett said. "Turn me loose, and I'll be out of town in half an hour."

"Maybe I will let you out," the man said with a laugh, "then put a bullet in you and take you back there for the five hundred reward money."

"Save the bullet," Everett said, "and I'll double the reward."

"Cowboy," the jailer said, "you ain't never seen a thousand dollars at one time in your whole life."

"Unlock that gate, and it won't take long to find out," Everett said. "Look, you can hold on to my gun, and if I don't come up with the money, shoot me and swear I was making a run for it."

"Where's the money?" the man asked.

"Open up, and I'll take you to it."

"No deal," the jailer said, then headed back into the office.

Later, Everett heard the marshal's desk drawers squeak open, papers shuffle, then saddlebags plop down on the desktop. The jailer was searching his saddlebags, no doubt. Boot heels scraped the wooden floor over to the office safe, which squawked opened, then slammed shut. Then things got quiet, and Everett slept until around two in the morning, when the rattle of keys awakened him.

"Get up, cowboy," the jailer said, "and poke your hands through the bars."

"Why are you cuffing me?" Everett asked, holding back.

"We're gonna take a walk," the man said. "Gonna give you that chance you asked for."

A chance for what? Everett asked himself. As likely as not, the jailer intends to take my money and put a bullet in my back. Even so, Everett stuck his hands between the bars.

With the cuffs snapped shut, the jailer swung open the iron gate.

When they reached the outside door, Everett balked.

"Where're we going?"

"To get your money."

"Bring along my gun belt," Everett said, motioning to where it hung on a wall peg. "And grab my saddlebags, too."

"What for?"

"When I hand over the thousand, I'm a free man and that means I get my gun back," Everett replied.

Keeping an eye on Everett, the man pulled down the gun belt, rolled it, and stuffed it into his coat pocket. He opened the safe and threw the saddlebags over his left shoulder. When he returned, Everett extended his handcuffed wrists.

"Nope," the man said. "Not 'til I see the money."

"It's back at the hotel, and the night clerk is gonna notice I'm a prisoner and become mighty suspicious," Everett said.

"I'll take 'em off at the hotel door," the jailer replied.

They eased out onto the quiet boardwalk, and headed north across the tracks toward the Dodge House, staying in the darkness along the storefronts. At the hotel, Everett turned and again extended his hands. The man twisted the key and slipped off the cuffs.

"I'll holster my gun," the jailer said, "but one false move, and you're gonna die escapin'."

They stepped inside, and Everett led the way upstairs, noting the desk clerk leaning back in his chair with his eyes closed. In his room, Everett grabbed his things and turned to leave.

"Where's the money?" the jailer asked, his frustration showing.

"Downstairs."

While the jailer stopped at the foot of the stairs, out of the night clerk's sight and his gun drawn, Everett awakened the man and handed him a slip of paper. Stretching his eyes open, the clerk disappeared into a back room. Soon he returned with a bulging leather pouch. Everett took it, signed the paper, and headed for the door as the drowsy man plopped back into his chair.

Sticking to the wall, the jailer eased over to the door and slipped out behind Everett who immediately turned on him.

"My gun," he said.

"First, the money," the jailer replied.

Everett reached into the pouch and pulled out a few dollars for the jailer to see. The man reached for the bag, but Everett yanked it away.

"Let's get back to the office," the jailer said.

"Not without my gun," Everett replied.

"I could kill you right here and take the money," the man argued.

"You fire your six-shooter, that clerk in there's gonna come running, then you'll have some hard explaining to do," Everett replied.

Reluctantly, the jailer pulled Everett's rolled-up gun belt from his coat pocket and handed it over. Everett slipped out his revolver, opened the cylinder, and checked the load. Satisfied, he strapped it on, took his saddlebags, and they headed for the jail where he counted out a thousand dollars.

"This don't look like no escape," the jailer said, pocketing the money, then motioning toward the open cell gate.

"Grab the coffee pot," Everett suggested, picking up a tin cup and leading the way to the long hallway.

Everett stopped midway through the cell door. Reaching inside, he pushed the cup between the bars with his left hand, then motioned the jailer to fill it. As the jailer poured, Everett suddenly pitched half a cup of steaming coffee into the man's face, snatched his revolver, and whacked the gun barrel against the side of the fellow's head. When the jailer collapsed to the coffee-soaked floor, Everett grabbed his legs and dragged him into the cell. Searching his pockets, he retrieved the thousand dollars.

"Wouldn't want the marshal thinking you took a bribe," he muttered, then pilfered the keys from the jailer's coat pocket, slammed the door, and turned the lock.

With the man moaning on the floor, Everett pitched the keys down the hallway, out of reach from the cell, and slipped out the front door. Moving swiftly along dark storefronts, he arrived at the livery, claimed his horses, and headed for the river bridge. Across, he hesitated. He knew he should ride west, away from Dodge and out of Kansas, but he turned east, following the river.

Ten miles later, he swung south to avoid Fort Dodge, then made his way back to the river. At daybreak, he reined in the black mare at the northeast bend in the river. After letting his horses drink, he turned to the southeast and headed for the red hills.

With the sun three hours up, he led his weary horses into a cluster of willows along a small stream. He removed the saddle and packs while they guzzled water, then staked them in a patch of grass. He chewed on the last of his dried beef, stretched out his bedroll, and crawled inside.

A couple of hours later, he awoke, saddled his horse, packed, and hit the trail again, guessing a posse from Dodge had been on his trail for two, maybe three hours. Likely Marshal Tilghman had telegraphed Caldwell, and another was riding toward him from the east. He was out of supplies, having planned to buy them in Dodge, and now lawmen would be on the lookout for him in every town.

The next day, tired, hungry, and with two spent horses, he came to the headwaters of Medicine Lodge River. He rested while his horses drank, then fed them the last of the oats and let them graze along the stream for half an hour. Back in the saddle, he followed the river toward the town named after the stream.

Sometime after noon, he spotted a house on a bluff along the south side of the stream. Climbing the slope to the edge of a thicket of trees, he took a closer look. Spotting sleeping quarters west of the main house and a wagonload of hunters leaving, he guessed it was a road ranch. When all seemed clear, he approached the building.

He tied his horses loosely to the hitching post and stepped inside. A woman, a young boy, and a teenage girl glanced up from the long table they were clearing.

"Too late for a bowl of stew?" Everett asked, noticing a handwritten sign tacked above the kitchen door offering a bowl-full for a quarter.

"No, sir," the woman said, then sent the girl to the kitchen.

"What about a few supplies?" he asked. "A week's supply of coffee, bacon, maybe some bread."

"We can spare that much, I reckon," the woman said.

Everett devoured the stew with two cups of coffee, then stepped over to where the woman had gathered his supplies.

"Hope you're not headed to Medicine Lodge," she said, handing over his bill.

"Trouble in town?" he asked.

"I'd say so," the woman replied. "Some fellas tried to rob the bank, killed poor Mr. Geppert and the owner, Mr. Payne. Townspeople hemmed up the thieves in a ravine south of town, then strung up them what hadn't already been shot to death."

"Who did it?" Everett asked.

"The leader was Marshal Henry Brown from Caldwell," she replied. "Now ain't that a shame, a lawman robbin' a bank, along with his deputy, Ben Wheeler?"

Startled, Everett managed a stammered response. "You mean Deputy Ben Robertson?"

"No, that was an alias he used to try to hide from his past. His name's really Wheeler."

"The marshal, Henry Brown, they hung him?"

"Shot 'im tryin' to escape. Riled townsfolk broke the prisoners out of jail, intending a hangin'. That's when Marshal Brown made a run for it. Bill Kelley, a farmer, blasted him with his shotgun, near cuttin' him in half."

Staring in disbelief, Everett tried to make sense of how this changed his situation. Caldwell without a lawman might mean no posse; however, it also freed Harrison to take the law into his own hands, an ex-marshal filling a void.

"Marshal Denn got on to their scheme somehow," the woman continued, referring to the Medicine Lodge marshal. "Some say he noticed one of that Caldwell marshal's cohorts, fella named Smith, standin' in the rain holdin' four horses just outside the bank door, and knew somethin' was up. One of the hunters that just left here said a fellow called I-Bar Johnson tipped off Marshal Denn some time earlier."

"I guess the town's pretty much in an uproar," Everett said.

"Lawmen from every township within fifty miles are there. They suspect some cowboys from the T5 were in on the plot, supplying relay horses and such, and they mean to round up every last one of them."

"Thanks," Everett said, paying for the supplies.

"They say that thievin' marshal had a new wife," the woman went on. "Married her a couple months back. He wrote her a note from jail sayin' he did it all for her, but if he'd got that money, he would've hightailed it out of this country, and she'd never have seen him again. They say his deputy has already run off and left two wives."

Everett stepped outside, thinking about Tabitha and wondering what she must be thinking about him. Had she already given up?

The T5 ranch was south of Medicine Lodge, so Everett crossed the river and headed north of town. When word of his jailbreak reached Caldwell, Everett guessed that vigilantes, likely led by Harrison, would get up a posse. If they caught him, there would be no trial.

That night Everett camped along the upper end of Bluff Creek. He chose a heavily wooded site, and after supper he doused his fire with sand. He was only half a day's ride from the Homestead Ranch. Tomorrow, he would know if Tabitha had waited for him.

Up early, he rode along the southwest bank of Bluff Creek. He remembered Jed Kimble telling about a buried treasure along the upper end of the creek. The story said there was another creek that joined from the north and a high bluff on the southwest side that overlooked their junction. On the bluff a large rock had a compass arrow etched on it, so the story went, and the arrow pointed toward the buried treasure. Nobody had ever figured out how far. Everett dismissed the urge to try his luck and crossed the stream.

He traveled in the shadows of trees when he could, but as he neared Bluff City, he left the creek and made his way toward the Homestead Ranch. About noon, he topped the ridge west of the house, slipped down from his horse, and using a big boulder as a shield, he watched for activity down around the buildings, hoping to spot Tabitha. Instead, a cowhand appeared, saddled a horse, then swung up and rode toward the tree-lined stream just west of the corral.

Everett mounted and headed down the slope, hoping to intercept the rider at the crossing within the cover of trees alongside the stream. As he rode up, the cowboy was relaxing in the saddle while his horse drank from the creek. Everett recognized Bob Jackson, yet approached with caution, his right hand resting on his pistol handle.

"Are you lost, cowboy?" Jackson asked when he noticed Everett approaching.

"Don't you remember me?" Everett asked.

"Everett Brook!" the man called out, reining his horse across the creek and alongside. "Where've you been? We'd given up on you ever comin' back."

"I've been on the run, out West," he explained, recalling their earlier conflicts and wondering if Jackson had mended his ways. He doubted it.

"Samuel Harrison has sworn to hang you on sight," Jackson said. "He led a bunch of his boys down into Indian Territory, searchin' for you. He came back, but I hear some of his bunch is still on your trail. You'd better be careful, real careful."

"Yeah, I've managed to stay a step or two ahead of them," Everett said.

"So, why have you come back to Caldwell?"

"I've got to see Tabitha," he explained. "I promised her I'd come back."

"Everett, I hate to be the one to tell you this, but Tabitha ain't here. She's been gone about three months."

"Where'd she go?" Everett asked, suddenly feeling sick.

"Family, I think. Old man Nichols died a few months back, and Tabitha went back East with her mother. Everett, I know it ain't what you want to hear, but she's married a banker back there."

Everett stared off down the stream, unable to put his feelings and thoughts into words. About to explode with hurt and anger, he wanted to scream.

Finally, nodding to Jackson, he nudged his horses into the stream, heading for the ranch house.

"Where're you goin'?" Jackson asked.

"I've come this far, I've gotta see for myself," Everett called over his shoulder.

With his gun handy, Everett swung down, stepped up on the porch, and knocked. When no answer came, he knocked harder and called for Tabitha.

Slowly he returned to his horses and swung up. After a lingering look at the porch swing, he reined his ponies back toward the stream, resisting the urge to put them into full gallop. He splashed past Jackson without a word and headed up the ridge.

He tried to concentrate, to think clearly. He felt sure that posses from Caldwell and Dodge City were searching for him, likely to converge around Medicine Lodge. He chose to ride north to the Chikaskia River, then turn west, staying well above the path he anticipated his pursuers would follow.

The sun was fading when he reached the stream. The air was cooling quickly, and a northwest wind made the evening feel even colder. Staring into the sunset, the image of his hooded father hanging from the gallows leaped into his mind. Was it memory or a glimpse of his future? A chill swept over him as he focused on the hooded figure. He pulled up in a cluster of cottonwoods, and tried to regain his senses.

After gathering wood, he sat by his glowing blaze, sipping coffee. Time seemed irrelevant. Surprisingly, he felt little concern about being discovered. In fact, he would welcome a fight.

Lying in his bedroll, visual clips of Tabitha popped into his head, bits of conversations echoed in his mind. He discarded them, yet he seemed unable to focus or concentrate on other things.

He remembered their last hug, sharing a peaceful sunset from the ridge west of the ranch house, sitting beside her in the porch swing, sharing supper with her family, and the hurried conversation just before he fled. Then other images came: the flash of Bandanna's hand to his gun, the sparkle of gold in his hand, the cow charging toward Vaquero. He remembered Brett Harrison's right hand slipping below the tabletop, and later that same hand grabbing his shiny, ivory-handled revolver. Then there were Bob Jackson's words, "She ain't here . . . she's married a banker." They burned inside his head.

Sometime late in the night, he finally dozed off.

Up early, he continued along the river until, late in the afternoon, it took a sharp turn to the northwest. He spent the night there, then continued west, hoping to make a dash across the Medicine Lodge River about noon and continue west as fast and far as possible.

Having seen no sign of a posse and with the sun now overhead, he urged his horses into the river, letting them drink while he removed the lid from his canteen and dropped it into the cold, clear water. After he and his horses had drunk their fill, they splashed across the wide, shallow stream. Emerging on the other side, he heard pounding hooves from down river. The riders had already spotted him and were spurring their ponies into full gallop.

Everett buried his heels in the flanks of the black mare, and she thundered across the open plain. The riders veered off in pursuit, some firing long-range shots. Two miles later, with his horses tiring but still in full gallop, Everett turned to check his back trail for any sign of pursuers. He saw none, but just as he faced forward, he spotted a narrow ravine a few feet ahead. With no time to stop or turn, he dropped the lead rope to the trailing chestnut and dug his heels into the black pony's sides. She leaped, barely clearing the gaping ditch. The chestnut tried to stop, stumbled at the edge, and tumbled into the ravine.

Everett spun the black around to check on his packhorse. She was up and limping down the gully, his supplies scattered over its floor. With the posse approaching and the chestnut too lame to keep up, he turned west and put the black mare into a dead run.

From the old map on the bunkhouse wall, he knew the Cimarron route of the Santa Fe Trail lay due west, breaking off the main trail somewhere west of Dodge City. Miles and miles of desolate country lay ahead, but he had no choice. If the ravine slowed the posse for a few minutes, the black would lengthen his lead, and she could outlast anything chasing them. That was his hope.

She did not disappoint him. For almost an hour the mare galloped across the flat plains, never wavering. Seeing no one on the trail behind him, Everett slowed her down, but she still fought the bit, wanting to run.

Half an hour later, they splashed across another river, the upper reaches of the Cimarron, Everett guessed. While his horse gulped down water, he thought about the chestnut. Lame, she would never survive on her own. Either a mountain lion would track her down or the posse would shoot her. When the black raised her head, he turned her downstream, following the streambed. He had to go back for the chestnut, his pa's mare.

Half an hour later, he cut back to the east, hoping to find the lower end of the ravine into which the chestnut had fallen. He made a dry camp that night, then continued with daylight, intersecting the gully midmorning.

He found hoof prints, certain they were those of his pony. He trailed along the ravine until it intersected with a stream. There he found her, limping along while grazing on blue stem. His horse back in tow, he headed upstream, letting the ailing mare set the pace. With dark settling in, he made camp in a deep, dry ditch about a mile later. A cold drizzle set in soon after dark, and having seen no sign of the posse, he made a fire for warmth, staked his ponies, and let weariness put him to sleep.

With morning's dismal dawn, he rebuilt his fire, and huddled around it while drying his bedroll. When he turned his backside to the fire, facing south, he noticed smoke rising into the dreary sky. He scampered to the rim of the ravine and stared at the gray column spiraling upward from a campfire, maybe half a mile downstream.

"It's them," he whispered to himself, "and they've seen my smoke, as surely as I have theirs."

Back in the ditch, he kicked dirt onto his fire, then glanced at his lame pony. He hesitated, then grabbed his rifle, checked his revolver, and crawled back to the rim of the gully.

"If you're coming after me, come on," he bellowed. "I ain't runnin' no more."

Angry, frustrated, and wet, he lay there shivering and waiting.

"What's holdin' you back, Harrison?" he yelled. "It's just me against your pack of wolves."

The distant campfire smoke faded and disappeared. They were coming, and Everett steeled himself, determined to fight to his last breath.

"They'll follow my trail along the stream," he muttered. "I'll pick off a few from up here before they can take cover. They'll get me, but it won't be easy."

Ten minutes passed, then fifteen.

"The rain must have washed out my tracks, and they guessed I rode downstream," he mumbled, while skidding down the steep bank.

Only minutes later, he was in the saddle, heading upstream toward the Cimarron River, arriving there a little before noon.

From the old map in the bunkhouse, he recalled a spring along the southern route of the Santa Fe Trail. It was called Lower Spring, and it fed the river.

About midnight, having allowed the chestnut to set a slow, often-interrupted pace all day, Everett noticed a small stream flowing into the river through a gash in the east bank. Low willows bordered the creek and a grove of cottonwoods filled the V formed by the streams' junction. He splashed his ponies across and into the tall trees where he slipped down, unsaddled, and staked the mares. His food lost when the chestnut fell, he rolled out his bedroll, and slipped inside, tucking in his saddlebags, too.

Before sunrise, he was up and back in the saddle. A hard day's ride should bring them to the Lower Spring along the famous trail, but with the lame chestnut, it might take two. He hoped to buy food and supplies from some freighter headed for Santa Fe.

It was two hours after sundown the following day when he reached the famous waterhole. He and his horses drank, his stomach gnawing at his insides. After a fitful night, he saddled up and started down the trail. Late afternoon, he spotted a train of twelve wagons ahead, most freighters but a few families in schooners. He followed patiently, though the chestnut was walking better, and caught up when they made camp at Middle Cimarron Spring.

"You look half dead," the leader of the train said, staring at Everett's gaunt face.

"Lost my supplies three days ago," Everett replied. "My pack horse fell into a ravine, spilling everything."

He bought oats from the wagon master, fed his ponies, and ate with a family from Missouri who refused payment.

Two days later, breaking camp at Flag Spring, a clear natural stream adequate to fill canteens, water barrels, and to satisfy the thirsty stock, he purchased enough food to repay the Missouri family and get him and his horses on to Camp Nichols. While the freighters were packing and harnessing their teams, he rode on ahead, hoping to make better time.

At the stone fort, he purchased more supplies, then set out early the following morning on a long, hard ride that, three days later, brought him and his ponies to La Junta, New Mexico Territory. The wild town, sitting beside the Mora River and often flooded by soldiers from nearby Fort Union, was the junction point of the Cimarron and Mountain Routes of the Santa Fe Trail. Everett left his mares at the livery, got a room, shave, and bath, then ordered a beefsteak. Too tired to worry, he slept like a day-old kitten.

Taking his time the next morning, he considered what he would do, where he would go. Getting back to Tabitha had been his focus, his purpose. Now he felt lost, his life a jumble of mistakes.

Las Vegas and Vicente Silva were not far down the road. That would be riding into the teeth of trouble. Elliot Bannister and Cimarron were up the road a ways, and Josh and the gold mine not much farther. Upriver was Mora and Mabel.

29

"Mabel doesn't care what foolish mistakes I've made," Everett mumbled while saddling the black mare, "and I don't care what she's done."

Riding out of La Junta, he followed the Mora River up through a shallow, winding canyon. In no hurry, he stopped and let his horses drink from the sparkling stream while he relaxed on a boulder.

The water, clear and pure, slid along without effort, laughed its way through rapids, and splashed into pools below like playful children. All around, birds flittered from tree to tree, perched and chirped their love songs, then darted to the ground to gather straw or to peck at a worm. Somehow their lives seemed so simple, nature so harmonious.

He remembered supper with Tabitha and her family, the table covered with warm dishes that filled the room with their delicious aroma. Laughter, the gentle touch of her hand, and the softness of her smiling brown eyes intermingled inside him.

The porch swing swayed to a rhythm only they shared, a soft breeze stirred strands of her dark hair, and the night choir sang its song of life. From the boulder on the ridge they took in the setting sun as it bowed low to the approaching peace of a restful night.

However, these things, once beautiful, were now marred; memories, once sustaining, were now depressing. He ached inside, but rather than producing tears of relief, the pain brought bitterness that gripped his heart and tortured his mind.

Everett gathered his rested horses, turned his back on the stream, and by mid-afternoon, he rode into Mora. After registering for a room, he stabled his ponies, then headed over to the adobe saloon. He ordered a drink and with it settled in at a corner table. His glass emptied, he stepped up to the bar, got a refill, and asked about Mabel.

"She'll be around about sundown," the bartender explained.

Everett gulped down the drink and headed for the door, coming to a sudden stop about five steps away. Pushing through the batwing entrance was the cowboy from Horse Thief Meadow, the one called Wolf.

Everett dropped his hand to his gun handle, then eased aside, hoping the man would pass by without noticing. Instead, Wolf glared.

"You're a dead hombre," the sneering cowboy said as he drew even. "Silva has put out the word to his boys."

"He put you on my trail?" Everett asked.

"I ain't no gunman, but I can draw a bead on a lowdown coyote as good as the next fella," Wolf said. "Think on that the next time you're out prowlin' the range."

"Back-shooters usually die by their trade," Everett replied, then glanced around the room. "And I figure there's one or two following your scent right now."

Wolf jerked his head around and scanned the room of faces as Everett walked out and made his way over to the general store where he bought a suit of clothes. Back in his room, he changed into the new shirt, pants, and boots, then walked down to the dining area. He ordered another beefsteak with fried potato slices and hot bread.

Finished, he stepped out onto the boardwalk and glanced westward. Sundown. He headed across to the saloon, stepped through the swinging doors, and surveyed the room. Wolf was gone, but Mabel was wiping clean a table near the bar.

"Hello, Mabel," he said, approaching her.

She looked up, hesitated briefly, then smiled.

"Hi, cowboy," she said. "Johnny, right?"

"That's right," he replied, feeling a rush of warmth. "And I'd like to talk to you, Mabel."

"Grab that corner table," she said, nodding. "I'll be right back with a bottle of whiskey."

Hanging his hat on the chair post, he took a seat. Facing the room, he watched her snatch a bottle from the shelf behind the bar, deftly scoop up two glasses, and start across the floor. Noticing his eyes fixed on her every move, she smiled, while emphasizing her every female charm. She slid her chair close, eased into it, then filled the two glasses.

"What brings you back to Mora, Johnny?"

"You. I came back to see you."

Though she had heard that line many times before, she leaned over and kissed his cheek, maybe even hoping he was different.

"It's been a while. Where've you been?" she whispered.

"Working cattle on a ranch south of Cimarron," he replied. "Did a little mining, and took a trip to Kansas."

"Got a girl back there?"

"Can't say that I do."

"Well, I'm glad you came back," she said, squeezing his arm. "I heard you not only quit Silva's high-meadow operation, but left them without a boss."

"Where'd you hear that?" Everett asked, thinking of Wolf.

"Some of Silva's boys have been in a time or two. But it was Red who said you killed Bandanna, all fair and square, mind you. Red likes you, Johnny."

"He still around?" Everett asked, concerned that the redheaded cowboy was spreading word about the gunfight.

"He left Silva's band and rode north. He mentioned a ranch in Colorado, and wanting to put some miles between him and trouble. You see, Silva requires an oath when a man joins his gang, and breaking that oath is sure death. Just last winter, he hung a man named Patricio Maes from the Gallinas River Bridge, calling him a traitor."

"I'm glad Red got out," Everett said, then paused, glancing down at his glass. "I ran into Wolf earlier."

"Some say he's all talk, but you ought to be careful of him."

"Right now I've got something else on my mind," he replied. "Mabel, I'm nothing but a no-good cowboy with more than my share of troubles, but I came back to see you, like you asked me to."

"Yes, I did," she said, her face beaming. "I'm glad you remembered me."

Embarrassed, he slowly lifted his eyes to hers. They appeared soft and warm, like those of a woman who knew men, one who could sense loneliness and drive it away.

"Johnny, I wish you could stay this time," she said, reaching for his hand, "but it's mighty dangerous for you in this town."

"Do you think we could talk somewhere more private?" he asked.

She looped her arm through his, and leaned her body against his side.

"I'd like that, Johnny. I'll be right back."

She crossed over to the bartender and whispered something. He nodded, and she motioned Everett to grab the bottle and come along.

He met her at the foot of the staircase and followed her up, somewhat embarrassed by the deliberate, inviting movement of her body. They continued down a long hallway to the last door on the left where he followed her inside and quickly closed it. Mabel made her way over to a hutch-like cabinet, then pulled out two small glasses, which she sat on a little round table beside the bed. She reached for the bottle and poured, smiling at him between glasses.

Stepping close, she looped her arms around his neck, looked into his blue-gray eyes, then kissed him. He hugged her tightly.

For a few minutes, they embraced, sharing light kisses and warm eye contact. Finally she stepped back, grasping his hands, and eased down onto the side of the bed, leading him to sit next to her.

"Now, what do you want to talk about?" she asked, smiling.

"Uh . . . about us. I'd like to know about you. Mabel, I don't even know your last name."

"Smith," she replied.

"Smith?" he asked, his eyebrows arched.

"Mabel Smith. And before you ask, I'm from nowhere, going nowhere," she said, the smile fading as her eyes shifted to the little curtained window over the table.

He released her hands and leaned forward, his forearms on his knees. She placed her left arm across his back and laid her head against his shoulder.

"I'm sorry. I didn't mean to make you sad," he mumbled.

"Johnny, names don't mean much to me. I hardly knew my parents. My mother worked in a saloon in Saint Louis. I met my father a few times, but they never married. She disappeared when I was eight years old. Later, I heard the man she ran away with stabbed her to death in a barroom fight."

After a deep sigh, she continued. "Mrs. Baxter raised me. She and Cal, her husband, owned the saloon where my mother had worked. I've been around these places all my life.

"When I was fifteen, the Baxters moved west, taking me along. They settled in Denver, opening another saloon. I ran off to Cimarron with a man who promised to marry me if I would come to his ranch down here. I was sixteen, never had nothing, and jumped at the chance. He left me along the trail north of here.

"A family headed for Santa Fe offered a ride, dropped me off at La Junta, and then I made my way here, doing the only thing I know how to do. So, you can see how a fancy name just wouldn't be fitting for a girl like me, Johnny."

Everett thought his life had been difficult, but watching her dab at tears in the corners of her eyes, he was overwhelmed with pity for this young woman. He had no idea what to say.

"Now, tell me about yourself," she said, lying back on the bed.

He stretched out beside her, staring at the drab board ceiling that in the far corner had two flies and innumerable gnats trapped in an enormous cobweb.

"Back in southern Missouri, my mother died when I was eleven. Pa was a roamer, and I followed him from camp to camp," Everett said, then hesitated. "A judge in Fort Smith hung him for horse theft and murder. I ended up at Fort Gibson, tending horses until I got out on my own. I've worked a few ranches and done some mining."

"Have you ever had a girl?" she asked.

He hesitated. "Yes, back in Kansas."

"What happened?"

"I had to leave for a while. When I went back, she had gone east and married a banker."

"Why did you leave her?"

"I killed a couple of boys in a saloon, a gambling fight. Their father, a wealthy rancher, would have had me strung up if I'd stayed."

"So you're on the run," she said, "from Silva, too."

He nodded.

"What was her name?"

"Tabitha Nichols," he whispered.

"And you loved her?"

"We planned to marry. She said she'd wait for me."

"I'm sorry Johnny." Mabel laid her head on his chest. "I'd like to run away, too. It scares me to think I'll end up like my mother, yet I know that's the path I'm on."

Everett wrapped his arms around her while she cried softly.

"My name isn't Johnny," he said suddenly. "It's Everett Brook."

She lifted her head, dabbing at tears.

"And my name isn't Smith. It's Mabel Harris. Somehow it's always seemed easier being somebody else."

"Mabel, if you were free to pick, where would you like to go?" Everett asked, raising to an elbow.

"Oh, it don't matter," she replied, slumping back on the bed. "I can't go anywhere and don't know anything else to do."

"But you could leave here, get married to some nice fella, and have a family."

"Oh, Johnny . . . I mean, Everett. I've given up on dreams like that."

Everett sprang upright on the side of the bed, pulling her up beside him.

"What is it?" she asked, startled.

"Have you ever been to Trinidad?"

"Just rode through once."

"Let's go!" he said, jumping to his feet. "It's a two-day ride, just over the mountains."

"What would we do there?" she asked, still seated.

"Why, you'd start your life over again! Maybe you'd buy a little house, get a job at a laundry or clothing store. You could meet a nice fella, get married, and have a family."

"Everett! I can't even buy a dress! How would I buy a house, even a shack?"

"I'll buy you a dress, a house, too."

Astonished, Mabel stared in silence, unable to fathom such a thing. She was afraid to believe it could be possible. A new life? She had chased that dream once.

"I'm serious, Mabel," he said, grasping her shoulders and lifting her to her feet. "I'll help you get that house and get settled in. I've got money enough, and I can get more."

She lifted her hands to her face, hiding a flood of tears, as he wrapped his arms around her and waited.

"Everett, are you sure?"

"As sure as your name's Mabel Harris, and mine's Everett Brook! I'll grab my things and be ready to leave when you've packed."

"I'll do it!" she said, lifting her chin from her chest. "I'll pack tonight and meet you at the backdoor tomorrow morning."

"I'll be waiting there at sunup with a pair of horses."

She tiptoed and kissed his cheek.

As the sun broke over the horizon, Everett was pacing back and forth at the rear of the saloon. He had bought a second saddle at the livery, and the black and chestnut mares stood ready to ride.

Soon the door opened, and Mabel stepped out, a carpetbag swinging from her right hand. Everett stepped over and grabbed the grip, tying the bag on behind the saddle on the chestnut. After helping her into the leather seat, he swung up on the black mare. Side-by-side they rode away in the dawning light, following the winding Mora River toward the Santa Fe Trail.

They spent the night in the Saint James Hotel in Cimarron, then hit the trail again, making Trinidad an hour after dark. They got rooms at the Sherman House, slept well past sunrise, then met for breakfast.

As they rode down crowded West Main Street, they soon discovered that every house was occupied, with new arrivals living in tents while waiting for permanent shelter to be completed.

"Let's check on jobs," Everett suggested, noticing a flurry of activity at Thatcher's General Store.

Inside the mercantile, they approached an elderly man, squatted down rearranging items on a low shelf.

"Sir, could we speak to the boss?" Everett asked.

"What can I do for you?" the man asked, raising himself upright.

"Would you have need of some help?" Everett asked.

"I certainly do!" the old fellow said, excitedly. "And you're a likely one for the job."

"Not for me," Everett said, then motioned toward Mabel. "This young lady needs steady work."

"It's a man's job I've got," the old fellow said. "People are buying up my inventory faster than I can stock it. I'm getting too old and stove-up to unload the freight wagon and get items on the shelves, some too heavy for my aching back."

Everett glanced at Mabel, then back at the man. "Thanks, sir, but we'll take a look about town," Everett replied, as they turned to leave.

"Hold on there. I just might have a job for her," the merchant said. "My wife died a few years back, and our only son is away in San Francisco. I'd sure like to have a woman around to cook, to do some sewing, washing, and such. Now, I can't pay much, but I can offer a nice room and regular meals."

"How much would it pay?" Everett asked.

"Maybe five a month," the man said, "spending money."

"She can make a lot more than that over at the Amusement Saloon," Everett said. "But wouldn't it be a shame for a nice, pretty, young woman like her to have to do that, when she could be doin' respectable work for you?"

"How much would she require?"

"Twelve a month," Everett said. "She's a good cook, handy with a needle, and mighty cheerful to be around. But she'll want time off on Sunday afternoon and for Saturday night dances."

The elderly man was rubbing his chin when a customer came up and asked about the price of a canvas cot. Another was interested in a tent.

"I'll be right with you," the merchant said to his impatient customers.

"Twelve a month, no less," Everett said firmly.

"Okay. It's a deal. Come back in an hour, and I'll take you out to the house," the man said as he rushed off to help the customer choose a cot.

Everett was smiling as they stepped out on the boardwalk.

"Everett Brook!" Mabel said, stepping in front of him. "If you'd lost me that job, I would have killed you!"

"Ah, I wish I'd asked for fifteen," he said, laughing.

"And what makes you think I know how to cook or would even recognize a sewing needle?"

"You grew up without a mother," he replied, his smile fading. "I know what that means."

She looped her arm through his, and they headed for the hotel, both smiling.

"Everett, I'm going to make you very proud of me," she said, lifting her chin.

He smiled down at her as he patted her hand. Inside, they took a seat at an empty table in the dining area.

"Well, it looks like the house will have to come later," he said. "But I'm gonna buy you some fine dresses with matching shoes and bonnets, and get you a good horse with a carriage. You're gonna be a proper lady, one this town's gonna take notice of."

"Oh, Everett. I can't thank you enough for what you've already done. I feel like a different person. Fact is, I may change my name! What would you pick for me?"

"Let's see. Maybe you should be Isabella, like that queen, or Catherine the Great," he said, laughing. "And I once heard of a woman named Cleopatra. What do you think of that one?"

"I'm serious, Everett! With a new start, I want a new name."

"Well, there is a name I've always liked. The name Penelope conjures up the thought of grace, someone fine, a lady to be admired for her natural beauty and kindness of heart. I think you should be Penelope Smith?"

"No, I don't think so. Penelope is fine, but I want a last name that folks will notice, rather than one to hide behind."

After thinking for a moment, he smiled. "My mother's maiden name was Hope. She'd be proud for you use it."

"I like that! I'll be Penelope Hope. That's something I haven't had much of, until now."

The hour passed, and they returned to the general store as the merchant was closing up for the night.

"I'm John McIntyre," the storekeeper said. "I don't believe I caught your name, Miss."

"Penelope Hope," she said, stealing a glance at Everett. "It's a pleasure to meet you, Mr. McIntyre."

"Well, if you two will follow me out back, I have a buckboard waiting," Mr. McIntyre said. "We'll get out to the house and let you get settled in."

"I'll get the horses and come around," Everett said.

He stepped out, and Mr. McIntyre locked the door behind him. Everett got the two horses and led them around to the back of the store where the storekeeper and the former Mabel were waiting. Everett followed them to a nice, roomy house about a mile west of town. Everett carried Penelope's cloth bag inside where Mr. McIntyre showed them the house, pointing out her room along the way. After half an hour of conversation, Everett excused himself to return to the Sherman House, Penelope following him out to the horses.

"When will I see you again, Everett?" she asked.

"I'll be back, bringing you that new carriage," he said, then reached into his pocket and counted out two hundred dollars, placing it in her hand. "Now, you get yourself some fine dresses and a few fancy things to go with them. The next time I see you, I want to have to ask your name!"

"Everett, I can't take your money. Soon enough I'll have earned my own, all I'll need."

"Please, just do as I ask. Get those dresses, shoes, and bonnets. I've never bought those things for a pretty woman, and I want to do it for you," he said, folding her small, soft hand around the money.

"Okay," she said, feeling overwhelmed. "I'll get the dresses tomorrow."

"And some of those pretty, lacy, white gloves," he said.

He rode back to the hotel thinking he needed a fresh start in his life, too. To do that, he thought, I've got to clean up my back trail. He would start with Josh, but eventually, he would have to settle with Vicente Silva and Samuel Harrison.

The next morning Everett bought a carriage and a gentle bay horse to pull it. Tying his black mare to the tailgate, he rippled the reins along the bay's back and headed for McIntyre's, arriving a few minutes later. Penelope answered the door.

"Step outside, my lady," Everett said, bowing with a long, low sweep of his right arm along her intended path, stopping when his open hand pointed toward the carriage.

Penelope took one step, then caught her breath.

"Oh, I love it, Everett!" she said, slowly approaching the black carriage.

He lifted her onto the seat, then slipped up beside her. Taking the reins, he guided the horse in a wide turn, then onto a narrow lane leading toward the foothills to the west. A mile later, he veered off the trail and turned the carriage onto a flat hilltop. He showed her how to hold the reins, how to turn the horse, how to brake the carriage, and how to lock the wheel.

"Now, it's your turn," he said, handing over the reins.

"I'm not sure I can," she said when he had come around and climbed in beside her.

"Ah, you'll do fine."

She slowly turned the horse and carriage and started back down the lane, rippling the reins as she had seen him do. The bay broke into a smooth, slow trot. The brisk morning air chilled her face as her long, brown hair fluttered in the wind. Down a sharp incline, she eased back on the brake handle, keeping the weight of the carriage off the horse, then made a smooth turn toward the house. She felt wonderful, experiencing a freedom she had never known before.

Back at the house, Everett congratulated her as she pulled up by the front gate. Her eyes sparkled as she brushed back her windblown hair.

"This is wonderful! I just can't believe it's mine!" she squealed with glee.

"Do you need me to unhitch the horse and put up the carriage?"

"Oh no! I've seen it done a hundred times," she replied. "Besides, it's mine, so I need to handle it for myself."

"Then I'll be going now," Everett said, hopping down, " but I'll be back soon."

"Where will you go?" she asked, a tinge of worry creeping into her voice.

"It's time I got some things straightened out," he said.

She slipped down from the carriage and met him at his horse. He swung into the saddle as she gazed up at him.

"Everett, please be careful. I'll miss you."

"Don't you worry none about me," he said, then cleared his throat. "I'll be back to see you when you're all dressed up."

Wondering, she waved as he rode away.

30

With his bags bulging with supplies, Everett headed south along the Santa Fe Trail. He reached the mountains bordering Moreno Valley the following day and started the climb toward Josh's mine. As he neared the claim, he hurried the pace, anxious to see his old friend and find out if he had a new partner.

Rounding a bend in the creek, he spotted the old cabin ahead and eased to a stop. The burro stood napping next to the west wall, and the campfire burned low with lazy blue smoke curling into the air and fading into a gray sky.

Everett smiled, and nudged his horses forward. Three strides later, he yanked them to a halt when a man ducked out the door of the cabin, a tall, lean fellow wearing a big brown hat, a fringed leather coat, and spurs that jingled with his every step. A revolver hung heavy on his right hip, tied low around his thigh, and his curious horse poked his head out from behind the cabin. In his gut, Everett knew something was wrong.

He quickly reined his ponies behind a rock shoulder jutting from the canyon wall and leaped down, yanking his rifle from the saddle scabbard. Hugging the cold wall, he peered around the boulder. The man stood by the campfire warming his hands. Moments later, he poured a cup of coffee from the familiar old pot sitting in the edge of the coals.

After several sips, the man dashed the remaining coffee from his cup onto the fire and tossed the tin aside, sending it rattling over rocks. Snatching up Josh's blackened gold pan, he tromped down to the creek's edge. After filling it with streambed sediment, he dipped the rim into the water and began an irregular circular motion, sloshing out water and dirt. Frustrated, he slammed the pan against the rocks with a sharp clatter, and stomped along the stream, cursing into the breeze.

Everett wanted to charge into the camp and find out what was going on, but the man might have a partner around somewhere, or maybe Josh had sold the claim to this cowboy. If so, he must have sold his burro and equipment as well, a development Everett considered farfetched. Josh was a miner, through and through, which means he still needed these tools of the trade. The clincher was the cowboy's awkward handling of the pan; he was no miner, nor ever likely to be.

With darkness approaching, Everett decided to move in and demand some answers. He grabbed his ponies' reins and led them around the boulder, sauntering casually toward the old cabin, whistling a tune.

When the cowboy heard Everett coming, he whirled around and grabbed his revolver. Everett pulled up and slowly raised his hands.

"Hello!" he called out. "I'm a friend of old Josh. Just dropping by to check on him."

"He sold out to me and moved on," the man replied, a sneer fixed on his face.

"How long back was that?" Everett asked, moving ahead at a casual but steady pace.

"Couple weeks." The man kept his gun leveled on Everett's midsection.

"Say where he was going?" Everett was maybe fifteen feet away now.

"Upstream, but he could have gone most anywhere after that." The man lowered his pistol.

Everett remembered that Josh had panned the upper part of the stream and was working his way down.

"That surprises me some," Everett said, shaking his head as he dropped the reins and eased away from his horses. "I'm certain he'd have moved downstream, and I just came up that way."

"No difference to me. I got no cause to worry which way he went," the man said, still gripping his ivory-handled pistol.

"I reckon you got a bill of sale," Everett said, sauntering two steps closer. "You see, I was his partner, and I figure old Josh owes me a fair share."

"Look!" the man growled, his face turning red. "I bought this claim from that old man! You got a part comin', you best get it from him."

"You make a good point there. But just so he can't cheat me, tell me this. How much did you pay?" Everett asked, glancing up at the digging on the canyon wall, which was plugged with brush.

"More'n it's worth. I ain't found no gold here."

"There's gold, all right," Everett said. "I expect Josh showed you our diggings."

"If you mean that shaft up there," the man said, jerking his thumb upstream, "it ain't nothin' but dirt and rock."

Everett laughed, rubbing the back of his neck with his left hand. "I'm afraid old Josh snookered you, cowboy."

"What do you mean?" the man asked, holstering his revolver.

"I mean you're lying, and I ain't leaving 'til I get a straight story from you," Everett said, his eyes suddenly fixed on the man.

"You'll move on, or I'll fill you with lead!" the man said, his hand still on the butt of his gun.

"Like you did the old man?" Everett asked, his right hand now hanging beside his revolver.

Glaring and riled, the man noticed and hesitated.

"Josh never wore a gun. Did you shoot a defenseless old man?" Everett asked, pushing a step closer.

Suddenly Everett feigned a turn back toward his horses, but as he did, his right hand flashed to his gun. Before the man could react, Everett had him dead in his sights.

The cowboy stood as if frozen. With Everett only eight feet away, even if the man could draw his gun, a shootout would undoubtedly leave both men seriously wounded, and the nearest help miles away.

"If you want to get off this mountain alive, you'll tell me where old Josh is and where your partner is hiding out," Everett said, his face hard, his jaw muscles rippling.

"I didn't kill him! I swear I didn't!" the cowboy replied.

"Where is he?" Everett asked, stepping closer.

"Hidin' out somewhere upstream."

"And your partner's gone after him?"

"I'm alone."

"Drop your gun belt, real slow like." When the man had unbuckled and let it fall at his feet, Everett continued. "Now head over to the cabin."

He followed, snatching up the man's pistol on the way.

"Step inside," Everett ordered, then peeked in after him, hoping to find Josh, maybe bound and gagged.

Instead, he found the cabin empty and no sign of a struggle. Then he noticed the old prospector's coat hanging from a nail on the back of the door, and his rifle resting across two wooden pegs on the back wall.

"Sit down and take your boots off, along with your socks," Everett said as they eased back outside.

"But my feet will freeze!" the man protested.

"Not if you hurry off this mountain," Everett replied with a slight smile. "And if you don't, you won't be needing boots, anyway."

Everett motioned the barefoot man around behind the cabin to his horse. The saddle boot held a rifle, which Everett slipped out and laid across the crook of his left arm, then checked the saddlebags.

"Climb up," Everett said, grasping the reins while the man stepped gingerly over and stuck a pale foot into the stirrup. "Now ride out of here, and don't come back. And if I find you've killed old Josh, I'll come after you. There won't be a safe place for you this side of the Mississippi."

Everett slapped the pony on the rump and watched him gallop downstream, horse and rider disappearing beyond the bend.

"God help you if you've killed old Josh," Everett muttered as he turned toward the gurgling stream.

Josh was out there somewhere without a coat, and with night coming on, the temperature was dropping rapidly, headed for the teens at eighty-four hundred feet. If the old prospector was alive, he had to be found quickly.

Everett scoured the area for leads, a hat, a glove, a tool, a bloodstained rock, but found none. He trotted upstream, calling out and darting into every nook and cranny along the way. Heavy cloud cover brought on early darkness, and Everett finally worked his way back to the cabin, fearing the worst.

After caring for his horses and unpacking, he warmed supper and sat by the fire, listening, thinking, and hoping. He poked at the fire, chunked on more wood, and kept the coffee hot. If I hadn't left Josh alone, he thought, remembering the old prospector's admonition, "A lone man can't make it up here, not anymore."

If I had come back sooner, just a few hours, I'd have been here when that dirty coyote showed up. My life must be destined for mistakes, for killing, stealing, and for hanging, just like Pa. I sure wish I'd given Josh his fair share of the gold money.

As he spread his bedroll the length of the cot, he longed to get his hands on that cowboy. Wish I had tied him to a tree and left him out in the cold, he thought to himself, like he did Josh.

After a restless night, Everett rolled out of bed, anxious to renew the hunt for his old partner. Outside, he instinctively searched around camp, hoping for any sign. After scanning up and down the stream, he stepped over to the campfire, quietly enjoying its lively flames.

Then suddenly it came to him. He grabbed his gun, staring at the fire that should not be there. When he had gone to bed a little before midnight, the blaze had about burned itself out. Who rebuilt the fire, and when? he wondered. The cowboy? If so, he's likely up on the canyon rim with a Winchester trained down on me right now.

After darting to the side of the cabin, Everett eased to the back edge and scanned along the top of the canyon walls. Nothing. Carefully, he eased out into the open and accounted for all the tools, pans, cookware, and his horses. Everything was there. He then searched for tracks in the sand around the campfire, but there were hundreds of them, his own, the cowboy's, Josh's. It made no sense.

Hungry and frustrated, he snatched up the old coffeepot. It was half full, though it had been nearly empty when he had gone to bed. He poured a cup. It was hot and black, more so than he preferred.

He spent the day searching up and down the stream for clues, a fragment of clothing, a fresh grave, anything, but found no answers.

Later that night, Everett sat by the fire, his rifle resting across his thighs, wondering who might be out there. Night noises, the murmuring wind, even the crackling and popping of the fire seemed exaggerated, causing him to back into the shadows and stare into the darkness. About midnight, exhausted and frustrated, he stepped inside the cabin, barred the door with a strong pole run through a couple of iron rings, one bolted into the wall on each side, pulled the canvas curtains tight across the windows, and went to bed. Lying still, a jumble of thoughts and emotions tumbled through his mind, driving away sleep.

Up early the next morning, he strapped on his revolver, pulled on his coat, and grabbed his rifle. Pushing the curtain back, he peered out, but saw nothing unusual. With the bar removed, he eased open the door, and slipped out.

As before, the campfire burned lively, and a swirling gray tail of steam rose from the spout on the old coffeepot. The frustration and worry were almost more than he could take.

After another day of fruitless search, he returned to the cabin, baffled and ready to pack up and ride out. Gradually he had come to the conclusion that the old prospector was dead, either killed by the cowboy or by exposure to the mountain's frosty weather. He took some solace in the fact that the mystery night visitor apparently intended him no harm. Maybe some rogue miner wants the claim, he thought, and is trying to spook me into leaving. Tomorrow, I'll climb up and see if the gold has played out.

Before retiring that night, he set a fresh pot of coffee over red-hot coals, and hung a tin cup on a fork of one of the stakes that supported the horizontal rod spanning the fire. He then swung a pot of beans from the rod, using the S-shaped iron hook that hung about a foot above the fiery bed. He wanted the mystery man to know he knew, and he hoped to send him a welcome message.

In bed early, he lay on his cot and listened, rising occasionally and peeking out at the campfire. About midnight, he added wood to the flames, and stirred the beans.

Rising early again, he rushed outside. The cup hung from an arm of the forked stick, just as he had left it. The pot of beans still swung over the small fire, and the coffeepot sat on a bed of red coals. However, removing the lid, he found most of the beans gone and the coffeepot half-empty.

After breakfast, Everett wedged himself behind some thick brush along the jagged canyon wall and pulled out the ladder from where he and Josh had always hid it. He wagged it over to the face of the wall and leaned it so the top rung rested beside the masked hole.

With a pick slipped inside his belt, he shimmied up the ladder, pulled out the bushes, and peered inside. Seeing nothing but darkness, he crawled in and found it several feet deeper than he recalled. Lying on his side, he took a few awkward swings at the back wall with the pick, prying away clumps of rock and dirt. Stuffing his pockets full, he backed out, and onto the ladder. Down by the stream, he found the bent pan, reshaped it the best he could, emptied his pockets into it, and dipped its upstream side into the current. After swirling away the dirt and tossing out the rocks, a bed of black sand gleaming with specks of gold stared up at him. He wished Josh were there to see it.

He continued working the claim all day, skimming off the gold into a leather pouch he found hanging on the wall. The quantity was not what it had been initially, but he guessed he had five or six ounces, over a hundred dollars, too much to walk away from.

That night Everett again left out coffee and food, and as he readied for bed, he took a brush-broom and whisked away all tracks around the campfire. Weary, he slept well.

With first light, he ducked through the doorway and gazed at the barren sand in front of the fire. Boot tracks stared back at him.

"Josh!" he exclaimed. "It's you, you old rascal! You're not dead, after all."

The prints were familiar, easily identified by the tack marks on the left heel, which he had helped the old prospector reattach.

Everett called out for his partner, first upstream, then down. No response.

Stiff and sore, he climbed the ladder and worked the mine. He had forgotten how tiring and backbreaking the work was. At day's end, he had another eight ounces.

That night, he put out food, but also hung Josh's old coat on the door front. Pinned to the coat, he left a note.

Josh, it's Johnny. Come on in. Your bed's waiting.

In the dark and cold, the door hinges squeaked, and Everett moved under his blankets. The door squawked again, and he opened his eyes to flickering shadows on the wall. When he raised his head, a short, bulky silhouette was framed in the doorway, a blazing fire in the background.

"Josh?" Everett asked, straining to see.

"Johnny?" the familiar scratchy voice responded.

Everett leaped from his bed.

"Where've you been?" he asked. "What happened?"

"Step on out by the fire," the old prospector said. "I want to see your face."

Everett rushed out, ramming his fists through his coat sleeves.

"Gosh blame," the old fellow said, "if it ain't you, Johnny."

"You're alive, partner!" Everett said, hugging his old friend and clapping him on the back. "What happened?"

"Well, one afternoon I was upstream there a ways, pannin' as usual, when I hears a noise from downstream. I turns and looks and a cowboy has me dead in the sights of his long-barreled shooter. I begun'st to run, and he fires at me, missin' by no more than a whisker stub.

"As you could guess, I didn't wait around for socializin', and I had no intention of being a target in a shootin' gallery. So, I heads for the nearest place where I can climb outta this canyon. Quick as a bear goes to honey, I scampers up that wall. Scramblin' to my feet, I hears that yeller-belly coyote bellowin' somethin' at me, but I wasn't stayin' for the dance. Just then a couple more shots ring out, but miss. Lucky for me, that cowboy must've been purty near blind, 'cause I was perched up there like a turkey on a naked limb. Anyways, I moves on as fast as these stubby legs will carry me.

"I know'd of a place upstream, a place with a cave. I decides to try to make it there, and with the help of the Almighty, I does just that. So I stays in that cave by day, and scavenges for grub by night. I finds a few berries, but mostly I stays hungry, bad hungry. Finally, at night I sneaks back here, and from that rim up there, I watches the camp, knowin' there's food down here. But, somebody was in my cabin. I know'd that for certain, too.

"When I knows he's asleep, I sneaks down, movin' quiet as a feather on the wind, and helps myself to my own grub, and warms by my own fire, all the time thinkin' that scoundrel is sleepin' in my warm bed while my teeth is a'chatterin'.

"Then one night I gets a surprise. A pot of beans sits there a'warmin'. I eats 'em, and drinks the coffee, to boot. The next night, coffee and food was there, intentional-like. Then there's my coat a'hangin' on the door, and this note. At first I thinks it's some sorta trap, but lordy, how I wants that coat. My old thumper about stops when I reads your name on that paper, Johnny. Makes me about the happiest man on this here mountain!"

"Same as me," Everett said. "I'd about given you up for dead."

"By the way, what did happen to that stinkin' skunk that came in a shootin' at me?"

"I got the drop on him," Everett explained. "Sent him packing, barefoot."

Josh cackled while smacking his hands together. "Got to have a partner up here, that's what I say."

"And there's still gold up there," Everett said, pointing to the hole on the wall. "I brought down eight ounces today."

Josh went quiet and stepped close. "Partner, that scoundrel never found my money, did he? I'd a rode out the first night, but I just couldn't leave my gold stash."

"I reckon not," Everett said. "He rode out with a real sour look on his face."

The old prospector motioned for Everett to follow over to the canyon wall, stopping at the foot of the tall ladder.

"Let's scoot it over there to that big flat rock stickin' out," he said, pointing up.

They moved the heavy ladder about fifteen feet to the left, and set its feet firmly in the dirt. Everett started up.

"Under that ledge," Josh said, "there's a hole about the size of a double fist. You'll find a sharp-edged rock stuck in its mouth. Inside there's a strip of rolled leather tied up with a rawhide string."

Everett scaled the ladder, being careful in the dark. When he reached the rocky ledge, he extended his left hand along its bottom edge until he felt the sharp corner of a rock. Taking hold, he pulled it out and laid it on the ledge. Then he stuck his hand in the hole and pulled out the makeshift pouch. Back on the ground, he handed it to his partner, who removed the string and unrolled it.

Everett whistled, having never seen such a stack of money.

"Gold money," Josh said with a big, gap-toothed smile.

"How much?" Everett asked.

"More'n twenty thousand."

"Partner," Everett said. "I've got two hundred and eighty dollars of yours to go with it."

"What do you mean?"

"That first sample I took to town brought seven hundred and sixty. I only gave you a hundred."

"I'll take it," Josh said. "And you'll be obliged to take half of this."

"That wouldn't be right," Everett said. "We were fifty-fifty partners when I dug up the sample. I was gone when you got this."

"The wind blows both ways, partner," Josh said, eyeballing the midpoint of the stack.

"Then I'll just keep your two eighty," Everett said.

"Suit yourself," the old fellow replied, re-wrapping the money.

With the money back safe under the ledge and the ladder stowed, the two went to bed.

For the next two weeks, they worked their claim, returns steadily diminishing.

"Looks like it's about played out," Everett said one afternoon.

"Yeah, but there's a bigger deposit right close by," old Josh said. "I think what we found is what washed down and settled on top of some soft rock."

"Think we ought to check higher?"

"That's my bet."

The next morning Everett moved the ladder closer to the wall and climbed up, a pick hanging from his belt. He began chopping away dirt and rock, Josh taking occasional samples. The second day, with the hole six feet deep, Josh washed some diggings, then called up to Everett.

"You're gettin' close," he said. "A fine sample, that last one was."

With renewed vigor, Everett swung the pick. As he shoveled out the loose earth, he saw gold glitter in the sunlight. A nugget.

Rushing down, he handed the bucket of dirt, rock, and ore to Josh, pointing.

"That's it, sonny," Josh said all bubbly, grabbing a fistful of the diggings. "You've found a good streak, all right."

Five days later, they had stuffed every container they could find with gold.

"Better close her up," Josh said, "and cash in what we've got."

In town, they set their yellow-filled pouches, cans, and jars on the counter, smiling. An hour later, they walked away with ten thousand eight hundred dollars.

"I've got more money than a cowboy makes in a lifetime," Everett said, adding his half to what he had in his saddlebags.

"What'll you do with it?" Josh asked.

"Partner, my heart's set on having a ranch, a good herd of beeves, and a string of cowponies," Everett said. "And I think I've got enough here for a good start."

"Sounds like you're leavin' again," Josh said.

"I came here to set things right with you, and I've about done that. Now it's time I clean up a few other things on my back trail."

"But we've just hit a good one, partner," Josh pleaded, motioning to the new hole on the wall. "I expect there's three times, maybe four, what we've taken out."

"It's yours, partner," Everett replied. "Always was your claim."

"I'll put some aside for you, just in case you come back," the miner said, smiling.

"I'll worry about you up here alone," Everett said.

"Won't be alone. There's a lonesome prospector across the way beggin' to join up with me."

That moonlit night, Everett stepped inside early and packed up, all except his bedroll, stacking his things at the foot of his cot. With Josh outside, restless, Everett slipped inside his bedroll while his partner pitched wood onto the fire, sending a firestorm of sparks into the night air.

Rising early, Everett saddled the black, strapped the packs on the chestnut, then slipped back inside where Josh was snoring. Everett reached inside his coat pocket, counted out two hundred eighty dollars, and poked it inside his partner's hanging coat. He whispered a goodbye and eased out.

Two nights later he registered for a room at the Plaza Hotel in Las Vegas. Handing his saddlebags to the clerk at the desk, he asked to deposit his money in the hotel safe.

"How much?" the clerk asked.

"About twelve thousand," Everett replied.

"I'd better count it," the man responded, motioning Everett to follow him to a back room where the heavy safe stood.

The clerk counted meticulously, making stacks of one thousand each. When he finished the eighth stack, Everett knew something was wrong. The uncounted stack was twice the combined size of the counted ones.

Upon completing the sixteenth pile, the clerk glanced up at Everett, then continued. When the process was done, the man counted twenty-two stacks, with four hundred dollars left over, ten thousand too much.

31

Las Vegas, New Mexico Territory
Summer 1884

The next morning Everett milled among the vendors and customers around the Las Vegas plaza, asking about Vicente Silva, but the responses he got were dire warnings.

"He ain't a man to go lookin' for," an old fellow advised. "Ever since Refugio Esquibel found his stolen horses out at the Monte Largo with the VS brand freshly burned on their hip, Silva's been hidin' out. Askin' too many questions is beggin' for the worst kind of trouble."

"You go snoopin' uninvited," another said, "and the best you can hope for is, you don't find him. The worst is, you do."

But Everett was determined to have an understanding with the man, so he could quit looking over his shoulder.

The second night as Everett sat pushed back at a corner table in The Imperial Saloon, sipping a whiskey and watching men come and go, two fellows barged through the door, looked around, then headed for his table.

"You want to see Silva?" the mustached one asked, standing to Everett's left while his partner waited on the other side, their hands resting on the handles of his revolvers.

"That's what I keep telling folks," Everett replied.

"What's your business with him?"

"Owe him some money. Want to settle up."

"Come with us," the man said.

Outside, the one in front suddenly turned, his revolver drawn. Everett grabbed for his, but it was gone. The man behind him was slipping it inside his wide belt.

"And they say he's a bad hombre," the outlaw said, laughing.

"You'll get it back, if the boss says so," the lead man said.

For two hours they rode into the mountains, then stopped at the mouth of a little canyon.

"Here, we blindfold you," the leader said, pulling out a strip of black cloth.

With Everett's eyes covered and his hands bound behind him, they rode on. He leaned forward in the saddle, countering the slope his pony was climbing. The smell of pine and spruce grew strong.

Sometime later with a sharp chill in the air, they reined up their ponies and swung down, leading their prisoner. Everett felt the wave of heat when they pushed him through the doorway. Then one of the men removed the kerchief.

As Everett's eyes adjusted, he recognized Silva but not the other two men sitting at a table across the room. Their leader was puffing on a cigar.

"You come back so I can kill you?" Silva asked.

"Would you shoot an unarmed man?" Everett replied.

"Wouldn't be the first time," one of the men beside Silva said, laughing.

"Some say you're a bad man, but none say you're yellow," Everett said. "Maybe they're wrong."

"Untie 'im and give 'im his gun," Silva barked, jumping to his feet.

Calmly, Everett spun the cylinder, checking the loads, then holstered his revolver.

"Your boy, Bandanna," Everett said, "tried to settle our disagreement this way. I figure you to be smarter."

"What we got to settle?" Silva asked.

"I stole a white stallion from you," Everett said, slowly reaching inside his coat. "Sold it for forty dollars and counted it my pay. The money's rightly yours, but you've got thirty of mine. Back wages."

With his eyes locked on Silva, Everett pitched ten dollars on the table. "Now we're even, so call off your bloodhounds."

“You’re a horse thief,” the badman finally said without moving, “tryin’ to buy your soul back.”

“My soul’s worth a sight more. I just figured to set things straight between us,” Everett said. “Now, I’ll be moving along.”

“Want me to plug ‘im?” asked the man with the mustache.

“Bandanna was quick,” Silva said, his steely eyes locked on Everett. “What chance you think you’ve got, Menguado? No, I think he’s worth more to me alive.

“Cowboy, how about you take Bandanna’s place up in the meadow. It pays fifty a month, victuals, and five extra for every wild mustang you bring in.”

“I’m on a different trail,” Everett said. “I’m not interested in back-tracking.”

“You’ve got no choice,” Silva said. “You know too much. I can’t let you walk out.”

“There’s only one way to stop me,” Everett said, waiting calmly.

Silva stepped back from the table, his eyes narrowing. Sweat beaded on his forehead.

“Think about it, Silva,” Everett said. “It’s been months. If I was going to talk, the law would already be hot on your trail.”

Silva hesitated. He was alive because he was careful. The slightest hint that one of his bandits might betray him, and that man died. So why was he waiting? The only man he had ever feared was Bandanna. Silva had heard about the showdown in Horse Thief Meadow, and now he was facing the winning side of that fight.

“You ever cross me again,” he muttered, “I’ll feed you to the coyotes. Now get outta here and don’t never come back.”

El Menguado, The Shrunken One, headed toward Everett, pulling out the blindfold.

“It’s no use. I know the trail,” Everett said, cutting his eyes over at the horse thief.

Menguado glanced at Silva who motioned him aside.

Everett then backed his way to the door and let himself out.

He had recognized the cabin as the hunter’s hideout, the one he had led the priest to. With the mare in a trot, he made his way down the mountain, glancing back occasionally to an empty back trail.

Everett packed his things at the hotel, picked up the chestnut at the livery, and rode north. After a night in the Saint James in Cimarron, he rode on to Trinidad, reclaiming his room at the Sherman House. Mid-morning the next day, he rode out to the home of John McIntyre.

"Everett!" Penelope cried out, running to meet him. "You're back!"

"You're looking good," he said. "Colorful as a ripe peach, and just as sweet, no doubt."

"Stop the teasing and come on in."

He swung his leg over a chair back and took a seat while she poured two cups of coffee.

"Tell me where you've been," she said.

He related his trip back to Josh Clawson, without mention of the gold find. Then he told about Silva, how he had set things square with him.

"I guess you're ready to settle down now," she said.

"I'll be looking for ranchland," he said. "How about you?"

"It's been wonderful," she replied. "Mr. McIntyre is such a nice man. And he has a son who's been away in San Francisco. He'll be here in a couple of days. I hope he's like his father."

"Sometimes it's that way," Everett said, thinking of his pa, "sometimes not. But I expect he'll fall all over himself to please you."

"Oh, Everett, don't say things like that."

"Why, he'll be in love with you in sight of a week," Everett went on. "I can already hear wedding bells."

"I'm so happy right now that I don't want to be married," she replied, smiling. "Unless you want to propose."

"I'm a failure at love, Penelope. But don't you miss your chance," he replied, looking down at his cup. "Now, how about those new dresses?"

"Want to see them?"

"I'll wait right here."

"I'll go change into the prettiest one," she said.

Five minutes later, she returned wearing an ankle-length blue dress, matching bonnet, and frilly white gloves. To Everett, she looked like she had just stepped out of a catalog.

"My, how pretty you are," he said, rising to his feet. "My favorite color."

She blushed, then lifted the hem of the dress slightly and stuck out her foot, revealing a fancy white shoe with three narrow leather straps crossing her arch and threaded through shiny buckles.

He extended his arm so she could loop hers through, and then they danced around the room. Finally, he stepped back and took a long look while she glowed with joy.

"Let's take a ride in the carriage," she suggested.

"I'll get the bay hitched and pull it around front," Everett replied.

She was standing on the front porch when he arrived at the gate, then started down the steps.

"Hold it right there, Lady Penelope," he said, jumping down and rushing toward her.

He took her hand and led her down the steps and to the buggy.

"Where to, my dear?" he asked with an exaggerated bow.

"My secret castle in the mountains," she replied, lifting her nose into the air and profiling her face.

They followed the trail to the foothills, but kept climbing to the edge of a high meadow with a gurgling stream twisting through it.

"Let's stop right over there under those trees," she said, pointing to a cluster of aspen on the side of the hill. Then gazing out over the waving grass, she continued. "What do you think?"

"Fit for a queen," he said, "or a fine ranch home."

"Maybe you should buy it and start your ranch right here."

"But what about your castle?" he teased.

"Oh, I've got others," she replied, playing the part.

For several minutes, they sat quietly enjoying the scenery and the solitude, their thoughts on the future.

"Everett," she said softly, "I've never known a kinder human being. If ever there is anything I can do for you, just let me know."

"It's enough that you're my friend," he replied. "Now, I reckon I'd better get you back to the house."

They rode back in silence, and at the gate he lifted her down and walked her to the porch.

"Gotta keep those pretty shoes nice and clean," he said, reaching down and brushing away some dust. "Leastwise until that McIntyre boy gets here."

"Goodbye, Everett," she said as he turned and headed for the gate. "And don't wait so long to come back."

Climbing up on his horse, he smiled, tipped his hat, and rode away.

For two weeks, Everett searched for ranchland. He finally set his sights on twelve thousand acres southeast of town, along the headwaters of the Cimarron River. He loved the rolling hills, the wide-open spaces, the towering mountains in the background. The Maxwell Cattle Company offered the ranch for fifteen thousand dollars, stocked with nearly five hundred head of cattle. He had only to ride to Cimarron, pay the money, and sign the papers to complete the deal, but he stalled.

West of town, along the Purgatoire River, he found excellent grassland east of the foothills of the towering mountains, reminding him of that on the Bannister ranch. In the distance stood a towering stone wall, a remarkable monument to nature's sculptor. It was called Stoner's wall, its namesake being James N. Stoner, a nearby homesteader and postmaster in Trinidad. Again he hesitated.

"I'm not sure why," he explained to Penelope on Sunday afternoon. "It's what I want."

"No need to fret," she advised. "You're young and there's land everywhere out here."

"Maybe I'll go back and check on Josh," he said.

The next day, he bought supplies, packed, and headed south. Arriving at the old mining shack, Everett found the prospector in great spirits.

"Best deposit of gold I've ever come across," he explained to Everett. "I'm minin' fifty ounces a week, and could do three times that except I'm so decrepit I can't work from that ladder more'n a few hours a day."

"What about that partner?"

"Ah, he was as lazy as that donkey over there. I run him off after two days."

"I'll stay around and help," Everett said. "After all, I owe you for the ten thousand you slipped into my saddlebags."

"I'd be much obliged to you," the old fellow said. "Though you don't owe me nothin'."

For three weeks, the two worked the mine, Everett climbing the ladder, hacking deeper and deeper into the wall, and lugging buckets of diggings down, shoveling it into the long tom while his partner sifted it through the rocker at the other end and washed it. With twenty-three pouches full of gold, they agreed it was time to go cash in.

In town they went directly to the bank. After assaying and weighing the gold, the teller counted out sixteen thousand two hundred dollars. They split the money, and headed for the Herman Mutz Hotel for a hot meal.

Their stomachs full and packs bulging with supplies from Kaiser's store, they mounted up and headed back. Everett kept a lookout over his shoulder, suspicious of two men he had noticed trailing them since they had left the bank.

"This mare seems to have a loose shoe," Everett said as they started up the mountain trail. "You ride along. I'll catch up."

After making sure Josh continued along the trail, Everett began picking at imaginary debris wedged into the cleft of the black's right front hoof. While doing so, he kept an eye on the valley trail, soon spotting the two men. He climbed back into the saddle and caught up to his partner.

"We're being followed," he explained to Josh. "A couple of fellows from town."

Halfway up the mountain at a sharp bend in the trail, Everett reined up.

"Josh, you pull off there in that thicket," he said, "while I double back and check on those two no-good skunks."

Everett hurried back to a rocky ledge overlooking the mountain trail. He soon spotted the two men stopped at a trail crossing below, studying the ground.

Keeping an eye on them, he eased down the slope, staying in the trees. Suddenly, he spurred his mount out onto the other fork of the trail, some fifty feet from the men.

"You fellas lost?" he asked, turning his pony toward them.

"We could ask the same of you, prospector," replied the taller one, wearing a much-soiled, red shirt.

"And what makes you think I'm a prospector?" Everett asked.

"Most everybody on this mountain is," the man replied.

"What about you two?" Everett asked.

"Just havin' a look around, thinkin' of stakin' a claim," the man replied, smiling as he glanced at his partner.

"I don't doubt you're looking for gold," Everett said, "gold somebody's already washed."

"We'll take it however we come across it," the man's partner said.

"And what if it was my gold?" Everett asked.

"Like my pardner said, we ain't particular," the one in the red shirt replied.

"A cowboy tried that a while back. I sent him packing, barefoot," Everett said, "but I was in a good humor that day."

While they hesitated, Everett slipped down from his mare and closed the gap between them to about twenty feet. He focused on the one with the red shirt, the bolder of the two.

"Either draw iron or get off this mountain. Either suits me," Everett said. "To my way of thinking, a gold thief's no better than a horse thief. Either way, it's a man's livelihood you're taking."

The two men stared at Everett for a moment, then climbed into their saddles and turned down the trail. When they were well out of sight, Everett rode up to the thicket where his partner waited.

"What'd you say to those two?" Josh asked, kneeing his mule back onto the trail.

"I told 'em you was hidin' in the brush with a buffalo gun trained on 'em, and that, though you was my daddy, you was the meanest and most ornery polecat that ever walked these hills. Then I told 'em I'd buried too many men you'd already killed, and I wasn't gonna dig two more graves today. They sent their apologies."

"You're gonna ruin my reputation," Josh said, shaking his head. "All the same, I'm right proud to have you around."

For the next several days, Everett kept a close lookout from atop the ladder. His caution slowed the digging process, but they were still bagging about twenty ounces a day.

Three weeks later, the mine was fading fast, but they had accumulated several filled pouches. They stuffed the gold into their saddlebags and headed to town.

The banker weighed their ore and declared that it was worth nearly seven thousand dollars. They pocketed the money and headed for Kaiser's Mercantile.

When they stepped outside, Everett was surprised to see an old friend.

"Zeb," he called out, rushing over to the chuck-wagon cook from Bannister's ranch. "What're you doing here?"

"Ah, I've given up the cowboy life," he said. "Thought I'd find a soft job here in town, sweepin' out or somethin'. I hear a man can make it fine with a broom, just sackin' up the gold dust spilled in the saloons."

Everett quickly introduced Josh, then turned back to Zeb.

"Sign on with Josh here, and you'll fill every sack you can find, but it won't be with a broom."

After Everett explained his past friendship with Zeb, the two old-timers got to talking. Everett noticed the sparkle in the old cook's eye and the smile behind the beard on Josh's face.

"Young fellas," he said with a clap on their backs, "I'm going to hit the trail. I've got some miles to cover." Then he explained he was headed for Trinidad, but would be back to check on them in a month or so.

After claiming a room at the Sherman House in Trinidad, Everett rode out to the McIntyre place.

"Everett! Come in!" Penelope said, beaming as she opened the door.

After a hug, they moved inside and took seats opposite each other. Momentarily, Penelope rose and walked over to his chair.

"Everett, Mr. McIntyre's son arrived a while back. He's nice, real nice. His name is Cole, and I think he likes me."

"He'd be a fool if he didn't. Maybe you've found the right man, after all."

"Maybe," she said, turning toward the window. "But he doesn't know about my past, and I'm not sure I can tell him."

"You've got to. If he loves you, your past won't matter none."

"I don't want to mess this up. I may not get another chance."

"Do you plan to question him about his bygone days?"

"No, of course not. I'm interested, I suppose, but I'm sure he's never . . . well, been bad like I have. But if he had, it wouldn't change things."

"So he won't care that you've made mistakes. We all have, Penelope."

Everett stood, and she looped her arm through his as they headed toward the door.

"Everett, if Cole asks me, I'm going to say yes. But, there'll always be a special place in my heart for you. You'll forever be welcome, wherever I am."

"Ah, Penelope," he said, his face flushing. "Marry this fella, and give him a house full of kids. You'll be the best and the happiest mother in town."

"I don't know about that, but I'm sure lucky to be Penelope Hope."

"Well, I hear good luck comes to them that deserve it."

Outside, they stood looking at each other, sensing big changes not far into their future.

"Penelope," Everett said, "I always said that someday you'd be the prettiest lady in town. Right now, standin' there in that lavender dress, your eyes sparklin' like a fresh raindrop, and your hair shiny and soft in the breeze, I'd say that day has come. This Cole gent had better marry you before some other fella comes along."

"Though all that's not true, thanks for saying it anyway," she replied, blushing.

"Well, I'd better be going. But I'll be back for the wedding."

"Everett, what about that girl back in Kansas?"

"Tabitha? It's too late now."

"I don't think so. She's no more forgotten you than you have her."

"She's got a husband, likely a kid or two by now."

"You've only got that cowboy's word on that. I expect someday you'll want to see for yourself."

Shaking his head, he told her goodbye.

32

Trinidad, Colorado
December 1884

After three more weeks of fruitless search for ranchland, Everett rode out to the McIntyre place to check on Penelope. Approaching along the winding dusty lane, he spotted her seated snugly against a neatly dressed young man, swaying back and forth in the front-porch swing. Seeing him, the couple stood and ambled over to the top of the porch steps as Everett opened the yard gate and headed up the walkway. The man appeared a little less than six feet tall with a slight frame and clean-cut features so similar to John McIntyre that Everett knew he was the merchant's son.

"Everett, I'm glad you've come by," Penelope said, looping her right arm through her companion's left. "I want you to meet Cole McIntyre. Cole, this is my friend, Everett Brook."

The two men shook hands as Everett removed his hat.

"Penelope has told me lots of good things about you, Mr. Brook," Cole said, motioning Everett to a nearby chair as he and Penelope returned to the swing.

"Right or wrong, I'm not about to contradict her," Everett replied, smiling. "And she's told me nothing but good things about you."

"And I suggest we leave it at that," Cole said with a chuckle.

"Well, do you plan to stay in town, maybe help your father with the store?" Everett asked.

"I do. I wasn't sure of that until I got back," he said, smiling at Penelope.

"Yeah, I can understand that. And this town is fortunate to have you around. Your father's about ready to bow out, and Frank Bloom will be glad to have you step into his place."

"Father will stay on until I learn the ropes. Then, I'll be glad to take over. You see, we're going to be married soon," he said, taking Penelope's hand. "I hope you can come to the wedding."

"Congratulations!" Everett said cutting his eyes at Penelope. "Have you set a date?"

"Two weeks from Saturday afternoon. It'll be here at the house."

"I'll be here. You can count on it. Now, where will you live?"

"In all your looking, have you found anything you'd recommend?"

"Places I've been checking on are too far out of town for your needs," Everett replied. "Have you considered settling here on your father's spread?"

"There's a meadow up there," Cole replied, pointing toward the mountainside. "Penelope likes it a lot."

"I know the spot, and I don't see how you could beat it. A house on that ledge on the west side of the mountain, overlooking the meadow, would be just perfect," Everett said, remembering when he and Penelope had ridden there.

"That's what I think," Penelope said. "Close to his father, not far from the store, and it's so beautiful."

"You two will be as happy as a pair of larks, wherever you settle," Everett said, getting up to leave.

After a handshake with Cole, he extended his hand toward Penelope.

"I'll walk you to your horse," she said. "I'll be right back, Cole."

"Everett," she said, standing by his pony. "I've told Cole about my past, and it's okay. I've never been so happy."

"I'm glad for you, Penelope. Cole's a lucky man."

"See you at the wedding," she said, smiling.

Riding back to town, Everett remembered when he had first met her in the saloon at Mora. She smiled a lot back then too, but differently, somehow. Now her eyes joined in, bright and alive. What a change has come over her, he thought.

But quickly the smile faded as he pulled his horse to a stop. His thoughts turned inward. I'm still a wanted man, an outlaw. If I don't set things straight with Harrison, I'll be looking over my shoulder until I die, most likely just like my pa. Suddenly, he knew why he had been unable to finalize a deal for a ranch. Until I clean up my back trail, I don't have a future, he concluded.

Back at the Sherman House, he made his way to the dining room for supper. As usual, his eyes quickly scanned the room. A dapper man wearing a fashionable hat and sporting a dark, well-trimmed mustache and a stiff-collared white shirt sat at a corner table. His dark suit coat was buttoned just below the neck and open at the waist, making his shoulders appear narrow. His gray-blue eyes fairly danced as he visited with two women hovering around his table, talking and gesturing excitedly.

Before Everett ordered his meal, he asked quietly about the fancy-dressed fellow.

"Bat Masterson," the waitress explained. "He still has an interest in a gamblin' house here in town, and only two years ago he was the town marshal."

"What's he doing in town?" Everett asked.

"I heard him say somethin' about a special assignment," the woman said. "Could be he's doin' detective work, or chasin' after some gunman. They say he's about the best there is at huntin' down outlaws."

Everett knew Masterson had spent years in Dodge City, filling various lawman positions. Could he be in Trinidad looking for him? If so, should he run or face the problem head on?

"I'll be back later," he told the woman, pulling his hat brim down and slipping out of the room.

For the next couple of weeks, Everett roamed the countryside, taking his meals at Red Bransford's and returning to the Sherman House only after dark. But the day of Penelope's wedding, he stayed in town. After a shave and bath, he dressed in his best clothes, then stopped at the hotel desk and asked for his money pouch. He counted out one thousand dollars and handed the remainder to the clerk to return to the safe.

Everett stuffed the money into an inside coat pocket, and rode the black mare out to the McIntyre home. A small group had already gathered.

The large front room was elegantly arranged and decorated for the wedding. When everyone was seated, a black-suited preacher stepped in from an adjoining room, followed by Cole and a man Everett did not recognize. Everyone turned when Penelope entered by a side door. She is beautiful, Everett thought. Momentarily, he wondered why he had not proposed to her himself.

The ceremony was short and simple. After Cole and Penelope kissed, Everett joined the guests in standing and clapping their approval.

At the small reception, Everett stepped over and offered congratulations. Then when Cole turned to accept compliments from others, Everett glanced down at Penelope.

"I want to give you a wedding gift," he said softly, reaching inside his coat.

He pulled out the envelope stuffed with a thousand dollars and handed it to her.

"Everett, I can never repay you for all you've already done," she said, tears filling her eyes.

"You waited a long time for your chance, Penelope," he replied. "Now, just be happy."

"What about you? Are you happy?" she asked.

"I suppose so," he said, his eyes dropping to his hands. "There's still something I have to straighten out in my life, but I'll soon take care of that."

"What about that girl you loved?" she asked.

"That was a long time ago. I hope she's happy."

"What was her name, Everett?"

"Tabitha Nichols. She lived on a ranch northwest of Caldwell, the Homestead."

"Do you still love her?"

"The girl I remember," he replied. "But she's somebody else now."

When other guests required her attention, Everett quietly slipped out the front door. Riding back to the hotel in late afternoon's stillness, the sun floated on the horizon like a heavily loaded ship in a calm sea. His mind drifted back to Caldwell, to Tabitha, and to the ridge west of the ranch house where they had shared so many sunsets. He could see her face, her eyes, and he could hear her pleading for him to take her with him.

With his mind swinging like a pendulum from one emotional extreme to the other, he stepped into the hotel dining room, fighting the turmoil inside his head. Weary, he slumped down at a corner table.

"Everett Brook," a tall man said, stopping at the opposite side of the table. "We met in Dodge City."

Everett jerked his head up, caught the glare off the marshal's badge, and grabbed for his pistol.

"Don't do it," Bat Masterson said, slipping up behind Everett with his gun drawn.

"Tilghman's my name," the man in front said. "I'm right curious to know how you got outta my jail. Suppose we sit and talk about it."

The marshal pulled out a chair on Everett's left, while Masterson took Everett's gun and seated himself to the right.

"That jailer still with you?" Everett asked.

"Nope, he ended up on the wrong side of the law, and then found himself on the inside of a jail cell."

"Truth is, I paid him double the reward to let me go," Everett explained.

"But his pockets were empty when I found him," Tilghman said.

"I had to lock him up to have get-away time," Everett explained. "And I knew it would look bad for him if he had bribe money in his pocket, so I took it back."

Masterson laughed. "Bill, you gotta admit you'd have strung that deputy up if you'd found a wad of money in his pocket."

"Problem is, now I gotta take this one back to Dodge with me," Tilghman said.

"Marshal," Everett said. "I killed those two boys, that's true, but they drew down on me. I swear it, and there are others who'll back me up."

"That might be, son," Tilghman said, "but there's a warrant out on you. My job is to bring you in, not to judge what you've done."

"I'll never get a fair trial in Caldwell," Everett said. "Samuel Harrison will see to that."

"Samuel Harrison, the old marshal?" Masterson asked.

"Yeah, and a wealthy rancher now," Everett replied.

"Harrison was a federal man, a bulldog lawman," Masterson said. "Once he gets you in his sights, he don't ever give up."

"A good lawyer might get the trial moved out of town," Tilghman suggested.

"Change of venue?" Everett asked. "The vigilantes would never allow it."

"Maybe you gotta hold him in Dodge," Masterson said to the marshal, "until his lawyer can get the trial moved."

"I've got no right to do that," Tilghman said. "But I can stall. First thing tomorrow, I'll telegraph Caldwell, tell them I have their boy, and suggest the trial be moved. Then I'll head for Dodge with my prisoners. Bat, you can wire their answer to me in Pueblo. We'll see if they feel different. But tonight, Brook is gonna spend the night in the local calaboose."

"There's no hurry," Masterson said. "It's New Year's Eve, so let the boy have supper, then lock him up."

Everett ate slowly. His appetite was suddenly gone.

Early the following morning, Marshal Tilghman and Colorado Vigil, the local lawman, appeared at Everett's cell door.

"Time to go, son," Tilghman said as Vigil unlocked the iron gate.

"I have some things in my room," Everett said. "And I want to ride my own horse."

"We'll take the seven o'clock train," Tilghman said, "but you're welcome to bring along your saddlebags and your pony."

The marshal escorted Everett to the hotel where he packed his things, got his money, and then went to the livery for the black mare.

"Glad we're taking the train. Looks like a storm coming," Tilghman said, glancing to the northwest where the sky was turning purple.

With everything gathered, they made their way to the train depot along with a second prisoner, a lean man the marshal called Broomstick. Boarded in the only passenger car, the marshal cuffed his prisoners to the metal frame of the seats in front of them, then eased into one right behind.

Only five other passengers, a family named Barlow, were aboard the freighter when it pulled out and gradually built up steam. Half an hour later the storm hit, sleet and then snow blowing in sheets against the train windows, and the temperature plunged nearly forty degrees. As the tracks coated over with ice and disappeared under snow, the train slowed, then stopped.

Huddled at a window the Barlow family peered out at a solid white landscape, thick snowfall limiting visibility to no more than fifty feet.

"What'll we do now?" Mrs. Barlow asked, wringing her hands.

"Wait 'til they can clear the tracks," her husband replied, "and that ain't likely until this storm lets up."

"You got a gun?" Tilghman asked Barlow.

The man nodded and pulled out a shotgun.

"These two are prisoners," the lawman said. "I'm going up front to see what's happenin'. Either of these tries to break loose, shoot 'im."

With that, Tilghman, slipped out of the car and disappeared.

"This is a bad one, and that marshal is gonna save his own hide and leave us to freeze to death," Broomstick said to Everett. "We gotta get loose."

"He'll be back," Everett said, though he had already been plotting how he might kick the seatback off the one in front, then work the cuffs down to a narrow gap at the bottom of the frame. If he could pry the pipe-formed support apart just half an inch, he could slip free.

"They're clearin' a drift that's buried the tracks where the railroad cuts up through the side of hill," the marshal said, slipping back inside the car. "We'll be movin' again soon."

But ten minutes passed, then fifteen, and the storm raged on while the train idled. Tilghman made a second trip up front. Half an hour later, he returned, worry etched on his brow.

"It's collectin' faster than they can shovel it. We'll just have to wait it out," he said.

The storm continued throughout the afternoon, snow piling up against the train's upwind side. The marshal pulled food from his saddlebags, sharing some with his prisoners as he chewed on some dried beef. He had anticipated being in Pueblo for supper, so had brought along a limited supply.

"If we don't move around some, our feet are gonna freeze," Broomstick complained to the marshal.

The lawman let one prisoner free, then the other, just long enough to move around the car for a few minutes. Side-mounted lamps glowed against the darkness, and the waiting continued, everyone bundling up the best they could. The wind howled, and so did hungry wolves in the dark distance.

"Papa, are we gonna freeze to death," the youngest girl of the Barlow family asked.

"No, honey," he replied, hugging her. "It'll let up soon."

When the children were asleep, Barlow eased down to where the marshal sat.

"Back in seventy-three," the man said, "people caught out on the plains froze to death by the tens and twenties. It lasted three days. A stage driver froze in his seat, still holding the reins. His passengers never knew it 'til they reached the station. Out on the prairie, a family burned all their wood, then their furniture. Still they froze to death, all huddled together in the same bed."

Daylight brought no letup in the weather. Snow against the north side of the car reached the bottoms of the windows.

Throughout the day, they nibbled from their meager food supply, stirred around trying to bring feeling to their feet, and napped as best they could. The little girl cried, even in her sleep, and unspoken worries preyed on every mind.

The second morning, the storm had slackened, but the train remained immobile.

"The engineer says it'll take a day or two to clear the tracks after the snow stops," Tilghman said returning from the front.

"We're about out of food," Barlow said.

"We'll share," Tilghman replied, "what little we've got."

"What about our horses?" Everett asked.

"I've been checkin' 'em, and feedin' 'em," the lawman said. "I stacked hay against the walls of the car. They're huddled and doin' okay."

"We could eat one of 'em," Broomstick said.

"They're our last hope," Tilghman said, "but not as dead meat. One of us is goin' to have to ride for help."

"I ain't gettin' out in this," Broomstick said. "A man wouldn't last a hour out there."

"I'm the one," Tilghman said, then eased down toward the family. "Barlow, do you think you can watch these two, feed 'em, and occasionally let 'em up to stomp around a bit?"

"Marshal, I've got my family to take care of," the man said. "And I ain't much of one when it comes to ridin' herd on outlaws."

"I'll go," Everett said. "I survived a blizzard back a few years ago, tending some cattle along Bluff Creek."

"You might not come back," the lawman said, shaking his head.

"I don't see that you've got much choice," Everett said. "I'll need some food, a second horse, and maybe some firewood from up front."

After studying it a while, Marshal Tilghman unlocked the cuffs and led Everett outside. They made their way to the horses and rigged up a supply pack out of canvas. The fireman allowed Everett to take a supply of wood, and he swung up on the black, then reached for his saddlebags.

"I'll keep these," the lawman said, handing him his gun belt instead. "You couldn't walk away from a thousand dollars on my deputy, so I reckon you won't drift too far from what's in here."

"I'll be back," Everett said, then smiled. "I just hope you're still alive."

The snow was the worst Everett had ever seen. The white landscape extended as far as the eye could see, broken only by snow-covered mounds where rocks or bushes lay in icy tombs, and by an endless windrow of snow that had collected against the thick cross-ties and elevated rails. He followed along the railroad to avoid getting lost, but in low areas deep drifts forced him to skirt around their edges. With the horses pushing through snow frequently up to their bellies, they required frequent rests.

As darkness settled in, he located a small grove of trees shielded by a slight ridge. Gathering what wood he could, he built his fire, using only enough from his cache to get it started. He blanketed the spare horse with the pack canvas and his black mare with his bed tarp. Even lying right beside the fire all night, warmth was impossible. He welcomed daylight and the precious heat the sun beamed down.

He trudged on, following the snow-crested rails. The storm was gone, but the wind blew relentlessly, while the terrain grew rugged and drifts deepened. Eight hours later, he estimated he had gone ten miles. The cold had numbed his mind, along with his hands and feet.

He made another camp and burned most of his wood, trying to stay alive until sunrise. His food gone, he hit the trail again. The wind had subsided, and by mid-morning, the sun restored feeling to his face. By dark, he had covered eighteen miles, maybe more.

Hungry, he searched the area until he found a frozen jackrabbit. He used the last of his wood to cook his supper, then with his stomach filled, he rolled up in his bedroll.

The sky had cleared, and what little heat existed rose quickly as the temperature plummeted. When he awoke, he had difficulty getting his bearings. Where am I? he wondered. What has happened?

Exhaustion, the incessant cold, and bleak isolation in an endless landscape entombed in snow had addled his mind. Sore, stiff, and numb from head to toe, he tried to crawl out of his bedroll. Finding the effort too great, he fell back.

You must find the will to live, a voice deep inside whispered, or like water seeping into a sinking ship, death will slowly close in.

33

Everett forced his eyes open and managed to work a hand out from under the blankets and rub some feeling into his face. Then he stretched his free hand to a charred stick from the fringe of his campfire and poked at the coals. When a flame sprang up, he repeated the process with other partially burned limbs until the growing fire threw off enough warmth he could feel it on his face. Gradually he pulled himself out of the stiff blankets, and crawled closer. Kneeling, he added to the fire and then hovered over it, bringing his hands and face dangerously close to the flames until the growing heat forced him back.

With his hands and arms regaining feeling, he tried to stand, but his numb legs refused. He pulled himself across the snow to the black mare and coaxed her into dropping her muzzle near his face. When he grabbed her mane, she jerked up, and he lost his grip. Again he got the mare to lower her head. This time he managed to loop his arms around her neck and interlock his fingers. As she raised her head, he hung on until his legs were beneath him. Gradually, he regained enough feeling in his feet and legs to stand.

Hobbling over to the fire, he thawed until he could complete two feeble knee bends. With renewed control, he packed, saddled his pony, struggled up, and headed south along the snow-covered iron tracks. A brilliant sun helped bring life to his limbs, and by early afternoon, he was moving along at a steady pace. Two hours later he tried to yell for help when he first saw the snow-coated top of the livery building on the outskirts of Trinidad, but his voice managed only a raspy whisper.

At the closed doors, he slipped down from the saddle and banged with his fist. The hostler peeked out from a barn packed with horses, then pushed the

door open and helped Everett lead his ponies inside, asking who he was and where he had been.

"Get the marshal," Everett whispered, then stumbled over to a chair near a roaring potbelly stove.

The man climbed onto the back of a haltered pony and headed out. Ten minutes later, he returned with Colorado Vigil, and Everett told his story.

"There are seven people, plus the engineer, fireman, and brakeman. Take all the supplies you can," Everett whispered into the lawman's ear. "And tell Masterson."

"Saddle four stout horses," Vigil said to the hostler. "I'll be back with help."

The lawman returned with four men, along with Masterson and Dr. Michael Beshoar.

"I'll show them the way," Everett said, rising to his feet.

"Nonsense, boy," Beshoar said. "You're in no shape to ride, and those boys can follow the iron tracks."

With buffalo hides draped over their backs like capes, the men climbed on the borrowed ponies and headed out, trailed by a wagon loaded with bundles of supplies and firewood.

After Dr. Beshoar had thawed Everett's feet and hands, he got him into his buggy, wrapped a blanket around him, and took him to the Sherman House. Soon a woman he did not know set a hot meal in front of him. He devoured it, then climbed the stairs, crawled into his bed, and fell asleep.

Two days later in late afternoon, Everett looked out his window and spotted the rescue group pulling up at the hotel with Tilghman, Broomstick, and the Barlow family huddled in the wagon bed. Everett eased downstairs to meet them.

"It's good to see you," Tilghman said to Everett. "I got a little worried before Sheriff Vigil showed up."

"I took my time," Everett said, smiling.

"We're all okay, thanks to you," Tilghman said.

"What about the train?" Everett asked.

"Still stuck out there, but the engineer and his men have food and blankets to hold them until they can shovel their way out."

"What're you gonna do about me?"

"I sent Broomstick down to the jail with Vigil," Tilghman said. "I'm goin' to get some sleep now, but come mornin', I'll take you along, too."

Determined to resolve the Harrison conflict once and for all, Everett resisted the temptation to run, although he wondered if the marshal was giving him that chance. Instead, he joined Tilghman for breakfast. Finished, they headed for Sheriff Vigil's office.

"Got a cell for this one?" Tilghman asked when they got to the jail.

"Yep, but you may not need it."

"What do you mean?" Tilghman asked.

"I got a reply from Marshal Phillips in Caldwell," the man said. "When he got our message a few days back, he requested a hearing. It seems that Samuel Harrison died a couple months ago, and when folks back there heard about the hearing, they raised a ruckus, swearing your boy here shot in self defense."

"When will we know the results?" Tilghman asked.

"I'm expecting a message any time."

"Let's wait over a cup of coffee," Tilghman suggested, motioning Everett to join them.

Soon a boy rushed into the sheriff's office and handed a telegraph message to Vigil. As he read, his eyebrows shot up, then he handed it to Tilghman.

"I believe these are yours," Tilghman said, handing Everett his saddlebags. "You've been cleared, son."

"You mean I'm free?" Everett asked, jumping to his feet.

Tilghman handed over the telegram. Everett read it hurriedly. He started for the door, then turned back and grabbed Tilghman's hand, thanking him.

He turned and ran outside, jumped on the black mare, and put her into a full gallop, headed for the McIntyre home. At the gate, he hit the ground running and bounded onto the front porch.

"Penelope!" he called out, as he rapped on the door.

When no one answered, he galloped back to Thatcher's store and rushed inside.

"Where's Penelope?" he asked Mr. McIntyre.

"Why they've taken a trip," the storekeeper replied. "I expect them back in about a week."

Three days later, a Friday afternoon, there was a knock on Everett's door. He opened it to the same messenger boy.

"Telegraph for you," the lad said.

Everett opened it and read.

Urgent.
Meet 3PM train, Sat. Jan. 16.
Penelope.

What's wrong? he wondered. Maybe there's been an accident. Should he alert Mr. McIntyre? Not wanting to alarm the elderly man, he decided against it.

At the telegraph office he learned that the message had been sent from Dodge City. What was Penelope doing there?

Everett was pacing up and down the depot boardwalk when he heard the train's whistle. The locomotive soon appeared around a bend some three hundred yards away. Slowly it puffed closer, then began its steamy, screeching halt. A man from the depot office came over and placed a stool on the ground to ease the passengers' step down.

Everett held back next to a large support post, unsure what to expect. As he watched travelers unload, Cole McIntyre filled the doorway, then stepped down and turned to help Penelope. Both appeared fit.

Cole immediately turned his attention to their baggage while Penelope scanned the waiting crowd.

Everett was headed her way when he noticed another passenger exiting the train, an attractive woman wearing a long coat over a blue and white dress. With her eyes on the footstool, the brim of her hat covered her face as she gathered her dress and eased down. Everett shifted his eyes to Penelope who had spotted him and was on tiptoes, calling and waving.

Just as Everett reached Penelope, she motioned his attention to someone behind her. He shifted his eyes over her right shoulder, then stopped cold. There stood the woman in the blue dress and long coat.

"Everett, I think you'll remember . . ." Penelope said, her eyes dancing between the two.

"Everett," the young woman said. "You've grown so, I hardly recognized you."

"Tabitha," he replied, confused and bewildered. "It's good to see you."

"I'll get the carriage," Cole said as he plopped the luggage down.

Seeing Everett's wide-eyed stare, he winked at Penelope and headed toward the livery stable.

In a daze, Everett gathered up the baggage and followed the ladies to the depot platform. She's a grownup woman, a beautiful one, he thought.

"There's so much to tell you, Everett," Penelope said over her shoulder, bubbly with happiness.

When Cole returned with the carriage, Everett stacked the luggage in the back, then helped Penelope step up. Turning to Tabitha, their eyes met. The same brown eyes, he thought. Her long, dark hair, her soft face, and beautiful skin, are all unchanged.

Everett took her arm and helped her into the rear seat beside Penelope.

"Everett, I want you to come to the house for supper," Penelope said. "And I won't take no for an answer."

Too baffled to speak, he nodded and watched the carriage pull away. For a few moments, he stood and stared after them, his mind a spinning blur like the wheel spokes of the buggy. Finally, he walked to his horse and rode over to a clothing store where he bought a suit, shirt, new boots, and hat. After a shave and bath, he dressed and headed for the McIntyre home.

Riding out, he relived his torturous journey from Caldwell where he had learned that she had gone east and married another man. Angry and resentful, he had been determined to drive her from his mind. But now she was here. What did it mean? Was she unmarried? He was confused, hopeful at one moment, unbelieving the next.

He tied his horse at the McIntyre gate, took a deep breath, and stepped onto the front porch. Before he could knock, Penelope burst through the door and grabbed his arm.

"Everett, this is wonderful," she said, stepping outside and closing the door behind her.

He stood dumbfounded, his eyes pleading for explanation.

"Aren't you glad to see her?" she asked.

"Penelope, what's going on?"

"Everett, I never believed that she had stopped loving you, so with part of the wedding present you gave us, I bought train tickets to Caldwell. There, we got directions to the Homestead Ranch and rode out.

"Everett, I had to do it. I told her that you still love her. She burst into tears, then asked a hundred questions about you.

"Tabitha's mother was scared for her to come with us. She knows you're an outlaw and can't return to Caldwell, but she also knows the love her daughter has for you."

"Penelope," Everett said, near tears. "Please ask Tabitha to come out here for a minute. I've got to talk to her."

"I'll send her right out," Penelope replied. "Everything's going to be okay."

Tabitha slowly pushed open the door and turned to face Everett.

"I know you came back for me. I'm sorry I wasn't there," she said, easing closer.

"I thought I'd never see you again."

"When Papa died, Mama and I went back East for a few months, but I left a note on the door telling you I would be back. Later, I learned that Bob Jackson burned the note. I don't know what he told you, but you left without knowing the truth.

"I waited for you, but finally decided you would never return. Then Penelope came, and she explained everything. I love you, Everett. I always have."

"And I love you, Tabitha," he said as he took her in his arms.

After a lengthy embrace, they moved to the porch swing, swaying back and forth with his arm around her and her head tilted against his shoulder.

"You didn't marry that banker back East, did you?"

"Is that what Jackson told you?" she asked, lifting her head.

"It doesn't matter now," he replied, pressing her head close to his.

"Everett, can I stay here with you?" she asked softly.

"I thought we might go back and see your mother," he replied. "I expect she'll need some help with the ranch, especially after I run off Bob Jackson."

"But they'll hang you if you go back there," she said, jerking her head up and staring at him.

"I've been cleared. Found out a few days ago," he explained, reaching inside his coat. "I've got the telegraph message right here."

"Everett that's wonderful!" she said, throwing her arms around him.

Everett glanced over Tabitha's shoulder. There resting on the towering mountain peaks was a brilliant yellow glow that exploded against the sky, painting it with a stunning mixture of red, orange, and pink. That tender, warm feeling had returned to his world.

"Look," he said, pointing west. "I hear there's one every day."

"And we'll see them together on our ranch," she whispered. "We'll call it Sunset."

Epilogue

Judge Isaac Parker—Appointed Federal Judge in the Western District of Arkansas in 1875, Judge Parker served until his death in 1896. His jurisdiction included the Indian Territory, currently eastern Oklahoma. He sentenced one hundred seventy two persons to be hanged of which only seventy-nine met their end on the gallows outside his Fort Smith courtroom. Largely due to his determination for sure and swift judgment, followed by punishment consistent with the crime inflicted upon the criminal's victims, Judge Parker brought law and order to a violent territory, once a refuge for outlaws. The price was not cheap. Over one hundred deputy marshals were killed fulfilling their duties within his jurisdiction.

Bass Reeves—A federal deputy marshal working out of Judge Parker's court, Bass Reeves served thirty-five years, arresting over three thousand outlaws while killing fourteen. His most difficult arrest was that of his son, charged with murder. Marshal Bennett of Muskogee offered to have another marshal serve the warrant, but true to his impeccable character and unflagging courage, Reeves took the assignment, returning with his prisoner two weeks later. A fearless man, Bass Reeves, as a slave in Texas, had knocked his master unconscious and escaped across the Red River into Indian Territory where he became one of the most respected and honored lawmen.

Fort Gibson—A stockade fortress, it was established by Colonel Matthew Arbuckle in 1824 along the east bank of the Neosho or Grand River, three miles north of its confluence with the Arkansas. The third river in what became known as the Three Forks area was the Verdigris, which joined the Arkansas just to the west of the fort. Arbuckle and the 7th U. S. Infantry moved upriver from Fort Smith at Belle Point to construct the fort, an eventual terminal on the Trail of Tears. Its purpose was to establish and maintain peace between the Osage and Cherokee Indians, to protect them from whiskey peddlers and encroaching whites, and to prepare the way for the relocation of more members of the Five Civilized Tribes to the area. Occupying a strategic location, it served various military purposes until 1890. Today the old stockade fort and remaining buildings are maintained as a National Historic Landmark, along with the Commanders quarters and the Garrett Home on Coppinger Avenue.

Colonel Matthew Arbuckle—Without the flamboyance and flair of better-known military commanders, he served on the frontier for twenty years, seventeen as the commander at Fort Gibson. He preferred restraint and understanding rather than force, though he firmly believed the presence and readiness of a strong military was necessary. The result, during his nearly two decades at the Three Forks in the heart of Indian Territory, his forces never killed one Indian and he lost only one soldier to Indian hostilities, a remarkable accomplishment. Throughout this time he maintained a firm and consistent approach toward the Indians, though the federal government repeatedly changed its leadership and policies.

Red Fork Ranch—Lying just north of the Cimarron River, or Red Fork of the Arkansas, this road ranch was ideally located between the Chisholm and the Reno Trails, thus providing supplies to both cattle herders and stagecoach traffic. Ralph Collins and his cousin, Fred Williams, nephews of Brinton Darlington who managed the Cheyenne-Arapaho Agency at Fort Reno, purchased it in 1881 from a man named John Hood and his partner Johnnie Blair, they having bought it two years earlier from Dan Jones. Eleven-year-old Hubert Collins joined his twenty-five-year-old brother at the ranch in 1883, traveling alone from Iowa by train and stagecoach. The cousins added a second floor to the store and built a circular corral to accommodate the large cattle herds moving north. Capable of holding three thousand head of cattle, the six-foot-tall corral fence was constructed of oak posts cut from the adjacent Blackjack Forest and sunk three feet deep, stockade style. Considered one of the best corrals in that part of the country, it proved to be a tremendous boon to attracting the cattle-drive business. Also, the cousins built their own herd from sore-footed cattle unable to make it to the Kansas railheads and from strays. Ralph's uncle, Ben Williams, became a deputy United States marshal in Indian Territory in 1874. Today, the town of Dover, Oklahoma sits near the site of the old ranch headquarters.

Hurricane Bill Martin—The noted outlaw led a notorious band of thieves who hid out in the Blackjack Forest and stole horses from surrounding ranches and Indians, then sold them in Kansas where they purchased whiskey and returned to peddle it to soldiers and Indians in Indian Territory.

Lizzie Johnson Williams—A schoolteacher, cattle dealer, and writer from the Austin, Texas area, Lizzie invested $2500 dollars in a Chicago cattle company that quickly grew to $20,000 which she used to purchase ten acres from Charles W. Whitis and her own herd. She is considered by many to be the first woman cattle boss to trail cattle north up the Chisholm Trail. She took her first herd to Dodge City in 1879. Her husband, Hezekiah Williams, whom she married in June 1879, ranched with her, but she maintained the land and cattle, along with her CY brand, under the name of Elizabeth Johnson. At the time of her death, October 9, 1924, she had investments worth a quarter of a million dollars.

Caldwell, Kansas—Lying along the Chisholm Trail just north of Kansas' southern border, the town's roots go back to 1869 when Curly Marshall's First Chance/Last Chance Saloon out along Bluff Creek served as its gateway to Indian Territory. A town company was formed March 1, 1871 by men from Wichita to encourage the continued flow of cattle up the old Chisholm Trail, thus routing business on to Wichita. C. H. Stone, treasurer of the company, built a mercantile store there, then Cox & Epperson added a similar one, which was run by and eventually purchased by J. M. Thomas. Catering more to area farmers than the passing drovers, the town grew, but its boom years began in 1880 when the railroad reached Caldwell, including a spur to Manning Peak south of town. With growing local concern about Texas tick fever carried by the longhorns, various bans prohibited cattle drives from reaching most Kansas cities, so having a railhead on the edge of Indian Territory proved extremely valuable to the little border town. As with all cow towns, the business benefits were offset by the violence and vice so characteristic of towns that opened its streets to the thirsty cowboys. For about six years Caldwell, the Border Queen, flourished and fought, welcomed and wailed, while reaping its whirlwind of wealth and bounty of Red Light Saloon killings.

George Freeman—A founding father of Caldwell, a blacksmith, photographer, and deputy marshal, he authored *Midnight & Noonday*, his story of early Caldwell and a treasure of recordings of the people and times of the frontier town. Freeman and Buffalo King arrived in May 1871 and established their claims on Fall Creek. His wife, Laura Pool, died September 17, 1874, but after a brief return to his family in Butler County, he married Emmaline Covert and returned to Caldwell where he remained an active citizen.

Johnnie Blair—Another '71er who arrived from Indiana with his parents, Enos and Margaret Blair, and younger brother, Marion, he clerked in Cox & Epperson's Mercantile and later purchased the business from C. H. Stone in 1874, the same year he married Katherine Wendell. The marriage produced two children, Mabel born December 3, 1879 and Marguerite in November 1885. He served as councilman and postmaster and was a prosperous businessman, one of Caldwell's most popular citizens. Once owner of the Red Fork Ranch in Indian Territory, partnered with John Hood, in 1881 he sold his business in town and turned to cattle, becoming one of the most successful ranchers in the area.

John Sain—Still another '71er, he ran the Mammoth Cave Drug Store and wrote a weekly local-interest column for the *Sumner County Press*, using the pen name of Don Carlos. In 1876 he followed Johnnie Blair as postmaster, running the postal service from his drugstore.

Mercantile & Drovers Bank—J. S. Danford, bank president, created quite a stir in late November 1881 when he locked the doors and left town. The bank's solvency was questioned, yet many trusted the institution's management and continued to make deposits there. Rumor was that Danford had gone to Emporia to exchange deeds to his Caldwell properties for $30,000 to add buoyancy to the sinking institution, but when he failed to return, depositors became angry. Learning the banker had returned to Wellington, concerned citizens raced their ponies there and brought the banker back to Caldwell to face his depositors. An inquiry, held to determine the banker's fate, determined that the $30,000, along with other assets and accounts payable, were adequate to payoff the depositors and a committee of trusted citizens was formed to oversee that process.

Mike Meagher—Once sheriff of Wichita, Kansas during its cow town days and later marshal with his deputy Wyatt Earp, Meagher was a lawman well seasoned in dealing with the most notorious outlaws of the West. Later he was a saloon owner, marshal, and mayor of Caldwell. In a major town shootout, he was shot to death by the outlaw Jim Talbot on December 17, 1881. Escaping into Indian Territory, Talbot was arrested in California in 1894 and brought back for trial. Though Tell Walton, Abram Rhoades, and W. D. Fosset identified Talbot as the gunman who led the gang, he was acquitted. The jury concluded that, among the firestorm of bullets thirteen years earlier, proof was not presented that Jim Talbot had fired the fatal shots. Then in 1896 an unnamed California gunman shot and killed Talbot. Some believe a brother of Meagher was the unidentified assailant.

Bat Carr—B. P. Carr, from Colorado City, Texas, was hired as Caldwell's marshal on June 27, 1882. A strong-bodied man, Carr dressed smartly, was courteous to women and children, but fearless when dealing with wild cowboys, who considered the lawman to be a holy terror with fist and firearm. Taking office on July 5, the new marshal hired Henry Brown as his deputy, and the two lawmen quickly brought order to the town. However, things changed in December when Carr returned from Texas with his new bride. Brown had brought in Ben Robertson (Wheeler), an old buddy from his Texas and New Mexico days. A disagreement ensued between Brown and Carr, eventually leading to the mysterious dismissal of Carr and hiring of Brown and Robertson. Carr left town and became a special policeman in Wellington.

Henry Brown—Hired as assistant marshal on July 5, 1882, he became Caldwell's marshal on December 21 of that year. He and his assistant, Ben Robertson (a.k.a. Ben Wheeler) were effective and respected by Caldwell citizens until a disastrous turn of events soon after the marshal had married Alice Maude Levagood on March 26, 1884. After buying a house and furniture for his new bride in May, Brown and Robertson, along with William Smith and John Wesley, attempted to rob the bank in nearby Medicine Lodge. Due to a downpour, an earlier tip from I-Bar Johnson, and resistance by the bank officers, the robbery was foiled. Wylie Payne, bank president, and George Geppert, cashier, were shot and killed. Marshal Sam Denn and local citizens pursued the fleeing outlaws and apprehended them in a canyon south of town. That night local citizens surrounded the jail, overpowered the marshal, and took the outlaws. Brown tried to escape, but was shot to death. His accomplices were hung. The betrayed citizens of Caldwell then learned that Henry Brown had run with Billy the Kid in New Mexico Territory and dealt in stolen horses around Tascosa, Texas.

Red Light Saloon—The most notorious spot in Caldwell, George and Mag Woods's saloon and dancehall attracted the cowboy and the outlaw. The site of numerous deaths, including Marshal George Brown and the saloon owner, it was closed by order of the city multiple times, but the popular establishment always managed to rebound until June 1882 when the citizens purchased the building, sold it to a grain storage combine, and thus ended its reign of violence and vice.

Charley Siringo—Born February 7, 1855 at Dutch Settlement, Texas, this wiry fellow lived a full and exciting life as cowboy, businessman, Pinkerton detective, and author. He trailed cattle up the Chisholm Trail for fifteen years, brushed shoulders with Shanghai Pierce, David Beals, Billy the Kid, Butch Cassidy, and Harvey (Kid Curry) Logan. After recording the events of his Pinkerton days in *A Pinkerton Cowboy Detective*, a book steeped in controversy, Siringo was forced by the Superior Court of Chicago to change the title of the book to *A Cowboy Detective*. Additionally, the court ordered that he delete significant portions of the work and that references to known western characters, as well as to the Pinkerton Agency, be made under false names. A truly colorful western character, he continued to battle the Pinkerton Agency through his writings (*Two Evil Isms: Pinkertonism and Anarchism* and *Riata and Spurs: The Story of a Lifetime Spent in the Saddle as Cowboy and Detective*) until his death on October 19, 1928 in Hollywood.

Little Texas—An area of the Llano Estacado in eastern New Mexico, settled by ranchers from Texas, thus known by many New Mexicans as Little Texas.

T Anchor—A ranch originated in the fall of 1877 by Leigh R. Dyer, brother-in-law of Charles Goodnight, it was located in the Palo Duro Canyon area with its headquarters in Spring Draw near the junction of Palo Duro and Tierra Blanco creeks. In 1880 Judd Campbell drove thirty-six hundred head of cattle from Kaufman County to Spring Draw from which he ran the ranching operation. Under Campbell's direction, the ranch is credited with being the first cattle kingdom in the Texas Panhandle to complete a major fencing project, enclosing some 240,000 acres. Late 1881 the ranch adopted the T Anchor brand, thought to have been created by Joe Harris near Saint Jo, Texas in Montague County. A drift fence ran along its northern border to stop cattle wandering to the south, often driven by deadly winter storms farther north. The ranch is credited with the largest single cattle drive on record, some 10,652 head.

LX Ranch—With headquarters on Ranch Creek just north of the Canadian River in the Texas Panhandle, David Beals and Deacon Bates started this nearly two-hundred-thousand-acre ranch in 1877. Charley Siringo worked on the ranch and Henry McCarty (Billy the Kid) was a visitor there.

XIT Ranch—In 1879 the Texas Legislature, needing a new Capitol building, handed over three million acres of Panhandle land to Mathias Schnell in exchange for constructing the state building. Schnell sold the land to investors who formed the Capitol Syndicate. From this the ranch was formed at an effective cost of over three million dollars. With headquarters at Buffalo Springs, Barbecue Campbell left his ranch on Medicine Lodge Creek in Indian Territory and became the ranch's manager. Abner Blocker scratched out the XIT brand with his boot heel, having driven the first herd of cattle to the ranch from the Fort Concho area. Some believe the brand stands for "ten in Texas" because the ranch spanned ten counties. With Joe Collins and Berry Nation as foremen, the herd grew to over a hundred thousand head by 1886.

Blizzard of January 1, 1886—The below-zero temperatures, sixty-miles-per-hour winds, and heavy snow threatened every living thing on the Midwest plains. Range cattle wandered south, trying to leave the horrid weather behind, but more often than not died when stopped by some impassable barrier, a fence, river, or elevated railroad. At winter's end, carcasses were found piled at such locations, as well as in the Texas Panhandle, some wearing Montana brands. One rancher reported finding only twenty-five hundred head of a twenty-thousand-head herd, and the Bay State Cattle Company of Nebraska folded after losing one hundred thousand of its herd. Death was not restricted to cattle. Ranchers, freighters, and travelers were caught out on the plains and many froze to death.

Cantonment—Established March 6, 1879 along the North Canadian River by Lieutenant Colonel Richard Dodge following a raid by the Northern Cheyenne in 1878, led by Dull Knife, its purpose was to help control the warlike Indians. But when the Northern Cheyenne were allowed to return north to their homeland in 1882, it served little purpose and was soon abandoned. Noted chiefs, Powder Face of the Arapaho and Little Robe of the Cheyenne band, located their followers near this agency.

Henry Keeling—Keeling became the sutler at Cantonment after working with his brother, Major William Keeling, the quartermaster at Fort Keogh. Henry's store goods, and possibly his life, were saved in 1881 by Black Wolf, a Northern Cheyenne chief whom the sutler had befriended years earlier when the chief had been seriously injured in a knife fight with a white man at Fort Keogh.

Dog Soldiers—Cheyenne braves who refused to accept a much reduced reservation area in Indian Territory as agreed to by most of the tribe, the Dog Soldiers continued to raid. Their hostilities are cited by some as leading to the Sand Creek Massacre in 1864 in which one hundred twenty of the peaceful group of Arapaho and Cheyenne were killed, mostly women and children. The surprise attack led by Colonel Chivington of the Colorado Militia further agitated the hostile band. Fighting continued until 1868 when Colonel George Custer's early-morning raid of Black Kettle's camp on the Washita River resulted in the death of the peace chief, along with fifteen men and thirty women and children. Still the Dog Soldiers fought until destroyed as a fighting unit in 1869 at the

Battle of Summit Springs. Renegade remnants of the band remained for years afterward.

Little Robe—A Southern Cheyenne chief and leader of a group of Dog Soldiers who settled his band near Cantonment, sharing a reservation with the Southern Arapahos about thirty-five miles west of Red Fork Ranch. His father had been killed at the Sand Creek Massacre in 1864, causing him to lead raids until he signed a treaty in 1866. Not even Custer's early-morning raid at Washita caused him to break the treaty. And to the surprise of many, he kept his followers at peace during the 1874 Red River War. However, in 1884 when Indian Agent J. D. Miles was replaced by D. B. Dyer, Little Robe and his Dog Soldiers became incensed with ranch companies who had leased a considerable portion of the reservation lands for grazing cattle. The Dog Soldiers began stealing company herds and threatening those Indians who had abandoned their traditional ways and accepted white-man's farming. The conflict reached a crisis in late 1884, when Agent Dyer agreed to allow Powder Face to go to Washington to voice the Indians' concerns. After an investigation President Cleveland dismissed Dyer and cancelled the cattle company leases on reservation land.

Powder Face—This Southern Arapaho chief settled about thirteen hundred of his band near Cantonment. Following the massacre at Sand Creek in 1864, he became a leading war chief, but when the Red River War broke out in 1874, led by Southern Cheyenne, Powder Face refused to participate. In fact, he protected the Darlington Agency from attack, thus creating a rift with the Cheyenne. By 1880 he had started a substantial cattle herd, and in 1883 he owned considerable cornfields and vegetable gardens as well. Dedicated to change, he enrolled his son, Clarence, in the famous Indian school at Carlisle, Pennsylvania.

Fort Supply—This stockade-style fort near the junction of the North Canadian River and Wolf Creek, near the east end of the Oklahoma Panhandle, was established November 18, 1868. Originally called Camp Supply, it was established to support Major General Phil Sheridan's winter campaign against the Cheyenne, Kiowa, and other Plains Indians. Designated a fort in 1878, it was abandoned in February 1895.

Tascosa—A Texas Panhandle cow town northwest of present-day Amarillo, Tascosa lay just north of the Canadian River amid huge cottonwood trees. Mickey McCormick and his wife Frenchy, the mystery woman who never revealed her true identity, were the town's most famous citizens. Years later, Lee Bivins of Amarillo purchased the LIT Ranch, which included the old Tascosa town-site. Its boot-hill cemetery still lies atop a rocky ridge, while its courthouse is now a museum. True to its tradition and with the help of the Bivins family, the Cal Farley Boys Ranch now occupies the land, operating an active cattle ranch.

Las Vegas, New Mexico—A key site along the old Santa Fe Trail, this historic town welcomed such notables as Doc Holliday, Kit Carson, Clay Allison, Billy the Kid, and Lucien Maxwell. Once the doorway to the Santa Fe trade center, the arrival of the Atchison Topeka railroad in 1879 signaled the beginning of the end of the famous trail. However, the next several years were marked with violence in which it was difficult to distinguish between outlaws, lawmen, and vigilantes. Vicente Silva, once an upstanding businessman, turned bandit leader, and some of his band included policemen. Mysterious Dave Mather, alleged train robber, became town marshal. In one month twenty-nine men died violently in and around the town. Gallinas Canyon, west of town, is the gateway to the Montezuma area with its 1885-vintage hotel and the famous hot springs that to this day continue to attract and sooth weary travelers.

Vicente Silva—This Las Vegas tavern owner came to Las Vegas about 1875. Later he was purported to be the leader of a forty-member band of outlaws noted for murder, theft, and livestock rustling. The bandits included Ricardo Romero or El Romo (The Roman), Guadalupe Caballero or El Lechusa (The Owl), Tomas Lucero, Martin Gonzales or El Moro (the Moor), Dionicio Sisneros or El Candelas (The Icicles), Manuel Gonzales y Baca or El Mellado (The Dull One), Antonio Jose Valdez or Patas de Mico (The Pussy-foot), Florentino Medran, Remigio Sandoval or El Gavilan (The Hawk), Librado Polanco, and Genovevo Avila or El Menguado (The Shrunken One). Silva owned the Monte Largo ranch, a remote spread where stolen cattle and horses were amassed and the VS brand applied. Also, Refugio Esquibel found his stolen horses at the Monte Largo, a key to identifying Silva as a horse thief and driving him to his mountain hideout, El Coyote. Also, he owned The Imperial Saloon on Moreno Street with his brother-in-law, Gabriel Sandoval the bartender. He and his wife Telesfora adopted an abandoned baby girl, named her Emma, and raised her. Silva, determined to kill his wife and her brother, kidnapped Emma and hid her in Taos. First he lured his brother-in-law to a remote old mill site with the promise to see the girl, then murdered him. But when he stabbed Telesfora to death in 1893, some of his band felt he had gone too far. One of his bandits, possibly Pussy-foot (Antonio Jose Valdez), shot Silva in the head as they walked away from the arroyo where the outlaw leader had just dumped his wife's body. After throwing Silva's corpse in with his wife's, the bandits divided up ten thousand dollars from his money belt and parted ways.

Horse Thief Meadow—A beautiful high mountain meadow in Pecos Wilderness, split by a narrow, deep-running stream and bounded on either side by steep slopes. High on the mountainsides are remnants of pole fences formed with two-foot-thick logs. The meadow was used as a convenient hideout by a band of horse thieves to re-brand rustled horses and to allow time for their scorched hides to heal. Horses stolen from east of the mountains were then sold west of the range. Those plundered from the west were likewise sold to the east, sometimes to the ranchers from which the thieves had taken horses, thus creating and filling a market on both sides.

Mora, New Mexico—This quaint little village sits on the outskirts of Pecos Wilderness, hidden deep in a valley through which the Mora River cascades eastward. Father Tafoya shepherded a little congregation there and, because of some unusual investments in land, some believed he had a fabulous gold mine hidden away in the wilderness. His regular trips into the wilderness to tend to the spiritual needs of the sheepherders there linked his storied riches to the mysterious mountains.

Cimarron, New Mexico—Once Lucien Maxwell's town, the area became the home of huge ranches, such as Manly Chase's fifty-thousand-acre ranch along the Vermijo River and a half-million-acre one farther to the east. Even in the early 1880s the Maxwell Cattle Company still controlled over a million acres for cattle grazing and was run by a Mr. Sherwin. Henry Lambert's St. James Hotel still stands, as does the old gristmill constructed in the 1860s.

Bat Masterson—Lawman, gunfighter, gambler, boxing promoter, and newsman, Masterson lived a long and exciting life. Here it is worthy to note that he met Bill Tilghman at Adobe Walls, and they became friends for life. Both were lawmen in Dodge City and both were buffalo hunters. In April 1882, Masterson was appointed marshal of Trinidad, Colorado and owned a gambling establishment there. In the winter of 1883 he escorted a prisoner, along with a sheriff from Iowa, to the train depot in Trinidad. At the age of seventy-seven, he died at his desk at the *Telegraph* on Eighth Avenue in New York City where he was a sportswriter.

Marshal Tilghman—Buffalo hunter and lawman deluxe, Tilghman lacked the flamboyance of many frontier marshals, but he was highly respected as a marksman, a fast draw, and a man with unusual courage. A former deputy of Wyatt Earp, he became marshal of Dodge City in April of 1884, appointed by Mayor George Hoover. He then turned his badge in after the devastating blizzard of 1886, which wiped out most of the cattle in western Kansas. Later he gained more fame as a lawman in Oklahoma, where he joined in the Land Rush of 1889, staking his claim near the present city of Chandler. Tilghman, Heck Thomas, and Chris Madsen became known as the "three guardsmen" of Oklahoma Territory. After having retired as a lawman, in August of 1924 the governor of Oklahoma asked Tilghman to go clean up the oil boomtown of Cromwell, a town some described as more violent than Dodge City. By fall Tilghman had the town under control; however, later that season, while eating breakfast in a restaurant, he heard gunfire. He rushed out and arrested a drunk. As he prepared to search the man, a federal prohibition officer, the prisoner slipped a concealed gun from his coat pocket and shot the lawman twice. Minutes later, Bill Tilghman, one of the best lawmen of the West, was dead.

Medicine Lodge, Kansas—The site of the attempted robbery of the bank by Caldwell's Marshal Henry Brown, his deputy Ben Robertson (a.k.a. Wheeler), William Smith, and John Wesley was also the location of the famous Treaty of Medicine Lodge Creek on October 28, 1867. After weather and brave bankers foiled the attempted heist, the infuriated townspeople grabbed their weapons, climbed on their horses, and gave chase. Included in Marshal Sam Denn's posse were Barney O'Conner, Vernon Lytle, Alec and Wayne McKinney, John Fleming,

Lee Bradley, Tom Doran, Roll Clark, Howard Martin, Nate Priest, George Friedley, and Charley Taliaferro. For the posse, capturing the murdering would-be robbers was not enough. Angered by the senseless killing of the two bankers, as well as a few townspeople, about nine o'clock at night citizens broke into the jail, intending to hang the prisoners. Marshal Brown, having slipped out of his leg irons, was gunned down trying to escape. The other outlaws were then strung up from an elm tree east of town. Humiliated by the actions of his lawmen, the mayor of Caldwell sent a letter of apology to the citizens of Medicine Lodge.

La Junta, New Mexico—Present day Watrous, New Mexico, the town lay along the Mora River at the junction of the Cimarron and Mountain Routes of the Santa Fe Trail. The Cimarron Route, or Dry Route, was shorter and more commonly used in the winter and after the Plains Indians were under control. The Mountain Route was longer but less dangerous and provided more access to water.

Printed in the United States
15852LVS00003BA/60

9 780865 343801